The Maul of Murgleys

Scott C. Ristau

PublishAmerica
Baltimore

© 2006 by Scott C. Ristau.
All rights reserved. No part of this book may be reproduced, stored in a retrieval system or transmitted in any form or by any means without the prior written permission of the publishers, except by a reviewer who may quote brief passages in a review to be printed in a newspaper, magazine or journal.

First printing

All characters appearing in this work are fictitious. Any resemblance to real persons, living or dead, is purely coincidental.

ISBN: 1-4137-7601-9
PUBLISHED BY PUBLISHAMERICA, LLLP
www.publishamerica.com
Baltimore

Printed in the United States of America

This book is dedicated to my family.

Chapter 1

After only three days, with less than twenty-five leagues put between Cullan and his former prison, death came chasing after him with terrifying speed. Death was hungry, vengeful, and relentless.

He escaped from Gairloch at nightfall and immediately fled north into the desert hills, it being the most inhospitable route and therefore, he hoped, the least predictable. Once outside the castle's walls, Cullan ran without rest, never pausing until he was outside Gairloch's sight, not even long enough to smile in celebration of his newfound freedom. But they found him anyway, a certainty reason had assured him of but against which his desperate heart had dared to hope. Unwilling to yield to the inevitable, Cullan ran on.

In the broad blue backdrop of its heaven, the sun beat down upon the arid land, its brilliance unimpeded by cloud or tree. Serpentine waves of shimmering heat radiated from every rock. The air was dead, the temperature suffocating. There seemed no movement anywhere upon the parched, sun-scorched landscape, as if he were the only living thing that occupied the desert. But that, of course, was wishful thinking. Far off in the distance, a plume of dust rose higher and steadily closer. To Cullan, it represented the herald of death's approach.

His breathing grew more labored, heavy gasps for air that seared Cullan's over-worked lungs. Blood, thinned by the heat, rushed like water through his veins and arteries in a quick, erratic pulse. Cullan wore nothing but a pair of loose shorts made of white cotton. But perspiration bathed his body. The precious moisture continued to leach from his sun bronzed skin, then refused to evaporate; so that rather than cooling him, the sweat hung over him like a heavy, sodden cloak. Hot and dehydrated, Cullan pushed on, still managing a steady pace, but slowing.

Running across the rugged terrain and climbing when necessary, his strong, athletic build served Cullan well. He was young and in his prime. But would that be enough, he wondered. Other questions plagued him as well. Had his pursuers already spotted him, or were they still merely chasing his trail? Was it possible that if he kept going and his strength held out, that he could keep his freedom? Such an optimistic prospect seemed inconceivable.

Hope and determination were alien to Cullan. Although physically powerful, he had always felt weak inside. He was afraid, and the feeling was a familiar one. It came as no surprise that fear had followed him in his hopeless flight from Gairloch. It would not be left behind. Fear clung to him, having been Cullan's one loyal companion for as long as he could remember.

His fevered head swam with dizziness. Already the hard land had taken a bitter toll. A mix of blood and sand encrusted Cullan's hands and feet. His abraded flesh, having been torn open repeatedly, exposed raw nerves that howled with pain. His tongue was dry, giving no comfort when he licked his split and swollen lips, blistered by the afternoon sun. Unrelenting, the sun offered him no mercy but continued to shine upon him like a searcher's spotlight. The sun also burned the delicate tissue of Cullan's eyes, leaving his vision blurred with pain and the disorienting effects of heat exhaustion. His muscles ached with overexertion, but his movements remained marked by a graceful strength. Though sorely battered, Cullan kept faith in his body. It was his courage he questioned. As always, his body was hard but his spirit soft.

Cullan's body defined who he was; it had always been that way. From the start, his existence depended on his physical appearance and ability. Tall, handsome, and muscular, that is what he was, and that fact allowed for a better life than that held by many of Gairloch's human populace. But it wasn't good enough, not by far, for none of it was his to control, not even his own body, most especially his body. Denied control of his physical being and personal destiny, Cullan had never been allowed to experience a will of his own. Until now.

For the first time in his life he felt a hint of freedom, a bittersweet taste of independence. Although its attainment brought a torment of its own, this bracing new experience was wonderful beyond expectation. The pain didn't matter. At least for once he was determining the time and circumstance in which it was inflicted.

"I won't give up," Cullan promised in a raspy whisper. "I'm never going back. I'm free. And, damn it, I'll die before I'll let them take me back."

He ran on, thinking only of putting one foot ahead of the other until a bird's shrill cry sounded in the air above him, sending a cold blast of terror through the marrow of his bones, freezing it to ice.

Overhead, a massive hawk suddenly occupied the azure sky, gliding on the air in effortless grace, cartwheeling in a series of wide circles that signaled the fugitive's position. It was the overlord's bird. It hunted for him and had found its quarry.

"No!" Cullan screamed in a dry anguished protest, refusing to accept the failure of his escape. After a lifetime of starvation under slavery, this feast of freedom would be lost to him before he could barely taste it. Panic consumed him, so crippling that it nearly drove him to the rocky surface of the hard-packed desert floor.

There were crags and small caves in which to hide. But it would do no good. So he kept running, struggling up a steep slope of rust colored rock blasted by the harsh elements.

The hawk flew in long swooping spirals that grew tighter and tighter with its lazy decent. Again the tranquility of the afternoon sky was shattered, filled with a cacophony of screeches and high pitched screams of excited fury. Then, breaking its flight pattern, the bird dove, feet stretched out before it, talons extended with deadly intent.

It struck. Claws, sharp as steel razors, sliced into the thick muscle of Cullan's shoulder. Its wickedly hooked beak slashed at his face, raking out a chaotic pattern of bloody furrows in his skin. The broadly spanned wings of the foul bird beat furiously as it tore away chunks of human flesh. Cullan flailed his arms wildly, desperately trying to fight off the vicious attack.

Once more the hawk took to the air. Released, Cullan ran without direction, blinded with pain and terror. Fat droplets of sweat and blood rolled off his forehead and spattered on the barren earth.

On the loose gravel, Cullan's feet slipped out from under him, throwing him to the ground under the force of his own weight and shattering his knee as it impacted against the unforgiving stone. A thunderous shockwave of intense, enervating pain roared up through his leg devastating his resolve, overwhelming his strength, and obliterating any remaining optimism.

It was over. Freedom was lost forever.

Cullan tried to crawl, digging his fingers into the soil and pulling his useless body forward. He wished for a drink of water, just one swallow to ease his dry throat. Knowing even that small comfort was too much to hope for, Cullan heard the savage baying of hounds. He looked back over his wounded shoulder just as the loathsome animals bounded up the hill, surrounding him. Cullen sat up and used his good leg to push his back up against a natural rock wall. The three dogs formed a semicircle around him, cornering Cullan and holding him in place. The hounds stood their ground with baleful, red eyes fixed on Cullan. They barked and growled and snarled, a mélange of terrifyingly ferocious sounds. The sun glistened off the thick oily fur of their greasy black and rust-red coats. Slaver dripped from their snapping maws and sprayed in every direction as they shook their heads in berserk fury. Their snarling teeth were long, yellow, and sharp. The dogs' big, thick muscled bodies shook with a rapacious need to tear Cullan apart. But they waited. Something held them back and Cullan knew what it was. They waited for their master. In the baking heat of the afternoon sun, Cullen leaned back against the rough rock and waited for him too.

Astride a green, wingless dragon, the overlord rode up the hill and into view. The dogs immediately quit barking and laid down, but their attention remained focused on Cullan. With the sun at his back and framed by the day's harsh, glaring light, the overlord cast a cool shadow over Cullan. The overlord, Chang, was one of the White Elves, from the ruling class in Gairloch, and a leader among Emperor Torrin's unholy horde of foul worshipers.

The twenty years spent under the influence of Torrin's rule and his growing, malevolent magic changed the elves. They were called the White Elves because their once dark complexions had been bleached away by some force of Torrin's magic or perhaps by other changes in their new way of life. Their culture, beliefs, and behaviors bore little resemblance to the elves of the ancient past or even to what the elves had been before they swore fealty to Torrin. They still possessed raven black hair and pointed ears but their skin was now a strange, milky white color.

The overlord's hair hung loose around his shoulders with part of it tied in a small braid that ran down the back of his head. His slanted eyes were almond in color and shape. They were eyes devoid of any compassion. The imperious expression on his long, high-boned face also bore a cruel joy, a sparkle of ruthless amusement.

Although their skin had been faded by corruption, the White Elves remained handsome. The strong, elegant features of their ghostly countenance and lavish raiment radiated a sense of superiority, a malicious form of refined character, and an aristocratic narcissism. Their patrician nature kept its strength and style while discarding any noble sentiment in favor of self-love and self-promotion. With a condescending attitude, they looked on all other life with distain. Absorbed with their own desires and the will of their emperor, the White Elves were a dignified but petulant people, easily discontented and irritated over trifles, with a penchant for cruelty.

Four more elves, these on horseback, rode up to join the overlord. Two elves came to a halt on either side of him. The five elves all wore the same thing. Their torsos were clothed in a leather overvest with a stand-up collar and cap sleeves that flared upward to a high point at each shoulder. The vests were dyed a rich crimson color. Metal had been affixed to the leather in vibrant decoration, a scrolling filigree of gold that formed the image of a griffon across the chest and back, and similar trim wrapped around the edges of the garment. Beneath the vests, they wore black shirts of fine silk. Their pants were crimson like the vests but made of soft, supple leather. Gold mesh belts encircled their waists and calf-high boots of black leather protected their feet. Each elf was crowned with an open-face helmet fashioned of blued-steel and gold laminate. Cheek-plates trimmed in gold swept down to a point at their chins. Overlapping metal lames formed the neck guard at the back of the helmet. At the helmet's peak, a gilded griffon crouched. The horses and lizard steed were also well dressed, clad in ornate trappings and harnesses. Each had an open bard with decorative breeching and breast collar made from wide bands of black leather that passed around the rump, flanks, and shoulders of the animals. Gold bits passed through their mouths and ornaments of the precious metal studded the bridles and breast collars. Black saddles adorned the horse's backs above red blankets with braided gold edging. Only the White Elves would be so vain as to dress in such regal finery to hunt a runaway slave in an empty desert.

Chang removed a handkerchief from his pocket and used it to wipe the sweat from his forehead and from the back of his neck. He looked pleased but also bored. After replacing the handkerchief, Chang extracted a flagon of water from his saddlebags. He took a long drink, swallowed and then took another. The second drink he swished around in his mouth before spitting the water out on the thirsty desert floor.

"Well slave," Chang said to Cullan. "Our hunt is over and your freedom is lost. I think we all enjoyed the sport, although it became somewhat tiresome toward the end. You seemed to have more enthusiasm in the beginning of your escape. During the first two days you at least gave us a little bit of a challenge. Then you became lazy. Complacency is such an shameful weakness, especially when you're fighting for you life. Well, we've had our fun. Are you ready to go back to Gairloch now?"

Cowering in the overlord's shadow, Cullan shivered with dread. "Please Master. I'm just one man and of little value to you really. You have others. She has others. Why do you care if I escape? What difference would the loss of my service be to you that you should trouble yourself to hunt me so?"

"I care because you're mine," Chang replied gently. However, his cordiality was unable to mask the menace he represented. "I acquired you to serve as my wife's concubine. You belong to me; and what is mine, stays mine. When something of mine no longer serves me well, I would rather destroy it than throw it away by setting if free in the desert. Because by destroying it, I might at least squeeze some last pleasure from its existence. But your days of service need not be over. Your life may yet have value. My wife was happy with your affections and I was happy that you and her other concubines kept her vile affections away from me. So if you can prove to me that you have seen the error of your ways, that you can recapture your love for your former duties, you don't have to die."

Cullan shook his head in dismal defiance. His body lurched with ragged sobs and shook from spasmodic muscles afflicted with the palsy of fear. "Please, don't take me back. I'm hurt. I'm exhausted. Please, can't you just leave me here to die? I won't last another day. I probably won't make it through the night."

"Stop," Chang interrupted, his anger piqued. "If you're going to beg, you should be on your knees. It's a position with which you should be very familiar."

"Yes Master, but I can't. My knee is broken. I can't move."

Chang rose up in his stirrups, swung his right leg up and over the back of the dragon, then dropped to his feet beside the beast. He lifted the helmet from his head and hung it on the saddle horn. His graceful stride brought him quickly to Cullan's side, where Chang then knelt himself. Cullan looked away, unable to bear such close scrutiny from the cruel eyes set within the overlord's pale face.

Chang rested his palm lightly upon Cullan's crippled knee and his fingers tenderly enveloped it. Then he squeezed with brutal force, bearing his weight down around his tightened grip. Cullan's eyes and jaw muscles clenched as he struggled against the pain rushing through him.

Chang spoke a single elvish word and made the broken knee magically whole again.

Instantly, Cullan scrambled to his knees, bowing his head and clasping his pleading hands together in front him. "Thank you Master. You are merciful and great. Please complete your mercy. Let me go or kill me now. But don't take me back to her."

But the resources of Chang's soul were unable to construct a genuine act of mercy. The inexorable overlord stood, brushing the dust from his neat leather pants. He met Cullan's great lamenting with a stern dismissal. "I'm a tolerant man but I'm growing impatient with your pleas and protests. Now, I can understand that having sex with my wife must be unpleasant, even painful. But you must accept and endure the pain for my sake. You can do that for me, can't you?"

"Oh Master, I would do anything for you. But it will be so much worse now than before. She will torture me beyond all human endurance for what I've done. I tried to escape; she'll see that as an insult and punish me for it. Please don't let her hurt me too much," Cullan pleaded in plaintive supplication.

"Yes, that's probably true," Chang confessed. He shrugged, easily casting off the weight of Cullan's plight. "But I don't like to get involved in my wife's trivial affairs. And you brought this on yourself. You should never have given action to your arrogant thoughts of escape. My wife is not a woman of ordinary passions; that is undeniable. And she is certainly unafflicted with any sort of kindness. I understand that the hard usage of sexual slavery under a woman of such gross character and monstrous desire must seem unbearable. But as you well know, so many in Gairloch suffer far worse fates than yours. The Pit comes to mind. Would you care to give up your duties and join your wretched brethren in the Pit. Or would you like to try your hand as a gladiator? I don't think you want that. So show me you can still abide the sadistic caress and cruel lust of my darling wife."

Cullan remained silent.

The overlord dug into his pocket and removed a red stone about the size and shape of a chicken's egg. Placing the stone into Cullan's hand, he closed the slave's fingers around it and spoke briefly in elvish. Chang let go his hand, but Cullan found he was unable to release the stone. Chang then withdrew a short sword from the scabbard at his belt. He held the sword out for Cullan to take with his free hand.

Cullan shook his head. "No Master. It is forbidden for me to touch a weapon."

"Take it," Chang insisted. "But I don't want you to use it, no matter what. Do you promise?"

Cullan nodded and Chang spoke another word in the elvin tongue. The stone pulsed and began to glow. Cullan's hand began to tingle and then to itch. His eyes widened as the itching became worse and worse. It now felt like thousands of serrated pins pierced and twisted in his skin. Then the imagined pins began to burn. The pain grew terrible and continued to worsen. Cullan screamed and dropped the sword. With his free hand, he tried desperately to pry his fingers away from the stone but they refused to move. Wild with agony, he slammed his fist against a boulder again and again, trying to knock the stone from his grasp but it refused to let loose of him. He felt his fingers break, the bones splintering into sharp jagged pieces, but it was nothing compared to the pain imparted by the stone, and still his fingers clung to it. He fell face down in the gravel and dust, then began thrashing in a mad prostrate dance of pain. He twisted and rolled, all the while screaming for help. But of course none came. When the fingers of his open palm touched the sword lying on the ground, Cullan snatched it up and without any further hesitation, used it to cut off his tortured hand. He held up his maimed arm, watching his blood pump from the stump, and felt only relief.

The overlord shook his head in disappointment. "There you go trying to be free again."

Chang took the sword easily from Cullan, who offered no resistance. The slave continued to stare at his arm and seemed to be in shock.

A string of elvish words passed from Chang's bloodless lips as he passed his hand over Cullan's stump. The bleeding stopped, flesh and veins accreted, knitting themselves back together and healing the mortal wound.

"What use is a one-handed concubine to my wife?" Chang asked half in jest, half in earnest. "Well, maybe I can graft a new hand onto your arm when we get back to Gairloch. Perhaps a goblin's claw would be entertaining. But if I am going to bother with taking you all that way, I should make sure you can still serve your mistress, that you can still pacify her virulent lust. We wouldn't want to disappoint that nasty bitch and get her hackles up. When that happens, she's as mean and ugly as these dogs," remarked Chang, gesturing toward the three savage hounds.

Grinning, Chang paused in his commentary. He glanced back at the other elves and they smiled with him.

"There's an idea," continued Chang. He reached down and grabbed one of the dogs by the collar and began walking it toward Cullan. "Romance this beast and it will prove to me that you'll still be able to do your job with my wife." As pet and master drew closer to Cullan, the dog began snarling and barking and pulling at its collar as if it knew what was being proposed and viciously opposed the obscene suggestion.

Cullan fell to his face again, pleading, overcome with fear and horror. "No, Master, I can't. I can't," he wailed.

The overlord stopped. He gloated triumphantly over the spectacle of Cullen's humiliation. "Very well, maybe that's too vile even for human scum. And this disobedient mutt doesn't seem too pleased with the idea either."

Cullan continued to weep in utter despair, moaning and muttering to himself in a mucous-clogged voice and uncontainable, terror-filled disgust. He had seen his life lose one day after another every feature of dignity, every shade of joy. Now even hope had vacated his soul and it would be eternally absent.

"Stop sniveling and look at me, you ungrateful worm. Watch, and learn what happens to disobedient animals." Chang flipped the dog over on its side and, before it could react, he pulled out a dagger and stabbed it deep into the animal's chest. There issued a loud, strangled bark and then it quieted. Chang plowed open the hound's belly as he dragged the knife back toward its hindquarters. He reached within the open cavity, hauling out the animal's disemboweled, bile filled intestines. Then he held it out, offering the grotesque meat to Cullan.

"This is your last chance, slave," Chang announced. "I always thought the taste of my wife's lips bore an uncanny similarity to excrement. Eat this and you'll at least prove to me that you can still stomach her kisses. If not, then you're definitely headed for the Pit."

Cullan crawled toward him. Tears streamed down his cheeks, the shed moisture of his eyes mixing with his blood and sweat, leaving his spirit desiccated. Hope and dignity dried up completely and blew away forever on the desert wind, forsaking his heart and leaving it as blasted and desolate as the burnt-out, lonely landscape to which he had escaped.

Miserably compliant, head bowed in pathetic submission, Cullan took the entrails and bit into them. His throat seized; his stomach gagged and convulsed as he forced himself to swallow the emetic meal, the putrid mix of blood, viscera, and feces.

The overlord nodded, finally appeased and satisfied with the slave's subservience. He gave the carcass of the eviscerated dog as a treat to the other two hounds. On command, they attacked their former companion's remains with ferocious glee. They ate greedily, their massive jaws rending and chewing, their snarls blending with the wet sound of tearing flesh and the hard snap of crunching bones. Ignoring the feasting animals, Chang hauled Cullan to his feet and tied a rope around his waist. He tied the other end to his dragon's saddle, tethering Cullan to the giant lizard.

Chang removed his helmet from the saddle horn and fitted it back upon his head. Remounting the dragon, Chang addressed the other elves. "I'm tired and I need a bath. Let's go home. The dogs will catch up when they're done."

Horses and dragon moved slowly down the hill.

Thirsty, hurt, and forlorn, Cullan followed behind the leisurely pace of the overlord's dragon. He wept, moaned, and muttered to himself, a wretched dirge sung in tribute to his physical pain and the emotional torment over his return to slavery.

The sound of Cullan's whining annoyed the overlord, stirring his impatience. He grew irritated by Cullan, by the heat of the sun, by the rocking motion of the dragon on which he rode, by the dust, by the snug fit of his pants, by the duties waiting for him back at Gairloch. He wanted to immerse himself in the cool, cleansing waters of a bath, and he wanted it now.

"Chkk, chkk." Chang clicked his tongue, instructing the dragon to quicken its stride. The horses kept up as they settled into a brisk trot. The rope jerked painfully at Cullan's waist, pulling him forward. His steps becoming more awkward, he stumbled repeatedly as he endeavored to jog over the rugged rock and rubble of the desert floor. Clinging to the lifeline, Cullan wrapped his hand around the rope and held on while struggling to keep on his feet. But in time, Cullan tripped and fell, stirring up a cloud of dust as he fought desperately to pull himself back up.

Although the whining had stopped, the yank and pull at the leash by the dawdling slave further aggravated Chang. *The selfish, time-consuming slug is keeping me from my bath*, thought Chang. The overlord scowled as he considered the value of the stupid, worthless human he had recaptured for his wife as well as for his own sport. It never occurred to him that they could move faster if Chang placed Cullan on the dragon with him. To do that would be too much like acknowledging that the human might be something more than a mere animal.

Chang intensely disliked humans, particularly those that made a pretense of being more than ordinary clay. Humans were nothing and should never be allowed to entertain the ridiculous notion that they possessed freewill. The destiny of all life was to be shaped by the hands of Torrin and the elves. It was theirs alone to manipulate and control. That was the truth they sought to establish in the world. And they were making great progress in gratifying that ignoble goal.

"It will take us forever to get home at this rate," complained Chang. "I think you were right slave; you're not that valuable."

Chang kicked his heels against the dragon's flanks. The lizard broke quickly into a gallop. Cullan ran, but not fast enough. He fell to the rocky earth and was dragged.

At his master's prodding, the dragon increased his momentum further. Cullan twisted and kicked, banging against rocks, bouncing over the rough ground. His ribs broke, stealing his breath. His skull cracked, blurring his consciousness.

Now headed swiftly for home and his bath, the hot air playing with his long black hair as it rushed past him, Chang laughed as he dragged the impudent slave, breaking Cullan's body apart, smearing bone, blood, and flesh across the barren land.

At his emperor's command, Chang joined Torrin in a high tower room that overlooked the main gate of castle Gairloch. On a broad terrace outside the room, Torrin stood leaning on a stone balustrade, watching as the sun removed the dark veil of night and reclaimed the day.

Gairloch had changed over the years, becoming a masterpiece of splendor and corruption. The castle had become a warped and wicked place, where anything was possible, where human flesh was bought and sold and virtually no form of decadence was considered forbidden. Two distinct worlds existed side by side with the castle walls. As the ruling class, the White Elves enjoyed a world of opulence, lavish luxury, and vile pleasure unhindered by any moral restraint. But the common hordes of Gairloch, on the other hand, lived in stark contrast to elvin eloquence and sophistication. They lived in a world of unending pain, crushing poverty, and ubiquitous mayhem imposed by the depravity of their masters, Torrin and the White Elves. Although different, both faces of the castle were an expression of flagrant evil.

In obeisance, Chang bowed on one knee, lowering his face to the floor. "My emperor, I am here as instructed and as always, ready to serve your will."

Torrin gestured for Chang to rise. "Where have you been," Torrin demanded of his overlord.

Chang stood but kept his eyes lowered humbly. "I went into the Barrens to retrieve a runaway slave, one of my wife's favorite concubines."

"A waste of time," Torrin said in chastisement. "Look, a new consignment of slaves is even now being brought to the castle."

Following the pointed line of Torrin's finger, Chang saw two large wagons pulled by horses, surrounded by goblins, and led by four elves. A cage of iron bars occupied the back of the wagons. Hungry, frightened, and hurt, people were packed cruelly inside each portable pen. A few members of the miserable cargo had already died during transport. The wagons passed through a colonnade of large poles driven into the ground on either side of the road. On these poles, people hung crucified or strung up and set afire in punishment for crimes and as a warning to others. Only corpses decorated these poles at the moment but a few still smoldered from the heat of Gairloch's atrocious brutality.

The horror in this spectacle of injustice was lost in the vacuum of Torrin's soul. He had become immune to the gentler and nobler tendencies of the heart.

"I'm told we need more clean, healthy slaves for domestic work around the castle," said Torrin, "but I plan to take a few of these recent arrivals for new experiments I have been considering. Although it wasn't quite right and we had to destroy it, something broke out of the Pit and got inside the castle a few days ago that inspired my creativity. I've been thinking about a creature similar to a goblin but with wings, like a bat. Such a creature might help our upcoming battle plans and give us a valuable strategic advantage; don't you think?"

"It sounds intriguing," said Chang. "And we need to increase production of the goblins and gnomes. Our forces are spread rather thin these days."

"Yes," Torrin agreed. "We now have a large population living at Prakrit, securing our occupation of the dwarves' old kingdom and mining its resources, particularly the magic of its interior. Many have been lost in trying to excavate and exploit the storehouse of raw magic contained in the life and material of Prakrit's core. But I don't want to leave them undefended nor scale back their explorations."

Chang nodded. "A significant number of our troops are also out scouring the land, doing reconnaissance and recovery work with the Seekers."

The Seekers were elves but born with rare and unique abnormalities. Their pigmentation had mutated in the opposite direction from the White Elves. The Seekers were unusually tall with black skin and misshapen features. But these oddities also possessed an aberration in their nature that was particularly useful to Torrin. They could smell magic. So Torrin dispatched the Seekers from the castle with instructions to roam the land sniffing out items of magic. What they found, they obediently brought back to Torrin for him to use in expanding his power and authority. Because of their special importance to Torrin, the Seekers held an elite rank and stature in Gairloch. But likely they would have been feared even without the backing of Torrin's favor.

"Yes," Torrin affirmed Chang's comment. "But we have already benefited greatly from what they've found. With those treasures we've already acquired and an increased fighting force, I'm confident that we will defeat Braemar this year. And I want Braemar utterly annihilated as a warning to the other kingdoms that I'll be coming for them soon and resistance is futile. Through Braemar, the other kingdoms must be taught a lesson. If they do not serve me, then their lives are a wasted existence that I shall put to a bitter end. Even their bodies shall not be buried but left as dung upon the land."

"All hail Emperor Torrin," Chang chanted in reverent support and obedience.

"I cast out my net and draw more power to me," said Torrin. "I consume it and my power is magnified. I release it and the world trembles. I will make them know the full measure of my might and supremacy. They shall know the name of Torrin Murgleys and shall serve me as a god."

"All hail Emperor Torrin," Chang repeated dutifully.

"I will accomplish all my purpose and ambition," Torrin continued with overflowing hubris. An avatar of oppressive arrogance, Torrin embodied a philosophy based on the concept of improving one's self worth through the conquest and domination of others. "By my great power, I will stretch out my arm and Braemar shall become a heap of ruins. Then I will lay a yoke of slavery over Parhelion, Garonne, and all the people of the land. I shall own the world and all that dwells upon its surface. Every knee shall bow down before me, even if their owners' legs must first be broken. All will swear loyalty to me, or have their tongues cut out. Every heart shall worship me, or have its beating forever stilled."

Chapter 2

"To the creek!" The ten-year-old child shouted his youthful call to adventure, an invitation promising the excitement of playful escapades to any sibling bold enough to follow. But it was merely as an echo of a more powerfully compelling summons, the irresistible lure of their valley wilderness, the soul-stirring attraction possessed by a meandering corridor of natural splendor sheltered in the foothills of the Tissama Mountains.

The children had spent all morning staring out the window of their rustic home, waiting for the rains to stop, annoyingly impatient and bristling with the vitality of youth. Finally, after an interminable wait, after anxious hours of restless captivity, the deluge ended and the gray-black thunderheads began to break apart; and in the broadening gaps left by their retreat, a brilliant blue sky was quick to take up tenancy.

Three of the children, ages ten, seven and five, burst from the house propelled with all the explosive energy of a coiled spring. In their wake, their mother was left shaking her head with muted concern for their health and their father wishing he were young enough to take part in their energetic foolishness. The sweet smell of fresh air slapped their faces, awakening the children's exuberant spirits all the more. Slipping and sliding over water-slick grass, they raced across the lush green carpet of the open vale, splashed through the grassy ditch that drained their farmstead, and sprinted past a grove of trees encircling a wetland crouched low amid the imposing rock cliffs that surrounded it at a distance.

A small forest lay between the farmstead and the wetland, a wide buffer of trees, shrub, and fragrant wildflowers that served to create an unaltered habitat rich in texture and variation, salubrious for man and nature alike. Burning through the dissipating clouds, the sun's radiant, golden glow fell in bright bands through the leaf filled limbs of buttonbush, black willow, and sycamore and dappled the ground with a patchwork of light and shadow. Nearer the wetland's irregular shoreline, where softstem bulrush and rice cutgrass grew in thick green mats, pickerelweed bloomed, proudly displaying the ephemeral beauty of its clustered purple flowers. Like dark galleons bloated and heavy with a pirate's bounty, reflected clouds sailed over the water's mirrored surface. As if spilled from the decks of these treasure-loaded ships, emerald duckweed floated on the water and littered it with a jetsam of priceless jewels. A pair of ducks took flight and the choral trill of songbirds competed with the sound of the children's laughter. Touching lightly over the land in an airy caress, a cool breeze soughed softly through the trees.

Sloshing through the link connecting the wetland's vegetated buffer to that of the creek's, the children left the farmstead behind them. Like the ramparts of some castle from their father's stories, stone fences surrounded the property and divided the farm into several enclosures, walls that stood as a protective barrier against the escape of livestock or that safeguarded the family gardens from hungry invaders. Behind one stone block fence, pigs marched and grunted within their defensive perimeter, patrolling the denuded ground.

Drawn by the stream's rhythmic cadence played by the water as it rippled and splashed in swift passage through its fluid course, the children reached its swollen banks and for a moment marveled at the vibrant condition of the rich riparian habitat, letting the vision wash over them. Like a snake, the stream moved with sinuous grace, its coiled body sequined by the sun, glittering bright as the flash of a serpent's iridescent scales caught beneath the eye of heaven. A mixture of sand, gravel, and cobble formed the streambed. Above it, fish darted in the clear water around the cover of boulders and fallen logs. The strong roots of willow and dogwood trees held the banks and their lush canopy overhung the water, shading its surface from the heat of the afternoon sun.

The children began to throw stones at the wooden boats carved by their father and now moored with string to the stream's edge and set adrift. As he cast rocks in an effort to sink the little toy boat, the ten year old, Kyle, thought of something his father had once said when the boy had asked him where the water went, what happened to it after it passed through their creek. His father said that it flowed down the mountain and across the plains into the Dunegall River, then south past castle Braemar and into the Purl River near castle Parhelion. After that he wasn't sure were it went, maybe out into the ocean and eventually to the other side of the world.

How connected the world is, Kyle had thought. He realized that the things we do here, in the lakes and streams of our backyards, affect not just us but possess a cumulative significance of global proportion. When he voiced this sentiment to his father in the more simplistic language of a child, Quinn smiled and told him something he never forgot. He said that it is a testimony to the power of human reason that we protect the resources upon which we depend and proof of our compassion that we do so by means that benefit lives other than our own.

Quinn stood on the porch of their house with one hand resting on the railing and his other arm wrapped around Midori. Both parents smiled as they watched their three children run beyond their sight.

"They'll all need baths tonight. That's for sure," asserted Quinn.

"They will if they want to come back in the house," replied Midori. "Otherwise they can sleep in the barn."

"The barn might be drier. I need to get up on the roof of the house and fix those leaks or we may all drown in our beds during the next rain."

"It's not that bad, just one leak. Don't work on it today," Midori urged. "Those wood shingles will be too slick after the rain. I don't want you to slip off the roof and hurt anything important." She turned to him, rising up on her toes to kiss his mouth, and moved her hand in a playfully caress over the front of his trousers, teasingly signifying what part of his anatomy she considered important.

Smiling, Quinn observed, "The ground's too wet for me to get much work done outside today. Maybe you and I should go back to bed." They had been together for twenty years and she still excited him like no other woman could, not that he had been with any other woman or even considered it during all those years. Quinn loved his wife and had committed himself to her completely. Their marriage was a harmony of passion and contentment, a synergy of desire and devotion.

"Sounds good to me. I'm up for it, and you seem to be too," she encouraged suggestively while continuing to massage the muscle hardening between his legs. She had kindled his amorous desire and now stoked its fire. It was a familiar flame yet one that remained intense. Theirs was a passion sanctified by marriage and glorified by love.

The years spent bearing and raising children in the rough mountain country had diminished little of Midori's striking beauty. An additional twenty pounds had been applied to her slender frame, but she still appeared limber and lissome, perhaps not as delicate as she once was but her matured figure was just as graceful as she had ever been in youth. The lines around her lips and at the corners of her eyes seemed to have been carved by years of laughter and smiles rather than by worry and the fatigue of age.

Quinn ran the fingers of one hand through her long, straight, glossy black hair, paused to trace the pad of his index finger around the pointed tip of her elvin ear before gliding his caress over the nut-brown skin of her cheek and neck, letting his palm slide leisurely over her shoulder and down her back before coming to rest at the inward curve of her waist. As they held each other, enveloped in the warmth of their embrace and enwrapped in the security of their love, Quinn looked into her eyes. Throughout their marriage Midori's eyes had sparkled with affection and joy, shining a radiant beam that drove out the shadows of despair from the corners of Quinn's heart, shadows of a distant past in which he had unwittingly fought on the side of evil and had foolishly helped to establish it as a powerful force in the world.

Physically, Quinn was quite a contrast to his wife. Time had washed much of the color from Quinn's blond hair and tinseled it with numerous strands of gray. He had a rugged, formidable appearance with a face most would call ugly, but he possessed a placid demeanor and handsome character. He was tall with a bear-like body in which dwelled the heart of a lamb. He was a man of calloused hands and a tender spirit, of tough muscles and a gentle soul.

"You're beautiful," she told him.

He laughed and answered, "That's just what I was about to say to you. Now I'm worried that your eyesight is starting to fail. I'll have to spend all my time following you around to keep you from bumping into walls or tripping over furniture."

"My butt may have started to sag but my eyes are as sharp as ever. I don't care what you see in the mirror; you're beautiful to me."

"And you're wonderful," Quinn sighed. He drew her closer into his arms and to his heart, cupped his hand around her diminutive derrière, and lightly squeezed her buttocks. "And your backside feels pretty firm to me." He grinned. "I'm so lucky to have you."

"We are both blessed, my love," Midori asserted. "Now, weren't we headed back to bed?"

"Hey Dad," their fifteen year old daughter, Shannon, cheerfully called as she stepped out onto the porch with her parents, breaking both the silence and the mood as the door banged shut behind her. "Do you want to split those logs we have stacked in the barn today?"

Feeling his chance for romance slip away, Quinn continued to hold Midori and longingly returned her gaze as he answered his daughter. "Do you really want to do that now Honey?"

"Sure, what else are we going to do on a sloppy, wet day like this?"

Midori and Quinn smiled at one another before she released him "Go on, your daughter has chores for you to do. I'll have to get my work out of you later tonight," Midori told him as she went back inside the house.

"So you want to chop firewood," Quinn asked.

"Sure," Shannon said with pleasure. "Why not?"

"Your brothers and sister are playing down by the creek. You could join them or just sit in the sun and read a book if you like. You don't have to work right now. It can wait."

"Naw, I've been sitting around all morning," Shannon complained. "I want to get out and do something useful."

"Okay, I can understand that. And I'm grateful. You're a big help to your dad, Baby Girl, especially lately." Quinn complemented his daughter, putting his arm over her shoulder as they walked to the barn.

"Thanks, but I'm no *baby girl*," Shannon demanded. "I'm fifteen years old."

Quinn directed his attention at Shannon and a wistful smile played at his lips. It was true; she was growing up. Her head now reached the height of Quinn's shoulders; already she was taller than her mother. Although she had a lovely face, Shannon had inherited much of her physical appearance from her father. She had wavy yellow hair that draped to her shoulder blades but was usually kept tied in a simple ponytail. She was thick bodied but not fat, with wide shoulders and broad, tapered hips. Her chest had bloomed into a pair of round, plump blossoms but her strength was equal to that of most men.

"I guess you're right," Quinn admitted. "Although it seems like only yesterday you were saying your first word, which had to be either 'no' or 'potato', because you love to argue and you loved mashed potatoes. I suppose you'll be wanting to leave us too before long. I know I can't expect you kids to stay here forever, but it's so hard to let go. Next time we meet up with the Rovers, I'll have to worry about you turning gypsy on me, taking off with their caravan to parts unknown and marrying one of those lighthearted charmers. I saw how some of those boys were looking at you already last year, paying a bit more attention than they did when you were younger, and a bit more than I felt comfortable with."

"Oh Dad," Shannon blushed. "You worry too much. I'm not running off with some silly boy."

"Not today anyway, maybe. But it won't be long. I just want you to know, when you do leave and get married, you can always come back here to live. I'd love to have my grownup children and their families all living here together in this valley. I hope your brother will come home soon with some pretty bride. I hope he's doing all right."

"He's fine," Shannon stated, dismissing the subject as together they pulled open the barn doors. "Enough talk about leaving and getting married. Let's get to work."

They set to cutting firewood. Quinn used an iron wedge and a sledgehammer to break the large logs apart while Shannon collected the split sections and employed an axe to break them into smaller pieces of fuel. They settled into an easy rhythm and the time passed comfortably in their pleasant, satisfying labor. The two worked well together and each enjoyed the flex and stretch of muscles put to productive work.

Riding a white horse, Aragon approached Quinn's farmstead. He observed the peaceful scene, the large inviting log home, the animal pens, the fruitful gardens, and the unaltered beauty of the wilderness neighborhood in which the farm dwelled. The man-made habitat and natural environment seemed at peace together. It struck Aragon as a healthy and a happy place, a place wholesome and pleasant, a place where he did not belong. As he surveyed the scene, he was distressed by the bucolic serenity that his presence would undoubtedly disrupt.

Aragon wore a dark blue cloak, perhaps in tribute to the long dead wizard Prelature even though he himself had left that institution well before its bloody demise, or perhaps it possessed no symbolism and was worn for the simple practicality of protecting him from the rain. The hood had been thrown back over his shoulders, now that the sun was again shining. He scowled both in anticipation of the meeting that lay before him and in discomfort from the morning's travel in the downpour. His potent abilities as a powerful wizard could not keep him dry, could not prevent the water and the chill from leaching within his garments and assaulting his skin. His magic skills were also incapable of filling an empty belly. He was hungry, weary, and worried. The stubble of a three-week beard concealed some of his careworn face in a tangle of short whiskers of red, brown, black, and gray, as if the hairs were warring with one another to determine a dominant shade. He was only forty-two years of age but his brow seemed furrowed in contemplation of ancient knowledge and concern for a troubled future. A tall, wooden staff hung holstered at his side, slid through a metal ring strapped to the saddle by a leather belt. Shimmering, spell-laden runes were carved into the polished, black surface of the staff. A silver cap protected the staff's base and its head was fitted with a silver, three-talon claw clutching a green gemstone. Behind Aragon, packed with supplies both mundane and mysterious, saddlebags rode the horse's rump. The pale horse leisurely walked its rider closer to their destination.

During the fall of Gairloch, some twenty plus years ago, Aragon spent two weeks imprisoned in an ancient temple located within the Barrens, the gateway to Mount Karakulrum. He went there to consult the Oracle of Gurrot, seeking knowledge of what his brother Torrin intended to do with the army he had somehow amassed. From the ancient oracle of the trolls, the Old Ones as they were once called, Aragon learned the frightening truth of Torrin's plans for Gairloch. But in his confinement he could do nothing to thwart the evil ambition of his younger sibling. By the time he freed himself, it was too late for Aragon to help Gairloch. Although he failed to understand much that he saw in the Oracle, Aragon learned many things before he gained his freedom from the temple. He learned that Torrin sired a child with an elvin woman who left Gairloch before the scion was born. Also, in her flight, the woman had been accompanied by another traitor to Torrin, a man named Quinn. Aragon kept this information filed away within his memory, knowing it may one day be of use. That day had come, the file had been opened and its contents would soon see application.

"Rider coming," Shannon said. Her words were casual even though visitors were a rare occurrence for them. She released the axe, leaving it wedged in an upright block of wood, then wiped a forearm across her brow, using the shirtsleeve to mop away her sweat. "I don't know who it is but his horse sure is pretty."

Quinn looked up to see the rider walking slowly toward them in the distance. The sight of the blue robed figure astride a white horse stirred ugly memories of a man who was once his friend, of a man who became a monster.

"Get the others and hide," Quinn rasped. "Do it now!"

"Why Dad," Shannon asked, her voice shaken with a sudden tremor. The sight of her father frightened, as she had never before seen him, greatly unnerved her. "Who is it? What's wrong?"

Quinn couldn't answer. Fear stole his power of speech, drained the color from his face, and froze the air in his lungs. Raw panic and noble purpose bubbled in his bloodstream. He was terrified of losing the life and people he loved, yet unwavering in his determination to protect his family at any cost. Without warning, he found himself witnessing the coming destruction of all that he held dear, all that was good and pure, innocent and joyful. The closer the rider came, the more it seemed the horror of his past had finally caught up with him. He felt certain that the man he saw approaching must be Torrin Murgleys and that he had finally come to collect his property and delivery his revenge.

With uncontainable vehemence, Quinn exploded across the yard, screaming like a madman and charging like a bull toward Aragon, fully committed to a ferocious act of self-defense. Wild-eyed with fear and fury, Quinn still held the sledgehammer. But now, with knuckles white and cramped around the shaft, he raised the hammer, zealously determined to shatter the rider's skull instead of breaking wood.

Surprise washed all weariness and worry from Aragon's facial features. He had expected that these people would not welcome him warmly but he had not anticipated such murderous rage to be so instantaneously aimed against him. Wanting to move from the path of the screaming attacker, the horse tossed its head, twisting and shifting its body as it fought Aragon's efforts to hold his ground. Griping the reins with his right hand, Aragon slid his staff from its holster, held it out, pointed it at Quinn, and prepared himself to use the staff to stave off the man's wild aggression. Seconds before Quinn reached Aragon, a brilliant shaft of coruscating emerald light burst from the top of the staff. The bright bolt struck Quinn in the chest and sent him flying in a backward arc through the air and fifteen feet across the ground. Landing hard, he was struck unconscious.

Aragon rode quickly to his victim, dismounted, and knelt beside him, putting his fingers against Quinn's neck to check his pulse. He was soon joined by Shannon and Midori, the latter shoved Aragon aside and clamped her palms over Quinn's cheeks, calling his name and pleading for his answer. When she got none from her husband, she demanded one of Aragon.

"Who are you," she spat at him. "What did you do to him?" Tears filled her eyes.

"He'll recover. It's not as serious as it looks, I assure you. I am truly sorry but I had no choice. He meant to kill me."

"It's true Mamma," said Shannon. "Daddy attacked him."

"Why?" she asked with a new kind of fear.

"I don't know," Shannon explained. "He didn't say anything. Dad just went crazy and charged after him."

"Maybe he's sick," Aragon offered. "Or maybe he just thought he saw something that wasn't really there. But I assure you, I mean you no harm. Please let me help you get your husband inside so we can properly care for him."

Midori and Aragon each grabbed Quinn under one of his arms. Shannon took his legs. Quinn was a big man, however, and it would be impossible for even the three of them to carry his limp body under normal circumstances. Discretely, Aragon employed his magic to temporarily lessen the burden of Quinn's considerable weight. Neither wife nor daughter took notice of the mysterious lightness, both being too preoccupied with concern for Quinn.

Once inside the house, Quinn's true weight returned as they laid him on the couple's bed, causing the mattress to sag beneath him and the frame to creak in protest. Midori sat on the bed next to her husband, checking him for injuries. Aragon and Shannon stood back, watching.

"I'll be right back," said Aragon, "if you'll allow me. I have an elixir in my saddlebags that should help him."

Her silence implied consent and Midori let him leave, but she had no intention of allowing the stranger to pour any unknown elixir down Quinn's throat. In Aragon's absence, she began using her own modest elvin magic to restore her husband to consciousness. Outside, Aragon retrieved his staff and tied his horse to the porch railing of the house, then he obtained a small glass bottle from his pack. As he entered the bedroom, Quinn began to stir. Seeing that his potion was no longer needed, Aragon pocketed the bottle and, leaning on his staff, bent forward over the recovering patient.

"He's coming around I see," Aragon observed.

Quinn's eyes slowly fluttered open and took comfort in the appealing sight of his wife hunched over him. Then he remembered his earlier terror. Whipping his head back and forth, he hastily took in the contents of the room before letting his gaze settle on Aragon. Quinn saw now that the man was not Torrin, and he relaxed slightly. His head ached painfully and an unpleasant tingling crawled over every inch of his skin, but other than that, Quinn felt well enough. However, the case of mistaken identity and the feral attack it provoked now made Quinn feel rather foolish. His embarrassment helped set aside his physical discomfort and extraordinary fear. But more than anything, he felt great relief that the man he feared most in the world was not among them and Quinn wanted to quickly push the despised image of Torrin Murgleys to the far recesses of his mind and bury the detestable memory of that hateful man.

Quinn swung his legs over the side of the bed. Slowly, he stood up. At first the room seemed to pitch and roll, forcing Quinn to grasp the bedpost for support. But after a second or two the room righted itself and felt more stable beneath his feet.

"I'm sorry about that out there," Quinn groaned, gesturing with a shaky hand toward the yard outside the house. "I don't know what came over me. Please forgive me." Quinn held his hand, which had now lost most of its tremor, out for Aragon to clasp.

Aragon took the offered hand and returned the firm handshake. "No harm done, at least none to me. I apologize that my arrival alarmed you so."

"No, it's my fault. But what brings you here? What can we do for you?"

"A warm meal would be wonderful, perhaps the chance to sleep in your barn. That rain last night made for unpleasant slumber. And some conversation would be very welcome; it's been a lonely road I've traveled lately."

Midori and Shannon exchanged uneasy glances but left the question for Quinn to decide.

"Certainly," Quinn announced. "We can do that for you. Let's go out into the main room and make ourselves more comfortable.

At that moment the other three children returned from their outdoor adventures. As they entered the house, Kyle called out so that he could be heard throughout the residence. "Hey Mom, Dad left his sledgehammer out in the middle of the yard." The children were always severely scolded when they committed acts of such irresponsible neglect, so the boy was a little amused at the prospect of turning the tables on his father. "And who's horse is that out there? She's a beauty."

Kyle and the other children fell silent as the two groups met in the living room.

"Hello children," Aragon said cheerfully.

The surprised youngsters failed to respond, so Quinn spoke. "Good, I'm glad you're back. As you can see, we have a guest. Children, this is …."

Seeing that Quinn had not the information to complete his sentence,

Aragon introduced himself. "My name is Aragon," he said to the father, "and it's a pleasure to make your acquaintance good sir." The two men shook hands for a second time while the rest of the family moved in to have a closer look at the newcomer.

"My name's Quinn. This is my wife Midori. Shannon here is my oldest daughter; we were just talking this afternoon about how she's fifteen now. Next in line is Kyle; he's ten but big for his age. Then there's Tim who's seven and our youngest Danielle, who just turned five."

Aragon tipped his head in a slight bow and shook hands with each person as Quinn went through the roll call of his family. He bent down on one knee to take hold of Danielle's tiny hand to regard her at the girl's own level.

"My," said Aragon. "You're a cute, little one aren't you? But you have a fine big family. How many brothers and sisters do you have?

"Four," Danielle answered simply but with a darling smile.

"Four?" Aragon repeated with incredulity. "I think you better spend less time playing and more time practicing your arithmetic with your mother. I count only three other children. Is there another one hidden in the cupboard?" Aragon gave her a wink and a smile of his own.

"No," Danielle giggled. "My brother's not in the cupboard. He's gone."

"That's enough Danielle," Quinn interrupted. "Stop bothering the man. He's hungry and doesn't have time for your games. You and the rest of the children go in the other room and leave us alone."

Danielle stared at her father quizzically, not understanding the cause of his peculiar attitude.

"That's all right; she's no bother," Aragon said, then turned his attention back to the little girl. "Your brother is gone, is he? I'm sorry to hear that. Did he die," Aragon asked gently.

"Oh no, he's not dead," Danielle answered. "Keenan just went away."

"Danielle," Quinn snapped, a hard edge added to his voice. "I said go in the other room. Now."

Midori intervened. "Come on children, go get cleaned up for dinner. The soup is done already. I'll bring yours in to you in a moment, after you've cleaned up and changed out of those filthy clothes. Go on, give your father and his friend a chance to talk in private while I fix their plates."

Quinn pushed the tools he was using earlier that morning over to the side of their dining room table, offered Aragon a chair, and invited him to sit at the table and have supper with him. Quinn poured glasses of mulled wine for the three adults, set bread and butter on the table, then sat himself opposite of his guest. Midori brought two bowls of hot soup to the table, indicating that she would have her own after she served the children in the other room. Aragon leaned over his bowl, eyes closed, and breathed in the delicious aroma. Mouth watering, he opened his eyes, picked up his spoon, dipped it into the bowl, and slowly stirred its appetizing contents. Fish, rice, and mushrooms floated in the thick, yellow broth along with celery, onion, and rosemary leaves.

"I hope you like it," said Quinn. "Midori is a great cook. This may not be her best recipe but we all think it's pretty good soup, even if it does have fish in it, which I've never cared for much myself."

Aragon nodded while eating greedily. A long time had passed since he last had the pleasure of a good, home-cooked meal such as he now enjoyed. "It's wonderful," Aragon praised around another mouthful, a trickle of broth dribbling down his bearded chin. The warm liquid filled his stomach and relaxed his muscles. He forced himself to slow his consumption and dine with more characteristic composure. With effort, he regained the habit of more elegant table manners.

Aragon noticed that the walls were adorned with paintings. Although artwork of high quality, Aragon suspected that they were most likely painted by someone within the household, probably the wife as the style and grace embodied in the painting seemed more indicative of a traditional elvin woman than of a frontiersman like Quinn. The frames that enclosed the paintings were also artistic, being large ornately carved creations polished with a gold stain. The elaborate, hardwood frames and the carpentry that produced them Aragon did credit to Quinn as they seemed a craft suited to the man and because they spoke of reverence and loving respect for the beauty they sheltered within their sturdy embrace.

Regarding Quinn, Aragon said. "I hope you're all right. I know I gave you quite a jolt outside but I thought you meant to kill me the way you charged at me with that hammer. You had murder in your eyes. Do you treat all strangers to such a welcome?"

"No. I'm sorry about that. I thought you were someone else."

"Well, I'm glad I'm not," stated Aragon. "He must be a very bad sort of person for you to want to swing a hammer at him like that upon first sight of his approach. Who was this man you thought me to be?"

Quinn shook his head halfheartedly as he tore a piece of bread from the loaf and dipped it in his soup. "No one. Just a ghost from a very long time ago," Quinn answered, bringing the soaked bread to his open mouth. Torrin Murgleys, the cruel conquerer of Gairloch, was well know these days and not at all well liked by anyone. It was not safe to admit any association with the evil emperor, even a distant one that had since turned to enmity.

"Nonsense," replied Aragon, dismissing Quinn's denial. "You thought I was Torrin Murgleys. Well, I'm not. I'm his brother."

Quinn froze. Utter shock immobilized him, halted the hand carrying the bread to his lips. The clenched morsel hung in the air inches from his mouth, dripping broth on his shirt and pants. An icy wave of fear washed over Quinn. Then the beat of his heart quickened to a wild tempo, forcing blood to surge through his veins and flushing him throughout with a frightful fever. A greasy sweat beaded on his forehead and abruptly dampened the underarms of his shirt. At his back, Midori was likewise caught off guard in the sudden grip of fear. She dropped her bowl of soup in a loud clatter on the floor and with dread backed slowly up against the wall behind her. The noise revived Quinn enough to set down his bread and lean back in his chair. However, beyond that faint response, Quinn could still do no more that stare with open alarm at Aragon.

Aragon shrugged and went back to eating his meal with calm indifference, offering his hosts no further sign of menace.

Quinn thought of attacking Aragon but remembered how easily the stranger had dispatched him before and, at present, Aragon appeared more interested in his soup than he did in aggression. So Quinn retaliated with denial. "I don't know why you would claim to be that man's brother; but I don't know Torrin Murgleys. I've never met the man and I hope I never do," rumbled Quinn in a coarse and rigid voice.

"That's not true," said Aragon casually. However, he held Quinn's eyes in an intensely penetrating stare, one so piercingly direct that it seemed to read every secret locked in Quinn's heart. "You knew him rather well. Don't deny it and don't worry; I'm Torrin's brother but I'm not his friend." Aragon relaxed, liberating Quinn from his concentrated gaze by raising his goblet and taking a leisurely sip of wine.

Quinn went on studying Aragon and realized that he did recognize a little of Torrin in the man before him. He was obviously a man of education and intelligence, of power and mystery; but was he an enemy? For some reason, although he feared it might be the influence of wizardry, Quinn felt he could trust Aragon or at least trust that the man was not an ally of Torrin's. And since the man admitted to being Torrin's brother, Quinn decided it might not be too grave a risk to admit having known Torrin long ago. He pushed his bowl aside. Worry gnawed at the inside of his stomach, stealing Quinn's appetite.

"I didn't know he had a brother," confessed Quinn. "Torrin never talked about his family much. I knew that Queen Bryana was his grandmother of course but that was about it. I tried to get him to open up about his family but Torrin was always evasive if not outright hostile on that subject. Besides, I know how family can be a sensitive issue, so if Torrin wanted to keep the matter private I saw no reason not to respect that wish."

"That's true," said Aragon. "But sometimes a person's heritage cannot and should not be kept hidden for it carries certain responsibilities with it that must be acknowledged. Tell me, other than your attempt to kill me, you seem like a peaceful man, a man of plain and wholesome interests, why did you help someone like Torrin? Why did you help him assault and capture Gairloch? And after you took the castle, why did you then leave?"

Quinn sighed and rubbed his face before answering. "You have to understand that the Torrin I knew, the man I called a friend, has been dead for over twenty years. The Lord of Demons who occupies Gairloch and spreads his plague across the land is not the Torrin I knew. It may in truth be the same man, but not in my eyes. It was wrong what we did. But until it was too late, I didn't understand what was happening; I didn't understand what Torrin was becoming."

"Tell me what happened," Aragon urged him.

Quinn looked gently over his shoulder at his wife, offering a confident expression that was enough to sooth her nerves and quiet her inner turmoil. Paroled from her prison of anxiety, she went to work cleaning up the spilled food but with a concerned ear still bent toward her husband's conversation.

"Torrin crowned himself king," began Quinn, "of a small community west of the Purl River called New Hope, although king is probably too grand a term for it. It was my idea for Torrin to become king, but he was good at it. He set up order, helped the people prosper, and gave them protection from the outlaws in that region. I was his second in command and I was proud of what we did there. Then one day Torrin and I and most of our humble army were away chasing down a large band of outlaws. We left the town pretty much undefended but we didn't think there was reason to worry about any sizeable force other than the outlaws we were chasing. We certainly never gave any thought to a threat posed by the royal army of Queen Bryana, who as you know ruled over Gairloch back then. We engaged and defeated the band of outlaws and headed back to New Hope, happy that we had served justice and made our little part of the world safer for our people. As we got closer to home, we rode into a stronger and stronger reek of smoke. Each of us prayed that there was some safe, ordinary reason for so much fire, but we knew in our hearts there was not. They had burned our town, killed our people, and destroyed what we had worked so hard to build. The bastards even left their flag flying over the ruins, as if Bryana should be proud that her royal army could destroy a poor, weak, defenseless town. And they killed Torrin's wife, Lenore. When Torrin found her lifeless body, his heart imploded, collapsing in upon itself under the extreme pressure of his grief and his guilt. He felt responsible because he wasn't there when she needed him. All his dreams turned to ashes. The woman he loved more than anything was dead, the town and people under his care were destroyed, and the future he'd been building was lost. Everything he valued had been burned to the ground and left smoldering. He was tortured by grief but also driven by a hateful need for revenge."

Quinn paused and drank the rest of his wine. Midori refilled his glass, rubbing his back in a gentle circular motion with her other hand. Then she took a seat beside him.

"Something foul stirred within the sediment of Torrin's soul," continued Quinn, "something growing below that murky unexplored spiritual substrate, a burgeoning malevolence. Madness took possession of his soul and would not depart. At the time, I didn't fully understand the intensity of his rage nor how dangerous a man it might make him. We were all outraged, but Torrin more than anyone and he was crazy enough to find a way to vent his extraordinary fury and achieve his horrific vengeance. When he spoke to the survivors of New Hope, the desire for revenge burning through him was bright enough to ignite the same fire in the crowd. And he did everything he said he would, though it seemed impossible at the time. Miraculously, he found elves in Cravenwood and convinced them along with the dwarves of Prakrit to follow him in an attack against Gairloch. It was exceedingly implausible and unbelievably audacious, but we did it. We beat the most powerful kingdom in the known land. We took Gairloch. But along the way, it started to seem less like a campaign in the name of justice for Lenore and our other dead, or even that we were fighting to give the survivors of New Hope protection against future attacks and secure for them a better future."

Aragon nodded with sympathetic appreciation. "You started out after justice, but in the end it was all about Torrin's pride and his lust for power."

"Yes," murmured Quinn. "I guess that's about right. Anyway, when we breached the castle, Torrin was already inside. It was rampant chaos. The riot of the victors struck me as ugly and obscene. So I went in search of Torrin in hope that he could bring order to the murdering, pillaging, and plundering mob our strange collective army had become. I found him in that great hall, the one used by the wizards. He had killed them all, seemed like hundreds of them. I don't know how he could have done it but there was no way it could have been a fair fight. It was as if those wizards had no choice but to be hacked apart. Surrounded by his victims' remains, Torrin lay unconscious on the floor. The floor was carpeted in blood, strewn with torn and mangled flesh. I walked into an abattoir of horrible carnage littered with shattered skulls and severed limbs, faces battered beyond recognition, throats split, and torsos ripped open and emptied of their organs and excrement. Torrin lived but I knew my friend was dead. I knew immediately, beyond any doubt or lingering optimism, that I could not serve this new king and I wanted nothing to do with the kingdom he would create. So amid the barbarous insanity, I fled from Gairloch."

"And what about her," inquired Aragon, gesturing at Midori.

"Along the way," said Quinn, "I found Midori. She was also escaping the castle. We needed each other; and later we grew to love one another. That's the end of it. That was the end of my involvement, though not the end of my shame. And that's all I know about Torrin."

"No," Aragon argued. "Even hidden as you are, here in your charming mountain hideaway, you can't be completely ignorant of what's been happening in the world over the last twenty years. You must know something of the horror that you helped create. You must have heard what Torrin's been doing to the lands around Gairloch. The pressure of his hate inspired vengeance may have formed and hardened the fanatic nature of his character, but the spirit he conceived within himself that night he destroyed the lives and liberty of Gairloch is now nothing but a blind and brutal ambition for power. You must be aware of some of the manifestations of his virulent aspirations. You must have heard of his more recent work."

"Yes," answered Quinn. "Torrin's all about death now. I'm aware of that."

"No," Aragon again disagreed. "Don't fool yourself that he's so simple as that. He's interested in life, not its meaning, certainly not its beauty, and not even the avoidance of its cessation, but rather in how it can be restructured, twisted and perverted, reshaped to serve his momentary whim or his ultimate purpose, his all consuming need for power, the drive to conquer and control, to dominate all life and force all to serve him."

Midori rose and walked silently away to toss another log on the fire burning in the hearth on the other side of the room. The afternoon sun waned. The light of heaven sank into the hills, filling the house with darkening shadow.

Using a splinter of burning wood from the fire, Midori lit seven candles in a large candelabrum. She brought the candelabrum back with her and set the illuminant on the table before returning to her seat.

Aragon savored another sip of the sweet wine and examined Midori with a brief, uneasy glance before continuing their grim conversation. "Torrin's elves abandoned their souls to corruption in their blind allegiance to him and in their own greed for the treasures he promised them. They gleefully pledged themselves to Torrin's foul will and committed themselves to his campaign of terrible conquest. He fed their pride, that most dangerous sin, just as he nourished his own, convincing the elves that they are the supreme race, superior to all others and destined to rule the world under his imperial leadership. Completing their voluntary surrender to Torrin's sinister madness, the White Elves enslaved the human and dwarven comrades who helped them capture Gairloch, and worse yet they began to pervert the fundamental essence and biological existence of these former allies. In their predatory need, their feverish and insatiate quest for power and evil pleasure, Torrin and the elves created things not human, not dwarven, but exotic monstrosities unnaturally born of those two races. From that base material and out of Gairloch's corruption, abhorrent life has been manufactured in frightening quantity and of a quality that is repellant in the extreme. From their degenerate experiments, Torrin and the elves created accursed creatures of morbid origin, malefic expression, and vile purpose. The human and dwarven roots are now barely recognizable in these creatures and the process of their generation has changed over the years so that it's become faster and less dependant on the natural seed.

"From the humans," Aragon continued, "goblins were created and from the dwarves, they fashioned gnomes. Both are fiendish beings of odd bodies and evil minds. Knit in an artificial womb, they are ferociously and woefully made. The goblins have large, round eyes that are a solid blood-red color and seem to lack a pupil. A pronounced ridge forms the brow above those unblinking eyes and below them is a broad, flat nose with up-curved, crescent-shaped nostrils. Their sense of smell is very keen, though their odor is very foul. Expansive jaws house upper and lower canine teeth so elongated that they are almost tusks, re-curved, yellow, and carnivorous fangs. They have thick, insensitive hides made of a slimy amphibian-like skin, almost the color of molded fruit, a greenish brown with a lacework of red woven sickeningly through their loathsome flesh. Their heads are characteristically bald but they have fine coarse hairs thinly scattered all over their bodies and thick tufts of it on their large, pointed, pig-like ears. The arms of the goblins are abnormally long and they can attain amazing speeds when running on all fours.

"The gnomes are also creatures of grotesque appearance and formidable strength, but have a more reptilian skin that is made up of tough yellow and black scales. Their heads are crowned with thick black hair, like a horse's mane, along with a pair of horns. Powerful, four-taloned claws constitute their hands. They have the eyes of a poisonous snake, green orbs slit by a black vertical pupil, with which to regard their prey, eyes that at night emit an eerie luminosity. Within their wide mouths lay two or three rows of wickedly sharp, serrated, triangle-shaped teeth. The babel of these obscene creatures, both gnome and goblin, is a blend of bestial cries and common words, and it is the latter of which that seems more frightening that they should be capable of uttering. I know you're isolated here, so perhaps you've been lucky enough so far never to have seen a goblin or gnome, but I'd be surprised if you've not heard of them before now."

"I've heard of them," grumbled Quinn. "And I've heard other vague, wild tales of bizarre and disturbing things that supposedly prowl around Gairloch these days. Most of it I'll wager is exaggerated country gossip."

"You'd loose that wager and you know it," Aragon assured his unwilling listener. "There's truth in what you've heard about the goblins and gnomes. Perhaps you've also heard that Torrin has grown an army of these vicious breeds and that the number of these gross atrocities continues to increase as does the destruction they wreak. These mutant species have been created by Torrin not simply for his depraved amusement but to invade the rest of the world and facilitate his total dominion. Torrin's infamy is spreading wide. Kin Slayer, Lord of Demons, Devourer of Souls, Plague Master, they are all his names now, titles Torrin has rightfully earned. With the White Elves, Torrin has led his accursed legions, his nightmare breed of goblins and gnomes, in campaigns to expand the territory under his control. Too many have already perished under his axe, the same axe he used to annihilate the wizard Prelature over twenty years ago. It has a name now you know; people call it Cleofan, the Maul of Murgleys. It is a weapon of unfathomable and unforgiving power. In time, Torrin's army and his axe will lay the world to waste and create an unending realm of horror. The kingdom of Braemar is growing weak and will likely soon topple. Others will quickly follow. Even you and your little family won't be safe here for long. Something must be done to stop him, or to at least reduce the enormity of his threat. And it must begin with that axe. It must be torn from his grip, so that in losing it, Torrin will lose a significant measure of his power."

"Yes," sighed Quinn, running thumb and index finger from the center of his upper lip, around each corner of his mouth, and down his chin. His hand repeated the circuit several times. "That axe is evil, of that I have no doubt."

"Its power is used for evil," remarked Aragon. "But it's still just a tool. Can an inanimate object really be evil, or only the intentions and deeds of the person who uses that object?"

"But that axe is not just an inert object," insisted Quinn. As he leaned forward on the table, it seemed to buckle slightly under his weight. "I felt it, I held it in my hands and it turned my stomach. It sickened my soul. It was as if it were somehow, at some level, alive. It seemed to have a deep underlying conscious purpose, a malevolent purpose ingrained within the wood and metal." Quinn reached over to the pile of tools at the far end of the dinner table, picked one out, and held it in front of his guest. "This chisel may be neither good nor evil. I used it once to build a crib for my children but I could also use it to kill. In its case, the quality of good or evil may lie only in the hand that holds it. But that axe is something different. It was changed by what Torrin did, as if it became possessed of a spirit, one with goals of its own."

"Perhaps," Aragon shrugged. "Regardless, it must be taken from Torrin. It is a thing of great power and Torrin already has too much of that. It must be taken from him and destroyed or at least secured against improper use."

"I agree, but if the world can't stand up against Torrin, there is nothing I can do. So why are you here looking for me?"

"I'm not looking for you," Aragon admitted. He stared intently at Quinn. "I'm looking for Torrin's son."

Terrible surprise drained the life from Quinn's face, leaving it a ghostly visage. "What son, and why come looking for him here."

"Because his mother is here," Aragon announced with dreadful certainty.

Quinn sprang to his feet, overturning the chair behind him. He leaned forward with his knotted fists resting against the tabletop, glowering at Aragon. "What are you saying? What are you accusing my wife of? How dare you come into my home, eat my food, and make such accusations against my wife's honor?"

Aragon stood up slowly, his manner calm but with the quiet threat of command and dominant capabilities hidden in his lesser stature. "I'm not accusing her of any crime or infidelity? She only made a mistake, the same one you did; she trusted Torrin. And that mistake resulted in a child, I believe your little girl called him Keenan."

"That's bullshit, you filthy maggot," Quinn cursed. "I'm Keenan's father."

Aragon held his ground surrounded by an aura of authority. "I understand why you would say that, but you and I both know that he was conceived by Torrin and not by you."

Midori righted Quinn's overturned chair. With comforting hands placed tenderly on his back and bicep, she gently urged her husband to recapture his seat and regain his composure. "It's all right my love," she murmured softly to Quinn as both men sat back down. "Clearly our guest is already acquainted with that part of our story. You might as well explain what he already knows."

Quinn sighed deeply and raised one hand to rub his eyes. He was tired but still full of anger. "They were together before Midori and I left Gairloch, before she and I were married, before we fell in love. But it doesn't make any difference. He's my son damn it! I raised him. I gave him love. I comforted him when he was hurt or afraid, made certain he ate his meals, did his chores, took his baths, did his studies. In every way that really counts for a damn, I'm his father. And wizard or not, I'll break your stinking neck, you meddling bastard, if you do anything to hurt him."

Despite the threats, Aragon sensed that Quinn was a very good man and no doubt a wonderful father. It troubled Aragon deeply that he must upset Quinn like this, that he had to use him, provoke him into revealing the hard truth and push him into action. But it was necessary. The stakes were high and Aragon could not afford too much sympathy at this juncture of the game.

"Does Keenan know that Torrin is his biological father," Aragon pried.

Quinn threw up his hands in disgust. "Of course not, who would want to know a thing like that. And what difference would such knowledge make other than to confuse and hurt the boy. He knows who his real family is, knows who loves him and where he belongs."

"It does make a difference. Keenan must understand where he comes from and accept the responsibility of his parentage and his heritage. He has a duty to perform, an obligation to society that only he can accomplish. If he hides from it, he turns his back on the world and a deaf ear to the cries of Torrin's future victims."

"What duty?" Quinn scoffed. "He's just a boy. What obligation does he have to society other than to live justly and to live well? Get to the point; what do you want with him?"

"Keenan must do it!" Aragon proclaimed. "Keenan must take the axe from Torrin. He's no boy, and you know it. Keenan's twenty; that's as old as Torrin was when the two of you took Gairloch."

"Why Keenan," Quinn asked roughly. "Why does it have to be my son? He's innocent in all this."

"It must be one of the Murgleys line," insisted Aragon. "Only a Murgleys could hope to control the power contained in that blade even for a short time."

"Then you do it. You're a Murgleys." Quinn pointed at Aragon.

"No!" Aragon snapped. "The thought of such power in my grip is abhorrent to me. That, together with the power already in my possession, would be far too dangerous. Too dangerous for me, and for everyone."

"You're damn right it's dangerous. Yet you want my son to assume that danger as well as others. No. I won't let you use him. I won't tell you where he is."

"Then I'll find him myself," replied Aragon. "I just thought it might be easier for him if he found out about his father from you."

"Bullshit, you don't care about his feelings. But it doesn't matter; you don't even know who you're looking for. You'll never find him."

"I found you didn't I?" Aragon answered ominously.

Quinn was on his feet again, shouting in a lethal tone, his anger and his fear flaring out of control. "Get out! Get out of my house and off my land. My family doesn't want anything to do with you or the name Murgleys. Now go, and don't come back!"

Aragon stood, collected his staff, and bowed to Midori. "Thank you for dinner, it was delicious." Not expecting a reply, he turned and with long, confident strides walked quickly for the door. They followed him out. Quinn and Midori stood silently on the porch as they watched Aragon mount his horse and ride off, relieved to see him go but worried about where he might be bound and what he might be planning.

Once Aragon was out of sight, Midori said, "You have to go after him."

"I know," groaned Quinn.

"You have to find Keenan, and do it before Aragon does. You have to tell Keenan everything. If you can, bring him home. Tell him it's only for a while but if he won't come, make sure he knows to stay away from that man. What he wants will get Keenan killed, and that's not all that frightens me about that man."

"I know," he agreed. "I'm scared too. I'll leave first thing in the morning. I'll explain things to Keenan and make certain he understands the danger he's in. But I'm worried about leaving you and the kids here alone."

"We'll be fine," she assured him. "You take care of Keenan. Go protect our son; he needs you more than we do right now."

Chapter 3

Braemar was dying. Alissa knew this was true even though her father, King Donovan, had spent his life fighting to save the moribund kingdom and prevent its ill-fated, premature demise. It was a torment to watch as a loved one died and to witness every effort at resuscitation fail. It was a torment she and her father had shared. For years they denied Braemar's terminal condition and kept faith in the possibility of recovery, that together its citizens could yet triumph over the disease that threatened Braemar's existence. But the evidence of its fading life was all around her, growing more obvious with each passing year, so that Alissa could no longer cling to naive hopes of a spontaneous resurgence in Braemar's health.

The wars had greatly diminished the numbers and strength of her people, leaving the halls and courts to seem so empty these days, so devoid of the vitality and splendor that once occupied the castle. The regular army, battle hardened men of extraordinary skill and bravery, was now only a skeleton of its former well-built body. The auxiliary army of women, old men, and young boys failed to instill much confidence and only contributed to the insidious foreboding of imminent defeat. Poorly tended, the farms now yielded a humble bounty, crops pitiable in quality and quantity. Their flocks of cattle and sheep had become thin and unhealthy, a herald of the destiny that would befall their masters.

During most of the twenty-three years since her birth, as Alissa's own strength and beauty increased, she saw Braemar grow steadily weaker and more decrepit. Alissa now understood that if there was any hope of a cure it would have to come from without as well as from within. If Braemar was going to be saved, it would need outside help, a transfusion of energy and might. Though it had been hard for a man of such independent pride, she knew her father had reluctantly come to the same realization.

Not long after taking Gairloch, Torrin Murgleys mobilized his forces in an effort to expand his conquest and broaden his realm. The countryside surrounding Gairloch was devoured and the rural folk displaced, decimated, or enslaved. Garrisons of troops dispatched from Gairloch and stationed there to maintain Torrin's control ruled the country farms and communities. These garrisons were made up of mostly human and dwarven soldiers governed by a seneschal who was always an elf. Most of these lands had previously been under the protection of Bryana when she sat as queen over Gairloch. So Braemar had not resisted much in the beginning of Torrin's campaign. However, Torrin's army grew and changed, and before long he began to encroach on Braemar's territories. At first, Braemar easily defended its borders but as the years passed, the enemy became more formidable and soon attacked even the castle stronghold of Braemar itself. Torrin led his army in these attacks against Braemar's castle, riding in a chariot pulled by a massive griffon. Braemar's soldiers had managed to kill the griffon but not the beast that held its reins. Torrin seemed almost immortal and he fought with a magical axe, the Maul of Murgleys, that was possessed of a power equivalent to a hundred warriors. Over the years there were fewer and fewer humans and dwarves in Torrin's army, but the ranks of his soldiers multiplied. The nature of his army underwent radical anatomical changes, mutating over time until it became almost entirely composed of goblins and gnomes, heinous monstrosities commanded by White Elves and the malevolent purposes of Emperor Torrin. In battle, Torrin extravagantly expended these revolting creatures, careless of his losses, but each year there seemed to be more and each new generation appeared stronger and deadlier than its predecessor. Braemar had managed to hang on to its castle and the lands immediately around the fortress, but they were still losing ground, losing people, and losing hope. What Gairloch had been unable to destroy all at once it would soon conquer through attrition.

King Donovan stood in his throne room, meeting with his treasury minister, army general, agricultural advisor, and others. They discussed the state of the kingdom, inventorying its wealth and military might. It was information Parhelion, their neighbor to the south, would want in anticipation of the union between their royal families. Also, Donovan had to find a way to amass a suitable dowry without crippling Braemar's already frail economy.

Beginning seven years ago, the kingdom of Parhelion had periodically sent soldiers to help Braemar in its border wars with Gairloch. No formal alliance existed, but Parhelion and Braemar had a history of friendship and cooperation, so they were willing to assist one another during times of need. However, last year the need and its associated cost had proven too great for Parhelion. In that last battle against Gairloch's invasion of Braemar's territories, Parhelion had suffered such a considerable loss of soldiers and military provisions that it gave them pause and made the kingdom more conservative with its forces. Parhelion declined Braemar's requests for further help, determining that it was in Parhelion's best interests to reserve its forces against the growing possibility that its own kingdom may require defense against invasion. All subsequent attempts by Braemar to persuade Parhelion that their interests were inherently linked had failed. Only one way remained to join the interests of the two kingdoms and unite them in defense against Gairloch while preserving Braemar's independence. A marriage was being arranged between King Donovan's only daughter, Alissa, and prince Tynan, son of Parhelion's King Cameron.

With Alissa married to Parhelion's prince, her younger brother, Nolan, would become heir to Braemar's throne upon Donovan's death. However, in order to save his beloved sister from matrimony to Tynan, Nolan would have gladly forfeited this opportunity to one day ascend the throne and receive coronation as Braemar's king. But that choice was not his to make. It was Alissa's decision. For even though he saw no other way to save Braemar, King Donovan could not bring himself to demand the sacrifice of her. However, there proved to be no need of demands. Although she would have preferred another, Alissa understood and accepted this approaching marriage of necessity.

Alissa entered the throne room quietly, so as not to disturb her father's dialogue with his chief civil and military advisors. Her father kept no secrets from her concerning the kingdom's affairs, so she knew that her presence was not a violation of the king's privacy. But not wanting to infringe upon their time and distract their attention from important matters of state, she took a chair behind the men and the table at which they stood looking over rolled out documents and maps. She sat with her hands folded neatly in her lap, content to silently wait and listen, confident that she would learn from what she heard. After a few minutes, however, they all seemed to sense her presence at once and with unanimous accord, all turned their attention in her direction. Not one of them appeared displeased by the interruption she had unintentionally imposed. Their expressions had been grim before but when they recognized Alissa, each face broke into a smile of sincere pleasure. Almost without exception, she had this same effect on everyone regardless of their social station; from peasants to princes, all felt their spirits lift and their virtuous natures enlivened by her company.

If they did not share so many of the same troubles as Alissa, most who encountered her might suppose that all her cares were light and her conflicts nonexistent as she was so often smiling with a pleasant air of calm tranquility. Her tender manner and positive attitude proved a reliable source of cheer and encouragement to all who came in contact with her.

Alissa possessed an aura of unique beauty, a luminous quality that seemed to make her shine brighter than the drab reality in which she lived. She was a woman whose exquisite physical charm was surpassed only by the radiant beauty of her heart, the imperishable jewel of a gentle and quiet spirit. Her body was a perfect setting for that brilliant jewel, a perfect chamber for such a kind and caring soul. Her face and body were an outward expression of internal grace. She was intelligent and confident, eloquent and self-assured, and enormously pleasing to the eye; yet all her charismatic qualities were above envy or reproach because of the genuine modesty that permeated her character. But she was not just a lovely flower with a quick mind and a compassionate soul. Her father had seen to it that his daughter was instructed in the use of weapons and she had been an apt pupil. Although she had not yet been allowed to participate in much actual combat, her strong, lean body was well trained for battle and quite capable with a sword.

Alissa stood and bowed slightly. "Forgive me gentlemen," she said. "I apologize for my intrusion. But please don't stop on my account; don't let me keep you from your vital business. I promise to remain quiet and ask that you simply ignore my presence here."

Blayne, the king's agricultural advisor walked over to Alissa. Taking her hand in his, he kissed the backs of her fingers and said, "When all are weary of the night, how could anyone ignore the rising sun."

"It's good to see you, princess," said Morgan, the king's general. "And with all due respect, I doubt you could remain quiet for too long. You have too many ideas and opinions for one mind to contain, views on every subject, even on how I should manage our army. And more often than not, they are good suggestions that we're wise to follow." He laid his callused hand on her shoulder in relaxed comradery. His scared, wizened face beamed with a gapped-tooth grin.

"Gentlemen, let's take a break from our planning and assessments," Donovan said to Blyane, Morgan, and the others. "We can resume all this later in the afternoon. Right now I want to spend some time with my daughter. She will be leaving for Parhelion soon and I want to take advantage of her company while I still can."

He walked them to the door. Behind him, Alissa bid them good day and again apologized. Donovan closed the doors and turned back to face his daughter.

"When I hear your voice I keep expecting to see my little girl. But you're all grown up," Donovan observed, his lips askew with a melancholy grin. "I see the woman you've become and I realize how much I've missed of your life. The pressures and demands of my office, the years of war with Gairloch, they all conspired to keep me from my family. I missed so much of your childhood and your brother's. I spent far too many days beyond the reach of your mother's loving embrace. There are so many memories we never had a chance to build together, so many experiences that were postponed for another day. But time, like a good soldier, kept marching forward into a future that would no longer allow those domestic experiences of innocent joy to ever happen."

Alissa took her father's hands in hers and squeezed them lightly with filial kindness. "Although far too rare, the time we were able to share with you was precious and we always made the most of it."

Donovan released her hands and his grin broadened a bit. "I love the woman you've become but I still miss the little girl you were."

"I will always be your little girl."

"And I miss your mother more than I can ever express," Donovan complained. "I especially wish she could be here now to help you as you prepare for this marriage. I'm sure you need comfort and counsel that only she could give, that I don't know how to offer you."

"You are a comfort," Alissa encouraged. "And although I miss her too, mother is always with me here." She folded her slim hands together and laid them on her chest over her heart.

"Your mother will always be a part me too," Donovan agreed. "The best part of my heart is reserved for her. I hope she knew how deeply I loved her.

I wish I would have told her more often. I regret so much being away, fighting the border wars with Torrin and his demons, when she fell ill and died. I regret leaving her here to die alone."

"She didn't die alone, Father," Alissa insisted patiently. "We were with her."

"Yes, I'm thankful for that but ashamed too that I had to leave my poor children to grieve alone, strangers their only hope for comfort."

"Father, they were hardly strangers," Alissa said, her mellifluous voice as soothing in its tone as in the content of her words. "We had the shoulders of loved ones here on which to cry. You shouldn't exaggerate the misfortune in order to punish yourself with excessive self-reproach. We all knew why you could not be here. We respect your office and the obligations it places on you. We respect you for fulfilling them. We know your love is with us, even when you are not. Mother knew this too. Her final words were of love for you."

"You are too kind to your father," Donovan sighed, still savoring the sweet honey of his daughter's speech. "My guilt might be easier to bear if you were angry with me and I was forced to defend myself against your condemnation. But no, I've taught you too well that the demands of duty must be honored and obeyed, that we must respectfully fulfill our royal obligations. Discipline, rather than desire, must be the determinant of a monarch's destiny. And I see that quality of me in you. I recognize it in your acceptance of this miserable duty, your willingness to sacrifice yourself before the alter and marry Parhelion's Prince Tynan."

"Oh Father, you're exaggerating again," she scoffed. "Marriage to Tynan isn't like being burned at the stake and it won't be the great and terrible martyrdom that you portray it to be. Tynan is a nice man, immature in some ways, but usually quite considerate and generous. Although perhaps largely for superficial reasons, he does regard me in very high esteem. And from what I know of him, he's never intentionally cruel. He is young and strong with a pleasant appearance. He should make a fine husband and produce fine children."

"But you don't love him," Donovan asked somberly, casting a doubtful look at his daughter.

"No," she answered flatly.

"I wanted you to marry for love, just as your mother and I did, and know our same joy."

"So did I," she expressed with restrained grief. "But that cannot be."

"How can I do this," Donovan inquired, the question directed more at himself than to Alissa. Anxiety and guilt twisted his words. "I'm making a whore of you. I'm selling my own daughter for peace and for protection against my enemies."

"Father, do not say that again!" Alissa commanded, angered by Donovan's aspersing comment. "Do not wound me with such an insulting analogy ever again. I am no whore. You know that I have never opened my body to any man, that I value my chastity and have preserved my virginity. You know my long held morality and motives for wanting to save myself for my wedding night, to be able to present myself as a pure gift to my husband. I just never imagined that it would be Tynan. But even if there is not love between us, it is not prostitution. I am not a whore because the sex will be sanctified by marriage and made holy by our vows."

"Yes, I'm sorry," he said. "I should not have spoken such thoughtless words. And of course I don't really think of you that way. I'm just ashamed of myself for not finding some way to spare you from this political marriage and give you the freedom to marry the man you love. There is someone, isn't there? I've seen you with one of the captains of my cavalry, a young man named Rorke. Neither of you are obvious in your attentions to one another but it's clear that there is love between you. Initially, the attraction surprised me a little but he is a good man and I would not have opposed your interest in him. You love him, don't you?"

"Yes, but it must never be spoken of," she said dolefully, her words quavering before her voice found solid ground on which to stand. "It would not do honor to my marriage to have rumors spread that another man occupies my true affections."

"After you marry, you could still see this Rorke secretly. Such things are done and royalty is often given greater liberty in such matters."

"No," she stated firmly. "That would be wrong Father. And I ask that in the future you not encourage or even suggest such infidelity. It is hard enough to resist temptation as it is. Remember, it is still a sin even if committed in the name of love."

"I hope your husband, Tynan, shares the same opinion."

"So do I," Alissa answered somberly.

Her grave admission and his own frustration set the king in motion. Donovan began to pace back and forth beside the table, the restless movements of his body an inept expression of the inner turmoil in his soul.

"I hate Gairloch and all the evil brewed in that infernal cauldron," he avowed vehemently. "But sometimes I think I hate the other kingdoms even more. I hate how they ignore Gairloch, ignore what's happening to us, ignore the fact that for years we have been under attack and that if we fall, they will be next. I hate how they use us as their defense without giving us help or even thanks. I hate how they have forced me into this position. I hate that I am making my daughter marry a man she doesn't love so that Parhelion will finally commit itself in complete resistance against Gairloch."

"Hate will not help," Alissa reasoned with him. "And you are not making me do anything. This marriage was my idea and my decision. And in a way, I am marrying for love. I'm marrying out of love for Braemar and its people. I've accepted it and so must you. There is no profit in dwelling upon the unhappy aspect of this union. We must focus on the greater good that will come from it, the hope and prosperity it will mean for so many people that are suffering far beyond what minor disappointment I may feel about this wedding. We must accept it and with a heart full of thanksgiving we must move forward with the preparations."

However, before they could continue to mine that vein of thought and excavate a final plan, the discourse of father and daughter was intruded upon by another. Nolan, the young prince, used his backside to push open a small side door, causing it to bang against the wall in an uncommonious announcement of his arrival. In one hand he held a silver plate filled with roast chicken, bread, and a viscous, brown gravy. The other palm cupped a goblet of goat's milk.

Three years younger than his sister, Nolan was a tall, handsome man with chiseled features and a well-carved physique. His thick, brown hair hung to his nape in loose, carefree curls that appeared stylish rather than unkempt. He possessed a boyish charm and a purblind outlook, his mental vision untroubled by much of the deeper colors and richer textures of life's complex tapestry.

After crossing the room to the clomping beat of his heavy boots against the hardwood floor, Nolan laid his meal upon the table. The impolite prince brushed the king's documents and maps aside, and placed a chair before his solitary table setting.

"Are we converting my throne room into a dinning hall," the king asked in lighthearted sarcasm.

Nolan raised and lowered his shoulders in a slow perfunctory shrug, used his fingers to tear a chunk of meat from a chicken leg, and dropped the ragged callop of poultry into his mouth.

"Oh well," said the king. "I suppose it won't hurt this once, especially since we so seldom have the opportunity to take our meals together any more. And it's good you're here for we were just getting ready to make plans for the wedding."

"I want no part of it," Nolan grumped sullenly.

"Nolan," Donovan barked. "You will behave as a member of this royal family should, fill the role you're given, and participate as necessary."

"Sorry." Nolan offered the single word as a brusque, inimical request for forgiveness and avoided any further reply by coughing into his fist. Although not remorseful of his attitude, Nolan made a cheap show of it in order to mollify Donovan's reproach. His father was normally gentle with his children but at times, like now when Donovan's eyes narrowed and his brow drew close, a tremor of fear rippled through Nolan's heart, not so much a fear of physical violence, as a fear of his father's disapproval, damning and difficult to revoke.

"The nuptials will be held at Parhelion," explained Donovan, "as is customary and in our case prudent given the somewhat compromised condition of our own castle. Alissa must be there in advance of the ceremony so that she can spend time with Tynan's family and assist directly with the wedding arrangements at their castle. Parhelion's queen will help Alissa select material for her bridal gown and have it sewn and fitted there. Alissa is leaving for Parhelion the day after tomorrow, accompanied by an armed escort of twenty of our best soldiers. That should be adequate since she will be bound southward away from Gairloch and isn't likely to encounter any significant hazard along that route. The rest of us will follow in two weeks with the gifts of wealth and property we shall present to Tynan as a dowry."

Donovan continued but Nolan lost track of his father's words, his attention drawn away by the provocative lure of his sister's pouting lips, the delicacy of her fine-boned face, the emerald fire of her eyes. Although he would deny it, Nolan is obsessively in love with his sister and has struggled for years to resist his forbidden fondness for her. The sight of her caught his heart, holding it with a love so intense it hurt, but with a pain not so great as the aching prospect of abandoning that love and accepting her marriage to Tynan.

Licking chicken grease from his fingers, Nolan allowed his eyes to feast on Alissa while she remained focused on their father. He admired the glossy sheen of her long, flowing auburn hair, a beautiful cascade that tumbled about her shoulders. His eyes slid along the graceful column of her slender throat, over the smooth roll of her shoulders, and down the delicate ridge of her converging collarbones. Suspended from Alissa's nape hung an elaborate necklace of lacquered brass cast in a dainty, interwoven network of scrolling curlicues and set with sparkling purple gems cut in ovals and marques. At the center, a triple tier amethyst teardrop dangled from the necklace's lowest point. Her ankle length, lavender gown was cut from luxurious velvet artfully worked with paisley brocade and encrusted with ebony beadwork. Black satin piping around the décolleté accentuated the deep, square-cut neckline. The gown laced in back behind a v-waist bodice that served to emphasize the pleasant proportions of her figure. The long sleeves of the elegant garment ended in a point at the top of her hand with a loop over the second finger. Foolishly, Nolan felt jealous of the dress for unlike him, it could hold Alissa in a tight embrace and feel the warm press of her body. He marveled at the fullness of her breasts outlined by the satin border of her gown, ran his probing gaze along the sleek, flared contours of her hips, and imagined the smooth, lithe lines of the long, supple legs concealed beneath the fabric of her clothes. If not for his unnatural love for his sister, Nolan could have virtually any woman he desired. But he wanted Alissa and the remoteness of the possibility had exaggerated the strength of the attraction.

My heart is so weak, thought Nolan remorsefully as he continued to stare at his sister. *I know it's wrong, but I can't stop loving you. Surely you must see how I feel, and it forces you to be strong for both of us and fight the mutual attraction. Or is it that you do not share my love, that I see only what I so desperately want? I remember when as young children our lips would touch, before we knew what kisses meant. How often and how wistfully I look back on those times now, longing for the lost purity and innocence of our transgressions and wishing for them again. I wish for those sweet lips pressed to mine with every breath I take, in every dream I have, in every waking hour's thought, and with every prayer I make. Now that we are older and it would mean so much more, why must our kisses be forbidden by the cruel dictates of traditional morality and the arbitrary rule of social custom? Why should these trivial formalities bar the path to love? In a world so full of evil and sin, how can love be called that too? It should stand out like a beacon in the night. But mine is not to shine. I must hide my love, deny it, and if possible extinguish it. This is not a rash or idle infatuation, but a deep and consuming love that has grown greater day by day for years. You must not marry Tynan. What chance is there for my happiness without love or at least the hope of love? What use is life without your love?*

"Nolan," said the king, rousing his son from his reverie, "How does all that sound to you?"

"Uhm, it sounds fine," Nolan replied. He had only a vague idea about what he was agreeing to and in actuality he doubted that it was fine at all. But there was little point in seeking clarification or in voicing his real opinion concerning the upcoming wedding.

"Good," Donovan asserted, closing the subject and opening another. "The smell of your chicken has made me hungry. And the roar in my stomach suggests I should get something to eat before I reconvene my meeting with my advisors. They think I growl at them enough as it is. Alissa, since Nolan didn't bring enough to share, would you like to come with me to get some food of our own?"

Alissa accepted her father's offer and the two of them took their leave.

The two days passed quickly and the time came for Alissa to depart her ancestral home and leave behind the life she knew and cherished. Soon life would change forever, the familiar would be replaced with the unknown, her view of family would take on new definition, her dreams would be remolded into new shapes, and nothing would ever again be what it was.

Alissa was alone with these troubling thoughts as she saddled her horse within one of the stalls inside the king's stables. After fitting the bridle over the horse's head, she rubbed her hand along its neck, feeling the soft plush of the sorrel's reddish-brown coat. It was a close match to the slightly darker shade of Alissa's own chestnut-colored auburn hair, a long mane now woven into a single, thick braid that hung down the back of her neck. She was dressed in simple tan pants and a white shirt with a ruffled collar and loose, flowing sleeves. Over the shirt, she wore a burgundy suede bodice with gold trim that laced in front.

After a few minutes she sensed that she was no longer completely alone with the horses. Two stalls down, a man stood quietly in the shadows, watching her. At first she stiffened in surprise and experienced a quick shiver of apprehension. But pretending not to notice his presence, she listened, waited, and gradually relaxed as Alissa somehow became certain she knew who was keeping her under his clandestine observation. Alissa let him watch, sympathetically giving him time to deal with his sorrow and determine how he wanted to deal with their imminent separation.

Clinging to the shadows, Rorke breathed deeply, letting the air flow slowly in and out of his lungs. The equestrian scent of horses, hay, and even the animal's manure was a balmy fragrance to the career cavalryman. It comforted him. It calmed him. So did the sight of Alissa, her wholesome, unadorned beauty. Seeing her made his heart swell with joy, even as the thought of a future without her was breaking it apart. He respected the courage and compassion that moved her to set her own desires aside and do what was best for Braemar, even though her decision would bury their chance for love. He desperately wanted her to stay but because of his love for her, he also wanted to make it easier for her to endure leaving. To do that, maybe he should leave her alone. What good would one last goodbye be to either of them?

Wiping away a tear and swallowing the lump in his throat, Rorke left the concealment of his hiding place and walked toward her. As he approached, Alissa turned and smiled. An inner voice shouted at him to sweep her into his arms and never let go. He ignored the clamorous impulse and settled instead for laying a tentative hand lightly over her upper arm.

Rorke was five years older and at least four inches shorter than Alissa. Rorke's shaved head possessed a face composed of blunt features, a flat, crooked nose, and thin lips set within a trim black goatee. Although a dull brown color, his alert eyes sparkled with acumen. His head seemed to sit on his brawny shoulders without the normal intervening interruption of a neck. Strong and squat, his thick body appeared as immovable as stone. His military attire further augmented the impression of obdurate strength conveyed in his solid build. Over his barrel chest, Rorke wore a chainmail hauberk beneath a soft, leather surcoat that hung to mid-thigh. The surcoat had quarter-sleeves and was died a forest green and decorated at the edges with interlocking designs stitched in heavy black thread. The front of the garment also bore the embroidered outline of a mountain lion. Vambraces of hard, thick cowhide protected his forearms and supple gloves covered his hands in black leather to match his knee-high boots. Circling his waist and supporting his double-edged sword was a studded leather belt with a silver buckle cast in the form of a roaring lion's head.

"Alissa, I had to see you before you left," Rorke told her.

"I'm glad you did. The last time we talked was far too sad."

"I know," he affirmed. "I'm sorry that in my selfishness I grieved you even further than you already were. I was only foolishly grasping for some way to keep you near me. I didn't want to hurt you with my words. That's the last thing I want. I would do anything to make you happy, even if it means letting you go. And I would do anything to keep you away from harm. With all my heart, with all that I am, I lo-."

She put her fingers to his lips stopping him before he could proclaim his love. "In time you'll find another," she said, her voice rich with tenderness, her eyes moist with restrained tears. "Don't waste on me those special, precious words you should reserve for her."

He kissed her fingers and she withdrew them.

"My feelings for you will never change," Rorke declared.

"I hope they will," she urged. "For my sake, you must try. I could hardly bear the knowledge that your feelings for me linger without hope of expression or the possibility of my returning them, and that the cruel constancy of that denied emotion should cause you torment for even one year let alone for a lifetime."

"I would do anything in my power for you," Rorke pledged. "But what you ask is beyond it."

"Try," she said and turned from him toward the sorrel. "What do you think of my horse. Did I saddle him properly? Does the captain of the cavalry approve of my work?"

Rorke made a show of carefully inspecting the horse's harness although he knew it to be unnecessary. She was a skilled rider and they both knew it.

"Looks good. You should enlist in the cavalry. I'd be proud to have you serve under my command," he joked.

"I'm sure you would," she replied facetiously. "But I think you would enjoy giving me orders too much."

Rorke made a show of exaggerated offense at her suggestion. "Never," he insisted dismissively. "I am always fair with my soldiers."

Their eyes held one another and they shared a warm, visual embrace. Then Alissa took the reins in her hand and began leading the horse down the aisle and out of the stables. Rorke followed alongside her, their fingers almost touching.

"You're not traveling in one of the king's carriages," Rorke asked. "Won't Tynan be expecting his bride to arrive with more pomp and grandeur than this?"

"No," she answered. "There will be plenty of that silliness later. We will save the pageantry for the wedding. Riding on horseback without all the ceremonial dress will be less conspicuous, and more comfortable."

They reached the stable gates and saw the twenty soldiers across the courtyard waiting to accompany Alissa on her journey. She turned and looked into Rorke's forlorn face. Then a mighty belch rumbled past her lips and her eyes twinkled with delight.

The unexpected treat of her gastrointestinal roar forced a loud bark of laughter from Rorke and he smiled with true humor and affection. "With manners like that you'll be the pride of Parhelion," he chuckled.

Alissa smiled back at him, her teeth a string of flawless, snow-white pearls. "Better to let go and bear the shame than stifle it and bear the pain," she said with a wink.

"I agree." Rorke's smile faded just as his laughter had ended its short-lived existence. His demeanor sobered and his words became earnest. "I want you to know that if there is ever something troubling you, you can always 'let go' with me. You know how it hurts me to see you leave, but my friendship is yours forever. If you're ever in pain, know that you can share your burden with me. You don't have to 'stifle it.' If you ever need me, I will always be willing to help you, freely and unconditionally, and I will never ask for more than you can give."

She touched his hand briefly. Then with a flourish of perfect grace she mounted her horse and rode away from him toward her escorts. They formed a protective barrier around her and marched on horseback through the castle courtyard and out the main gate.

Chapter 4

His father thought that Keenan left his childhood home in hope of finding a wife, and that was certainly part of the young man's impetus to roam. Few women found reason to come near their family farm in the mountains and Keenan had been interested in the fairer sex for several years. But in addition to a growing sexual appetite and dreams of a wife, and one day children of his own, boredom also gave motive to Keenan's escape from a home that in recent years had come to seem about as exciting as cold oatmeal. Although he loved them, Keenan wearied of the same scenery, the same company, and the same daily routines of home. He longed for excitement and adventure, and the thought that such exotic things were out there in the world waiting for him was as seductively compelling as the tantalizing attentions of all the beautiful women that Keenan also fancied must be anxiously awaiting him. Being young and naive, such immature notions were understandable if not all together rational. His father understood the necessity of Keenan's travel but hated to see his son go and hoped he would soon come back bringing a good wife with him and leaving behind his youthful appetite for the vanities and cares of the outside world.

Quinn worried to excess about his children, for their happiness and well being, and out of that extreme loving concern, he conditioned the terms of Keenan's departure before bestowing his blessing upon his son's decision to leave. Quinn refused to allow Keenan to journey to Braemar for that kingdom was too much at war with Gairloch these days and he did not want his son to get caught up in their battles. He ruled out the kingdoms of Parhelion and Garonne as possibilities because they were simply farther away than Quinn yet felt comfortable permitting his child to move from home. That left the west, but Quinn also excluded the town of New Hope from consideration. He did not know what the place was like now, but Quinn's old memories of the town made it unpleasant for him to think of his son taking up residence in New Hope, the site where so much of Quinn's own trouble and sorrow began. They agreed upon the town of Abandon, for the time being or at least as a place to start his introduction into the larger world.

Keenan had been in the town now for several months but had yet to experience the thrill of romance or any stimulating escapades fit to earn him even modest heroic fame or palmary fortune. In truth, he still felt ill at ease around so many people. He did not know how to connect with the town's folk and hadn't made many friends yet, or even many familiar acquaintances. The people seemed so different and so preoccupied with their own lives that occasionally he experienced the imagined sensation of invisibility. Most people regarded Keenan, or any stranger, with cold contempt or wary mistrust. It was difficult for Keenan to project an image stern enough to cause unscrupulous people to leave him alone but gentle enough that the honest ones were enthused to welcome him. Often he felt lonelier here, surrounded by countless, nameless faces, than he did back in his family's secluded mountain home. But he remained hopeful that things would change for the better, and his new life was still thrilling at least in its potential.

Keenan found employment at a humble orphanage, helping with meals, custodial duties, and repairs along with teaching and supervising the children. The job also afforded him a free room in which to live. The wages were meager but he enjoyed the work and at times he felt it paid him a moral fortune. Although the populace of Abandon had swelled somewhat in quality and quantity after the fall of Gairloch, receiving an influx of refugees from all strata of society, Abandon remained a perilous town with an abundance of social ills. Violence and neglect left many children forsaken by their parents and in need of surrogate care.

Marketa, a kind, gray-haired woman of at least sixty years of age, ran the orphanage. She was married to a quiet man a few years her junior named James. He owned a general store in town that he managed during the day. The store no doubt supported the couple and provided the primary financial means by which Marketa was able to maintain her orphanage. But the burden of this economic disparity inspired no ill will between the two; in fact James clearly took great satisfaction and joy from his wife and her altruistic occupation.

Both were gentle and temperate people of simple tastes and modest pleasures. Marketa was more socially engaging than her husband but each provided pleasant company. Keenan developed a friendship with Marketa quite easily and already felt a close bond to the woman. But only mere chance brought them together. Although they may have unconsciously sensed some kind of connection, neither had any idea that Marketa was biologically Keenan's paternal grandmother. In fact, Marketa's character had matured so much over the years that even Torrin Murgleys might no longer recognize the woman as his mother.

Keenan's only other co-worker was a thin, gangly, rigid woman that was twice his age and in no way a candidate for his romantic interests. From time to time, the orphanage also helped out women who were hiding from abusive husbands. Keenan felt sorry for these women, and some were attractive despite black eyes and bruises, but he never considered that it would be wise for him to court their affections.

Although it became clear to Keenan that love would not be found at his job, it was less apparent to him where or how he would discover the passion and romance he craved. Tonight, out of this insecure uncertainty, he elected to settle for a cheap imitation of true affection.

It was early evening. The setting sun left a chill behind in the night air. Keenan left work with nowhere to go and nothing to do. Carrying a lonely heart, needled by unquenched desires, Keenan walked the dirty streets. He told himself that he was just out for a stroll, that he had no particular destination in mind. But in truth he knew where he headed, knew where his peregrinations would lead him; he just did not want to admit it to himself. He wanted to be able to tell himself that this trip to the tavern he had heard about, one that offered more than alcohol, came as a spontaneous decision, that it was only a lark that sent him inside as he happened to be walking past the tavern's door.

Hands stuffed into his pockets, head tucked down against the cold, or perhaps to hide himself, Keenan stepped quickly inside the tavern's entrance. A big, brutish man stopped him with a hand to Keenan's chest.

"Two groat." The brute said.

"What," Keenan asked with tense, total incomprehension, as if money were an utterly foreign concept to him.

"Two groat," the man repeated impatiently. "You want to come inside, it's going to cost you two groat sonny, that's eight pence."

Keenan fished the hard earned money from his pocket and paid the toll. Once past the guard, it seemed uncomfortably warm inside the tavern, but that could have been a byproduct of his nervousness. Standing in the middle of the room, he felt vulnerable and exposed. So he quickly located an empty table and sat down, trying hard to blend in with the other patrons.

The enclosure held several tables, each set with a small oil lamp that cast a dim, circular pool of light amid the dusky interior landscape. There was a bar with a barkeep behind it on one side of the room and a small stage set against the other wall. Tongues of flame flickered excitedly and licked the logs lying on iron andirons in the large hearth near the stage. The firelight cast peculiar shadows that leapt and swayed in wild swarms against the walls and upon the faces of the crowd. The air was fragranced with the stale, bitter odor of tobacco. Over in one corner of the room, musicians played a lively tune with dulcimer, flute and drum. But no one seemed to take much notice of them.

"What would you like handsome," a woman's voice purred in Keenan's ear. The warmth of her exhaled breath caressed his skin. Then a soft hand stroked his cheek, turning his head in the direction of the voice. She leaned into him with one hand resting on his leg. Keenan's eyes fell easily from her comely face to the point where her gown was cut lowest yet fullest. Admiring the smooth, soft texture of her skin, the roundness of her breasts, their full and resilient weight, his eager gaze lingered over the woman's generous bosom before descending along the voluptuous curves of her body, gliding over sensuous thighs and down the silken flesh of her legs.

"What would you like to drink," she asked.

Keenan reluctantly dragged his eyes away from her body. Swallowing the knot in his throat, he said, "A pint of ale, please."

"That's a good place to start, Darling. Maybe we can work up to something more interesting later on," she enticed in an inviting, throaty voice. "I'll be right back with your ale, so don't you wander off."

Keenan smiled weakly and watched the young woman walk away toward the bar. He watched the way her legs scissored, each buttock alternately rising and falling in a seductive rhythm. Her short, curve-hugging dress revealed her legs nicely, and when she bent over to take another customers order, Keenan saw it revealed even more.

Other, similarly underdressed barmaids worked the room, most were young women, pretty and slender, but there seemed to be something here to satisfy every man's taste. Although he didn't drink much alcohol, Keenan had visited taverns before but he had never been in a place like this where the barmaids dropped their clothes for money, and would do more than that for a higher price, so he was told. Until last week, the callow youth had not even known such establishments existed. It had not taken long for curiosity and frustrated desires to get the better of him.

Opportunities to find more virtuous employment were scarce for women in Abandon and competition was high. It was a rough, decadent town with few decent men to take care of their women. Husbands and boyfriends were frequently killed, ran off, or failed to provide for their mates. Keenan had not given much thought to why these women worked here, and at the moment he was too preoccupied with simply enjoying the fact that they did to consider the motives of their profession.

An enticing woman with wheaten hair and sultry eyes stepped on stage wearing cerulean pants made from a sheer, diaphanous fabric and a long-sleeve, lace jacket dyed in the same rich shade of blue. The jacket draped to her knees in a graceful cascade that almost resembled falling rain as the material shimmered and flowed against the creamy background of her flesh glimpsed through the fine holes of the lacework's delicate web. Near the edge of the stage, she placed a small, wide-mouth pale on the floor to receive monetary tokens of the audience's appreciation. As soon as she did, an overeager admirer tossed in a coin. She rewarded him with a salacious smile, then rolled her tongue along her upper lip and blew him a kiss. Returning to the center of the stage floor, she began to dance.

She worked her body, swiveling her hips and rolling her shoulders, getting lost in the music and the hypnotic movement of her libidinous dance. Slowly, gracefully, she began to shed her clothes. Hooking her thumbs inside the waistband of her pants, swaying languorously and bending at the knees, she eased the pants over her hips, let them fall in a puddle at her feet where they hugged her ankles briefly before she stepped out of them and kicked the fallen garment to the back of the stage. She danced for a while longer under the intermittent cover of her lace jacket before it too was abandoned, revealing the exquisite proportions of her magnificent body. Men moved closer to the stage and more coins dropped into the bucket. Sometimes, to encourage higher denominations in their pecuniary applause, she gave special attention to those individuals around the stage, bending toward a man and squeezing her breasts together, bending away from another man and shaking her bottom provocatively, and using her mouth to take the coin from the hand held out by yet another man.

The barmaid with the lush figure who had fawned at Keenan with such overt coquetry when taking his drink order returned with his cup of ale. She stood in front of him, blocking Keenan's view of the stage. "Here you go Darling," she said passing the cup to Keenan, then held out her palm for payment. Leaning to his left to regain sight of the dancer while setting the ale on the table, Keenan deposited a coin in the barmaid's hand.

She shifted her stance to again occupy his field of vision. Then without warning, she sat in Keenan's lap and wrapped her arms around his neck. "I'm glad you're enjoying the show, Darling, but don't ignore me too much. You'll hurt my feelings and make me jealous."

Her fingers played in his short, black hair then drew his head to the cleft of her bosom. He found her cleavage fragrant with perfume and perspiration. Despite the mixed bouquet presented to his olfactory sensitivities, the position suited him as being quite agreeable. However, Keenan hoped the woman would not notice the pointed ears he had inherited from his mother. There was no way anyone would mistake him for a White Elf of Gairloch, but any link to the elves met with suspicion if not hostility these days. People feared the growing threat that lay to the east and of the strange things seen more and more frequently in their own lands. Such fears often made people dangerously intolerant of even small differences.

The music stopped. The dancer left the stage and the barmaid left his lap. Keenan gave her another coin. Her venal affections were counterfeit but pleasant nonetheless.

"Thanks," she replied. "I knew you liked me. "My name's Amy. If you need anything, Handsome, you just ask for me." She winked. The insincere amorist then walked away to perform her bawdy ritual on someone else.

Keenan did not mind though as another dancer had taken the stage. One after another, he watched the women and their salacious choreography, almost studying them. Like most of the other patrons, he stared shamelessly, grinning like a hungry fool as he tried to memorize every scintillating line and vulgar curve of the twirling, twisting forms of naked feminine beauty that paraded before him. With increasing fervor, he longed to touch the velvety soft contours of the girls on stage or those prowling the floor scantily clad in erotic attire. Each one appeared different, mystiques ranging from playful innocence to that of the wild and dangerous temptress; and each one was perfect. Yet to Keenan's unbiased, inexperienced mind there seemed no contradiction in this assertion. Like Amy, the other barmaids flirted and teased, giving the customers every penny's worth. But their affections would idle down when the money ran out and the only attention given then was merely advertisement for another rental. But the men seemed satisfied with that and everyone appeared to understand the arrangement and accept its limitations.

This was new and exciting for Keenan. He had never seen so many women without the burden of their clothes. The experience thrust from within him an ebullition of lust. But the outburst of this ripe emotion was tempered by embryonic feelings of guilt, and an indistinct sadness lurked in the back of his heart. Although aroused, strangely he felt lonelier now than he did before he entered the tavern. However, he could not bring himself to leave just yet even though his finances and his pleasure were dwindling.

From behind him, a pair of large, powerful hands grabbed Keenan's arms and hauled him savagely to his feet to the coarse accompaniment of a man's vicious snarl. On his way up, Keenan bumped the table, causing his third cup of ale to rock precariously back and forth, sloshing the alcoholic brew over the lip of the glass.

"Get up," his attacker growled. "You're leaving. Now!"

Mortified, Keenan recognized the misshapen face that towered over him. Wide-eyed, he regarded the familiar features, now contorted in anger, with his own expression of surprise and fear.

"Dad," Keenan exclaimed. "What are you doing here?"

"The question is what are you doing here," Quinn insisted, his voice ferocious with disapproval. "I must have been a damn poor father if I raised you to think this is a suitable place for you to spend your time. You've got some explaining to do boy. Let's go."

Quinn let go of one arm but kept possession of Keenan's other and turned him forcibly toward the tavern door. They moved only a few steps before a massive bull of a man blocked their passage. The man's stupid, brutish nature was accentuated by his unkempt and grim appearance. The tavern employed the man as hired muscle to keep the peace in the tavern, to make sure the establishment's few rules were followed, and that the female merchandise was not abused. But he was also obviously a man of turbulent inclination, prone to violence and quick to enjoy a fight should the opportunity arise.

"Hold it right there, fella," the bull demanded, holding up his hand, which he then pointed at Keenan. "He's a paying customer and he stays if he wants to. You on the other hand, your face could curdle milk and its scaring the girls. So, I think I'll boot your ugly, fat ass to the street."

Undaunted, Quinn took a step forward, still dragging Keenan by the arm, his grip tightening, his nails biting painfully into Keenan's imprisoned bicep. "He's not a customer any longer. He's my son." The hard, confident sound of Quinn's deep-toned voice, as sharp and deadly as a sword blade, carried throughout the room. "And if you want to try to come between me and him, go ahead. But it'll be last thing you do in your sorry excuse for a life. Now shut up and start swinging, or get out of my way you worthless pile of hog puke."

The whole room gawked at them. For the moment, this drama became better entertainment than the dancers. The two men continued to stare menacingly at one another for a long, tense minute.

Feeling the unwelcome and unaccustomed sensation of fear in the presence of Quinn's seething intimidation, the tavern man backed down. "Go on and get out," he grumbled, "both of you."

Outside, they walked up the street together in silence. A hundred questions banged around inside Keenan's head, but he did not think it was safe to say anything yet. His father still looked too angry to answer questions or to tolerate hasty excuses for Keenan's presence in the disreputable tavern.

Half way up the dark, deserted street, Quinn stopped in front of a closed shop with a bench set outside its doorway. He pulled Keenan into an unexpected embrace and hugged him tightly. It was like so many other comforting hugs given by his father during the course of his life but with an unusual, desperate quality added to it that was somewhat frightening. When Quinn finally let go, Keenan saw his father's eyes were moist with restrained tears.

"Sit down," Quinn croaked gently, and the two occupied the bench.

"What's wrong Dad. Has something happened to Mom?"

Quinn laid his hand over Keenan's leg just above the knee and squeezed lightly. "No, no. Everyone is fine back home. They miss you, but they're doing well. Shannon really misses you since she's had to take over most of your chores since you left. But she sends her love. They all do."

"Then why are you here Dad," Keenan asked fearfully. "Why are you crying. Is it me? I'm sorry about where you found me. I'm sorry I let you down but..."

Quinn wiped the moisture from his cheek, tilting his eyes toward the stars. "Remember how we used to sit like this on our porch back home? We would talk for hours about everything. There were no secrets between us." His tears tried again to escape the prison of his eyes.

"Sure Dad. It wasn't too long ago we sat on that porch talking about my leaving home. That was a long conversation as I recall." Keenan didn't understand what his father really wanted to talk about but he gave him the time he needed to find his way to the subject, a subject that clearly threatened his father's security more than the bull back at the tavern. "How did you know where to find me Dad?"

"I've been here for two days, asking all over town for you, asking if anyone knew you or knew where I could find you. Tonight I asked at that orphanage where I guess you work. That Marketa, she told me you live there but that you were out and she didn't know where. That other woman, the skinny one, she said, 'All men are pigs and most head for the same diseased wallow.' When I asked what she meant by that, she told me about the tavern where I found you."

"Dad," Keenan blurted. "I've never been in that place before. I swear."

"Yeah, that may be, but you were there tonight. I understand its appeal son but it's a deception, one that can hurt you without you even realizing it. It's nice you working in that orphanage. I wish there had been some place like that for me when I was a child. But you shouldn't polish your character with good works during the day just to soil it again with vice at night." Quinn paused, releasing a heavy, weary sigh. The tears had dried up, talking helped; it was sort of like old times. "I'm sorry about the scene I caused back there at the tavern. I suppose I was a little harsh, maybe a little too intense," suggested Quinn.

"You scared the crap out of me, and I think that fella dropped a load in his trousers too."

Quinn let loose an unexpected bark of laughter but grief quickly choked it off. The laughter sounded sweet in Keenan's ears and he regretted hearing it die so soon.

"You're an adult now," Quinn continued solemnly. "And of course you can do what you want. But you really shouldn't go to places like that. It empties your pockets and drains your dignity. The time and money you spend there doesn't help those girls build their character or help them build healthy relationships. And it doesn't help you any either. I understand your desire to look at those girls. It's natural, but being natural doesn't make it right. And I understand that you want to do more than just look. But ogling those girls while they dance or paying for their sex isn't harmless even though it's consensual. It may seem pleasant at the time and without any lasting consequence. You may think it doesn't hurt anyone. But you're wrong; it does. For one thing, it fills your memory with experiences and images that will stay with you even if you no longer want them. Then one day, when you're married and you're kissing your wife or holding her in your arms, those dirty old memories will sneak up on you to pollute the purity of your love. All those vacant, corrupt experiences will diminish the excitement and degrade the virtuous ecstasy of intimate relations with your wife. You'll be denying her the thrill you squandered on women that meant nothing to you, while she, your beloved, is left with the tainted, tattered remains of your carnal desires. And what if you use some woman who you value for sex and nothing else and through that meaningless union you contract a disease? Then later you meet the love of your life, the woman of your dreams, but you can't consummate your love because you would injure her with the disease you contracted from your worthless night of base pleasure. It may sound like the advise of a silly, old man but please believe me son; it's better when you're married, in love and unblemished by a sordid past. If you can't abstain until you're married, at least promise me you won't lay with any woman unless you honestly believe you could marry her, that you can see the two of you together as husband and wife forever."

"I promise," Keenan pledged. Some of what his father said made sense but it was also embarrassing and he wanted to change the subject. Any topic would be better than discussing fornication with his father. "I'm sorry about the tavern; I won't go back. But Dad, why are you here?"

Quinn believed that what he had been telling Keenan was important but to continue would be avoiding the matter he really needed to address. Thinking about it brought the lump up in his throat again and caused his eyes to well with the water of the heart.

"I love you Keenan. From the day you were born to this moment and every second in between, I've loved you with all my heart. I delivered you and I held you in my hands as you took your first breath of air. You've filled my life with joy, filled my heart with pride. You were a good boy and you're growing into being a good man. In every way that matters, you and I are father and son. Nothing can change that; I'll always love you as your father." Tears were streaming down his face now. Quinn gave up trying to hold them back.

"Dad, what are you talking about," Keenan inquired with stomach-turning apprehension.

Although difficult, Quinn laid the truth bare for Keenan. He explained his lost friendship with Torrin Murgleys, explained how Torrin had known Keenan's mother, and that Keenan had been conceived by Torrin rather than by him. It was a distasteful revelation, as nauseating for Keenan to accept as it was for Quinn to confess. Being an outsider, being different, and having an elf for a mother, made it hard enough to find his place in the community, to find acceptance and friendship. How do you fit in after you have learned the Lord of Demons is your father? He felt contaminated and ashamed, and angry that he should be made to feel this way because of something he had no control over, something that had been done to him rather than by him. When Keenan asked why he was finding out about all this now, Quinn went on to explain that a wizard had showed up at their farm claiming to be Torrin's brother and asking about Keenan. He told him that Aragon wanted Keenan to join him in some damn fool crusade against Gairloch. Keenan had heard much about that evil realm, particularly since his move to Abandon. Thought of the place sent an icy prickling along his spine and unconsciously made him look warily at the dark buildings and alleys around them. During his time in Abandon, Keenan had also heard whispered stories and nefarious legends about Torrin's axe, how it could decimate armies and devour souls. So the idea that Aragon wanted him to journey to Gairloch and steal that infamous axe seemed ludicrous considering its scale of enormous difficulty and the immense magnitude of its danger.

"What do you want me to do, Dad," Keenan asked after a long silence.

Hearing his son call him 'Dad' in a voice, although confused and afraid, still filled with love and respect was a supremely glorious sound. It felt like being wrapped in a warm, comforting blanket of serenity.

"Your mother wants you to come home," Quinn answered. "It's not like you'd have to come back and hide out forever. You could just stay with us for a while, a few months, maybe a year, until this Aragon gives up and finds something else to interest him. Then you could come back here if you want, or I suppose you could go somewhere else, maybe Garonne. I didn't want you so far from home but maybe it would be a good idea to put more distance between you and Gairloch."

"That's what Mom wants," Keenan said. "What do you want me to do?"

"I've had some time to think about it on my way here," Quinn answered poignantly. "You know I'd like to have you come home one day, have you settle near us so the family stays together. But I'm not going to drag you back against your will, and I'm not going to try to guilt you into coming back or frighten you into running home. You're a man and what you do with your life is your decision. If you want to stay here, I'll support that decision, even though I'm the one who'll have to explain it to your mother. But I had to warn you. That Aragon is a dangerous man and what he wants you to do is crazy. Any association with him will almost certainly end in death."

"I'll stay," Keenan pronounced. He was worried and confused but he wanted to be brave. "I'll keep a low profile for a while and keep an eye out for this Aragon. In a few months, I'll come home for a visit to let you know everything is fine, which I'm sure it will be. He may be a wizard but I don't see how he could make me go with him to Gairloch and retrieve that axe against my will even if he does find me."

"All right, but be careful," Quinn admonished and put his arm around Keenan's shoulder. "Please be careful. And if you do need help, know that I'm always there for you."

"I know. And Dad, it doesn't change anything. None of this changes anything between you and me," Keenan said, staring into the dark street, hoping his words carried conviction.

Quinn remained silent but his arm hugged Keenan's shoulder tighter, communicating agreement as well as love.

"It's getting late," Keenan observed. "Let's go back to the orphanage, have a bite to eat, and get some sleep. You can stay with me in my room."

After their meeting, Aragon suspected that Quinn's first move would be to find and warn Keenan. So Aragon had waited that night and followed Quinn when he left home the very next day, certain that the concerned father would lead him straight to the son. As he tracked Quinn, Aragon succeeded in keeping himself hidden from his quarry but on a few occasions it seemed as if Quinn sensed he was being stalked and made some effort to shake off his unseen pursuer. But Aragon managed to stay with him the entire way, and tonight he watched in wonder as Quinn left the orphanage to take advantage of the direction he had received there. For Aragon, the trail had taken a rather unexpected turn.

Responding to Aragon's knock, Marketa opened the door. "Well what a pleasant surprise," she exclaimed. "It's about time you came back to visit your mother. I haven't seen you in over a year, almost two."

"These are strange days, Mother, and I've been busy. But it's good to see you."

"Come in," Marketa invited. "Let's go sit down in the kitchen and get caught up. Are you hungry?"

At the kitchen table, Aragon immediately got down to business. "That man who was here before me, do you know who he was looking for?"

"Yes. He was looking for Keenan, a very nice young man who works for me."

"Amazing," Aragon murmured. "It is absolutely amazing. What a coincidence that he should be here, right under my very nose. There are forces at work that even I can't predict." He shook his head, and then asked, "What is the boy like?"

"Keenan, well he's nice," explained Marketa, perplexed by Aragon's interest in her hired help. "He works hard, cares about doing a job well regardless of what it is. He's smart and seems to have good morals. He's always been honest with me."

Aragon arched his eyebrow and laughed a little. "I'm glad you like him. Do you know who he is? Do you have any idea of his true identity?" Seeing that she did not, Aragon continued. "He's your grandson."

Marketa's face lit with joy. "Aragon, why didn't you ever tell me you had a son."

"He's not mine," Aragon replied flatly. "He's Torrin's son."

The light in Marketa's face dimmed under the shadow of fear and her smile fell. Aragon explained Keenan's history and the reasons both he and Quinn were searching for the boy. The information troubled her, but gradually Marketa regained her joy over the news that she had a grandson.

When Keenan and Quinn entered the room looking for a small morsel to quiet their stomachs until the morning meal, Aragon was pouring himself a cup of tea with his back to the new arrivals. Marketa ran to Keenan and hugged him.

"Oh Keenan," she exclaimed as she stepped back from him, holding only his hands now. "I had no idea who you were but I'm so happy. I've always wanted a grandchild and I couldn't have asked for better."

They stared at her with shared expressions of perplexity, although Quinn's also held shadings of grim distrust. As Aragon turned to face them, Quinn's expression changed to outrage and he shouted, "You! You son of a bitch!"

"That's no way to talk about Keenan's grandmother," he returned calmly, "particularly since you've all just met and introductions have hardly been completed. Even though civilization is growing perilously close to destruction, let's try to talk like civilized people while hope remains."

Quinn could not speak. The world was closing in on him and choking off his breath. He pulled Keenan away from Marketa and started moving toward the door. "You keep away from him! I warned you, and I meant it. We're leaving. Don't try to stop us, and don't follow us either."

"Dad," Keenan resisted. "He's already found us. We might as well let him have his say so we can put an end to this here and now. We can't keep running. Once he makes his plea and realizes his entreaties are useless against me, he'll give up and leave us alone. He'll have to move his attentions on to some other plan to fulfill his deluded ambitions."

"What a extraordinarily reasonable young man," Aragon observed. "That is an excellent suggestion. Let me talk to the boy, explain his destiny and his duty. If he refuses to take part in the noble quest I offer him, so be it. I'll walk away and out of your lives forever. Although we will all suffer the penalty of such a craven choice, there will be no retribution from me. The doomed world may punish you, punish us all, but I will bring no harm to you whatsoever."

Grudgingly, Quinn agreed and they all took seats around the table. Never having seen a wizard before and knowing that almost none still existed, Keenan was fascinated by Aragon. Almost reverently, he scrutinized Aragon's aristocratic manner and his tenebrous appearance. Aragon's angular face and slender build were unremarkable but Keenan was struck by the imposing image the wizard presented. Aragon projected an aura of authority, his expression masterful but not arrogant. Clearly, the wizard was a man of uncommon intellect and superior breeding.

Keenan stared into Aragon's dark visage, into the entrancing thrall of his eyes, listening intently to the sonorous pitch and resonance of the wizard's droning, hypnotic voice as Aragon began his tale and unveiled his claim on Keenan. He told Keenan about Torrin's unholy brood of monsters, described the atrocities Torrin and his servants committed against innocent people, how Torrin used his axe to wage war and inflict destruction upon the inhabitants of the lands around Gairloch, that his need for power would not be complete until he held the whole world under his cruel domination. He described the nightmare country of Gairloch, reaching into Keenan's thoughts to construct every inch of the appalling vision, every hue, every shadow, every texture, making the monstrous realm a reality in his mind. Filled with menacing omens, his words painted the landscape surrounding that forbidding empire as a place of darkest terror in an age of dire peril. He explained that if something were not done to stem the evil tide of Torrin's spreading ruin, it would not be long before the creeping devastation swallowed everyone. He explained why Keenan had to go with him to Gairloch and capture Torrin's axe, preventing its use for further foul conquest and striking an important blow against Torrin's growing power.

"And if you refuse to help, it won't just be other people who suffer," Aragon averred. "Not just other innocent families, but yours too. Think about your home burned to the ground, your mother's eyes gouged out by the White

Elves for her failure to see Torrin's greatness. Think of her being used against her will in unspeakable ways for Torrin's amusement and evil purposes. Think about your brothers and sisters, some murdered, some brutalized and enslaved. All this and more will come to pass if you shirk your responsibility, if you fail to help me. Their fate is in your hands."

Quinn let loose a trenchant snort and shook his head in disgusted disbelief. Keenan, however, felt immobilized by a petrifying horror that froze his soul and crushed his heart under the immense pressure of its cold, heavy weight. He was haunted by a presentiment of doom but also crippled by his fear; he felt helpless to defy it. And strangely, he did feel responsible. Now that he knew Torrin was his father, he felt that the only way he could make things right, the only way that he could cleanse that taint from his blood would be to fight against Torrin, maybe kill him if such a thing were possible.

Ignoring Quinn's incredulity, Aragon continued with his persuasion. "Do this Keenan and you'll be a hero to the people, to your family. History will remember your name for years, immortalize you as a brave champion against oppression and enrich you with esteem."

Keenan's face turned as cold and pale as a gravestone. "I don't care." He forced the words through a clenched throat but they gathered strength now that the path was cleared. "I don't want to be anybody's hero. I never wanted to be anybody's anything."

"Don't lie to me boy," Aragon spat back, his mordant tone corroding the mock courage Keenan had exercised to refuse him. "Your head is full of self-important dreams of greatness, just like Torrin's was at your age. If you turn away from this challenge now, it's not because you don't care, it's because you're a coward. And you know it."

Quinn sprang to his feet and grabbed Aragon, pulling him out of the chair and slamming him against the wall. His hands fisted in the chest of Aragon's shirt, Quinn roared at him. "Shut up! He's given you his answer; now shut up. You have no right to condemn him, no right to accuse him." Quinn shook with murderous rage.

"No Dad, he's right," Keenan shouted. "He's right. I want to help; I want to be a hero. But I'm scared."

There was shame in Keenan's admission. Quinn heard it, and wanted desperately to remove that burden from his son. "You don't have to do this," Quinn insisted. He looked back over his shoulder at Keenan, still holding Aragon in a tight grip with the wizard's back pinned to the wall. "It's not your responsibility."

"Then whose is it Dad?" He seemed to be almost begging for an answer, for some honorable way to escape the demand that the name Murgleys had placed on him. "If not me Dad, who?"

As Quinn turned his attention back to Aragon, he swore to himself that if he saw a self-satisfied smirk on the wizard's face he would kill him right then and there. But there was no smile, no fear either. Quinn let him go and walked over to his son.

"Keenan, do you really mean to do this," Quinn asked.

"I don't want to," he answered. "But I think it's the right thing to do."

Quinn sighed heavily. His arms hung limp at his sides and his shoulders slumped in defeat. "Then I'm coming with you. Maybe I can still talk you out of this madness along the way. I'm sure once you've had time to think about this a little more, you'll see how crazy it is. And if not, we will face the danger together."

"That is acceptable," Aragon announced boldly. "We may even have a use for you Quinn. We should leave tonight. I'm known in this town, so our departure in the morning would likely draw too much attention to ourselves, and I may not have been the only one who followed you Quinn. I have the feeling that others have been sniffing around about us. Get your things together but pack light. Do you own a horse Keenan?"

"Yes, it's stabled out back."

"Good," said Aragon. "That will save us some time. I'm going out for a little while. I'll be back in a few hours. Be ready to leave when I return."

"We'll be ready to leave," answered Quinn. "But you're a fool if you think any of us are ready for what awaits us at Gairloch. I think that will become obvious to everyone as we get closer. But we'll go if that's what Keenan wants. However, we are going to stop by my home on our way so we can let Keenan's mother know what happened."

"Very well," Aragon reluctantly agreed. "But we will take a different route than the one we followed to get here. We'll go north along the Purl River then cut east through a pass in the Tissama Mountains to reach your home and then continue on to Gairloch."

Aragon left. Marketa said good night and went to bed, leaving Keenan and Quinn alone. Although neither felt very hungry, they ate before going to Keenan's room to pack. There they began laying out on his bed the items they thought Keenan would need.

"Why are you doing this Keenan," Quinn asked.

Keenan shook his head weakly. "I don't know. I'm half elf; maybe I want to prove that not all elves are evil like Torrin's White Elves.

"You already know that's true," stated Quinn. "The elves were not always what they are now. They were not always evil. Your mother is an elf and the most beautiful, kind, and loving woman I have ever known. The elves were perverted by Torrin. They gave up their god, choosing to forsake Navar and worship Torrin instead. And in so doing they became changed, became creatures of evil like their master, his most devoted followers. Torrin deceived a lot of people and they all paid because of it. I don't want you to be used like Torrin used those people, like he used me. You don't know if you can trust Aragon. There are plenty of reasons not to. It's hard to know what people are really made of even after you've known them for some time, and you don't always want to assume the worst. In dealing with others, with strangers, it's necessary to make judgments, but judge carefully. My own experiences have taught me that appearances deceive and the heart often misleads us, for often it fails to see the whole truth of another's character. Remember this my son, and that I love you. And you don't have anything to prove, not about the elves or about yourself."

"Maybe I do," said Keenan. "Maybe I have to prove that I'm not like Torrin just because I'm his son. Maybe being his son makes it my responsibility to try and stop the evil he is committing."

"It doesn't," Quinn insisted. "Your blood relationship to him means nothing. I know I've always tried to impress upon you the importance of family, but he is not your family. You are not responsible for him."

Next to his change of clothes, Keenan dropped a bow and a quiver of arrows on the bedspread, a confused patchwork of cloth squares varied in color and design. Quinn added Keenan's sword and scabbard to the pile.

"Remember when I got you that sword," Quinn asked. "You wanted one for so long, nagging me constantly, wanting me to teach you how to fight. Finally I relented and I bought one for you with blunted edges. You were so excited, so eager to learn. But you thought a sword should have sharp edges. I told you to wait, that you should get familiar with it first, learn to use it safely. But you went off behind my back and put a keen edge to that blade."

"Yeah," Keenan admitted sheepishly, "and damn near cut my own leg off as a result."

"That's right, and watch your language. You were rash and undisciplined and you scared the shit out of your mother. Lessons can be painful to learn, don't let this one be fatal. There's nothing for you at Gairloch, nothing for any man. Torrin is not your responsibility."

"Maybe." Keenan told him. "But then again, maybe we are all responsible for the evil in the world if we do nothing to try and stop it, if we do nothing to fight against it."

"We do something just by living moral and loving lives," Quinn observed.

"I know Dad, but sometimes that isn't enough. Sometimes I think we have to fight for what's right, fight against what's evil. Going to Gairloch sounds crazy, I know; but it also seems right. It just feels like the right thing to do. And if I don't try, I think it will haunt me for a long time. Maybe forever."

When Aragon returned, they were ready. Without any fanfare, the three men mounted their horses and rode out of Abandon into the dark unknown. They rode slowly at first with Aragon in the lead, but their pace quickened as they left the town behind them and entered the open countryside.

A day and a half out from Abandon, they had covered many leagues, having rested very little since their midnight departure. Their anxieties and the weather had not proven conducive to sleep. It had rained heavily, leaving the ground soaked and making it an unattractive bed. So instead of making camp, they resolved to keep riding, dozing as they could while staying in their saddles. The rain stopped during the early morning hours but by midday, heavy, swollen clouds still filled the sky, gray-black thunderheads, pregnant with precipitation.

"Do you smell that," Aragon inquired of his companions, new worries drawing his compressed features into a tighter knot.

"Yes," Quinn affirmed, sniffing at the air and wrinkling his nose in distaste. "It smells like rotting fish. We're not far from the Iyar River. Maybe something poisoned the water, causing the fish to die in large numbers."

"I don't think so. We should ..." Aragon began but left the thought unfinished. He was interrupted by a soul-upheaving sound, the savage barking and howling of many inhuman voices, bellowing and braying with a mad, terrifying bestial ecstasy.

Three hundred feet away, a pack of fifty goblins and gnomes charged into view over a rise in the undulating land. Led by a Seeker, they were searching for magic items and had caught scent of Aragon's staff or perhaps of the wizard himself. In their crouching, simian gait, the goblins ran toward them with ferocious speed. Gnashing their teeth, their red unblinking eyes bulging in heinous expectation, the goblins ran at them on all fours, their abnormally long arms striking and rebounding against the ground. The gnomes followed closely behind their quicker brethren.

Keenan stared with disbelief at the ghastly marvel of Torrin's demented experimentation, abnormal life that in a healthy world would never have drawn a breath. Wild-eyed, Keenan's horse whinnied, tossing its head and stamping its hooves fitfully. Keenan shared the horse's terror as he gaped in wonder at the nightmare incarnate lopping swiftly toward him.

"Curse it all, they've found us," Aragon hissed. Then he shouted, "Run you two! Head for the river as fast as you can. I'll follow but don't wait for me. Now move!"

Keenan and Quinn spun their horses around and put their heels to their flanks. Aragon held his position against the rushing tide of unhallowed creatures. Letting his reins hang on the saddle horn and taking hold of his staff, he raised his hands into the air. In the arcane language of the ancient elves, Aragon invoked his magic. A great tempest stirred in the heavens. The clouds overhead began to boil and roll, growing darker and more threatening, amassing greater density, gathering force. From the concentrated might built up in the cumulous mass overhead, that great, turbulent storehouse of natural power, thunder detonated and lightening discharged. A bolt of blinding energy exploded from the clouds and blasted the ground in the midst of the enemy. The staggering fulmination shook the ground like an earthquake. The blast killed only a few goblins and gnomes but the others panicked. They scattered off in all directions, covering their heads against falling chunks of blasted earth, and casting fearful glances at the heavens in dread of greater threats. Another lighting bolt struck the ground, this one missing its mark.

Torrential sheets of rain fell, a deluge so thick and heavy that Aragon could barely see anything beyond a distance of three or four feet in front of him. But he knew the horde of living abominations would soon regroup and resume their attack. The goblins and gnomes were easily startled but the ruthless command of their master along with their own mad, innate bloodlust would overwhelm their fear, setting them in aggressive motion once again.

Gripping his staff in his left hand, Aragon took hold of his reins with his right, then fled at a full gallop from the momentarily confused enemy and in pursuit of his companions. The storm-lashed sky continued to bellow with thunder and flare with lightning but without the purposeful direction that Aragon had put to it with his magic. However, it seemed that wizardry still fomented and propelled the merciless intensity of the blinding rain.

With a residual of the magic called forth by Aragon, the green stone at the staff's apex glowed with an inexplicable light that caused it to act as an unwanted beacon in the rain darkened air, giving a luminous track for the goblins to follow. The voice of the storm boomed like the shouting of the World Spirit, angry and threatening. But the goblins and gnomes now ignored the warning and as they chased after Aragon and the other quarry, they began issuing a berserk admonition of their own, guttural growls and haunting shrieks of fury.

Leaving the open plain, there were more trees as Aragon came nearer to the river. Suddenly from this growing cover, a goblin that had somehow overtaken Aragon sprang out in front of him biting at the air with his ugly tusks, brandishing a falchion, a thick clever-like sword, and preparing to strike.

Aragon swung his staff like a sword, arcing over his head and around his back before impacting the goblin's chest. The prodigious force of the blow lifted the goblin off his large feet and sent him sprawling across the rain swept grass. Another goblin leapt onto the back of the horse, clawing at Aragon and sinking his fangs into the wizard's shoulder. The horse reared up on its hind legs, its front hooves flailing at another attacker on the ground. Aragon twisted back and forth, punching his elbow into the side of the creature and dislodging it from his back. As the goblin fell, Aragon spurred his horse forward again toward the river.

When Aragon reached the river, he saw through the driving rain that Keenan and Quinn waited for him on the other bank. He reined in his horse. The animal pranced nervously in a tight circle, splashing water and mud over its fetlocks, as Aragon fought to regain control of the beast.

"You fools, don't stop," Aragon shouted. "Ride as fast as you can."

A goblin with a spear and two gnomes swinging maces charged the wizard. Ignoring his sword, Aragon again used his staff as weapon of percussion to block their assault and deliver violence of his own.

"Wait here," Quinn hollered to Keenan over the deafening downpour. Quinn unsheathed his sword and rode down the slippery riverbank and charged across the water to offer armed aid to Aragon. When Quinn reached him, Aragon had already killed one gnome. He backed off, raising his staff and calling forth his magic in the fluid, mysterious speech of the ancient elves. He left the other two adversaries for Quinn to deal with, which would have been fine except that more goblins and gnomes broke through the trees and swarmed around them.

In answer to Aragon's invocation, the river began to rise rapidly. The volume and velocity of the flowing water quickly increased.

"Quinn, make haste; we have to cross the river now, before it's too late,"

Aragon cried. Without waiting for an answer, Aragon rode across and up the other side, joining Keenan on the opposite bank.

Quinn backed his horse slowly toward the river, continuing to exchange blows with the massing goblins and gnomes. Blazing arteries of light pulsed within the sky's dark skin, the flashes casting a fitful illumination upon the repulsive faces of Quinn's enemies. They surrounded him in the water, swinging weapons and clutching at him, forcing him to defend himself and preventing him from escaping.

Suddenly a massive wall of water crashed around an upstream bend in the river and barreled toward him, carrying boulders and logs as easily as leaves in its furious flow. It swept Quinn's horse out from under him and tossed him into the tumultuous current. With unnatural force, the devouring water raced through the widening channel, scouring its banks of soil and vegetation. It also swallowed up most of the goblins and gnomes. Quinn saw them bobbing and thrashing in the water around him, grasping for roots or floating debris to save themselves from drowning.

At the river's edge, Aragon and Keenan rode swiftly downstream over the rain-bent grass calling out to Quinn and hoping to get ahead of him so as to offer some rescue. Rain pounded the earth. Water poured through the channel. The roar of the river competed with that of the falling rain, dueling sounds, maddening in their relentless volume.

Up ahead, Aragon dismounted and took position at the rim of the riverbank, reaching out over the water with his staff, waiting as Quinn was swept nearer. Quinn grabbed the staff, his hands slipped and slid over its smooth surface but then hung on. He was caught in a tug of war between the water and the wizard. Aragon dug his heels into the muddy ground, his arms strained with tension as he struggled to pull Quinn free. Then the earth fell away beneath Aragon's feet. The piece of ground he had been standing on sloughed off into the eroding river, dragging Aragon with it and dropping him into the water. Quinn released the staff but Aragon maintained his hold on it. Gurgling and burbling, the water swirled around them.

The cataract overflowed its banks, churning wildly around the surrounding trees. Branches snapped, surrendering to the rapacious power of the flowing water. Keenan had to move further back from the river and could no longer see Aragon or his father clearly. At times he lost sight of them completely.

Pulled down by the cloying grip of the river's many undercurrents, forces unseen but menacing, Aragon and Quinn fought to keep their heads above the water's surface. Waves of muddy froth slapped and splashed their faces, choking them. They coughed and gagged on the dirty, sediment-laden water. They grew frightened by the unyielding entrapment of the river and grew weary from struggling against its greedy hunger. It snapped and pulled and sucked at their bodies as if it were a living thing trying to consume them.

The two men were swept beyond Keenan's view but he had no time to weep. Behind him, a group of six goblins and gnomes managed to escape the water on Keenan's side of the river and set to chasing him with a seemingly inbred, all-consuming, single-minded focus on murder. Downstream, four more of the gruesome creatures clawed their way out of the river with bloodthirsty eyes likewise fixed on Keenan. He hoped his father would also be able to free himself from the flood but there was no time to look for him, no chance to help him now. Keenan was forced to forsake his companions and take flight away from the river and beyond the hateful reach of the fiendishly misshapen creatures that pursued him.

One week later, Quinn and Aragon arrived back in Abandon. Both had managed to get out of the river. After the water receded they were able to locate one another and then find both their horses. However, Quinn's horse was dead, stuck in the riverbed, half buried in sediment and drowned by the flood. Quinn's pack had broken free of the horse and was nowhere to be found. The flood also left Quinn unarmed as he had been forced to drop his broadsword during his desperate swim for survival. They came across the ghastly corpses of several goblins and gnomes. Gagging and shuttering, Quinn passed by them with his hand cupped over his mouth and nose, trying to filter out the filthy, fishy stench of their degraded biology. Even the flies seemed to avoid the bodies, as if their unnatural flesh was too foul even for insects of such undiscriminating tastes to regard as agreeable nourishment or to accept as a suitable environment for their maggot children. But they saw no sign of any living enemy, and saw no sign of Keenan either. Reluctantly they gave up their search for him. They concluded that Keenan would probably return to Abandon. The town was closer than Quinn's home in the mountains and it was downstream, the direction Quinn and Aragon had been headed when Keenan last saw them. So sharing Aragon's horse, they made their way slowly back to Abandon and Marketa's orphanage.

"Yes, Keenan was here," said Marketa. "And he left three days ago."

"He left," Quinn asked in disbelief. "Where did he go?"

"He was very upset," Marketa explained. "He was pretty sure that you two would be all right, that you would get away from the goblins. But he was terribly worried about you. And he felt responsible for what happened to you. He said those monsters must have known who he was and that was why they were chasing you. He thinks Torrin is determined to kill him along with anyone who helps him."

"That's insane. Isn't it," Quinn asked. "Torrin doesn't know, does he?"

"I doubt it," Aragon answered. "I don't think he is aware of Keenan's existence. And even if he is, I doubt he would be very interested. Torrin has more important things to concern him at the moment."

"Nothing is more important than my son," Quinn snarled.

"Yes, yes," Aragon replied apologetically. "I didn't mean it that way. And I think those monsters more likely sought me instead of Keenan. There was a Seeker among them. Torrin has them scouring the land, looking for magic items they can steal and take back to their master. The Seeker probably smelled my staff and sicked his goblin dogs on us."

"Damn you." Quinn cursed and began to pace nervously. "I knew you'd be trouble."

"Well Keenan didn't see it that way," Marketa interjected. "He thought the goblins were after him and that his presence put the rest of you in danger. That's why he left and that's why he didn't go back to your home in the mountains, because he didn't want to put your family in danger."

Startled by this news, Quinn stopped pacing and looked intently at Marketa. "If he didn't go home, then where in the hell did he go?"

"I'm afraid that is exactly where he's headed. He said he was going on to Gairloch by himself, straight into the heart of hell."

"What," Quinn gasped in horror. He could barely speak and managed only one additional word. "Why?"

"I told you, Keenan felt responsible. Those monsters he saw put a frightened determination into him. He thinks he is putting everyone in danger. He wants to eliminate that danger, eliminate all the evil in the world he now knows exists and somehow feels a part of."

"How, by stealing that damn axe from Torrin?" Quinn asked.

"Maybe," replied Marketa. Her voice grew heavy with despair, weighed down by a nebulous foreboding. "Or maybe by using it."

"We can't let him do that," Aragon insisted.

Quinn grabbed Marketa by the shoulders and shook her. "Why did you let him go? He hasn't got a chance of even getting inside Gairloch. He'll be killed for certain. Why didn't you stop him?"

"I tried," Marketa groaned with pity. "You must believe me. I know it's crazy for Keenan to try this on his own; and I tried to stop him but he wouldn't listen. My husband, poor James, even threatened Keenan. But neither of them had the heart to do violence to the other. Keenan left and we could do nothing but stand here and watch him go. We hoped that you two would have shown up sooner so you could go after him before Keenan got too far. And he's scared too. You could see it in his eyes. He told me which way he intended to go. So I think he is secretly hoping you will go after him. He may give up after he's had time to think about how hazardous the journey really is."

"What route is he taking?" Quinn's breathing was too rapid, his heart pounding. He looked like he had already started racing after his son.

"He's headed north to Gairloch on the east side of the Tissama Mountain's this time."

"That doesn't narrow it down much," Quinn moaned. "But I might be able to find him, if I can catch up to him. And he may still go home, at least he may stop there. Marketa, do you have a horse I can borrow?"

"No," said Aragon. "You're going to require a strong, fast horse, something better than anything Marketa has to offer from her stables. You'll need other supplies as well, particularly a sword. Wait here while I get you these things. I will hurry."

"Get two horses," Marketa said. "I'll go with you Quinn. I feel somewhat to blame and four eyes have a better chance of spotting Keenan than just your two."

Quinn ignored her, not really wanting her help and assuming the old woman would fail to keep up and would eventually be left behind.

"That's a good idea," Aragon remarked, surprising them with his unexpected support of Marketa's offer. "I fear Keenan may stir up more trouble than any of us can deal with alone, even me. I won't be going with you. I'm going to Braemar to see what help they can give us. I'll be able to travel much faster alone and I will have no need of my horse. So Mother, you may have him and I'll find another for Quinn."

Quinn did not understand how Aragon hoped to involve the kingdom of Braemar in this mess. But it made no difference because frankly, he did not believe Aragon. He thought the wizard was making excuses to run off and leave them now that his original plan, whatever it had been, had turned sour. But in a way Quinn did not care; he was glad to be rid of the wizard. All Quinn wanted was to find his son and take him home before the boy ended up dead.

"Get me a horse and a sword," Quinn demanded as he fell into a chair. "Be quick. I won't wait long. My boy is out there and he needs me. If you're not back very soon, I'll steal the first horse I see and I'll be rid of you for good."

Chapter 5

After the first day of their journey south to Parhelion, Alissa learned almost all the names of the twenty soldiers who served as her retinue and armed escort. Through casual conversation, she came to know something of each man's individual character and discovered pieces about their lives and personal history. It was now the third day and earlier that morning the troop had bathed in the Dunegall River with Alissa modestly secluded from the others. The bath had helped to refresh their spirits as well as cleanse their bodies but a melancholic discontent still clung to the soldiers.

Alissa felt sorry for the soldiers. Like her, none of them really wanted to be on that lonely road that led away from home, family, and friends. Setting contemplation of her own troubles aside, Alissa wished for some way to improve the general mood. Conversation did not seem to be helping much today even though it was truly a splendid afternoon and there was much for which they could be thankful. The sun sat bright in a cloudless, azure sky but a gentle breeze kept the escalating heat at bay allowing them to enjoy the ascending light without having to endure an allied uncomfortable rise in temperature.

The road passed through a shallow valley. Bejeweled in a hundred shades of green, a dense woodland filled the gently sloped terrain on both sides of the wide road of hard packed earth and stubborn, stubby weeds. A lush herbaceous understory of grasses and sedges crowded around the dark columns of rough, gray-brown bark. These living pillars of maple, sycamore, and oak supported a broad, lace canopy of leaves above the forest floor. The woodland architecture was also built with the spiny shafts and limbs of locust trees, the pale, celadon trunks of birch, and the soft-needled boughs of pines. Other variants of woodland design adorned the rich foliage including blueberry bushes and rose brambles decorated in small red and white buds. Swayed by the soft breeze, the susurrant leaves brushed and played against one another in intermittent spasms of whispered frenzy. Through the trees could be seen the flashing flights of red-winged blackbirds and other aviary occupants. And within the botanical edifice, Alissa heard the determined tapping of a woodpecker, the twitter of swallows, and the low-pitched, rolling croak of frogs.

However, the soldiers were today immune to the optimism communicated by these subtle, ecological pleasures and the ubiquitous joy of nature as displayed in its rich colors, varied textures, and momentary serenity. So to enthuse felicity, Alissa sang a cheerful ballad about a victorious army returning home to the celebration of their countrymen and the joyous welcome of their wives. She sang more to cheer the others than from an attempt to make herself feel better. But she sang with a blithe aspect and sweet enthusiasm.

An exquisite physical beauty that surpassed fair description complemented the magnificent splendor of her voice. Even after three days of traveling and camping in the rugged outdoors, Alissa remained breathtakingly lovely in her appearance. After her morning bath, she left her long hair to hang loose and open for the sun to dry. Her soft, auburn tress shimmered in the refulgent light of the afternoon sun. A healthy glow seemed to inhabit the smooth, lineless skin of her face and within her alluring figure dwelled an enchanting purity and poise.

When the first song ended, she followed it with another merry tune. Gradually, the dulcet tones and buoyant rhythms of her melodic voice did manage to sooth the soldier's cares and relax their dour expressions.

Then the forest became quiet and the only accompaniment to her third song was the metronomic beat of the horse's hooves and the jingle of their bits. The birds and other animals were hushed in an unnatural silence that was undoubtedly not inspired by reverence for Alissa's performance. Unaware, Alissa continued to sing. But the soldier's noticed the strange stillness of the woods and became suddenly alert to their surroundings. Large, fleeting shadows seemed to dart between the trees on either side of them, quick, furtive movements that were threatening in their vague nature and unknown origin.

Alissa became conscious of the escalating tension rippling through the cavalcade of soldiers, noticed that their hands had settled over the hilts of their swords, detected their new wary interest in the forest. They kept their horses moving forward, not changing their easy stride; but the soldiers were alert, watching the trees with suspicion, casually on guard against an uncertain, unidentified threat.

She drew the curtain of her lips, ending her song and closing the last act of her musical performance. The shadows stirred with greater number amidst the trees, moving with increasing speed in the opposite direction as the soldiers. Whoever or whatever it was, they now moved without much effort given towards the pretense of stealth. Bushes rustled violently, twigs and branches snapped. The mad gibbering and muttering sound of many inhuman voices rose up all around them. The light wind shifted and a hateful, putrescent odor assaulted Alissa's olfactory senses. In seconds, the strange stench expanded to horrendous proportions.

The soldiers drew their swords but commanded their mounts to maintain an unhurried, measured pace. The horses and their riders were well trained. All possessed the steady nerves developed through previous battle experience with creatures like those swarming around them.

All at once the woods erupted in a loud cacophony of bestial wailing and wild bellowing. Out of shadow, crashing through brush, goblins and gnomes charged into the light of the open road. Their scrofulous hides were clad in ragged clothes, soiled leather with brass studs, and mismatched armor, much of which were spoils of war that had been stolen from their victims and unevenly distributed among their ranks. One hundred in number, they bristled with weapons. The creatures filled in on every side of Braemar's twenty soldiers, surrounding them, crowding the road, blocking advancement as well as retreat, and closing in quickly in a furious wave of aggression. The monsters punctuated their sadistic stampede with shrill cries, hateful, deep-toned howls, and an insane chittering laughter.

The soldiers closed ranks in a tight circle around Alissa, like a clenched fist gathering force and preparing to strike. They were hopelessly outnumbered and they knew it. If they broke and ran, some of them might have been able to escape to safety on their horses. But none of Braemar's soldiers were willing to abandon the princess. Neither would Alissa abandon them to fight alone. She drew her own sword, equipping herself in defense against the rushing horde of living abominations, the grisly onslaught of murderous fiends.

The goblins and gnomes collided with the soldiers and the battle detonated in a clangor of armor and clashing weapons. Wielded with fury and fear against shields, body armor, and flesh; axes hacked, swords slashed, spears jabbed, and maces smashed. It was a fearsome sight capable of draining the valor of even the most stouthearted man, but Alissa found her courage and gripped it tightly. She stiffened her spine and let lose her sword, dropping its lethal cutting edge against the body of a goblin and opening a ghastly wound in its side.

The elevated height of being on horseback afforded Breamar's soldiers a slight advantage but it was a momentary one and an inadequate protection against the greater force of their adversary. The monsters attacked the horses, chopping at the poor animals' legs with swords and other edged weapons, stabbing spears into their exposed bellies. Killing or crippling their mounts, they brought the riders to the ground.

A gnome rammed an ahlespiess, a spear with a long, square metal shaft that came to a point, into the chest of Alissa's horse. It expelled a screaming whinny and reared, kicking its hooves at its assailant, the staff of the spear still protruding form the equine animal. The horse fell forward, dropping to its knees and pitching Alissa out of the saddle, over the horse's neck and onto the road. She landed on her left shoulder blade and rolled to mitigate the impact of the fall, but the shock still stole her breath and it took a moment for her ragged gasps to find enough air to fill her lungs. However, she kept hold of her sword, her fingers clamped around its hilt in an unyielding grip as rigid as rigor mortis.

She saw her horse lying on its side, struggling to get back up. Snorting with futile exertion, its nostrils flared. Its hooves flailed wildly against death but its legs were useless; it could not stand. Its body heaved in deep inhalations that came at more widely spaced intervals.

Managing what her horse could not, Alissa sprang to her feet, swinging her sword in a deadly arc against a pair of gnomes pressing in on her. She experienced a surge of satisfaction and adrenaline as she nearly cleaved off the scabrous arm of one gnome. The damaged appendage hung loosely together, poorly connected by broken bone and mutilated muscle. A spray of dark, putrid blood splattered Alissa's cheek and colored her clothes. Wasting no time, she impaled the other gnome's throat with the tip of her sword.

Sensing another adversary at her back, Alissa whirled in a graceful pirouette to face the challenger. She planted her feet in a fighting stance, her arm raised with the sword cocked over her shoulder and primed to strike.

The sight of her enemy caused Alissa's bowels to squirm in revulsion and froze her with fright. Before her stood a Seeker, seven feet tall with midnight skin and long, stringy white hair. He had high, abnormally pronounced cheekbones, an almost nonexistent nose, and a large jutting chin. His sword remained at his side sheathed safely in its scabbard. Yet he radiated an aura of deadly menace. The cruel, yellow starburst of his eyes regarded her with amused delight and his glistening teeth smiled with pleasure. Palm up, he held his hand out toward her. In it he grasped a small, white stone. Its surface seemed to swirl and stir like a cloud in the dark sky of his black hand. He held the Orb of Empathy. They had found it along with other magic devises and were taking it back to Torrin at Gairloch when they happened to cross paths with Alissa. The Seeker, named Tenchi, had already discovered the use of the Orb. He had enjoyed its application in simple games but suspected it could also prove to be a tremendous tool for gaining greater power. This thought occurred to him often enough that he sometimes wondered if he should perhaps keep it for himself. But now, as he stood looking at Alissa, a creature of gloriously stimulating appeal, hopes of new pleasures that might be derived from the Orb's use took possession of his desires.

The Orb of Empathy was an ancient elvin relic of great magic. With it, the user could feel the exact emotions of another person. But in addition to this, the Orb contained a more sinister purpose. The magic of the Orb could also be exercised in reverse to force the emotions of the user's choosing onto another person, making them feel whatever the user wished—love, fear, remorse, hate, anything at all.

Alissa had no idea what the Seeker was or what he held; but she knew instinctively that he was the leader of these monsters and that he was uniquely dangerous. So she was determined to kill him. She inhaled deeply, took a step forward; the muscles of her raised sword arm flexed in anticipation of her swing.

But it was too late. The Seeker had already called upon the magic of the Orb, filling Alissa's mind with an immobilizing sense of exhaustion, a lethargic detachment from the perilous reality of her situation. She suddenly felt too tired to move. A strange lassitude took possession of her and would not let go, a deep listlessness that left her weary to the bone. Her head rolled to the side. She saw the gleaming metal of her raised sword blade catch a slice of sunlight. But Alissa stared at the weapon as if she had forgotten what it was for. Surrendering to the lethal sleepiness, her fingers relaxed and uncurled. The sword dropped from her hand and buried its point into the ground. Through this dazed stupor imposed by the magic of the Orb, she let her arm fall and her distant, placid gaze shift further off to her right.

There she saw Cole, a soldier who had told Alissa about his five-year-old daughter back at the castle. She was sick and he was worried about her. Cole screamed his little girl's name as a goblin's broadsword struck his shoulder at the base of his neck, shattering his collarbone, spouting blood, and digging into his chest.

Not far away she saw another soldier named Trevor. During an earlier conversation he told Alissa that he had fought with his wife before they left the castle. He had said some unkind words to his wife that he later regretted and he was anxious to get home so he could apologize. A gnome wielding a massive spiked club smashed the soldier's jaw.

To her left, another soldier, she couldn't remember his name, was stabbed in the belly by a goblin while a gnome hammered the soldier's leg with a wicked, iron pickaxe. Bright crimson blood rose up and poured out of the soldier's mouth as he toppled over on the road.

Nearby, a soldier named Raymond fought valiantly against three goblins. Raymond had told her that when he was a child a cat had bitten him on his left hand. The wound had become badly infected and Raymond had to have the last two fingers of that hand removed. Yet he would not let his parents get rid of the cat. With a teeth-bearing snarl, one of the goblins pounced on Raymond's back and wrapped its long, powerful arms around him. The carnivorous thing sunk its tusk–like fangs into the soldier's neck and tore out a chuck of meat around his jugular. His flesh ripped and the soldier's blood spurted over the ghastly, feverish face of the goblin.

It was horrible. Alissa wanted to help all of them but she felt too tired to do anything except weep, and even in that she could only manage to move a few tears. Through her enraptured ennui, a muffled voice deep inside her mind shrieked for her to do something; but her body would not listen. It could not summon the energy necessary for movement. All she could do was passively watch as her people died.

In a trance of increasing, unimaginable drowsiness, she surveyed the horrific scene with growing disinterest, like she was viewing a jejune play that had become too tiresome to bear. The weight of magical somnolence pulled at her until she could resist no longer. A total loss of consciousness overtook her and Alissa collapsed into sleep on the ground at the Seeker's feet.

Keenan had been traveling from Abandon to Gairloch along the eastern edge of the Tissama Mountains. But along that route, he had spotted a caravan of some sort. He elected not to risk a close enough inspection to ascertain who they were but fearing that it might be more goblins, Keenan fled south away from the mountains and toward Dolmendie Forest north of Braemar. From there he planned to continue on to Gairloch under the cover of the deep forest.

Up until yesterday he had been making excellent progress and had reached the dense woodlands along the outer boundary of Dolmendie Forest. Propelled by fear, Keenan had been riding fast and for long hours each day. So he managed to cross considerable territory in a short period of time. Yesterday, however, he suffered a significant setback.

At various hours during the past few nights, the silence had been broken and sleep interrupted by a strange canine howl. Last night the noise increased in proximity and proportion to an extent sufficient enough to frightened Keenan's horse into a fit of extreme terror causing the animal to break free of its tether and run away into the dark. Keenan waited until morning to search for his craven horse but by then the animal was nowhere to be found. At a greatly reduced rate, Keenan was now forced to travel the rest of the way on foot. Fortunately, the horse had been striped of its saddlebags and supplies before making its cowardly escape. So Keenan was not left totally empty handed. But he was only able to take with him what he could carry and was forced to leave the rest behind.

Today's hike had been lengthy, hot, and exhausting. Keenan made camp earlier than normal, then hunted, cleaned, cooked, and ate a rabbit for his dinner. Emotionally dejected and physically sore, he went through the motions of these necessary chores without enthusiasm or pleasure.

The day drew to a close, the shadows deepened, the colors darkened. After his meal, he shoveled dirt over his cooking fire, extinguishing its telltale light. Then he prepared to bed down for the evening. He rolled out a blanket on the ground and, for security against the night howls, he placed his bow and arrows nearby. Keenan laid down on the spread blanket. Curled on his side, he pulled his cloak over him and hugged his scabbarded sword to his chest. But even though he was drained of energy, worn out from the all day march, sleep eluded him.

Lying on the ground, Keenan stared at the darkness, listening to the wind blow softly through the trees, a lonely, mournful sound. It whispered to him, not his name but his fate. He felt isolated and doomed. He missed his family and, wondering if he would ever see them again, he worried about them. He despaired about the likely prospect of a brief and friendless future. But these musings by themselves were not all that troubled his sleep. For the third night in a row, the unsettling feeling of being watched beset him. He sensed an unseen menace lurking amidst the haunted shadows of the darkened forest that was more, not less, threatening by its inexplicable character, its indefinable identity. It started with the wolf howls in the night, but he also felt the odd impression of being surreptitiously observed even during the day. Maybe he was simply getting more paranoid as he got closer to Gairloch, but he felt certain that something was stalking him.

It took a long time for him to find sleep and when he finally crossed into the elusive land of dreams it seemed to pass too quickly. The morning came and Keenan grudgingly awoke, his body aching from having walked too many miles the previous day and from sleeping on too hard a bed. He wanted to pull his cloak over his head to block the light of the rising sun and go back to sleep. However, the noise of the birds singing in the trees and the pressure of his bladder would not allow further slumber.

He tossed off his cloak, then sat up rubbing his eyes and combing his fingers through his hair. Blinking to clear his tired, grainy vision, Keenan saw someone perched on a large rock twenty feet away from him. The unannounced visitor startled Keenan to his feet. He snatched his sword from its sheath and sprang from his bed in one quick motion. However, the visitor did not react to the gleaming threat of Keenan's sword, but remained seated on the rock calmly watching Keenan.

A girl, around seventeen years of age, she was pretty and petite, about five feet, four inches in height. Her dark brown hair was parted in the middle and cut just above her shoulders. The crescents formed by her straight, silky mane bracketed her face like parentheses. She was dressed in a black, sleeveless suede jerkin with a broad strap over each shoulder. The jerkin laced in front, gathering the material at her waist and accentuating her svelte figure, then broke into a skirting of hanging vertical bands that encircled her hips. Beneath this, she wore a pair of brown, tight-fitting cloth pants that hugged her legs and were tucked inside her calf-high, black leather boots. The shoulder straps and skirting of the suede jerkin were decorated in silver studs and her belt was adorned with a sword, dagger, and a few pouches.

"You snore," she announced for no apparent reason. "Not all night but enough to call attention to yourself."

"What," Keenan asked in wary confusion. "I do not. And what difference does it make? Who are you?"

She ignored his sword along with his question, asking inquiries of her own instead of offering any answers. "What's a kid like you doing out here on the edge of Dolmendie Forest? Are you lost," she goaded him.

Keenan stood his ground with his guard up, but he lowered his sword. "I'm no kid. I'm a man, and I'm certainly older than you. What are you doing here and why are you spying on me?"

"These lands are under Gairloch's rule. It's not a safe place to be for a nice boy like you," she chided.

"I'm not worried; and I told you I'm a man, not a boy. I can take care of myself. And if it's so dangerous, why are you here?"

She shrugged. Rising and falling with her shoulders, the fabric of her jerkin tightened around her breasts in an enticing display. "Maybe I'm part of the danger," she said casually.

"You're a friend of Gairloch?" Keenan demanded she answer, his tone turning angry and suspicious.

In disgust, she turned her head and spat. "No, I hate everything about that place. If I could, I'd burn Gairloch down to the ground along with everyone in it." Despite her seeming innocence and inability to execute her threat, the hate in her eyes made Keenan shiver.

"Then it sounds as if we share a common foe. So perhaps you and I shouldn't be enemies to one another." Keenan shifted his sword to his left hand and extended the palm of his right. "My name is Keenan. And any foe of Gairloch is a friend of mine."

With a lupine agility borne of impressive strength and balance, she leapt from her perch onto the ground. Almost without stirring any sound as she walked, she padded lightly on her feet toward Keenan. The lithe lines and muscular curves of her body moved with a sinuous grace. Keenan took notice of her lean and limber build, the allure of her strong, slender figure.

When she reached him, she slipped her palm over his and shook his hand in a firm grip. The skin of her hand was rough and thickly calloused. But her touch sent sweet sensations of desire up and down Keenan's spine.

"My name's Lukos," she informed him.

"It's a pleasure to make your acquaintance," Keenan replied with sincerity and a smile. He studied her face, searching for traces of deceit and danger while also appreciating its simple, lineless beauty. She had a pert little nose set on a fresh, honest face; thin dark eyebrows; and the most amazing pale, gray eyes. Her eyes were like multi-faceted crystal with an incandescent magnetism that he found irresistible.

"You trust people too quickly," Lukos admonished him sternly, as if by entitlement of some vast superiority she had the right to judge him. "Around here that will get you killed, if your snoring doesn't do it first that is."

She smiled thinly and let go of his hand. Keenan regretted losing hold of her so soon but delighted in the glimmer of white teeth revealed by her weak yet pleasant smile. She was bold to the point of being rude, but Keenan still found her rather adorable.

Lukos could tell that Keenan underestimated her. She could read it in the attitude of his face and frame, in the way his body relaxed and easily set aside his defensive readiness. It was stupid of him and it made her angry. To him she looked sweet and innocent; so he considered her safe. But she knew he was making an unwise assumption about her. A wolf could look like a lovable, friendly dog but it is really a wild creature, unpredictable, dangerous, and sometimes savage. Only someone who had not been bitten much in life put such quick trust in outward appearances. Anyone with the scars of experience would know that to mistake a wolf for a common dog could be fatal. Lukos learned at an early age not to trust appearances, or much of anything else for that matter. To stay alive you had to be careful and callous. She had been watching Keenan for days before she risked this introduction. Everything he did suggested that Keenan would be no threat to her. But she still felt foolish making contact with him. It was not prudent; she did not belong among normal people. She did not belong anywhere. But she found him interesting, was intrigued by the kind of man he seemed to be. And although she hated to admit it even to herself, she was lonely. So after stalking him for days, studying him, considering him, she summoned the courage to hazard talking to him.

"Are you hungry," Keenan asked. "I'm afraid I don't have very much I can offer you but I'll share what little there is."

"No," Lukos answered, shaking her head. "I ate very late last night."

"All right then," said Keenan. "I thought I saw a raspberry bush over there. I'll go pick some for myself and be right back." He actually wanted to relieve his bladder but he could not think of a gentlemanly way to excuse himself for that purpose. "Wait here."

She nodded, encouraged that he at least had sense enough buckle his sword belt around his waste before leaving her. Keenan also slung his quiver of arrows over his shoulder and picked up his bow, although he glanced guiltily at her as he did it, afraid that the action would betray a lack of trust and offend her. In truth, she would have been more offended if he had walked away unarmed while leaving her alone with his modest arsenal of weapons.

After a few minutes, he returned empty handed.

"No berries," Lukos asked.

"Oh, no. I decided I'm not that hungry either." To occupy his hands and to hide his mild nervousness, Keenan began packing up his blanket and a few other supplies. "So do you live around here?"

"No," she responded simply. She paced about leisurely, stopping from time to time to stretch her arms and legs, all the while keeping Keenan in the corner of her eye.

She was not very communicative but Keenan persisted. "If you're traveling, which way are you headed? Maybe we could journey together for a while, keep each other company, at least until our paths go off in different directions."

Lukos ignored his offer but tilting her head to the side, she focused her attention on him more directly than she had been. "Are you a runaway farm slave? You look like you could be a farmer; although you don't seem like you've had to spend your life working under the whip of Gairloch's garrison masters?"

"No, I'm no slave," Keenan assured her. "My home is in the west, in the Tissama Mountains, but I'm headed north. How about you?"

"North!" Lukos exclaimed incredulously. "We're on the edge of Gairloch's territories now, you fool. If you go north you'll be walking right into the thick of his lair, where Torrin Murgleys rules and nothing but pain and death await. Only an idiot would willingly venture into Gairloch's territories. Are you really as stupid as you look? Are you really dim-witted enough to go there? They'll eat you alive before you know what's happening."

She frustrated and infuriated him. Yet strangely, for some reason he wanted to impress her. "I told you before that I can take care of myself. In fact, I'm going right into the heart of Gairloch. And when I get there, I'm going to kill this tyrant named Torrin and steal his infamous axe, the Maul of Murgleys." It was true but it sounded like a fool's boast even to his own ears.

"Hah," she laughed at him with an air of condescending jubilation. "I've been in Gairloch. I have first-hand knowledge of what lives there. You haven't got one whisper of a chance of even getting inside the castle gate. And you sure don't stand a chance against that lord of demons, Torrin Murgleys."

"You've been in Gairloch," Keenan asked with dubious excitement. If what she said was true, perhaps she could help him. Besides, he might very well die at Gairloch; and if he did, it would be nice to spend his last few days in the company of an attractive girl, even if she was as bad mannered as she was interesting. "Come with me, not all the way inside, but show me the way to the castle. You can always turn around and leave if you get scared along the way."

There were daggers in her eyes when he suggested she could be scared. Then she shook her head as if she pitied him, as if he were a dense child that did not understand the grownup world he was operating in. "You're going to kill Torrin Murgleys but you don't even know where the castle is. That's great. What are you going to do, just ask for directions as you go? Try asking those nice fellows with the pale white skin and the pointed ears. I'm sure they would love to help you find your way."

"I'm not afraid of the White Elves," Keenan bragged, "and I have a good idea of how to get to Gairloch on my own. I don't need your help. But I wouldn't mind your company, even though you're not the most pleasant person I've ever met. And if you could give me some information on how best to reach Gairloch and get inside, I would very much appreciate it. If you've really been there, your knowledge of the castle's layout could be of great help to me."

"What will you pay me for it," she inquired.

Keenan held up his hands in empty defeat. "I don't have anything of value on me. But I could repay you after my work at Gairloch is complete."

She laughed at him again. It was a mocking laugh, but because she was so pretty Keenan did not mind the insult too much. "Dead men seldom make good on their debts," Lukos told him.

She had no desire to leave the relative security of the woods and return closer to Gairloch. It cost her too much to escape from Gairloch to ever risk coming in sight of its detestable walls ever again. She knew what horrors lived there and what it took to survive them. Few people could say that. Keenan's boast insulted her and all that she had accomplished. She did not believe him, not his bravado nor the mission he claimed to be on, and she wanted to force him to admit his lie. Such an admission would validate her own strength. But that was not all. Although she would not admit it even to herself, she would not mind his company either, at least for a little while. There was something about Keenan that she liked, some indefinable quality that drew her to him. Maybe she could spend a few days with him and let herself pretend she had a friend. The charade might be entertaining, might help ease her loneliness if only for a short time. Other than his professed desire to go to Gairloch, he seemed harmless enough. So the short-term companionship he offered did not appear to present very much peril to her.

"Okay, give me your cloak," Lukos demanded. She did not really want the garment but she was not about to help someone for nothing, or at least not for something as intangible and most likely worthless as companionship. "I'll go with you for a ways, tell you some of what I know about Gairloch. We'll see how it goes, but I'm not promising anything."

"My mother made me this cloak," Keenan protested.

Lukos shrugged as if the sentiment meant nothing to her. And in truth she had very little understanding concerning the emotional bonds between a mother and her children, and therefore little sympathy for Keenan's reluctance to part with the dirty, tattered cloak.

"Fine," Keenan relented. "It's yours. We'll have to walk. I lost my horse."

"Yeah," she said. "I'm sorry about that."

"What do you mean," Keenan asked.

She shrugged again. It was a rude gesture but Keenan still enjoyed watching how her body moved when she did it.

"Nothing," Lukos explained. "I'm just sorry you lost your horse." Then she considered her answer a little more thoroughly and added. "A horse is worth more than your mother's cloak."

By mid afternoon, Keenan and Lukos had not traveled very far but surprisingly they had made considerable progress on their path toward friendship. Throughout the day they had joked and teased one another in a playful manner. They kept some secrets about themselves, Lukos more than Keenan but for the most part they were open and honest in their conversation and attitude. There was some kind of connection forming between them, a nascent affection that made it possible for even Lukos to feel the stirrings of friendship and trust.

They made camp early in a secluded hollow amid the timbered ridges and valleys. Keenan kindled a small fire, assuring Lukos that he would extinguish it before dark, then he ventured off with his bow to hunt them dinner. He brought back a pheasant, which they plucked and dressed together before putting it on a spit over the fire. Keenan also brewed them some tea to drink.

After they finished eating their simple meal, they put out the fire and sat side by side together, watching as the sun began its slow decent toward the horizon. The sunset washed the sky in a warm crimson glow and tinted the few scattered clouds in rich shades of violet. As the light of day ebbed into night, Lukos became more quiet and Keenan sensed an unusual introspective sadness come over her. Eventually, she released a heavy sigh then touched his arm lightly, almost as if it had been by accident, and stood up.

"I'm not going to sleep here tonight," she announced.

Keenan stood up too. He thought that perhaps she still did not trust him, that she was afraid he might try to attack her in her sleep when she was especially vulnerable. And he felt confident that he could not convince her that such fears were unnecessary. It was too soon for mere words of assurance to have any real meaning for a girl who clearly regarded the world with such profound suspicion. A budding friendship may be developing between them, but it was tenuous and still bound by understandable limits. Spending the night alone together, sleeping so near one another, was apparently one of them.

"Will I see you in the morning," Keenan asked hopefully.

"Probably." It wasn't much but it was the only promise she could give him.

Lukos started to leave. Then abruptly she turned back to Keenan. She grabbed him around the neck and pulled his face down next to hers. Then she kissed him.

The kiss was no quick peck but one that was lingering, deep, and probing. Her protracted kiss was hungry with a kind of animal urgency to it. Yet despite the fervor of her execution, she seemed to be exploring uncharted territory, as if she did not know what kissing was all about. But she experimented enthusiastically and seemed very eager to learn. She pressed her mouth hard against his; her tongue pushed past his teeth and thrust deep into his mouth.

When Keenan pulled her body closer, however, she pushed him back, gently disentangling herself from the firmer embrace he attempted. Reluctantly, he released his hold on her, still savoring the frantic tenderness of her lips. He had never tasted lips so soft, so sweet, so passionate.

"No more," she insisted softly. Something like fear filled her voice. She stared intently into Keenan's eyes, hopeful he would respect her limits and obey her demand but on guard in case he did not.

Keenan stepped back and Lukos relaxed a bit, both of them still breathless from their kiss. "Will I see you in the morning," he asked again, with a new longing infused into his voice.

"Probably." She echoed her earlier reply and started to walk away.

Keenan called after her. "Don't forget your cloak."

"Keep it," she answered. "It's too hot and it itches anyway." She shot him a playful wink and then, as the sun touched the western horizon, she disappeared into the trees.

Lukos returned the next morning and the morning after that. The bond between the two grew stronger as they made their way slowly toward Gairloch. They shared a few more kisses, each initiated by Lukos. But the physical expression of their mutual affection went no further. Keenan believed he was falling in love with Lukos, and he felt that she returned a similar fondness for him. However, at times her mood would suddenly shift and she would withdraw from him emotionally. She might be standing right next to him but her heart would seem a million miles away, or as if she had locked it securely inside some fortified prison where no one could touch it. Then she would kiss him and Keenan's own heart would boil over with hope. If the relationship continued as it had been, Keenan thought he might even want to marry Lukos provided of course his mission to Gairloch did not get him killed.

"Keenan, I'm not what you think I am," Lukos said suddenly.

Her statement came from nowhere. It was spoken with profound feeling but completely out of context with the conversation they had been having. So the enigmatic pronouncement startled Keenan, as did the shimmer of tears that tried to coalesce around her eyes before the heat of her inward anger forced them to evaporate through sheer strength of will.

"I have within me a latent malignancy," she continued, "a curse of evil that prevents me from ever having what you would call an ordinary life. I'm no good to anyone." She spoke with shame and regret, but it was backed up by an angry, stubborn pride. "I may be rubbish but I'm also dangerous. It's not safe for me to be around people."

"What are you taking about," Keenan asked. "You're not rubbish; you're extraordinary. Why do you criticize yourself that way? Are you sick? Do you mean that you have some kind of illness?" Even the mere thought of disease provoked an agonizing sympathy within him.

Lukos was plagued by guilt over who she was and afraid of how he would react to her once he knew. But she was determined to reveal the truth. She wanted him have this information in case she allowed herself to become any more involved with him, or perhaps to prevent increased involvement. These alien feelings of love, if that is what they were, scared her as few things ever had before.

"I was born in Gairloch," she began. "Or maybe I should say I was created there, for if I had a mother and father like normal people I never knew who they were. They make all kinds of creatures in Gairloch. Those that seem to have a purpose, they use, like the goblins and gnomes. Those disgusting monstrosities Torrin considers useful. So he continues to manufacture and 'improve' them. But he and the White Elves make other things too. They do a lot of experimenting inside the walls of Gairloch and their efforts have produced frightful creatures that they consider victorious accomplishments. The failed experiments like me, the ones they consider too weak or too worthless, they discard into the Pit." She shuddered at the memory of it.

"What do you mean 'experiments like you.' What did they do to you?"

"They made me. Aren't you listening," she snarled impatiently. "I said they made me. From what, I don't really know but somehow they created me. There were others like me. But I don't think any of them survived. As far as I know, I'm the only one of my kind. Are you sure you want to know any more?"

"Yes," Keenan pleaded, anguished by the pain that obviously lay behind her revelation. "Please tell me so I'll know how I can help you."

"You can't help me," she insisted coldly. "I'm a werewolf."

Keenan's eyes narrowed but he looked at her without any understanding of what she meant. "A what?"

"During the lunar cycle of full moon to new moon, about two weeks a month, when night falls I change." Lukos pushed herself to continue. "My body is transformed into a wolf during the night and in the morning I change back into the woman you see before you. During the other two weeks, from new moon to full moon, I appear as a normal woman both at night and in the daylight hours. When I was little, they kept me penned up along with the other werewolves to see what I would become, how I would develop. But eventually my keepers decided our value wasn't worth our cost or that we weren't useful enough or violent enough to serve Torrin adequately. So we were discarded. I was thrown into the Pit, the charnel bowels of that awful castle and a place of true horror. As I said, to the best of my knowledge I'm the only one of my kind to have survived. My time in the Pit was brutal but I didn't let them kill me and although it cost me dearly, I managed to escape."

"You poor thing." Keenan groaned. He ached with compassion for the plight she must have suffered both in Gairloch and after she was free of it, because she could never be free of what they had done to her. However, Lukos misunderstood his meaning.

"Yes I'm a thing, a perversion of nature, a wicked creature," she growled at him. "Don't you think I know that? Torrin is evil and I am evil because he made me. I'm cursed with the malign imprint of his power. His malevolence is woven into the fabric of my flesh. It's in my blood and I can't escape it."

This statement struck a special cord with Keenan as they were both born of Torrin's potency, she of his magic and he of his flesh.

"Just because Torrin made you, it doesn't make you like him," Keenan argued, using warmhearted kindness to combat the withering fury of her icy, gray stare. "You're not a demon simply because you were fashioned by one. He may have determined the type of body you have, but he doesn't control what you do with it. He can't create the type of character that will inhabit the unusual body you inherited from his magic."

"You don't know that. I don't even know if that's true. When I'm in the form of the wolf, it's so strange. I lose myself. I don't know that I can control what I do and in the morning it's hard to remember what I've done. My mind changes, not as radically as my body; but I can feel the power of the beast pulling at my mind too."

What she said was grave and disturbing in the extreme, but Keenan could barely believe what he was hearing. It was impossible for him to think of her as a monster. She was so pretty, so strong, and her healthy nature seemed so unaffected by any inborn perversion. To him, she was still the girl with whom he thought he might want to spend the rest of his life. Keenan could not think of anything to say that would reassure her. He could not find the words to convince her that he still cared about her and did not consider her a freak or a fiend. So for the first time, he initiated a kiss.

She welcomed it. She wrapped her arms around him in a tight embrace, clinging to him like a lifeline. Tears broke free of her eyes, flowed down her cheeks and around the union of their lips. Their bodies still embracing, Keenan moved his lips beside her ear.

"I love you," he whispered.

She twisted and pushed him away. She shoved him hard, almost violently. Keenan staggered back, nearly falling, surprised by her reaction and its intensity. Her nature was infused with an almost genetic instinct to resist any kind of cage, causing her to rebel even against the emotional captivity imposed by someone who cared, someone who would use the bonds of affection to put a leash on her freedom.

Lukos turned, ran into the woods, and was gone.

Keenan called after her but only his lonely echo returned to him.

Alissa awoke to the aroma of cooking meat but that normally pleasant smell was overlaid and tainted by the acrid odor of burning hair. Without opening her eyes, she concluded that the goblins and gnomes must be eating the slain horses. At least she hoped it was only the horses and not the soldiers too. Her wrists were locked in iron cuffs linked by a short chain. Another chain connected to her shackles bound Alissa like a dog to a tree, preventing her escape and limiting the expanse of her universe to a five-foot radius around its trunk.

She lay on her side, her cheek resting on a grassy pillow. Through half-lidded eyes, Alissa saw that the tree to which she was chained was set back at least thirty feet from the main body of the goblin camp. Just as she was drawing some comfort from this relative isolation, long fingers tipped with elongated nails tickled the back of her head, tousling her hair. Instant terror jolted her nerves. Frantically, she scuttled away from the abhorrent touch. Rolling, kicking wildly against the ground to get away, she saw her unwelcome attendant with alarmed recognition. The Seeker, Tenchi, had been crouched beside her while she slept. Standing up, he straightened his tall frame to its full height, flexing his powerful muscles like a threat. He stood stark naked, his dark, twilight skin a harsh contrast to the bright light of day.

Inconceivably hideous, the ugly warning implied by his nudity made her dry throat tightened like a vice, choking off an urgent impulse to vomit. She scrambled to her feet, pulling at her chain to put as much distance between them as possible. Tenchi smiled with optimistic cruelty and took a step toward her.

"You belong to me," Tenchi rumbled. His gravelly voice seemed to scrape the inside of her ears, abrading her auditory nerves.

A visceral loathing twisted in the pit of her stomach, stirring the bile of her disgust, causing her to gag and sending a terrified shudder throughout her body. Forcing down her fear, defying her moral nausea, Alissa invoked her courage, determined to marshal all her might in defense of her life and the purity of her flesh.

Tenchi reached out with his large, heavily veined hand. In his palm sat the Orb of Empathy. He called upon its magic and all of Alissa's repugnance and resistance were swept away like clouds in the wind, replaced by an intense involuntary arousal of her carnal passions. Through the Orb, her emotions were unwillingly possessed by an overpowering sexual titillation, imbued with irrepressible lust. The power of her will slipped from her control and suddenly, maddeningly all she wanted was to please him.

Trusting in the pliant state he created in Alissa through use of the Orb, Tenchi gave her the key and permitted her to free herself of the restraints. He instructed Alissa to disrobe and she eagerly complied, too eagerly. So he struck her across the face and commanded her to undress slowly for him.

Alissa licked the blood from her lip and did as she was told, pulled by the insistent drive of the Orb.

Tenchi kneaded the meat of Alissa's heavy breast then gripped her nipple tightly between his thumb and forefinger. He pinched the skin brutally and twisted, making her moan with pain. Turning up the volume of her simulated, erotic emotions, Tenchi made her crave it. Puppet master of her emotions, Tenchi used Alissa mercilessly to exercise the callous strength of his own depraved desires and explore the rich catalogue of his barbaric lust.

"Why are you still headed north," Lukos asked Keenan. "Are you actually serious about going to Gairloch, about wanting to kill Torrin? I thought that was just a bunch of hot air to try and impress me."

Thrilled that she had come back but trying not to intimidate her with his joy, Keenan controlled his emotions and continued walking as Lukos fell in step alongside him. "I'm not sure that anything I do can please you or impress you. But yes, I'm serious. I meant what I said about Gairloch, and about you."

"You're insane," she grumbled sourly.

She remained as rude as ever, but Keenan was glad for the chance to have her company again. "It's been almost two days," he observed. "I wasn't sure I would see you again. Why did you come back?"

She shrugged in her old familiar way, trying to imply apathy as well as ignorance with her impolite gesture. "I don't know, maybe I felt sorry for you."

Keenan was still hurt that she had left him but he smiled in spite of himself. "At least you feel something for me."

"You don't know what you're doing," she grumped with exasperated distain. "Your mother should have kept her cloak and kept a better watch on her son. Anyone stupid enough to go to Gairloch needs someone to protect him from himself."

"Is that what you're doing," Keenan asked. "Is that why you came back?"

She failed to reply. So Keenan slid his fingers around hers and held her hand. Without resistance, Lukos granted him that simple pleasure and with it gave him a complicated hope for the future of their relationship.

Around midday the two overheard a voice as they walked up a wooded ridge within the outer edge of Dolmendie Forest. Stealthily, they crept to the top of the ridge and saw that it overlooked a stream, a large tributary to the Dunegall River. A naked man stood waist deep in the middle of the stream's cool, clear waters, repeatedly raising his arms toward the heavens and then lowering them again. He spoke loudly, confidently, but Keenan and Lukos could not make out what he said nor could they see anyone with whom he might be conversing. He seemed to be alone.

"What do you make of it?" Keenan whispered his confusion to Lukos.

"He's talking to himself. He must be crazy. Maybe the forest drove him mad. We should be careful. He's unarmed in addition to being undressed; so he doesn't look too dangerous but he may not be alone. You stay here and I'll circle around for a closer look, then I'll come back."

Lukos started away, her movements astonishingly silent and swift. Keenan wanted to protest against her plan but she was already out of range of his whisper and he did not want to risk disclosing their position by raising his voice.

Careful not to disturb the hush of the forest, she worked her way through the trees. Once satisfied that no others lurked nearby, Lukos took cover in the shadows behind a thicket of bushes and hanging tree limbs so that she could observe the man more closely in order to make a final judgment of his nature.

The man stopped talking and seemed to have finished whatever it was he had been doing. She watched as he left the stream, his body shedding water. He looked to be in his late thirties. His stature was short and compact. In fact, he was only a couple of inches taller than her. His sandy blond hair was trimmed close to his head and he wore a shaggy beard across his face. Scars laced the majority of his copper skin but his movements advertised that he was a man of relaxed self-assurance whose body maintained a hearty vigor.

On the stream bank, he stood quietly for a few minutes, letting the warm sun and mild breeze dry the river water from his body. He was also listening, attuning his senses to the natural world around him as he departed a higher plane of contemplation and returned from his communion with an elevated presence. Once dry, he donned a voluminous garment of a thin, light brown fabric. Then he looked in her direction.

"Hello young lady," he said serenely. "It isn't morally suitable for a woman to spy on a man while he is taking a bath, especially one of ritual purification. But now that I'm dressed you are welcome to improve your manners by exiting your ineffective concealment and introducing yourself properly."

Son-of-a-bitch, how could he have spotted me, she thought. It was impossible. When she wanted to be, she was all but invisible. *He must be talking to himself again,* she concluded. *There is no way he could see me.*

"Come on, don't be shy now," he urged her. "And tell your friend up on the hill to come out of hiding too."

Crap, she cursed inside her mind, astonished by the man's keen perceptions. *He's not talking to himself. He knows right where I am and what's more he knows about Keenan.*

The guy was good, but she was not about to let some crazy fool get the better of her. So she unsheathed her sword and walked boldly out to face him. Keenan followed her lead.

"Who are you," Lukos demanded. "And what business do you have in these woods?"

"Put that thing away," he said with phlegmatic confidence, calmly referring to her sword, "before someone gets hurt. That goes for you too young sir. My name is Jeroboam. And I'd be pleased if you'd be willing to share your names with me as easily as you were willing to show me your weapons. They are impressive blades but I don't think you will have need of them at the moment."

Keenan nodded at Lukos and returned his sword to its scabbard. Hesitantly, she did the same.

"My name is Keenan and she is Lukos."

Lukos shot a reproachful glare at Keenan before turning her attention back to Jeroboam.

"Who were you talking to when you were in the water," she demanded. The man's calm demeanor now made Lukos doubt her earlier assessment of his sanity. But if he was not crazy, then she was certain that anyone this relaxed when confronted by two armed strangers must have allies somewhere close at hand to back him up.

"I was talking to God," Jeroboam answered.

Lukos scowled, her features twisted with antipathy and mistrust. "What god?"

"There is only one true God," Jeroboam instructed her. "And if we are to continue discussing Him, I must ask that you speak with greater reverence."

"He's talking about the World Spirit," Keenan put in quickly in an effort to deflect Lukos' pugnacious nature and prevent her from countering Jeroboam's admonishment with any insulting response. "The ancient elves worshiped it as the source of all magic. My mother taught me about it."

"Not exactly," Jeroboam corrected. "The World Spirit is only one expression of the face of God, only a part of the great I AM, not His total being. The Lord God resides in the earth just as His spirit also resides in His people. But no temple, not my body nor the world itself, can contain the totality of the Lord. He resides in the firmament. The infinite universe is all that could be home to the all knowing, all-powerful God, all that could house his infinite knowledge, power, and presence. The power, or the magic if you like, of God that lives in the earth, the World Spirit, can do amazing things, great things. But another power, a lesser but seductive power lives in the earth too, the power of the evil one. The evil one rejects the truth and corrupts with lies, using pride, the greatest lie and our greatest weakness, to turn us from the truth. The evil one tells how man is autonomous, free and powerful. The evil one has the ear and the heart of the man who rules Gairloch."

"You mentioned the elves," Lukos observed, "is that what you are? Are you some kind of elf?"

"No child," Jeroboam explained patiently. "My people live far from here. I come from across the Barrens, from the far north. We are distant from the people here and our ways are different. Even when the elves were ancient, the people here in the south had already lost the true religion and the centuries since have done little to improve their knowledge. Ignoring more important matters, they became preoccupied with magic. Instead of studying the Word, they devoted themselves to the study of magic. But magic is not a religion. It is merely a manifestation of the spirit of truth or the spirit of lies. My people in the far north preserve the genuine faith and worship the one, true God. We observe His teaching and honor His will. And we are troubled by what is happening at Gairloch. It is an insidious plague that poses a greater threat with each passing day."

"So why don't your people do something to stop Torrin, the man who rules Gairloch?" Lukos snarled the question at him like an accusation. She despised the way he somehow made her feel inferior even though he had said nothing in real criticism of her. It was against her nature to trust him and she had no use for his sanctimonious preaching. "If they're so holy and they care so much, why don't your people send help?"

"They did," Jeroboam announced with a placid composure. "They sent me."

Jeroboam made his declaration with profound sincerity but without any trace of arrogance. Lukos threw back her head and laughed at the outrageousness of his audacious claim.

"Ha. What are you," she asked mockingly. "I could take care of you without breaking a sweat. What is one small man against the awesome might of Gairloch?"

"Lukos," Keenan interjected harshly. "There is no reason to act that way. This man has done nothing that you should treat him with such scorn. Must you try so hard to alienate everyone?"

Jeroboam ignored the words Keenan's offered in his defense, keeping his sensitive gaze fixed on Lukos. There was an immovable kindness in his eyes mingled with a hint of pity, and it seemed to infuriate Lukos' distain all the more.

"I am a pilgrim," Jeroboam answered Lukos. "Some might call me a paladin priest, a warrior monk, or a knight cleric. But you are correct; in truth, I am nothing. However, I can do all things through Him who strengthens me. And I have been sent here to fight Torrin's minions, to dispute their master's authority, to battle their evil, and deny the corrupt dominion they seek to impose upon the world. It is the duty I have been given."

"I have a similar duty," Keenan remarked. "We are on our way to Gairloch. It is my intention to gain access to that castle. Once inside I am going to take one of Torrin's most powerful tools of destruction, a thing of evil magic. I'm going to take his axe. It's called the Maul of Murgleys."

"You say that the source of this axe's power is evil. What will you do with the axe once you have it," Jeroboam inquired.

"The main thing is to prevent Gairloch from using it," Keenan answered. "But I suppose it should be destroyed."

"Is that all that you intend?" Jeroboam spoke without emotion but a force seemed to be building behind his words.

"No," said Keenan. "If I get the chance, I'm going to end Torrin's reign of terror. I'm going to rid the world of the pain he causes and the danger he presents."

"You will kill him?" Jeroboam pushed Keenan to admit his true objectives.

"Yes," Keenan stated firmly. "It won't be easy, I know; it's a bold plan. I could use your help. You said you were sent here to oppose Torrin. So it would seem we share a common destiny, perhaps we were meant to join together in this cause. Come with us to Gairloch."

"Perhaps," Jeroboam murmured, contemplating the matter, weighing its moral meaning and practical significance. "I will travel with you today. Tonight I will pray and ask God for His guidance in this matter. If it is His will, I will go with you all the way to Gairloch and help in what you purpose."

Lukos' eyes smoldered as she glowered her disapproval at the two men. Keenan felt the heat of her caustic glare blister his skin. He hoped he would be able to smooth things over between them later. But it would not be safe to try and reason with Lukos now, given the unreceptive mood she was clearly in.

Jeroboam went to collect his meager supplies. He picked up a harness and strapped it over his shoulders and around his waist. Along with a pack, affixed to the harness were two scabbards that rode on Jeroboam's back and formed an X. Into each scabbard, Jeroboam placed a sword, one half the length of the other. Both were backswords having a single cutting edge with the back side of the blade being blunt except for a few inches at the tip where it was double edged. Long enough for use with both hands, a hilt stuck out over each of Jeroboam's shoulders.

They marched for several hours in relative silence then broke for the day. Once the simple chores of preparing their camp were completed, Jeroboam sat on the ground and read aloud from a tattered, leather-bound book he removed from his pack. He continued reading for over an hour. At first, Keenan tried to give Jeroboam his privacy by ignoring him. Lukos also tried to ignore him, being irritated by the uninvited recitation and the droning sound of Jeroboam's voice. But gradually, both of them took a greater interest in what he read and found the passages intriguing.

When he finally stopped and closed the book, Keenan asked, "What were you reading?"

"It is the Holy Book," Jeroboam explained, "the source of all truth. It is the sword of the Spirit. I hope you gained something from it. Given our circumstances, I believe these verses have a particular significance for us."

Jeroboam looked meaningfully at Lukos, then rose to his feet. He seemed to have gained strength from his reading, as if the words were a sustenance that refreshed both body and mind.

"I will leave you now," Jeroboam told them, "and I may be gone for several hours. I require seclusion as I pray for God's direction concerning this cause you have placed before me." He returned the book to his pack, slung it over his shoulder, and strode confidently away into the isolation of the dense forest.

"Oh he's something else," Lukos scoffed. "Keenan, we should leave while he's gone and take this chance to get away from that lunatic."

Keenan took her hand. "Give him a chance. He seems all right to me."

Umbrageous, she pulled from his grasp. "He's not all right. That guy is as dumb as dog dirt or he's as crazy as a loon. Why let him travel with us? Don't we have enough problems as it is?"

When she dropped his hand, Keenan was hurt again by her withdrawal from his affection. "I'm serious about going to Gairloch," he told Lukos, "and I need all the help I can get. As far as I know, I'm all on my own here. I still don't know if you're going to help me. I don't know if I can count on you. You haven't made me any promises. You may disappear again at any time."

"Do you want me to stay?" Her question was tense and timid.

"Of course I do," he assured her. "I told you I love you. But you left me once. I'm worried that at any moment I'll look for you and you'll be gone and that the next time will be the last. Worrying about the possibility of losing you is killing me."

"No," she argued despondently, "going to Gairloch will kill you. If I stay, will you give up this idea of killing Torrin?"

"I can't. I know after what you've been through, it's all but impossible for you to trust anyone. And you have every reason to stay as far away from Gairloch as you can get. I don't want you to get hurt either. So if do you leave, I'll understand. Although the idea of losing you hurts beyond belief, should that happen, even through that pain, one thing would remain. If you go, you can take with you the knowledge that I will always love you."

The wall around her heart began to crack for the first time in her life and Keenan's words touched her where no one else ever had. But even more than in his words, she saw the proof of his love written in his eyes. She was overwhelmed by it. She trembled with a fantastic fear, a frightful hope. This time Lukos did not run away. She was determined to face her terror and meet the threat that Keenan held before her. She wanted her own lips to echo his, but she could not force them to say 'I love you.' It was too soon and the impulse too new for her to understand, too foreign for her to trust.

Instead she hugged him tightly and simply said, "I'll stay."

Keenan's heart lifted. "What about tonight, when the sun sets?"

"I can stay," she whispered. "Last night began the new moon, so I won't change tonight. For two weeks we'll be safe from the wolf."

Lukos and Keenan chose to not yet share sexual intimacy with one another, each feeling that it was too soon in their relationship. But Keenan fell asleep with her body nestled next to his, her head resting on his chest, her arm draped over him, the scent of her hair mere inches from his nose. As he closed his eyes, he felt enwrapped by the warmth of her touch, the comfort of her fragrance, the sound of her breathing; and he thought it to be the nicest sensation he had ever known.

In the morning, as Keenan built a fire and brewed tea for their breakfast, Lukos confronted Jeroboam privately. She hated to ask a favor of anyone. It was contrary to the essence of her self-reliant nature. But Lukos was determined to humble herself in that or any other way if it was necessary to protect Keenan and safeguard the love evolving between them.

"Jeroboam," she began. "Don't go with Keenan to Gairloch."

"That is not for you to decide," Jeroboam responded patiently. "Why are you opposed to our alliance?"

"It's doomed for one thing." The sneer in her voice dug into him like claws. "If you want to get yourself killed, that's your prerogative. But don't encourage Keenan to do the same. He doesn't understand the danger he'll be facing. He doesn't know what he's getting himself into. It's suicide."

"His cause has merit," Jeroboam told her. His tone communicated unremitting confidence. "I believe it is God's will that I should join with Keenan on his mission to Gairloch."

"Stop all that damn god talk," she growled at him through the pressure of her escalating frustration. "That stupid, useless blather is only promoting his heroic fantasies, foolish daydreams that will accomplish nothing but his death. I care about Keenan; I don't want to see him killed because he was naive enough to believe in some imaginary hope."

"God is real and the dangers of the world are nothing compared to the danger present in a life lived contrary to the Lord's will. The death of the spirit is worse than the death of the flesh. I also care about Keenan. And I care about you too. I want you both to live. To do that we must follow the path God has set before us. No matter how perilous the road may seem, I assure you that walking in the will of God is the path to life."

He infuriated her. Exasperated, Lukos wanted to scream. Her body was as tense as an overdrawn bowstring. Aggravated rage cause her fingers to ball themselves into tightly clenched fists and she trembled with the suppressed, aching desire to use them like a cudgel to beat some sense into Jeroboam, to violently instruct him about worldly dangers and the significance of the flesh. She may have attacked if at that moment Keenan had not approached them.

"Good morning Jeroboam," Keenan remarked cheerfully. "The tea is ready. Come have some. You too Lukos."

The three of them sat by the fire, warming away the morning chill and sipping tea as the sun slowly climbed up the trees and into the soft blue backdrop of the sky.

After a few minutes, Keenan could wait no longer and put forth the question that was at the forefront of his mind that morning. "Have you reached a decision, Jeroboam? Will you unite with us against Torrin Murgleys? Do we have your word that we can trust you to help us in our fight against Gairloch?"

"The answer to each of your questions is yes," Jeroboam pronounced solemnly. "As the Lord lives, I swear it."

"Wonderful," exclaimed Keenan. He smiled brightly, reached one arm around Lukos and hugged her briefly, oblivious to the sharp glint of bitterness in her beautiful gray eyes. Then Keenan stretched out his arm and shook hands with Jeroboam as if the gesture were necessary to close the deal and seal their agreement.

"What's that mark on your hand," Keenan queried in reference to the symbol tattooed on Jeroboam's right palm. "If you don't mind my asking."

"I don't mind," Jeroboam answered, holding his palm out for the other's inspection. "It says 'The Lords.' It is permanently printed there as a promise, and to remind me that my hand should be utilized only for good works that honor God, and that my hand is available for Him to grasp, to move, and to apply however He sees fit. All that I am I owe to Him and He is free to direct me where and how He chooses. I must remember to never put my personal needs or desires before the will of God. I belong to God, for Him to employ to subdue His enemies or to heal His children, all in accordance with His will."

"What are you going to do, pray the goblins into submission," Lukos asked, her question snide as well as rhetorical.

Jeroboam appeared unfazed. His sanguine manner expressed grave dignity. "We will need God's help, more than anything, if we are to defeat Gairloch."

"I have more faith in steel and strength," Lukos retorted in a querulous voice. "I don't believe what I can't see."

"When it comes to God, a bird in the bush is worth two in the hand," Jeroboam advised her.

Lukos expressed her skepticism with a contemptuous snort and a roll of her eyes.

"Tell me, Lukos," Jeroboam asked. "When the clouds build and hide the mountain peaks, are the mountains still there?"

"Of course," she replied grudgingly.

"Although worldly thoughts may obscure the truth of God from your mind, He still exists, more solidly and timeless than any mountain."

"But I can see the mountain before and after the clouds come," she argued, her pride and resentment making Lukos unwilling to let the issue drop. "So I still say if I can't see it, it isn't real."

"Close your eyes," Jeroboam urged her, "let me demonstrate my point."

She did not trust him but she was determined to prove that she had no fear of him. So Lukos draped the curtains of her eyelids over her piercing steel gaze.

It took only a second or two and she never heard him move. But somehow

Jeroboam silently bridged the gap between them and stood before her without her even suspecting he had left his seat. Lukos was caught completely off guard as Jeroboam slapped her hard across her cheek, unceremoniously knocking her off the stump where she sat and leaving her sprawled on the dirt.

Keenan gasped. Still slumped on the ground, Lukos touched her red, stinging cheek in consternation. Goggle-eyed with disbelief, she looked up at Jeroboam and heard him say, "Just because you can't see something doesn't mean it doesn't exist. If you forget that, you're going to get hurt."

The blow excited the ferocious sensibilities of her animal nature and her cheeks now flushed with an uncontainable rage. Lukos sprang to her feet, liberating her sword from its scabbard in a flash of steel aimed with deadly intent at Jeroboam's throat.

Deftly, he stepped back from the arcing path of her blade and let it harmlessly slice the air in front of his face. Again she pounced at him, seething with murderous wrath. Jeroboam drew both his swords over his shoulders just in time to counter another lethal assault from Lukos.

"You bastard," Lukos snarled at him, her voice dripping venom. She looked feral, predatory. Her lips curled back like she intended to tear him apart with her teeth. "Nobody hits me. You're dead! Let's see if God can save you now."

She looked rabid, frothing with rage. Seeking to drive home the point of her sword, she lunged at his heart. But Jeroboam turned her blade aside inches from his chest.

Still stunned by the sudden conflict, Keenan prepared to use his own weapon to protect Lukos. But he first shouted for both combatants to stop their fight.

They ignored his pleas and continued to exchange blows.

Keenan stepped into the fray and struck Jeroboam's sword, hoping to dislodge the blade from his hand and begin disarming him. Jeroboam hung on to the hilt but Keenan succeeded in driving down his weapon and sending painful shockwaves from the mighty impact quivering through Jeroboam's arm.

Jeroboam pulled back his arm, cocked his elbow, and shot out with the edge of his fist, cracking the butt of his sword hilt against Keenan's forehead. Dazed, Keenan staggered from the concussion and dropped to his knees. In a sweeping roundhouse kick, Jeroboam planted his boot against Keenan's temple, knocking him unconscious and leaving him prostrate on the ground.

Swinging her sword with berserk fury, Lukos attacked Jeroboam like a gale force wind.

Jeroboam countered, blocked, parried, or avoided each stab or swipe she made at him. But all his moves were defensive. He made no effort to strike back with mortal or maiming violence of his own. Yet Lukos kept fighting with an atavistic hunger for blood, irrationally intent on hacking Jeroboam apart. The fervid savagery of her attack was thwarted by the eloquence of his expert defense.

As he defended himself, Jeroboam tried to reason with Lukos, to also deflect her assault with words. "I did not even draw blood from you and yet you would take my life in revenge. Does that seem just to you? You are a formidable opponent Lukos and I respect your skill if not the manner in which you apply it. I ask that you put down your weapon before someone is needlessly injured."

Unaffected by his appeal, she continued to assail him. As if every move had been choreographed in advance, Jeroboam easily thwarted every attack, his swords an impenetrable blockade that prevented Lukos from cutting him. Gradually, she slowed, becoming weary from the fruitless battle. Sucking air, her breathing grew increasingly ragged and labored. Her pulse roared in her ears, beating at her temples like a war drum. Grudgingly, she was forced to admit to herself that Jeroboam was an exceptionally superior swordsman and her enthusiasm for vengeance began to bleed away with her strength. She was good but he was better, a lot better. Lukos panted with exertion, her arm now straining at the effort of even holding her sword.

She swung at him and Jeroboam turned the blade easily aside, rolling his body to the left as he did. Quickly he side-stepped in toward Lukos, raised his arm, and brought his elbow crashing down like a pile-driver on her wrist. The sword fell from her hand. Jeroboam spun around three hundred and sixty degrees back in the other direction, sweeping his leg against the back of her knee. Lukos collapsed onto her back, frantically scuttling backward on the ground with her feet and reaching out her hand in search of the fallen sword. Her searching fingers found it but before she could get up again, Jeroboam laid the tip of his blade over her throat, stilling her movement.

His head throbbing, Keenan revived and saw Lukos immobilized beneath Jeroboam's sword. However, Keenan was afraid to act. It would require only one quick thrust for Jeroboam to pierce her neck.

"I am not your enemy," Jeroboam cautioned her. "It is your ignorance that threatens you, not me. Open your heart to the truth. Let God receive you and embrace you in His mercy and His righteousness. Trust in the Lord. I will not harm you; I have given you my word. Let us forget this conflict and continue now as friends. You made a mistake, but I believe your honor will prevent another unjust attack."

Jeroboam withdrew the blade from her throat and tossed his swords out of reach, one to the left and one to the right of him. Then he offered her his hand to help lift Lukos up. For a moment Lukos did not move. For a moment she considered her sword and her unarmed opponent. But to everyone's relief she chose to abandon her anger and the violence it provoked. Still scowling but with a new respect for the man she faced, she took Jeroboam's hand and regained her feet.

"Let's stop wasting time and get moving. It will take the three of us forever to get to Gairloch at this rate." It was the best Lukos could do by way of an apology and as an agreement that they should work together.

Alissa's captors hurried to get to Gairloch and pushed her hard to keep up. When she became too exhausted to run anymore, the goblins took turns carrying her in their massive arms. Alissa hated their touch along with the eye-watering, nose burning stink of them. So she tried to postpone being carried for as long as possible. But dragged by the chain binding her wrists, she had been running for hours and her endurance had about exceeded its limit for the day. The iron cuffs around her wrists chafed her skin and hurt bitterly, but it was nothing compared to the raw ache between her legs.

Because of the Orb's magic, Alissa could not control her reactions while it was happening but once it was over she remembered every detail of the rapes with perfect clarity. She had been grotesquely used. The unmentionable acts Alissa had been compelled to perform to satisfy the madness and perversity of Tenchi's lust filled her soul with indescribable anguish. The torments fell upon her like rain, each drop of hurt joining together to drown her in a flood of suffering.

Alissa's outward beauty excited Tenchi's sexual desires and he wantonly used her flesh for the gratification of his bestial lust. Thrilled by the experience of her, Tenchi reveled in Alissa's debasement. Yet no matter how much base pleasure she granted him, something about her kindled his wrath and Tenchi would end up beating Alissa ruthlessly, as if he sought to destroy the very beauty he hungered after. It was the indwelling light of righteousness that seemed to burn within Alissa despite all his efforts to extinguish it that enraged Tenchi. And since he could not seem to beat out that pure light of her internal strength, he beat her body instead.

She ached with revulsion and the agony of her helplessness. Alissa's shame made the cuts and sores sting all the more profoundly and they seemed to fester with a moral infection. She felt crippled, broken in body and soul, but slowly she gathered strength from her hatred, used it to concentrate her energy, to focus her thoughts, and keep going.

Through the day, the truce formed between Lukos and Jeroboam held and after the evening meal there seemed to be real peace in their camp. The mood grew more serene as Jeroboam played a variety of soothing melodies on a small wooden flute. Keenan and Lukos appreciated his talent with the instrument. Jeroboam's talents continued to surprise Lukos. She was intrigued by him and remained impressed by his abilities as a warrior, but she could not yet honestly claim to like the man.

Returning the flute to his pack and removing his Holy Book, Jeroboam prepared to read aloud again. But Lukos interrupted him before he could begin sharing the Word of God with them.

"Tell me something, Jeroboam," Lukos urged, her voice mildly taunting. "If god is all powerful, if he can do anything, can he make a rock so big he can't pick it up?"

"Lukos, don't start," Keenan appealed to her. "That's rude. It's a paradox, there's no answer to a question like that. Don't start another fight."

Ignoring Keenan, Jeroboam's face assumed an expression of bemused tranquility as he replied. "Lukos, it brings me great joy that you seek to understand the nature and ways of God. A desire to know Him is as important as loving Him. If you would like me to help you in your pursuit, ask me anything and I will gladly share all that I know about our God."

Lukos snorted with smug distain, thinking she had at last found a way to defeat him. "Thank you so very much; I'm eternally grateful," she said with vulpine insincerely. "So what's the answer to my question? If God can do anything, can he make a rock so big he can't pick it up?"

"Of course He can," Jeroboam replied, waving his hand dismissively. "In fact, He already has. The rock is sin. Although God didn't create sin, He created the environment for its formation. God created the world and made the people in it capable of sin by giving them free will. God loves us and desperately wants us to willingly turn away from sin. He's created the opportunity for that to happen but also grants us the opportunity to choose not to. He can't make us willingly turn away from sin because then it would be forced and not done through our own free will. Also, God could sin because He is all powerful however He won't sin because He is all holy."

Lukos had not expected his response, but more significantly she was not prepared for how it had affected her. It made her think about her own sin and the possibility that she might somehow be able to eliminate it from her life. She was touched by the possibility that there might be a God and that he might love her despite her sin, despite the corrupt nature of her being. Jeroboam's words seemed to cast a light on feelings she had not known she possessed and seemed to awaken something mysterious within her. Perhaps it was her soul, if such a thing existed. Whatever it was, it yearned for more and cried out for release against the shackles imposed by her mind and body.

As Jeroboam began to read, Lukos listened more intently. Part of her hoped that what Jeroboam read would prove God to be a lie and allow her to forget that there might be anything more in life than an earthly struggle for survival. Another part of her prayed for further revelation of the truth of God. After Jeroboam finished reading, the issue remained unresolved in Lukos' mind and when she laid down to rest, the matter kept her thoughts active for hours before sleep finally granted her troubled mind peace for the night.

"Where's Jeroboam," Lukos asked Keenan the next morning.

"He left early," Keenan answered. "He's down by the river."

"I think I'll go check on him," she said. "I won't be long."

Keenan looked worried but he tried to sound jovial. "Be nice. Don't try to drown him or anything."

Lukos found Jeroboam standing in the river saying prayers of ablution, once again engaged in ritual purification. Despite Jeroboam's nudity and the solemnity of his spiritual communion, Lukos took a seat on the stream bank to openly observe him.

After a while, Jeroboam concluded his prayers and acknowledged Lukos' presence. "Good Morning Lukos," he said amiably. "I see that you thirst for God's cleansing waters, that you have begun to hunger for his Word."

"Not really," she remarked with a shrug, making a show of indifference. "I was just curious about what you're doing. It's good to wash the stink off every so often, but why make such a performance out of a simple bath? I don't understand you."

"It's more than a simple bath. It helps to wash away the stain of sin," explained Jeroboam. "I know I seem strange to you, but it's not me you're really interested in. You have not come here to know more about me; you came to know the true God."

Lukos shook her head. "I don't know. Maybe, but God wouldn't be interested in knowing me. I'm not normal, not a good person." Her words gathered weight as well as momentum as she spoke, pressing on her heart and squeezing a drop of moisture from her eye. "I'm born of evil, a perversion of nature. I can't escape my sin. I can't change. I'm beyond hope."

"No, child, God is your hope," Jeroboam expressed compassionately. "We are all sinners. Your sin is not beyond God's grace and mercy. His love can cover your sin; you need only ask His forgiveness. Repent and accept Him as your Lord."

"My sin is who I am; it's what I am," she insisted. "I'm not worthy."

"It's not a question of worth. It's a matter of God's love and it's a question of your faith. The Lord stands before your heart waiting for an invitation to enter. Fling wide the gates of your heart. Come to me, Lukos. Come to God."

In her life, Lukos had not known kindness, mercy, compassion, or forgiveness, no parents to comfort her, no friends she could trust. Before Keenan, her stoic existence had lacked any experience with love. But now she sensed an indefinable yet extremely compelling presence that seemed very real despite its foreign and invisible nature. It was a presence that seemed to embody all those noble qualities that her life had lacked. She felt that this presence, this God, possessed something wonderful that even Keenan could not offer her. The hand that Jeroboam held out to her appeared to hold the promise of unconditional love and the prospect of redemption. Its inexplicable summons was so powerful, her yearning so deep, she could not resist. Desperately her soul cried out for the possibility of a love without limits, for forgiveness for what she was, for the removal of her guilt, and for acceptance. Knotted doubts gave way within her.

Lukos left the bank and waded into the river. Up to her waist in the water, she stood before Jeroboam and sobbed with expectant urgency, "How can I know God? What do I do?"

Jeroboam placed one hand on Lukos' cheek and raised the other hand in the air. "Open your soul to the Spirit of the Lord and answer honestly the questions I put before you. Do you, Lukos, desire to be baptized and to accept God as your savior?"

"I do."

"Do you place your whole trust in God's grace and love?"

"I do."

"Do you promise to obey His Word and follow Him as your Lord, to love Him with the entirety of your being?"

"I do."

"Will you proclaim your faith by word and example, loving all God's people as you love yourself?"

"I will."

"Do you renounce the forces of evil that rebel against God?"

"I do."

"Will you resist wickedness, promising that when you succumb to sin, you will repent and return to the Lord?"

"I will."

"Will you diligently endeavor for justice and peace among all people?"

"I will."

"We thank you Lord for the water of baptism," Jeroboam intoned reverently. "As your Spirit moved upon the water in the beginning of creation, I ask that you sanctify this water so that Lukos may be cleansed of sin and reborn as a child of God.

"Lukos," Jeroboam continued, "as His emissary, I baptize you in the name of God."

Jeroboam moved his palm to the dome of her head and gently pushed Lukos beneath the water's surface, immersing her completely in the stream.

After a few seconds, she stood back up, dripping wet. A new light shown brightly in her eyes.

"By the purifying water of God's grace and mercy," recited Jeroboam, "the Lord bestows upon His servant Lukos the forgiveness of sin and the promise of new life as an adopted child of God. We thank You for this precious gift and ask that You preserve and sustain her in her faith. God grant her courage to follow You, wisdom to discern Your truth, joy in the wonder of Your works, and above all, love."

Lukos felt sin pour out from her, down through her arms and out through her fingers, into the water and washed away by the current. She felt truly clean for the first time, overcome by a salubrious sense of mystifying purity that seemed to absolve her of her unholy nature and free her from condemnation and shame. She was aware of God's boundless love and the opinions of others no longer weighed upon her heart. Although she cared for him deeply, even Keenan's love was no longer required to justify her worth. Somehow, that change further encouraged her affection for Keenan, liberated her ability to feel a deeper emotion for him.

Her face held a beatific expression of hope as she turned her eyes toward heaven and proclaimed, "My heart is Yours Lord; my life is Yours. You've given so much, what can I do for You, my God?"

Lukos sobbed, her body trembling, her tears mingling with the dripping moisture of the stream. She seemed to pull the words from her body like a thorn as she said, "I'm frightened."

Jeroboam nodded. "God has striped away your guilt, redeemed you of your sins, and recruited you in His service. You have been walking in darkness and have been shown a great light. It will take time for your eyes to adjust so that with each step you can walk in confidence."

Jeroboam put his arm around her back and led Lukos from the stream. On the bank Jeroboam dressed. He allowed Lukos time to consider the changes within her and regain her composure, before taking her back to the campsite.

"Are you ready," Jeroboam asked. After she nodded, he added a word of caution. "You have been saved by His grace but the vestiges of your old sin-nature still reside within you. Try not to let them hinder your spiritual growth and your sanctification, your walk toward righteousness. Don't let old habits impair your desire to do as God wills."

"What should I pray for," Lukos inquired, her voice still tremulous but gaining strength.

"Pray for help in knowing the will of God and for the strength to carry it out. Pray for all good things consistent with his Word."

When they got back, Keenan was concerned for Lukos, troubled by the odd transformation in her demeanor as well as by the baffling change in attitude that had suddenly developed between her and Jeroboam. But his anxieties fled and his joy was exalted when later that morning, Lukos confessed her love for Keenan.

Alissa was bone weary from the day's grueling march. But as she saw Tenchi approach, she knew it was now his turn to push the limits of her endurance just as he had done relentlessly at the end of each day when the mob of monsters paused in its rapid advance on Gairloch. Stripping off his clothes, dark impulses coursed through Tenchi and a sparkle of evil humor glimmered in his cruel eyes.

With the Orb of Empathy, Tenchi could torment Alissa with any ignominious emotion he wanted and incite her to act out any madness or perversity he chose to impose on her.

"Alissa, I have something for you," Tenchi bragged, indicating the eager intensity of his male organ. Through his ragged respirations, a malicious lust echoed in his raucous voice.

Alissa groaned with the deep despair formed by unremitting grief and imprisoned rage. Because of the overwhelming physical pain and the punishing shame she now carried with her constantly, Alissa almost came to want Tenchi to use the Orb as the illusion of its imposed emotions began to seem like a relief from the crushing horror of her reality. Although afterward it magnified her distress, temporarily, the Orb was becoming an artificial surcease from suffering and the soul-destroying memory of Tenchi's abuse.

Nonetheless, she recoiled as Tenchi's tongue licked loathsomely along her neck. Her body heaved with convulsions of extreme revulsion. However, when Tenchi invoked the Orb's magic, Alissa's disgust and defiance dried up like mist in the rising sun leaving a compulsory craving in its place. Tenchi forced her to beg for her own degradation and to express boundless gratitude for the beatings and torture he inflicted. Propelled by the exuberance of his dire need, Tenchi drove himself into her, trying to violate not only her flesh but to reach deep enough inside Alissa to forever defile her spirit.

"How long have you been here," Keenan inquired of Jeroboam. "How long have you been fighting Gairloch?"

"For over a year I've been patrolling the lands around Gairloch's castle, until circumstances brought me further south where we happened to cross paths. During that time I did what I could to disrupt Torrin's power and diminish his forces."

"What's it like?" Keenan continued his questions. "Is there a safe way into the castle? Lukos has been there but I have not, and things may have changed from what she knew. What can we expect?"

"The castle and the land around it are alive with unnatural horrors," Jeroboam observed. "Torrin Murgleys and the White Elves have fashioned unholy abominations that are contrary to God's law, blasphemous variants of the corporeal and spiritual form of man. The goblins, gnomes, and other degenerate beings produced at Gairloch are a mockery of the design God gave creation. For those monsters, if they have a heart at all, it is one untenanted by love, compassion, and decency. The products of Torrin's experiments flout the sanctity of life, its intended pattern and its meaning. Gairloch is the womb of sin. It must be destroyed along with all the iniquitous, unclean creatures it has given birth to."

Unintentionally, Jeroboam's words stirred the ire and anguish of his companions. Lukos felt betrayed by what he said and a tear of resurrected sorrow leaked from her eye, trying to dissolve her faith in redemption.

"Don't judge all of them the same," Keenan snapped angrily. "Don't lump everything that comes out of Gairloch into the same category. Lukos was born in Gairloch and she's a good person, decent and beautiful. It is not her fault, but as a result of what they did to her in Gairloch, between full moon and new moon, at night she takes on the semblance of a wolf. But she's no abomination; you even called her a child of God. She is not a demon simply because she was made by Torrin, and neither am I. You see, although I reject his evil, more than anyone I am born of it. I was raised by another man, a good man; but Torrin is the father who sired me."

The revelation utterly shocked Lukos. However, her shock was quickly consumed by anger. It flared at the implications of Keenan's confession.

Just as she believed in the Lord's salvation, she believed that Keenan had come to accept what and who she was, and that despite her curse of lycanthropy, he honestly considered her to be a person worthy of love. Now she wondered if Keenan's profession of acceptance, his defense of her character, and his justification of her value were only a means by which he might try to convince himself of his own virtue. Again Lukos felt betrayed.

"It was all a lie," Lukos howled at Keenan. "The only reason you don't consider me a monster is because you're worried you might be one too. Is that the reason you want to kill Torrin, to prove you're not like him. You're an idiot. And I'm a bigger fool for thinking you might actually love me for who I am."

Keenan made a placating gesture, his eyes full of concern. "Stop. I do love you. The fact that I'm Torrin's son doesn't determine what I thought about you. It only helped me to understand your problem. I'm not trying to prove anything by going to Gairloch or by loving you. I want to oppose Torrin because it's the right thing to do, because I feel responsible and I think I can do something to help resist his evil. It's true that loving you makes me feel like a better person. But that's because somehow, you bring out the best in me and make me want to be more than I am. I want to be worthy of you. But I'm not using you to prove my worth. I don't have any hidden motive, I just love who you are. And I will, no matter what."

Jeroboam interceded. "Please do not be angry with each other. It is I who am at fault. My sweeping generalization was unfair. I spoke foolishly, judged wrongly, and I sincerely apologize. I ask that you both excuse my insult and Lukos that you would put aside your anger at Keenan."

Lukos refused to answer his conciliatory plea. Anger poured off her like lava from a volcano, incinerating everything in its path.

"Lukos, be kind and compassionate to others," Jeroboam appealed to her again. "Forgive others as God has forgiven you."

She turned on him "Why is everything still so hard? If God has saved me, why I am still hurt by condemnation, why can't there be peace in my life?"

Jeroboam expressed his answer tenderly. "Although you have received the blessing of God's saving grace, trials and hardship may still assault you. Don't rely on your own understanding to make sense of these tribulations but trust in the Lord and rejoice. Remember, it is not the Lord who is to serve you, but you who are to serve the Lord."

Keenan reached out to Lukos, his fingers tentatively enveloping hers. "I do love you. And you said that you love me too. Don't turn away from me now," he pleaded earnestly. "We can fix this. Let's talk it through. Let me explain my feelings."

Her heart softened and she agreed. The two hopeful lovers went off together, hand in hand to talk in private, granting Jeroboam seclusion for his prayers.

After a few hours, Keenan returned to Jeroboam alone. Keenan took a seat beside him. Having finished his prayers, Jeroboam played his flute. The melody was sweet and light but the musician appeared weighed down by bitter meditation.

"I asked Lukos to marry me," Keenan announced. "She has agreed and we would like you to perform the ceremony. Would you be willing to marry us?"

Jeroboam stopped playing and set down his flute. He sighed heavily before answering. "I've been giving the matter of your relationship some thought. This condition of lycanthropy, of turning into a wolf, it's not natural. It is a violation of God's will. But it was imposed on Lukos, she exists, and she has been baptized in the name of the Lord. So what do we do? How shall we deal with her? Should she be killed because she was bred in hell and given an unclean form? No. She is a decent person, and now a child of God. Should she be forced to live with wolves? No, she is not merely an animal. If Lukos were to breed with a real wolf, that would be an abomination. Should she be forced to live in isolation from other people? No, that too would be wrong, against man's humanity, its inbred need for fellowship. So what does that leave us? All people have a naturalism, a beast within them, but we must rise above our animal nature through our relationship with God. It is that relationship which is the true definition of our humanity. So, although I still find your romantic relationship somewhat distasteful or at least problematic, it doesn't appear to be sinful. However, if you were to engage in sex with Lukos while she is in her wolf form, that would suggest you are a deviant, a sinner in love with her animal self."

Keenan recoiled at the idea. "No, I would never do that," Keenan swore.

"Good," said Jeroboam, "then it is her humanity that you are in love with. I will perform the ceremony."

The wedding took place later that day, after Jeroboam had taken time to consult with each of them both individually and together. Time was also spent on ceremonial logistics and decorative preparations for the modest event. Having bathed and adorned themselves as best they could given their remote setting far from the comforts of civilization, Keenan and Lukos joined Jeroboam in a small open glade amid the forest. Four tall branches had been staked in the ground and Keenan's cloak draped over the vertical poles. Two sides of the open enclosure were festooned with garlands of flowers strung between the poles. As Jeroboam played his flute, and in accordance with his instructions, the couple took their positions underneath the cloak. As she was told to do, Lukos circled Keenan seven times before taking her place at Keenan's right. Jeroboam stopped playing and put away his flute.

"We lack many of the required elements of a traditional wedding ceremony," Jeroboam explained. "So we will have to improvise. The cloak over your heads is the wedding canopy, representing that this union comes under the holy covering of God and symbolizes His protection, mercy, and grace."

"Keenan," Jeroboam began, "do you take Lukos to be your wife, promising to love, honor, and cherish her, and forsaking all others to remain true to her as long as you both shall live?"

"I do," Keenan pledged.

Jeroboam turned to the bride. "Lukos, do you take Keenan to be your husband, promising to love, honor, and cherish him, and forsaking all others to remain true to him as long as you both shall live?"

"I do," she answered.

Taking each other's hands, bride and bridegroom faced one another.

"Keenan, please repeat after me," Jeroboam instructed. "I Keenan take thee Lukos to be my wife, promising as a covenant before God to be loving and faithful in wealth and in want, in joy and in sorrow, in sickness and in health as long as you both shall live."

Lukos, please repeat after me," Jeroboam asked. "I Lukos take thee Keenan to be my husband, promising as a covenant before God to be loving and faithful in wealth and in want, in joy and in sorrow, in sickness and in health as long as you both shall live."

Before continuing, Jeroboam smiled with genuine pleasure, infected by the couple's bliss. "Bride and bridegroom, having been consecrated unto one another and your covenant of marriage consecrated under God according to the law of His Holy Word, I hereby pronounce you husband and wife."

Keenan and Lukos sealed their union with a kiss.

"For this last part of the ceremony," Jeroboam stated, "we would normally use a glass. However, we do not have one and Keenan's small pewter cups won't serve here. So we will use this dry stick. It is a symbol of the fragility of life, something we must remember even during the best of times. It is also a symbol of your past. Keenan, please break the stick."

Following the brittle snap of the stick, Jeroboam said. "Forgiveness ends a shattered past. May your lives from here on be prosperous and full of happiness."

That night, Jeroboam left the newlyweds alone, granting them privacy to consummate their nuptials. They made a bed of Keenan's blanket and their clothes. Under the dark cover of the night sky and the dim light of the partial moon, they laid down beside one another, nervously talking in undertones and smiling with delight. At first their kisses were tender and tentative. Slowly, Keenan's hand glided over the concavity of her belly and the undulating ripple of her ribs. With his palm coming to rest cupped around her breast, his thumb rubbed across her stiff, turgid nipple. Lukos pulled him closer. Scraping his lips with her teeth, Lukos' kisses took on greater urgency, overcome by a passionate eagerness. Teasingly she tugged at his lip with her teeth, then moved on to nibble at his earlobe and nip at his neck. Feeding on her firm, luscious bosom, Keenan's tongue left a trail of moisture that glistened in the moonlight on the slope of her breast and across her dark nipple. Feral and insistent, Lukos clutched him, raking her nails across his back as Keenan explored her body and inflamed her erotic appetites.

Moving with a wild animal grace, she pushed Keenan onto his back and climbed on top of him, slipping him inside her. Keenan's fingers squeezed the round impish curve of her buttocks, slid up her sides, caressed her breasts, and ran through her dark, silken hair. Redolent with the incense of womanly passion and mewling with pleasure, Lukos arched her body, grinding her hips against him, flexing and contracting her muscles. Rising and falling with the sound of her breathing, Lukos' slow rocking motions quickened to more frenetic rhythms. Every nerve exited, Keenan's throaty groans and grunts kept time with his thrusts, quickening as he prepared to loose himself with her. Riding the crest of their ardent passion, Lukos panted, "I love you."

Shaken by orgasm and slick with perspiration, they laid enveloped in each other's arms. As they gradually drifted off to sleep, their bodies still entwined, Keenan whispered his promise into her ear. "I love you."

Chapter 6

"Wake up, my friends," whispered Jeroboam, gently shaking Keenan's shoulder. "We have unwelcome company in these woods. So please be quiet lest they discover us."

"What is it? What's wrong," Lukos asked in a hushed voice edged with fear.

"Come with me," instructed Jeroboam, "and I will show you."

Keenan and Lukos dressed hurriedly, pulling on their boots and strapping on their weapons. Wordlessly, Jeroboam led his companions into the deep dark of the night-shrouded forest, wending through trees with silent grace and a grave purpose. After crossing several hundred yards, Jeroboam finally motioned for them stop as they reached the base of a large hill. Beneath the pale light of a partial moon, Jeroboam placed his finger to his lips, warning Keenan and Lukos to proceed with even greater caution. Keeping low to the ground as they crawled up hill, Lukos heard the sound of their threatening company coming from the valley on the other side of the rise. Over the too rapid beat of her racing heart, she detected the eerie, loathsome noise of inhuman voices mumbling and muttering in the dark.

Concealed by the night and screened by thick foliage, the three travelers took cover at the top of the hill overlooking the shallow vale and its dreadful occupants. In the clearing below, they saw a large, military encampment of perhaps eighty soldiers. Loosely organized, their ranks were spread out around three large bonfires. The wind blew through the valley, scattering leaves and stirring up a swarm of sparks above the fires as the flames whirled about in a fitful ecstasy of heat and light. Some of the soldiers were sleeping, others eating or tending to various chores. A few quarreled amongst themselves while others issued coarse laughter in enjoyment of some form of recreation that was hidden from view. However, even at this distance Jeroboam and the others could discern that the soldiers were not human despite a vague resemblance in the size and general shape of the figure's silhouettes.

"Goblins," hissed Keenan. His face twisted with revulsion.

"Yes," Lukos affirmed, "and gnomes too, scaly little vermin. We should get back to our camp, collect our things, and get out of here as quickly as we can."

"That would seem wise" Jeroboam added quietly. "However, in addition to the goblins and gnomes, there is another down there. Look, off to the left, there is a woman chained to that tree. She is human and obviously a prisoner of these monstrous beasts. We must help her."

"There is nothing we can do," Keenan responded hopelessly. "There are too many of them. We could never sneak past them all and rescue her without raising an alarm. We'd be killed or captured ourselves."

"You said you're traveling the road to Gairloch in order to help the world," stated Jeroboam. "How can you so easily ignore the distress of this individual that you pass along the way? If you love your neighbor and want to do good, how can you turn away from the torment of the person you see before you. Would you have us abandon this poor woman to the continued horror of her captivity without attempting to offer her any form of comfort or assistance."

"I don't want to," groaned Keenan, weighed down under the heavy pressure of his guilt. "But what can we do?"

"We can pray," Jeroboam answered with confidence.

"Oh," replied Keenan. "Yes, of course, you should pray for her. But hurry, we are all in great danger here."

Jeroboam stood up and unsheathed the pair of swords from the scabbards strapped across his back. He stabbed the swords into the ground before him and then knelt between the blades, head bowed and hands clasped together. Lukos mimicked Jeroboam's posture and joined him on her knees while Keenan kept a watch out against discovery by their enemies.

"Lord God Almighty," intoned Jeroboam reverently, "Please grant this woman release from her captors. Lay Your comforting hand over this woman, heal her injured body, fortify her spirit, ease her troubled mind, and restore her freedom. Provide her with the peace and protection of knowing You and accepting You as Lord of her life. All this we ask in Your holy name, amen."

Lukos regained her feet and moved to stand beside Keenan. Quiescent, Jeroboam remained on his knees, concentrating his awareness more fully upon the armor of God in which he dressed. Clad in truth, righteousness, faith, salvation, and the Word of God, Jeroboam called again upon the Lord. "Oh mighty God," he quietly continued his orison, "Give me wisdom and strength to know how I should act in this time of trouble. Help me to be a messenger of Your love and peace, a guardian for the weak, an encourager to the dispirited, and a healer of the afflicted. Help me to honor You through acts of love and mercy. As Your humble servant, I ask that you reveal Your will to my heart so that I may carry out Your bidding, whatever it may be. So that I may glorify You, make me an instrument of Your will. I commend my flesh and my soul into Your hands and ask that You allow this evil foe no power over me as I fulfill Your command. Amen."

Invigorated by prayer, Jeroboam rose, straightening to his full height. With one gripped in each hand, he plucked his swords from the ground. Holding the blades before him and without explanation or warning, Jeroboam charged forward. Bold in his faith, zealous in his service, Jeroboam ran down the hill into the waiting valley of death.

"Son of a bitch," cursed Keenan under his breath. "What's he doing?"

Shocked and too late to stop him, Keenan and Lukos rushed forward to follow the mad decent of Jeroboam's suicidal assault. However, they followed him only with their eyes, unwilling to forsake the security of their hiding place.

Confident, knowing God was with him, Jeroboam ran without fear.

As Jeroboam reached the clearing inhabited by the goblin encampment, he shouted "The Lord lives!"

Too surprised to react, two goblins immediately gave up their lives to the flash of Jeroboam's swords. But three others and a gnome nearest to Jeroboam's fallen victims quickly snatched up their weapons and moved in to avenge their comrades. Under the command of the erudite warrior, Jeroboam's swords whirled around him, biting and slashing at his odious adversaries. He fought with quick reflexes and a superb skill deeply ingrained in the fiber of his muscles through years of training and difficult testing.

More monsters hurried toward him. The goblin's cerise eyes reflected bright red in the firelight; their pestiferous bodies trembled with vicious excitement and their porcine ears wiggled with homicidal glee. Stabbing and slashing, the spawn of Torrin closed in around Jeroboam. Yet none of their blows touched him; they could not break through his impenetrable defense.

Lukos and Keenan continued as passive spectators of the hopeless conflict, the outrageously imbalanced skirmish between one small man and a horde of hideous creatures. Both were amazed by the fantastic fighting ability of Jeroboam, surprised that a man of such inner calm could suddenly express himself with such explosive lethal grace. In repose, Jeroboam seemed as meek as a fawn but in battle he exhibited the ferocity of a lion. He fought against impossible odds but with triumphant dignity and a skill so beautiful that it was almost an artistic expression of martial talent. Lukos was again impressed, so much so that she drew her own sword and ran to assist the knight cleric in his desperate cause.

"Lukos, stop. Come back," Keenan screamed after her.

Ignoring her husband's heartfelt plea, Lukos continued her charge into the deadly fray.

Although certain he and his cohorts would all die, Keenan raced after Lukos, unwilling to let his wife face that unfortunate fate alone. But he tripped over a tangle of roots and fell in an inelegant tumble down the hill, rolling several feet before he could right himself and continue his desperate pursuit. His ankle twisted when he fell; now each step Keenan took exploded with a blinding flash of pain. But he kept moving, not allowing the injury to slow his stride. Carrying his bow in one hand, Keenan reached over his shoulder with his other and withdrew an arrow from his quiver. Still running, Keenan fitted the arrow's horn nock over the bowstring, his thumb and forefinger pinched behind the feathered flights glued at the back of the narrow shaft of ash. At the other end of the shaft, the broad-bladed arrowhead pointed the way forward.

Lukos moved in beside Jeroboam, adding her sword to the fight. The pell mell of the small battle erupted with greater shouts of anger and agony. Just as a goblin turned Lukos' sword aside and a gnome reached back his hatchet to strike at her unprotected head, Keenan burst from the trees into the clearing. He saw the mortal threat poised before his beloved bride and his heart howled with terror. Keenan drew back on the bowstring, aimed, and released the deadly dart. His senses heightened, Keenan felt the bowstring slap against the leather bracer protecting his left forearm and heard the arrow hum as it shot through the air.

Borne upon all his hopes and directed with the legendary skill of elvin archers, the arrow hit its mark with fatal precision. The gnome that threatened Lukos was struck in the eye. A third of the arrow buried itself inside his skull, leaving the remainder to protrude from the ruptured socket as a putrid fluid dripped from the crude opening. The gnome fell dead at Lukos' feet.

Firing one arrow after another, Keenan joined Lukos and Jeroboam as the growing circle of enemies closed in around them. Filled with a courage inspired by his confidence in God and energized by the indwelling presence of the Lord, Jeroboam continued to contend with the powers of darkness. He fought with an unquenchable fire, the inextinguishable light of God's spirit. Valiantly, his friends fought with him. Keenan soon exhausted his supply of arrows and was forced to exchange his bow for his sword. The adroit swordplay of the three companions sliced, ripped, and pierced the ugly hides of the goblins and gnomes. But the trio was surrounded, wounded, and still outnumbered by more than fifty. Even the indefatigable Jeroboam began to appreciate the inevitability of their defeat.

Wielding his long-handled scimitars with unfailing passion, Jeroboam raised his voice up to Heaven. "With joy and thanksgiving," he shouted, "I cry out to the Lord, grateful that He has used my hand in righteousness and to ask Him, that if it be His will, to deliver His servants this day from death."

A minute later, they heard the blast of a horn followed by a roar like thunder. Their barbarous ecstasy interrupted, the goblins and gnomes cast uneasy glazes into the night shadows. But they continued to press in upon the three doomed, would-be rescuers who were now in need of rescue themselves. The ram's horn sounded again and the thunder rolled closer. Out of the dark, the phantom voice of a devastating storm took shape as its source entered the light of the bonfires. Into the clearing stampeded thirty cavalry soldiers dispatched from Braemar and led by Rorke, Alissa's abandoned love. Alissa's brother, Nolan, also rode with them.

Hooves pounded the earth, tearing out clods of dirt and sending them flying like hail around the horses and their riders. Following the hail came a rain of steel as the soldiers unleashed their weapons upon the goblins and the gnomes. Panting for air and lathered in sweat from the arduous ride, the horses carried the soldiers into the heart of the camp. As the combatants clashed in a fury of violence, Keenan, Lukos, and Jeroboam cheered the cavalry's arrival, welcoming their unexpected allies, and fighting with a new hope of victory.

Alissa heard the earlier clamor of Jeroboam's fight with the monsters but she had little attention to spare for it. Her enslaved thoughts were preoccupied with the villainous passions of Tenchi. The Seeker was again entertaining himself by sadistically manipulating her emotions and immorally handling her flesh. Enraptured by the soul-devouring pleasure of his sin, Tenchi did not stop in his abuse of Alissa until the soldiers were upon him. Naked and unarmed, the Seeker stood up, turning to run just as a mounted soldier overtook him and planted his sword in the small of Tenchi's back. His spine cracked and his stygian flesh ripped open in a gout of rich, red blood. Tenchi dropped to the ground and the Orb of Empathy rolled from his hand. His broken body twitched with involuntary spasms, wracked by an uncontrollable shaking. Then a final, gentle tremor washed through him as he drew his dying breath. As Tenchi died so did the emotion that he had embedded in Alissa's mind.

Free to feel for herself, Alissa began to quiver with fear. Ignoring the furor of the battle around her, she was frantic to find the Orb of Empathy, the instrument of her unbearable torment. She had seen it fall from Tenchi's hand but now it had slipped from sight and Alissa could not locate where the hateful object had come to rest. Terrified that someone else would find the Orb before she did, Alissa crawled on the ground rummaging through the leaf litter, grass, and dirt for any sign of the small, cursed sphere.

Panic-stricken over the possibility that the Orb might be lost, Alissa began to weep and wail hysterically as she continued her desperate search. Finally, her fingers touched the smooth, cool shell of the Orb. Instantly, she curled her hand around it in a death-grip, pulling it to her chest and covering it protectively with her other arm. Amid the screams and fallen casualties of the bloody confrontation, Alissa scuttled along the ground back toward her clothes and Tenchi's corpse. Never letting go of the Orb, she hastily pulled on her shirt and pants. Curled in a fetal position, she then huddled at the base of a large oak tree, hiding from everyone. Ignoring the storm of battle raging around her, Alissa cried with abandon but the torrent of tears could not wash away her grief over what she had lost. No amount of crying could cleanse the horror of her experience from her mind.

The greater force of the goblins and gnomes was outdone by the vengeful fury of Braemar's soldiers. Together with Jeroboam, Keenan, and Lukos, they vanquished their common enemy and defeated the insufferable band of miscreants born of Gairloch's evil.

"Search the camp," shouted Nolan. The prince dismounted, releasing his horse and walking through the wreckage of the battle. "Leave no stone unturned. Find my sister and bring her to me."

After a time, a young soldier hurried over to Rorke. "Captain," the youth exclaimed, breathing heavily. "We found her. She's alive but not well. You should come right away."

Standing nearby, Nolan overheard the exchange and interposed himself between the two men, grabbing the young soldier by the arm to get his full attention. "Where is she," Nolan demanded. "Take me to her."

Nolan and Rorke followed where they were led, both men immensely relieved that Alissa was alive yet still raw nerved with concern for her well-being. Night began to melt into day as the morning sun again embarked upon its ritual ascent over the eastern horizon. As they approached Alissa, the light of the coming dawn clarified the vision of tragedy that lay before them.

Two soldiers stood guard over the princess with their backs to her and their faces respectfully turned away. However, Alissa seemed unaware of the men and their deferential stance, her blank stare fixed on Tenchi's dead body. Tenchi's nude corpse and the naked horror in Alissa's face made it clear that she had been raped. It was a hard truth for both Nolan and Rorke to accept but not nearly as harsh as the reality that Alissa had to bear.

Alissa stopped crying. In silence, she sat by the tree with her bent legs pulled up to her chest and her head turned so that her right ear rested on her knees. Her arms were tucked in tightly at her sides and she kept her hands rigidly fisted. Alissa's impassive face held a fixed expression, an unchanging look of resignation to an internal torment too powerful to fight, much less overcome. She looked disassociated with reality, locked inside some inner world, a world of agonizing indignity and unforgiving despair.

Disheveled, Alissa's clothes were darkly mottled with sweat and caked with dirt. A shirt, once pure white but now irrevocably stained, hung loosely over her shoulders. Carelessly dressed, her shirt lay partially open. Her dishabille revealed lean ribs with deep scratches scraped along her side. The auburn mane that was normally so lustrous and lovely now hung in matted clumps of greasy, ragged hair adorned with leaves and mud instead of ribbons or a crown. Her sallow skin had lost the pink flush of life; her sunken eyes were articulate with memories of degradation and an outlook of shame. Dark purple and green, a massive bruise the size of a large fist ringed one eye although both were puffy and swollen.

Nolan saw her ruined beauty and knew that it was lost forever. Rorke saw Alissa's ruined spirit and desperately hoped that there might be some way to rebuild it.

"What did they do to you," Nolan croaked in a voice knotted with grief. He choked on broken dreams and lost love although by their selfish and forbidden nature both had been corrupt from their beginning and had no possibility of resulting in anything but destruction. In a complicated weave of honest and immoral affections, Nolan grieved over his sister's pain and the defiled splendor of her innocent body, a body that he had for so long daydreamed of one day intimately romancing.

Nolan fell on his knees beside his sister. He reached out slowly with one hand to brush a lock of soiled hair away from her cheek and clear his view of her damaged face. She flinched and pulled back from his touch, whimpering softly and clenching her fists with greater rigor. Nolan bowed his head and began to cry.

"You men go help the others," Rorke dismissed the soldiers. As Nolan began to babble his sympathies and his own laments to Alissa, Rorke also departed, leaving the royal siblings alone. He desperately wanted to help Alissa but now was not the time. Now he had to leave her with Nolan and give them the privacy entitled of family and royalty. For the moment, such things took precedence over the duty and desire of friendship.

Rorke went to find the strangers they had encountered fighting with the goblins when the soldiers rode into the camp. He was curious about their presence here but grateful for their help. The one man in particular was a remarkable warrior who had made the cavalry's job of defeating the monsters and rescuing the princess much easier. He did not have to go far before locating Keenan and Lukos.

"My name is Rorke," he said, extending his hand in greeting. "I'm a captain in Braemar's cavalry."

"I'm Keenan, this is my wife Lukos, and that is Jeroboam," Keenan said, clasping Rorke's palm and with his free hand pointing to the ground. After the battle, Jeroboam had fallen on his face before God. He lay prostrate on the ground, giving praise to the Lord.

Rorke leaned over to touch Jeroboam's shoulder. "Sir, I'd like to thank you and your friends for your help in defeating these monsters."

Keenan interrupted him. "Don't bother trying to talk to him now. When he's praying, he's deaf to everything but the voice of God."

Rorke straightened back up, returning his attention to Keenan and Lukos. "I am indebted to you all for your assistance. But, tell me, what brought you into this fight?"

"We discovered the camp," explained Lukos, "and saw the woman they had prisoner. Our friend, Jeroboam, was determined to save her."

"Against so many," Rorke asked with evident disbelief.

In answer, Lukos shrugged.

Keenan attempted to clarify Lukos' explanation. "Jeroboam is unusual, not ruled by the common sense that guides the behavior of most men. He doesn't always see things like a mortal threat the way a normal man might."

Rorke regarded the answer with curiosity. But the approach of another soldier prevented further inquiry.

"Captain," the soldier interrupted with solemn formality. "I have accounted for all our casualties."

"How many did we lose," asked Rorke.

"Ten," the soldier informed him succinctly.

"So many," Rorke sighed with true regret. "But they fought bravely and fulfilled the mission given them by their king. Their lives will be remembered with the glory of this victory."

The soldier nodded. "Shall we prepare our dead to take their bodies back to Braemar?"

"No," Rorke told him. "I'm afraid we can't take that luxury. Their families will have to grieve without a funeral. Record their names and bury the bodies here."

"What about the goblins and the gnomes," queried the soldier; his face wrinkled in disgust. "Should we throw their filthy carcasses on the bonfires and burn them?"

Rorke shook his head. "No. Leave them were they fell. We are too conspicuous here as it is already without lighting a brighter fire for our enemies to see. We don't want any more of Gairloch's forces to discover us. As soon as the princess can be moved, we'll collect our belongings and head upwind, put some distance between us and the stink of this battlefield. Then I'll give the men a chance to rest while we decide our next course."

Concluding his prayers, Jeroboam stood up. He brushed off his clothes and turned to address Rorke.

"I have thanked God for sending you to help us," Jeroboam told Rorke. "Now I offer my thanks to you for responding to the Lord's call and coming to our aid."

"You're welcome," Rorke responded. "But it was Braemar's King Donovan who sent me. We've been searching for that young woman over there, to save her from these marauding monsters."

Jeroboam nodded sympathetically. "Yes, that was our intent as well. I am relieved she is alive. I'm certain that the poor dear has been through a horrible ordeal and has suffered greatly. Her wounds will be difficult to heal. But it is very important that you try."

"Yes, it's important. She is important," stated Rorke. He informed them that the woman was Princess Alissa. He related the story of her ill-fated journey to Parhelion and the betrothal arranged with that kingdom's Prince Tynan. "When word came to Braemar's king that Alissa had not reached Parhelion," explained Rorke, "we were sent out to look for her. We found evidence that she had been attacked by goblins and we tracked the trail they left behind them in their march back to Gairloch. That man with her now is Prince Nolan, Alissa's brother. I am truly grateful for your help in rescuing Princess Alissa," continued Rorke. "I invite you to return with us to Braemar. I'm sure King Donovan would like to reward you for the valor and kindness you displayed in helping to save his daughter."

"No, our path lies in a different direction," Jeroboam stated.

For reasons not entirely clear to himself, Rorke was reluctant to part company with the three strangers so soon. "By midday, we will leave here, head north, and make camp for today at least. There is much that will need to be discussed with Prince Nolan and decided before we go home. You are welcome to stay with us for as long as you like. And perhaps we can give you safe passage to your destination before we journey back to Braemar."

"That would be much appreciated," Jeroboam admitted, "but I fear it may not be possible for you to do so. However, we can talk more about that matter later. For if my friends Lukos and Keenan are in agreement with me, we would be pleased to share your camp tonight." Seeing no disagreement from his companions, Jeroboam continued. "I can see there is much that demands your attention at the moment. So we will let you do your work while we go get our things and rejoin you here."

After a few hours, the bonfires were extinguished and the noble dead were laid to rest within the permanent embrace of the good earth. Jeroboam recited a prayer over the deceased and the survivors seemed to draw some comfort from his words. The wounded were treated with bandages and field sutures. The horses were watered and allowed to graze and rest. They had been driven hard and served their masters well. Six horses died in the battle. It grieved the cavalry soldiers to abandon the bodies of their equestrian comrades to the mercy of the forest's predators and scavengers. But there was nothing else that could be done. Time was short, danger still present, and their mission not yet complete. The soldiers still had to return Alissa to her father. Given Alissa's mental and physical state, that responsibility carried with it unique challenges and the promise of grim consequences that Braemar's soldiers were reluctant to initiate.

Leading two horses by the reins, Rorke approached Prince Nolan and his sister. Beside her, Nolan sat on a large exposed tree root with his face buried in his hand. He seemed oblivious to everything and everyone.

"My Prince, we are ready to move at your command," said the cavalry captain.

Nolan lifted his head slowly to stare at Rorke. He nodded as he stood. "Alissa will ride with me on my horse." Turning to her and bending down, Nolan spoke to Alissa in a gentle yet wooden voice. "Come my sister; it is time for us to go."

Nolan reached down to take Alissa's tightly clenched hand. But when he touched her, she screamed, a bloodcurdling sound of darkest agony and deepest rage. Having refused all Nolan's efforts to get her to speak, it was the first sound that Alissa had made since her rescue. The high-pitched wail halted everyone in their tracks. All eyes turned in the direction of her tormented, icy keening and filled with heartbreaking sympathy for the poor, hopelessly wounded girl. Her scream continued as did Nolan's attempt to pull Alissa to her feet. Alissa laid her spine back upon the forest floor and kicked. The heel of her foot connected with Nolan's groin. Eyes widening in shock and pain, Nolan released his hold on Alissa's hand. He dropped to the ground, moaning.

Silent now, Alissa hunched her shoulders and huddled her body into a defensive ball curled around the fist she held clenched in a death-grip. Only Alissa knew that hand held the Orb of Empathy. And she was not about to disclose that knowledge or share the evil treasure.

After a minute or two, Nolan struggled to get up and recapture his dignity. The others waited for him and his instructions. Rorke wished that he were alone with Alissa or at least that Nolan had stayed back at the castle.

"She's lost her mind," Nolan judged. His voice possessed a rough wheeze and a higher tenor than was normal. "If we are going to move her, we will have to bind her hands and tie her in the saddle. She won't like it but it's for her own protection." Nolan pointed at two soldiers and ordered them to bring him a leather cord and help him with the princess.

"No." Jeroboam interjected the one word command in a calm, flat tone as he walked forward to face the prince.

Nolan bristled at having his authority questioned. His anger flared and he filled with an instant hatred for Jeroboam, an intense and irrational loathing.

Disregarding Nolan's hostile reaction to his intercession, Jeroboam regarded the prince with an expression that was stern yet tranquil, relaxed yet resolute. When he spoke again, Jeroboam's voice was firm but issued with genuine tenderness. "Your sister has been touched in a way no person ever should be, handled in an unspeakable manner by a heinous creature. Is it so surprising that she should recoil now at any form of physical contact?"

Nolan backed down from the harsh scrutiny of the ascetic priest and the truth of Jeroboam's poignant criticism. But inside, Nolan's anger grew stronger.

Jeroboam knelt at Alissa's side but at a respectful distance outside her aggrieved comfort zone, making it clear that he would not attempt to lay a hand upon her. Bright against the pallor of her skin, madness blazed in Alissa's red-rimmed eyes, full and furious flames fueled by an inner pain of unbearable intensity. She regarded Jeroboam warily from the corner of her wild eyes.

Jeroboam cleared his throat. "My dear, I know you've been hurt beyond all human ability to endure. But you haven't been conquered by evil, not unless you surrender your control to it on the inside. You are defeated only if you let evil take over your life from within and allow it to direct the expression of your soul. You must instead turn to the guidance and comfort of the World Spirit that resides within you."

Alissa turned her head to more directly meet Jeroboam's level, uncompromising gaze. She struggled to focus on Jeroboam and allow him at least some temporary, tentative access within the withered realm of her fractured reality. She observed that the skin of his face was worn by weather and worked into a tough hide creased with scars and wrinkles, evidence of a long, hard life but proof of his ability to survive adversity. His words transmitted a gentle insistence but it was difficult for her to keep hold of their meaning.

Jeroboam continued his compassionate appeal. "You believe that all hope is lost; but that is not so. God is your hope and He is steadfast and faithful. Hope in the Lord and your strength will be renewed. Let me show you how God can turn the dust of your broken life into holy ground. We could do that here as well as anywhere. But this place is not safe. Your friends have risked much to liberate you from the wretched beings that held you captive. Some gave their lives for your deliverance. They want only to lead you away from the foul carnage of this site and secure a sanctuary in which to provide for your needs in greater safety. But you have my word that no one will again touch you against your will, not while I am here to prevent it. Take this horse that your friend has for you. You may occupy its saddle alone but please travel with us from here to somewhere that is safer for all of us."

Rorke reached out his arm and dangled the horse's reins in front of Alissa. Beyond that simple gesture of encouragement, no one moved for several minutes, each member of the party attempting to give Alissa adequate time to join them on her own. Everyone seemed to hold his breath in hopeful expectation. When Alissa finally stirred, she lifted her head and stretched out one hand over the ground for added stability as she moved to stand. Her legs were shaky and her frail body swayed like a reed in the wind. But not a soul moved forward to hold her up, abiding by Jeroboams dictate that she not be touched and accepting the prudent wisdom of this restriction upon their care of her.

With hesitant, halting steps Alissa stumbled toward the tall, black horse. Keeping the unrelenting grip of her right hand securely clamped around the Orb of Empathy, Alissa opened her left palm and placed it upon the animal's rump as she reached the horse. Using the beast to steady herself, she was still for several moments. Then, as if in defeat, she bowed her head and rested her brow against the saddle.

Sensing Alissa's distress, the horse began to shift nervously, stamping its hooves and tossing its head in uncertain agitation. Holding its muzzle, Rorke stroked the horse's neck and prevented the animal from shying away from its troubled rider. He further quieted the horse by whispering soothing words of reassure to placate the animal's sensitive nerves.

But Alissa remained reluctant to move. Like a statue carved in illustration of a crushed spirit, she stood immobile with her head lowered submissively. She seemed to have forgotten what she was doing or how to do it. Or perhaps the exertion of walking those few steps had drained her of the strength and will required to mount the horse.

"You think that you have lost everything," Jeroboam expressed compassionately, "that there is nothing left to sustain your existence. But believe me when I tell you, better is the little that the righteous have than the prosperity of the wicked. The Lord is faithful and steadfast. He did not forsake you. He has not hid His face from you but has heard your cries, witnessed your affliction, and reached out to you with mercy. But you must accept God's hand and you must open your heart to receive Him. The Lord did not turn His face from you in your suffering but was there as your refuge and salvation. Allow Him now to restore your soul and set you on the path of righteousness."

Alissa lifted her head, revealing a countenance that was lost and haggard. The others watched patiently as she stepped back and sluggishly walked around to the other side of the horse. Once there, Alissa grasped the saddlebow with her left hand and fitted her left foot into the stirrup. Pulling with her left hand and pushing with her left foot, she managed to swing her right leg over the back of the horse and land securely on its sturdy back. Rorke flipped one rein over the horse's neck, then tied the leather straps together so that if Alissa let go of them during the ride, the reins would not drag along the ground but would instead rest on the horse's neck. Wordlessly, Alissa accepted the knotted reins from Rorke and leaned back in the saddle against the cantle.

Nolan then mounted his horse, a pretty animal with a beige coat and a cream-colored mane. Rorke, Jeroboam, Keenan, and Lukos were left standing beside the three remaining horses.

"We are one horse fewer than the number of people we have," said Rorke to his new companions. "One of you is welcome to ride with me."

"Thank you," said Keenan. "But that won't be necessary; Lukos and I can ride together."

Rorke nodded and with that settled, they all saddled up. Lukos sat behind Keenan with her arms wrapped around his waist. It was a pleasant comfort to Keenan to have Lukos so close. Despite their decent behavior, having so many other men around began to make Keenan feel jealous and protective of his wife.

The company moved north at a careful pace. Eventually, when no one was looking, Alissa furtively slipped the Orb into her pant's pocket. She left it there but surreptitiously checked on it with incessant frequency. Every few minutes, she felt for the lump in her pocket to reassure herself that the Orb was still there, safely tucked away. Alissa wanted to make certain it remained within her reach and to tenaciously guard it from all the others, unwilling to ever risk such power falling from her protection into the hand of another. She did not trust anyone with even the knowledge of the Orb's existence. But her obsessive behavior gradually provoked suspicion in those most concerned with Alissa's welfare and they grew interested in the nature of the concealed possession that so preoccupied her attention.

"You said your journey leads you away from Braemar," Rorke said to Jeroboam. "What then is your destination and what course do you take?"

Jeroboam smiled with pleasant humility. "Keenan is the leader of our expedition and he would be better able to answer your question than I."

"Oh," Rorke acknowledge with some surprise. He looked across to Keenan and offered his inquiry to the young man. "Would you mind sharing your plans with me? As I said before, we may be able to offer you some aid."

Omitting the personal details concerning his parentage, Keenan explained his intention to break into castle Gairloch and steal the Maul of Murgleys from Emperor Torrin. Although he mentioned that Lukos had once been a prisoner of that vile castle and escaped, Keenan refrained from disclosing that Lukos had been born in Gairloch. He also kept her lycanthropy secret, unwilling to expose the strange duality of his wife's nature, her regular transformations from girl to wolf set in accordance with the timing of the moon's cycle.

Listening politely as Keenan laid out his impudent scheme to rob the emperor of his deadly prize, Rorke displayed no reaction that might communicate ridicule of the outlandish plot. The cavalry captain had fought in battles against the forces of Gairloch in which he had seen Torrin wield the Maul of Murgleys. He had witnessed first hand the awesome power of that axe and beheld with his own eyes the destruction it was capable of wreaking.

"That is a noble mission," Rorke pronounced. He also thought it was an impossible mission but that it would do little good to point out that fact. "I wish you luck and hope for your success." Although doubting they would prevail, Rorke was sincere in his encouragement. It would be a great victory for Braemar and all the free kingdoms if Torrin could be striped of his magic axe. "What will you do with the Maul of Murgleys when you have it?"

"Destroy it," Keenan stated confidently. "I'll burn the wood to ash and melt the metal into vapor. No one will ever have use of it again."

Rorke respected Keenan's answer and the determination with which the youth delivered it. "You'd be a hero to a lot of people," Rorke commented. "It will be a joyous day when that axe is removed from this world and I would love to see it happen in my lifetime. So many of our people have died from the sting of Torrin's axe or fallen victim to the army he leads behind that cursed blade."

"You and your men should come with us," invited Keenan. "In light of what we're up against, we could use the help. And it may even help the princess if she is given a chance to fight against Torrin's monsters at Gairloch, to strike back at them for what they did to her. After all, nothing heals like revenge."

"No," Jeroboam interjected. "Man's revenge does not heal. True healing comes from the comfort and strength of the World Spirit. And vengeance belongs to God."

Rorke was not sure how he felt about Jeroboam's assertion. In truth, he wanted revenge himself. Killing the goblins and gnomes that had taken Alissa helped ease his anger but it was not enough to extinguish it. However, at the moment Rorke was more concerned with treating Alissa's wounds, both physical and emotional, than he was in punishing those responsible for inflicting them.

"I don't think the princess is ready for battle yet," Rorke observed. "Her father is worried and will want word that she lives as soon as possible. But given Alissa's present state, the decision of what we do next is Prince Nolan's to make."

As the day declined into evening, Rorke gave the order to halt and make camp. Alissa, having been mute all day, now slid silently from her saddle. Almost semi-conscious, she shambled away from her horse, leaving it to fend for itself or for someone else to tend. After tottering uncertainly for a few steps, Alissa stopped as if she suddenly realized that she had nowhere to go. Weakened by her ordeal, bereft of her vitality, Alissa foundered. Her legs gave out and she slumped to the ground where she sat for a moment or two before falling over on her side.

Rorke expected Nolan to go to her but for some reason the prince chose not to. Nolan dismounted, gave his horse to one of the soldiers, and walked off by himself. Rorke wanted to go to Alissa in Nolan's place but he had other obligations to fulfill as cavalry captain, to make sure the soldiers took care of the horses and put the camp in order to protect against attack.

"Jeroboam," Rorke turned to the small weathered man to ask his help. "Would you sit with the princess for a little bit while I take care of other things? I only want you to make sure she doesn't hurt herself or wander off."

"Of course," remarked Jeroboam. "I would be happy to keep Alissa company while you're busy. Take as much time as you require. We will be fine and I will protect her from any harm. As the Lord lives, I swear it."

Rorke accepted the oath and left them. Lukos and Keenan went along to give Rorke and the other soldiers whatever help they could. Taking off his backpack and long-handled swords, Jeroboam sat down beside Alissa and crossed his legs. He noticed the princess remove something from her pocket and cling to it intensely. But the poor girl seemed oblivious to everything else, including her concerned companion. Alissa swam against despair's whirlpool for as long as she could but finally her strength gave way to that ravenous vortex. Deep within a well of soul-sickening memory, Alissa plunged to unprecedented depths of appalling misery. Wearing an expression of aggrieved resignation, Alissa felt herself engulfed by an overwhelming sensation of spiritual ruin.

Jeroboam took his book of holy scripture from his pack. He caressed the leather cover and seemed to meditate upon the closed tome before opening it, as if seeking insight in how best to exercise the Word. Once the book was opened, he flipped through the pages until his fingers found the words of truth he wanted to expose to Alissa. Without preamble or explanation, Jeroboam began to read the passage he had selected for Alissa's ears to hear and hopefully for her tortured heart to embrace.

Nolan stopped when he reached the hedge of trees marking the edge of the clearing in which they were to camp. However, being frustrated and tense, he continued to pace back and forth along a short line at the glade's perimeter. Running his fingers through his handsome hair, Nolan thought about how the dream of his sister's love had been stolen from him. He fumed at the injustice of it, thinking it intolerably unfair that another had taken the pleasure he had for so long coveted and left the instrument of that longed-for joy forever destroyed. There would be no joy now in knowing her, in touching her. It would be like drinking a cup of fine wine aged to perfection after someone else had opened the cork and polluted the bottle with dirt. In Nolan's mind his sister was now ruined and worthless. He could never have the relationship with her that he wanted because he no longer considered Alissa to be the same person he once so fiercely desired. The cauldron of Nolan's selfish heart bubbled with bitterness and boiled with rage. Killing the goblins and gnomes had felt good to him but now where was his anger to turn? Rorke and Jeroboam provided Nolan with a convenient outlet for his animosity. The prince enjoyed the escalading feeling of contempt for the two short men and despised them for their meddlesome interference in his unhappy affairs.

Seeing the priest sitting with his sister and watching as Rorke walked toward him, Nolan's wrath sang to him. It was a harsh, discordant song of indignant, irrational vengeance.

"May I speak with you my lord," Rorke inquired of the young prince.

Nolan glowered at him, looking down his nose. But he consented to the conversation. "Yes Captain; what do you want?"

"I need to know your plans," explained Rorke, "so I can instruct my men and provide for the princess. How soon do you intend to return to Braemar? Your father has been worried and will be eager for a reunion with his daughter."

"You idiot," Nolan berated him without warning or preamble, speaking loudly enough for the other soldiers to overhear their discussion. "We can't take her home like that; it would break the king's heart to see her in that state."

"Yes, my lord. The king will be greatly saddened over the abuse his daughter was forced to endure," Rorke conceded. "But he must know the truth, and I'm certain the princess will improve on the way home."

"She can't improve," Nolan spat acerbically. "She is useless now. It would have been better if the goblins had killed her."

Rorke gapped at him in shock. Staggered by the impact of the pitiless statement, he felt as if Nolan had slapped him. Others paused in their work and stared momentarily at the prince with similar stunned expressions of angry dismay.

"You're upset my lord." Rorke's tone sharpened but remained deferential. "I know you don't mean that."

"Of course I do you stupid fool!" Nolan's rancor and the volume of his ruthless words continued to escalate. "We can't give her to Prince Tynan now. What kind of man would want her for a bride after that elvin freak has used her flesh in every horrendous way imaginable? Now that she's been soiled we can't trade her to Parhelion for their military protection against Gairloch. She is lost and so are we. Maybe if she had died, Parhelion would see her as a martyr and since she was betrothed to their prince maybe Parhelion would feel as if one of their own family had been murdered unjustly. But alive and despoiled, she is incapable of stirring anyone's love or passion. Tynan won't marry her. And Parhelion will give us their sympathies but not their protection."

"You're her brother; how can you say these things," Rorke asked in a clenched growl. "She deserves better from you."

"I say it because it's true," Nolan answered callously. "She'd be better off dead. Perhaps we should put her out of her misery. You're a soldier; you've seen horses put to death on the battlefield for that reason, because they are hopelessly crippled or too severely wounded to survive."

As Nolan spoke, Rorke knotted his fingers into a tight fist and drew back his arm. Rorke intended to reprimand Nolan for his heartless suggestion by knocking out his teeth. Although Nolan rightly had it coming, the assault on a member of the royal family would certainly end Rorke's career and quite probably result in his execution.

But before Rorke could deliver the punch, another soldier grabbed his arm, forestalling his attack and saving him from Nolan's inevitable revenge.

"Captain, I need your help regarding a problem we have with the horses," the soldier said quickly. Still holding firmly to Rorke's arm, the soldier positioned himself between the two men and pulled at Rorke in an effort to lead his captain away from trouble. Rorke stood immovable at first but then he grudgingly allowed himself to be led away.

After reading for a while, Jeroboam closed the Holy Book and rested. Alissa did not speak; so Jeroboam listened to the noise of the camp and the sounds of the forest. He lifted his face and studied the heavens. The day was drawing to a close. As it slowly set, the sun touched the treetops, igniting the sky in a brilliant blaze of vermilion fire and turning the clouds to violet smoke.

"Alissa," said Jeroboam, asking for her attention and speaking to her now as a concerned friend. "Terrible as they are, do not dwell upon your distressing circumstances but focus instead on God. He is calling you. He is the light that can lead you out of the darkness of your despair and provide you surcease from suffering. He delivered you physically; now allow Him to provide for your spiritual deliverance. Accept God as the Lord of your life. Place your anxieties, your afflictions, and your grief at His feet. Let Him carry the burden of your suffering because He cares for you and God works all things for good for those who love Him."

Jeroboam paused, waiting to see if Alissa would respond, hoping that she would. Unfortunately she did not say anything. She wore the mask of a corpse, hollow-eyed, lifeless, disintegrating. Alissa kept her vacant stare fixed forward yet her watery gaze focused on nothing as she contemplated a miserable existence.

"Alissa," he said her name again, "please listen to me. We are often moved toward deliverance by the very thing that would seem to be our destruction. While God would never cause the harm that has been done to you, He is capable of making it work toward good. I know you would do anything to save your people from the threat of Gairloch; perhaps this hardship was part of what needed to be done for their salvation to occur. If that is true, and I think it may be, don't let your suffering be in vain. Don't withdraw from life or curse God for what was done to you; but ask God for the strength to bear it and for the courage to build your soul into an even brighter mirror of His image."

Jeroboam's words penetrated the barrier of her despair but Alissa struggled to make sense of them. Her thoughts stumbled in all directions, colliding with pain and horror at every turn. Her mind tried helplessly to cling to sanity but it continued to slip away, like the shifting of fine sand through her fingers.

Faithfully believing that his words were getting through to her, Jeroboam continued. "Through calamity, the truth of one's soul is revealed. Adversity can often break down the walls we set around our hearts and allow God to enter in more completely. All the pain you endured will be forgotten when at last you receive the reward He has set for you beyond this present life, the glorious joy of being in His presence, of dwelling in His house forever and beholding the beauty of the Lord. All earthly trials pale in comparison to the everlasting joy of God's love and forgiveness, the salvation and redemption by which His children can enjoy the supreme blessing of sharing eternity in His amazing presence."

Jeroboam observed Rorke approaching them from the other side of the camp and he knew his time with Alissa was nearly over.

"You have been called by God to lead your people," Jeroboam told Alissa. "A righteous queen shall sit upon the throne. Trust in God; let Him be your refuge and your fortress as you carry out His will. Your land has been in spiritual famine, starved for the Word of the Lord. You are the one He has chosen to free your people from the oppression of their enemies but also to feed them the sustenance they need most."

A little time passed since his infuriating conversation with the prince. After working with his men and their horses to prepare the camp, Rorke was calmer now. Jeroboam rose to greet him. Rorke clasped Jeroboam's shoulder and shook his hand.

"Thank you for sitting with the princess," stated Rorke. "I can take over for you now."

"No thanks are necessary," answered Jeroboam, "I was happy to do it."

Rorke turned his worried gaze to look on Alissa's blank stare and her battered cheeks where Tenchi's fists had marred the gentle character of Alissa's face. The sight wrung his heart. "How is she," he asked.

"She is quiet," Jeroboam remarked. "But she is strong. Don't give up hope."

"I won't," Rorke swore solemnly. "Where there is life, there is hope." Rorke turned back to Jeroboam. As he continued, Rorke let most of the gravitas drop from his tone and allowed a friendly camaraderie to replace his serious demeanor. "My men have prepared a meal. Nothing fancy, but it will satisfy an empty stomach. Go get yourself something to eat and then get some rest."

"Thank you," Jeroboam told Rorke. Then the priest faced the princess one last time before departing. "Good night Alissa and God be with you."

Rorke held a plate of food out to Alissa and encouraged her to eat. She ignored the food and the man who offered it. Her slack expression revealed no evidence of recognition or interest in either. Rorke set the plate on one side of Alissa and took a seat next to her on the other. With obvious, genuine concern, he asked her questions about what had happened, about her injuries, and about her needs. Lost in her profound dejection, she answered none of his gentle queries. Being patient and kind, Rorke did not badger her for information. Instead, he told Alissa about their search for her, about how worried her father was, and about how he wished they could have found her sooner.

Alissa remained unresponsive. For a while Rorke stopped talking but he did not leave her. He was there to provide Alissa whatever she needed and would allow him to give. Resolute in the commitment of his love and devotion, Rorke waited by her, ready in his company to be whatever comfort or protection she might want.

Gradually, the night wrapped the camp within its dark blanket and almost everyone fell asleep beneath it. A few soldiers were still alert, set as sentries to keep watch against attack. Rorke and Alissa also remained awake. With his face tilted up toward the boundless firmament, looking at the twinkle of the stars and the shine of the crescent moon, Rorke spoke to Alissa in a whisper. His words were strong but not loud enough to disturb the hush of the camp.

Unsure of what to say but feeling that conversation would help draw Alissa out of her silent world of internal anguish, Rorke told her stories of his youth. He related tales of humorous mishaps and touching family events. Alissa's own memories of a happy childhood, like so many other gentle recollections, now seemed forever blotted out by the cruel experiences forced upon her by Tenchi. Rorke hoped to reconnect Alissa with her past and build a bridge over her present misery into a brighter future.

But hope departed Alissa and left the domicile of her heart vacant, free to be inhabited by darker emotions. Predatory, opportunistic sentiments such as anger and hate began to sneak into her heart in an effort to quietly take up residence. Despite Jeroboam's warning, Alissa failed to provide much defense against these destructive trespassers. Faith and love had been so abused that Alissa could no longer find those things she needed to protect herself from the insidious emotional interlopers that now preyed upon the broken home of her heart.

"My father yelled a lot," Rorke recounted. "But he was a good man and I miss him. He died in a battle at Gairloch over seven years ago. Yet, sometimes I still expect to see him, or even think I hear his voice. As a boy, I hunted deer and other game with my father. He always wanted me to go with him even though he knew I hated it. I would have been willing to eat only fruits and vegetables for the rest of my life if he would just leave me out of his hunting trips. But time and again he took me, making me an unhappy witness to the grisly spectacle of death. Many times I had to help dress the kill, standing half naked in my uncle's barn around an eviscerated buck hooked to the rafters. I'd be covered in the deer's blood and bile, bits of fat stuck in my hair, slipping on an ugly soup of organs, urine, and feces that lay pooled upon the floor. It made me sick but he wouldn't let me go until the job was done."

Rorke paused and wiped away a tear. "And he was always making me train with the sword. It started when I was quite young and never stopped. We dueled for practice and he fought hard against me. My dad never took it easy on me and he never let me win. Growing up, bruises always covered me. He even broke my arm once. I told him I hated him and I didn't want to be a soldier. But the training didn't stop. One day, I asked my father why he loved being a soldier so much. His answer shocked me. He said he didn't. He said he hated it and that he would rather pull a plow than be a soldier. He said he wished that the metal of every sword and spear would be turned into some peaceful implement. My father said, 'I don't like fighting, I don't enjoy killing, and I don't love being a soldier. But I love my son and I want him to live.' He knew what was happening in the world. He knew that Braemar would be fighting for its life against Gairloch for years to come and that my future would be unavoidably defined by war. The hunting and the weapons practice were intended to prepare me so I could survive the battles he knew I would some day face, so I could handle the adversities he knew life had in store for me. I guess that's what a father is supposed to do for his children."

It was getting very late. The sentries changed shifts. Rorke was enormously tired but neither he nor Alissa slept.

In the pale light, Rorke looked into the emptiness of Alissa's swollen, watery eyes and whispered to her. "For as long as I live, I'll love you with every fiber of my soul and every beat of my heart. I'll love you until my dying day, no matter how much it hurts."

A glimmer of awareness seemed to creep into Alissa's desolate gaze. "I asked you not to," she croaked weakly. Trying to swallow the lump in her throat, Alissa coughed, choking on the putrid taste of rotting dreams and decomposing dignity.

Rorke was chilled by the tone of her voice but still thrilled to finally hear it. "I know," he answered, "but you might as well ask water to run uphill or the sun to set in the east. I love you, and it is a love eternal, one without condition or end."

Alissa reached out to him and laid her hand lightly over his. The touch was faint, her skin cold and waxy. But it warmed Rorke's desperate heart.

"Tell me what happened," Rorke begged tenderly.

Her eyes lowered humbly, beaten down by shame, Alissa told Rorke about the Orb of Empathy and revealed the full extent of her abuse. Haunted by pain, her voice held a hollow sound, emptied of all hope. As Alissa disclosed the details of her horrific exploitation, each admission of Tenchi's mistreatment seemed to further degrade her honor, break her sense of purpose and security, shatter her peace of mind, and decimate her spirit of gentleness.

Rorke was tormented with sympathy for his beloved but he did not interrupt her. The blunt features of Rorke's world-weary face tightened with anguished compassion. He wept, holding her hand and waiting for her to finish. When she was done, Alissa pulled her hand from his and turned away from Rorke, withdrawing once again from reality.

Rorke tried to call her back by repeating his earlier affirmation. "For as long as I live, I'll love you with every fiber of my soul and every beat of my heart. I'll love you until my dying day, no matter what."

"Don't," Alissa whimpered. "I can't feel your love anymore and I can't return it. I've lost whatever it was within me that was once sensitive to love."

"I don't believe that," Rorke insisted. "It's there within you still, buried under all that pain. We can find it together. Let me use the Orb to help you, to ease your pain and to recapture the love we once shared."

"No," Alissa spat at him in abject horror. "Never!"

Following her vehement declaration of refusal, Alissa snatched the Orb from her pocket, clinging to it desperately and regarding Rorke with a wild, angry fear. She could never trust the Orb to anyone, not even Rorke. Unwilling to ever let go of the Orb and again be subjected to possession by another, Alissa crawled away from Rorke and appeared as if she were poised to run.

Reaching out in a desperate, placating gesture, Rorke begged her not to leave. "Alissa, don't run," Rorke pleaded. "I won't touch you, I swear it on my life. I won't take that thing from you either. I promise I won't make you give me the Orb of Empathy. Just please don't leave me."

The morning began to rise, lifting the sun into the light blue heaven above the trees. The dawn of a new day was greeted by the ululating coo of a morning dove. Slowly, the men of the camp started to stir, throwing off blankets and beginning their required chores. But granting them the privacy each had earned, the men purposefully ignored the discussion they saw taking place between Rorke and Alissa.

"If you won't let me use the Orb to help you heal, then you use it on me instead," Rorke urged her passionately. "Use the Orb on me, so I'll know what you feel, so I can understand what you're going through. That way maybe I can find a way to help you or at least then I won't do or say the wrong thing and make your torment any worse. Show me what your words alone could not, make me feel everything you felt when that creature used you and all that you feel now. Please Alissa. I want to help you but I don't know how."

Something inside Alissa responded to Rorke's plea. Her coiled body relaxed slightly and she crawled back a step closer toward Rorke. "You don't know what you're asking," she warned him.

Rorke answered with confidence, bold in his love for her. "Show me."

Her fingers loosened around the Orb, then unfolded to reveal the small sphere cupped within her dirty palm. Quickly becoming stronger, an unnatural light pulsed and swirled within the Orb.

Drawing on the Orb's magic, Alissa cast out her feelings into Rorke and shared the appalling experience of her torture, let him drink in the terrifying totality of her torment. His mind's eye opened on eidetic images of degradation and pain inflicted by Tenchi. Suddenly the ruinous ordeal Alissa had gone through was happening to him. Alissa inflicted Rorke with all the emotion she felt in being raped and imposed upon his heart the suffering of rape's emotional aftermath. Adopted as his own, all of Alissa's humiliation and hurt were depicted in his expression. His face became a mirror of her misery. She turned the scene of her abuse over and over again in his mind, fully exposing its deep psychological impact and inner consequence. Heated by Alissa's emotional fury, the crucible of Rorke's heart became a vessel filled with concentrated grief, distilled despair, and pure pain.

Reliving it all through her communion with Rorke, Alissa grew even angrier at what she herself had been made to endure. Moistened by tears of rage, Alissa's emerald eyes began to sparkle with malicious intent as she started to enjoy the empowering act of forcing her suffering upon another, making someone else feel the hideous extremity of her own outrageous agony.

Subjected to the excruciating intensity of the emotive trial, Rorke screamed out in pain and despair. Unable to summon the strength to continue his fight against the onslaught of inexhaustible misery, Rorke fell on his face, weeping and wailing in an uncontainable lamentation of extreme wretchedness.

Hearing Rorke scream, Nolan sprang into action. He snatched up his sword and started advancing swiftly toward Rorke and Alissa. However,

Jeroboam quickly moved in front of Nolan, blocking his path and obstructing the prince's hostile intentions.

"Your sister is in no danger," Jeroboam assured him. The warrior monk's words and manner communicated a strong conviction but with a mild delivery. "Your cavalry captain, Rorke, is a gallant gentleman of noble spirit. He would never harm the princess. He is attempting to help her."

"Bullshit," Nolan barked fiercely in reply. "But whatever is going on between them, I'll put an end to it once and for all. Now stand aside you little maggot or I'll cut you down."

Unarmed, Jeroboam opened his palms and held them out in a gesture of peace. The middle-aged man appeared small and insignificant in the shadow of Nolan's wrath and the young prince's tall, well-built frame. But Jeroboam showed no evidence of intimidation. Facing Nolan with a stoic determination and refusing to give way, he answered, "I cannot allow you to interrupt your sister at this critical moment."

Without any further warning, Nolan swung his sword at Jeroboam's midsection, empowering the blow with all his strength and intending lethal recompense for the paladin priest's defiance.

Jeroboam ducked into a low crouch and Nolan's blade sliced the air above his head, narrowly missing him. From that squatting position, Jeroboam shot up, bringing his fist into the underside of Nolan's chin. His teeth met with a loud crack as Nolan's jaw slammed shut and his head pitched violently backward. Staggered by the impact, Nolan fell back a step.

"Sir, I ask you to please put down your sword," Jeroboam beseeched his adversary with unruffled equanimity. "There is no need for us to fight."

Nolan swung again. This time Jeroboam pulled back from the deadly sweep of Nolan's blade, but the tip of the sword caught his flesh and cut a thin red line across Jeroboam's chest.

Ignoring the superficial wound, Jeroboam kept focused on his attacker. "Without cause you seek to kill a man who is not your enemy," he observed critically. "Don't disgrace your royal heritage; put away your sword."

In reply, Nolan thrust forward, now aiming to use the length of steel to impale the priest rather than hack him open. Jeroboam pivoted, shifting the left side of his body backward and out of the path of the plunging sword. Then he cocked his elbow and drove the bone against Nolan's sternum with devastating force. A split second later, Jeroboam's fist sprang up like a trip hammer and broke Nolan's nose.

Bewildered and blood spattered, the prince stumbled back again. Against the scarlet of Nolan's outraged face, a darker stream of red flowed from each nostril.

With their weapons drawn, Keenan and Lukos stepped from the quickly gathering crowd. Ready to defend their friend, they stood between Jeroboam and Nolan.

Looking to the soldiers ringed about him, Nolan issued orders in a congested snarl. "These people have threatened me, a member of the royal family. I demand they be taken into custody and hanged immediately."

No one moved. Disgusted by Nolan's attitude toward their princess, by his treatment of their captain, and his attack upon an unarmed holy man, the soldiers were reluctant to execute his unjust command. Whereas Nolan had only inherited the soldiers' respect, the others had earned it. And within the hearts of the cavalrymen, the authority of the latter warred against the influence of the former.

A soldier named Eric with gray, close-cropped hair and a hooked, beak-like nose withdrew his sword and strode forward. He looked at Nolan as if he faced a guillotine. Then Eric turned to Jeroboam and handed him his sword hilt first. After arming Nolan's opponent, the soldier dropped back a pace in rank with the other men.

"Traitor," Nolan bellowed with furious indignation. Then addressing the other men, he shouted, "Kill him too! Do it now, or I'll make you cowards pay."

Eric snapped to attention and the other soldiers followed his example. They stood rigid and immobile. Deaf to his command, none obeyed the prince.

In a puerile response to the soldiers' disobedience, Nolan sheathed his sword, mounted his pretty horse, and rode away from the camp.

"Where do you suppose he's going," one soldier asked as they all relaxed their positions now that Nolan was gone.

Eric snorted derisively. "I guess he's running back to the king to tell him what bad boys we are because we wouldn't play his way."

"Yeah, and I suppose now he'll have us hanged too once we get home."

"Probably," Eric answered dismissively, "but our days are numbered anyway. At least we'll die with honor, which is more than that royal pain in the ass can say."

Throughout Jeroboam's confrontation with Nolan, Rorke continued to cry helplessly. By using the Orb of Empathy, Alissa had completely confided all her secrets to Rorke. She inundated his mind with her tortured feelings, submerging him under the full depth and intensity of the emotional pressure she felt by all that Tenchi had done in ravaging her body and soul.

Wrapping her gaunt arms around him, Alissa dragged Rorke's head and broad shoulders onto her lap. She rocked him like a baby, crooning to him, "I'm sorry. I'm so sorry, I'm so so sorry." Her once musical voice now badly out of tune, Alissa spoke in a thick, slurred speech. But her tremulous words were gentle and infused with love. And no sweeter sound had Rorke ever heard. Under the power of her words, he gradually grew calmer and his distress passed into something new.

Rorke and Alissa began to shake with internal tremors of a burgeoning hope rejuvenated by the compassion they discovered in the magical unity they shared with one another. The burden of their psychic communion had been hard to bear but it enabled real love to break free from the chambered confines of Alissa's heart, a salubrious emotion with a strong restorative power over both their souls. In the presence of Rorke's sacrifice, love and hope swelled within her heart once more and awoke anew to the possibility of life's beautiful glory. Within her bosom stirred a resurrected belief in a world capable of virtue.

She looked physically wasted and mentally drained. Sheathed in a sallow complexion, the features of her slack face hung limp. Adding to her sorry appearance and testimony to her exhaustion, Alissa's face was marked by livid bruises and dark shadows beneath weary-laden eyes, which the unhealthy pallor of her cheeks made all the more pronounced. The once beautiful tumult of her auburn hair hung in a dull, dirty mat of greasy tangles. But as love poured into her hollow gaze, once more filling her eyes with life and hope, the magnificent aura of her gentle spirit returned and Rorke was struck by her superlative beauty.

Rorke looked at her and Alissa could tell that he knew exactly how she felt. Sharing the profundity of Alissa's despair, the couple had been uniquely joined by the experience, thoroughly bonded by a deep understanding, and forever unified by love. It was an affection invested with a steady resolution to honor the duty owed those we love, to persevere all for the other's sake.

"You're not alone," he said, kissing the back of her fingers. "I am with you. I am here for you and I'll never leave you. I will love you forever, no matter what."

Alissa treated him to a dazzling smile brightened with genuine pleasure and true warmth. Then in a burst of tears, she said, "I love you too."

Chapter 7

Aragon flew to Braemar on the dapple-gray pegasus named Helicon, a winged horse that the wizard had befriended years ago. Although characteristically opposed to serving any man, the magical steed agreed to Aragon's petition for help, acknowledging the deep-rooted bond of respect that existed between the two. But the esteem and familiarity they shared could sway the pegasus to tolerate only a limited imposition upon his autonomy. Once they reached Braemar, Helicon quickly took flight again, returning home and indifferently abandoning Aragon to whatever fate awaited him. Taking flight, the pegasus spread its great, feathered wings; they billowed and flapped like the white sails of a ship caught in a mighty wind upon a midnight sea. Through magic, man and beast telepathically said their goodbyes. Aragon understood the ancient creature of natural magic and bore him no ill will for the conditional loyalty produced by Helicon's intractable spirit and independent disposition.

At midnight, in order to facilitate the wizard's clandestine approach, the sky bound stallion left Aragon a mile outside Braemar's castle. It would not take long for Aragon to walk the rest of the way, but nonetheless he felt the pressure of time running out on him, a prescient sense that this singular opportunity to seize the Maul of Murgleys, Torrin's evil talisman, would be forever lost if he failed to act quickly.

Aragon was experienced with augury. During the course of his life, Aragon occasionally received visions of the past and present as well as glimpses of the future, and he also discovered himself capable of interpreting omens. Often the talent seemed a curse but his most recent experience had proved to be a comfort. The mystical mental picture Aragon had witnessed in his psychic dream revealed that Keenan was still alive and doggedly making his way toward Gairloch. Hope yet remained but only if Aragon hurried.

Having called upon his magic to cloak himself in a mantle of secret power, it was easy for Aragon to reach the castle and pass within its gates unseen. The reality of his flesh that was perceptible to the eye dissolved into a spectral illusion, transforming his physical shell into an amorphous phantom of the night. Like a ghost, an invisible apparition, Aragon moved through the castle streets and corridors, passing undetected as he navigated from room to room, traversed the halls, and scaled stairwells. An elf or another wizard might be able to pierce his illusion and perceive his presence but the mundane humans surrounding him were completely unaware of their uninvited visitor.

Aragon searched for Donovan first in the king's royal bedchamber. But when he failed to find him there, Aragon moved in silence to the throne room, continuing his hunt. It was in that august enclosure that the wizard found his quarry.

Aragon entered through an open door of thick, ironbound mahogany and saw the king sitting at a large table. To the left, General Morgan sat beside his king. Neither man spoke, both stared in quiet contemplation at the documents spread across the tabletop. But their thoughts seemed elsewhere, preoccupied by something other than the parchment scrolls and maps they intended to study. Alone in the massive throne room, the two men looked small, helpless, and lost.

In physical structure, Braemar's castle had the face of a soldier and the heart of an artist. Designed to emphasize a practical outer defense, the stronghold's exterior was austere and unadorned in vain ornamentation with its architectural poetry reserved for the castle's more confidential interior. The greatest expression of that private artistry was perhaps found here, in the king's throne room. The polished oak floor was flooded in a claret-colored stain, the wood drunk in a warm, wet-looking pool of reddish brown. And the glossy shine of the floorboards mirrored an even more intoxicating room.

The morning sun began to whisper at the expansive stained-glass windows making them blush with multi-colored light. Woven together with stone tracery and lead mullions, brilliant panes of rainbow glass formed exotic geometric patters along with dazzling images of heroic figures and natural wonders such as butterflies, peacocks, grapevines, irises, and more. Two rows of columns ran the center of the room and the head of a lion was carved into each side of the square capitals and a luminous globe enclosed within a filigreed brass cage hung suspended by a chain from the beast's chiseled roar. Assisting the light of these lamps were a series of six-foot tall, iron candlesticks of exquisite metalwork placed in strategic positions to promote art as much as vision. A gallery of marble and verdigris bronze statues stood in magnificent glory on flat-top corbels, stone projections attached to the square pillars built into the limestone walls at regularly spaced intervals. The rectangular pillars and interior columns soared vertically to meet elaborate vaults that fanned out across the lofty ceiling in a complex web of ribs and intervening cells. Detailed moldings encrusted the arches and balconies in a rich, decorative profusion of bold emblems and ornate imagery. Gilded pediments of elaborately carved mermaids and water foliage perched atop vivid tapestries emblazoned with valiant battles and scenes of genteel social order. The king and his general sat in upholstered chairs before a stylish, mahogany table of substantial proportion and profligately carved with boasting lions, rosette embellishments, and scrolling designs.

No longer careful to suppress the whispery rustle of his robes, Aragon approached the king and his general. Distracted from their languid meditation, the two men looked up as they heard the soft scrape of Aragon's footsteps and the rhythmic tapping of his staff against the floor. Donovan and Morgan cast uneasy glances all about the room but they could not identify the source that produced the unsettling noise.

Startled, Donovan and Morgan leapt up as Aragon's ghostly specter began to gradually assume visible form, slowly becoming a transparent image like a reflection cast in a window illuminated against the dark backdrop of the night sky. Little by little, Aragon began to materialize, progressively rebuilding his disembodied spirit into an imposing physical form that was fully visible. The two troubled men met Aragon's extraordinary arrival with both anger and alarm.

"Aragon," cried Donovan, regaining control of his gaping jaw, "how dare you enter here?"

"Filthy wizard," General Morgan cursed in indignation, freeing his sword from its sheath and rounding the table in a rush toward Aragon. "Stay where you are and drop your weapons; you're under arrest for trespass and treachery."

With a sharp, resounding crack, Aragon struck the heel of his staff against the floor. At the wizard's command, the irradiant gem clutched perpetually within the silver claw at the staff's apex flared to life in a brilliant green light.

"Hold your step and bind your tongue, Morgan," Aragon demanded coldly.

In the face of the wizard's withering stare and the menace of magic Aragon implied, the general obeyed the command. But, although he stopped dead in his tracks, Morgan squared his shoulders and raised his sword, determined to defend his monarch at any cost.

"I am here to address your king," Aragon said, dismissing the general and turning to face Donovan. "And I ask that your majesty grant me the courtesy to do so before your servant again threatens me with injury and incarceration. I apologize for the rude necessity of my unannounced visit but it is imperative that I speak with you."

Donovan gestured for Morgan to put away his sword and await further orders.

"What do you want," Donovan asked without hesitation. The king regarded Aragon with a censorious countenance, his dark eyes full of disapproval. "You're not as welcome in Braemar as you once were, certainly not enough to easily tolerate such insolent intrusion and at such an offensive time as this."

Beneath the evident disapproval, Donovan's face appeared sick with grief and worn by failure. Plaintively contending with this burden of sorrow, Donovan caressed the black armband that circled his bicep and inadequately symbolized his state of bereavement.

"I see that you are in mourning," Aragon observed. "Why? Who has died?"

"My children," Donovan answered. "At least that is what I'm told in the reports I have received concerning their fate. Court gossip along with more reliable yet equally grim tidings have it that they are both dead, along with any hope of a permanent alliance with Parhelion and any real possibility of military help from that faint-hearted kingdom. And the emptiness in my chest tells me these dire rumors are true, my children and my bloodline have died."

"How did they die," Aragon inquired.

"By the same plague that threatens us all," Donovan complained with bitterness. "They were caught in a net of marauding monsters cast by Gairloch."

Although Aragon felt genuine compassion for the king, he appreciated the selfish truth that this news about the death of the royal offspring might make it easier for him to persuade Donovan to the wizard's cause.

"I am sorry to hear about your children. I offer you the heartfelt truth of my condolences," Aragon thoughtfully intoned with sympathy. "I was particularly fond of your daughter, Alissa. She was a truly remarkable girl. The world is diminished greatly by her passing. And although I hate to impose upon your grief, I need your help."

"In your arrogance, you presume too much," Donovan grumbled, "too much in coming here let alone to come here asking favors. As I recall, I needed your help once and you turned your back on me."

"That is not true," Aragon patiently insisted, ignoring the vitriol in Donovan's accusation. "We are friends and I have helped you when I could."

"It is true," Donovan snapped. "Years ago when my wizard died, back when maybe Braemar still had a chance against Gairloch, I asked you for help and you denied me. And it was *your* brother who killed him. My wizard, Gaelan, was devoured by Torrin's axe. The Maul of Murgleys drank Gaelan's blood and fed his wizard's power to its master, allowing Torrin to consume Gaelan's magic and strengthen his own." Donovan shook his head in disgust at the memory of Torrin's predatory killing; then he nodded brusquely in Aragon's direction. "You better watch out. There're almost no wizards left; but Torrin's hunger for them is undiminished. He'll come hunting you one of these days, to take your life and your power too. But I wager that is precisely what you were afraid of, and it was your fear that kept you from helping us resist Gairloch."

"It was not fear and you know that." Aragon defended himself against Donovan's captious contention. "I was never meant to serve as a court wizard, not to you or any king. And over the years I have given you aid. You cannot deny that I have assisted you in the past and still be a man loyal to the truth."

"Maybe," the king conceded with reluctance. "But it wasn't enough. Keep that in mind when you ask your favor. What is this help you now want me to give you?"

Without pausing, Aragon boldly made his request. "I need you to attack Gairloch."

Donovan shrugged as if Aragon's petition were as trivial as the wizard's simple appeal made it sound. "Fine," the king announced with almost casual indifference in answering Aragon's bold behest. "I'm ready to ride into Gairloch alone. I'm ready to die. A man should not outlive his children. A king should not outlast his kingdom. There is no hope left for Braemar. I should be glad to die so that I will not live to see my people dispossessed, forced to abandon their home, to wander the land like exiles or to beg for sanctuary from our uncaring neighbors, those who ignored our misery as Gairloch ate away our strength over these many years."

With severe displeasure, Aragon responded to Donovan's consent. "I don't want one broken man who is ready to lay down and die. I want a king who will lead the full might of his army in a defiant attack on Gairloch." Aragon did not believe that Braemar could defeat Gairloch, but he hoped such an attack would provide a necessary diversion for Keenan's mission to capture Torrin's axe and offer a potential source of rescue for Keenan's escape from Gairloch.

Donovan waved off Aragon's insult. "My people don't have the heart for war anymore, and I suppose I don't either. I only want to join my family on the other side of death. With my family gone, Braemar is like a jewel that has lost its shine; its gold has grown dim. Soon all its children will lie in ash heaps or labor under the yoke of Gairloch. Torrin will make Braemar his footstool and it will become a place of mourning and lamentation forever. Look around; it has already begun. Like mine, Braemar's heart is desolate, its soul bereft of peace. Its glory is gone and ruin is its future. What would be the point of attacking Gairloch now? We cannot defeat those monsters. I may be ready for the grave, but I can't sacrifice my army for nothing and force all my people to forfeit their lives in vain."

"It would not be in vain," Aragon insisted irritably. "I tell you there is a hope of victory, if you're brave enough to undertake it. Torrin is Gairloch's head. If we can break through the castle's defenses and kill Torrin, the body of his empire will fall. Don't lie down now in your prison of defense and wait for your executioner to call upon you. Fight! Show Torrin that you are a lion, one ready to pounce. Pour out your anguished fury like fire against the forces of Gairloch in this final campaign. Although the other kingdoms have abandoned you, you need not do the same to them. Be the kind of friend and neighbor to Parhelion and Garrone that you would like them to be to you. Defend their future as well as your own by taking the offensive and attacking now. And if Braemar dies, then the world will remember that your kingdom unselfishly gave its life so that others might live. This is the moment that will define your legacy and that of your kingdom. Rise to the occasion. Be the champion of justice that a king should be and compel your kingdom to do the same. Surely the total strength of Braemar is capable of killing one man, of rooting Torrin out and destroying him once and for all, and thereby putting a final end to his tyranny."

"He is not just a man," Donovan spat impatiently. "And you should know that, since that beast is also your brother. Do you really want him dead?"

Aragon answered calmly. "Our kinship ended long ago. Although I had once hoped to save Torrin from himself, I know that is no longer possible and our brotherhood is forever lost."

General Morgan cleared his throat, drawing the others attention to him. "As much as I hate to agree with Aragon," said Morgan, "he's right. Gairloch may be the heart of evil, but Torrin is the heartbeat. He is the malevolent force that gives life to all Gairloch's evil. So let's do it. Let's have our revenge and exact our retribution. Let's throw everything we have at Gairloch in one final battle of legendary consequence. Let's make this last stand to commemorate the honor of your children's memory and to eternize Braemar's noble reputation."

"You really agree with him?" Donovan asked skeptically. "You honestly believe we should do as he proposes, that we should march against Gairloch?"

"I do, your majesty, with all my heart." General Morgan affirmed, his answer resolute. "I believe that it is the best way to end our years of struggle. I know the cost will be high, but to me, it seems the right course for us to take. And I'm confident the people will support it as well. Although they are tired of Gairloch's oppression, our people are not as weary of battle as you may think."

Donovan nodded as he clasped his hand over Morgan's shoulder in a unifying gesture of solidarity and companionship. "I trust your instincts my friend, as I have almost always in matters of war." The two men smiled at one another before Donovan turned to face Aragon once more. "And what will you do, Aragon? Where will you be when we take arms against your brother's stronghold?"

"I will join you," Aragon promised solemnly. "I will be there with you, by your side as you storm the gates of Gairloch. You have my promise. In this battle, your army shall be reinforced by the strength of my magic."

"Then so be it," Donovan bellowed with stern enthusiasm. "I don't know if it will end in triumph or tragedy, but Braemar shall have its day of reckoning."

"Good," Aragon spoke in quiet encouragement. "But how soon will that day come? When can your soldiers and support troops be equipped to move?"

"Immediately," General Morgan bragged honestly. "Our military has been at a heightened state of readiness for quite some time. And the possibility of a mass exodus has been something the general populace was prepared for, although I doubt they anticipated the direction we will be taking. In a day or two, the march to Gairloch can begin and Braemar will be empty except for those too old, weak, or young to be of any help to our army."

"What are you thinking about," Lukos inquired, whispering softly to Keenan through the early morning hush and the mellow, lambent light of the night's fading darkness. Her words were sleepy, infused with a dreamy quality born of the deep contentment she felt at that moment. Cuddling with her husband in the quiet, pre-dawn hours, Lukos lay on her side with her back nestled against Keenan's chest. His arm curled around her bare stomach, Keenan could feel her relaxed respirations and drew comfort from the peace implied by the smooth rhythm of her easy breathing, as well as from the gentle warmth of her skin. They had just made love a little while ago, concealed beneath their blankets and struggling to suppress the noise of their sensual ardor, the passionate enthusiasm of their tender coupling. It was the last night before the full moon, the last they could share together before Lukos would again begin her nocturnal cycle as a wolf, a change that would be repeated each night for the next two weeks.

"I was thinking about Princess Alissa." Keenan answered Lukos' question.

"Oh," grumped the suspicious stripling. "That's a fine thing, to have your thoughts wrapped around another woman while you're holding your wife in your arms. Should I be jealous?"

"Never; you're the only woman for me," Keenan pledged truthfully. "I was only wondering about the pain she has suffered and what it might have done to her, how it will affect the person she will become."

"You pity her," suggested Lukos. Her experience with cruelty acquired during her time in the bowels of evil at Gairloch made Lukos harder to impress when it came to the ruthless offenses people were capable of inflicting upon one another. Still, Lukos felt sorry for Alissa and was disgusted by what the princess had been made to endure.

"I suppose," he replied hesitantly. "I mean, after what she went through, it seems natural to pity her. But it's strange. I think more than pity, I've come to feel an unusual respect for her, almost an admiration. She has weaknesses, human frailty like anyone, but Alissa seems to have summoned the courage to overcome her ordeal and focus on a commitment to something outside herself rather than upon her inner torments. It is a remarkable thing to have been so abused and yet regain such nobility, not pride but a dignity reborn. I don't know exactly what passed between them, but Rorke appears to have restored Alissa's sanity and her sense of purpose."

Lukos nodded. "Yes. And Jeroboam has helped her too. Alissa is attentive when he reads from the Holy Book and she asks him many questions about our God and Jeroboam's faith."

"But," Keenan murmured his doubt, "I also wonder if her recovery can last. Do you see her over there? She's sitting all alone in the deep shadows amid that thick stand of junipers, on her knees with her head hung low. In that mournful pose she still looks so vulnerable, so at risk of surrendering to the inner demons placed inside her by that monster that raped her. What do you suppose she is doing there all by herself?"

"She is praying," asserted Lukos tenderly, "just as I have learned to do. And I think she can continue to resist corruption and despair. I've learned much can be accomplished through love and strength of faith. And they are good people, Rorke and Alissa. Before meeting you and Jeroboam, I didn't believe people of such kindness and decency existed. I'm glad I had the chance to meet them too."

"So am I," Keenan agreed. "But we will have to separate soon and bid them farewell. Rorke says they will be leaving for Braemar today, that Alissa intends to be baptized this morning by Jeroboam just as you were and that they will depart immediately following the ritual."

"I know, and I'm glad for her. Only I'm sorry our time with them has to end so quickly. I was beginning to discover what it might be like to be a normal person with friends and family, to have something more to care about than mere survival. Never having had it before, it's hard not to cling too tightly to such hope and happiness."

Keenan swallowed the lump of guilt lodged in his throat and asked ruefully, "You still don't want me to go to Gairloch, do you?"

"No," she sighed. "I don't want either of us to go there, because if we do, I'll lose you, I'll lose what we have together, a life filled with something so wonderful I never before believed it possible. We'll die at Gairloch, I'm certain of it. But you are my husband, the one I have promised to love and honor. I have accepted your decision; and where you go, so will I."

Keenan hugged Lukos tighter and marveled at how quickly their relationship had evolved, how dramatically their love had deepened, how profoundly they had devoted their lives to one another. He now placed her above all others and trusted implicitly that she valued him in the same manner. As husband and wife, they were friends, confidants, and lovers, partners in everything.

Keenan wanted to please his young wife, very much wanted to make Lukos happy, but he could not rid himself of the need driving him to seize the Maul of Murgleys, destroy Torrin's axe, defeat that lord of demons, and absolve himself of any blame that he might have inherited through his biological association with the evil emperor. Lukos may be right, failure and death may be inevitable if they continue on this impossible quest, but for Keenan, the possibility of abandoning his mission, even for her, remained unthinkable.

"The camp is beginning to stir," Keenan remarked, changing the subject. "The soldiers are waking up. We should get dressed while we still have some privacy."

Birds greeted the day with song as the sun slowly drank up the evanescent night. The darkness dissipated, forced to relinquish its hold over the land by the insistent, inescapable power of the rising sun's bold illumination. Little by little, the silken black sky with its dimming constellations of glimmering diamond stars receded from sight, fading into an emerging field of pale blue that gradually began to engulf the heavens.

Several dozen paces away from the position of relative seclusion held by Lukos and Keenan, Rorke approached Alissa. The cavalry captain advanced slowly, reluctant to disturb her focused meditation but now assured as never before that she would always welcome him.

Alissa's improvement and the deeper bond that now inextricably connected their individual lives pleased Rorke. But he still anguished over the injuries Alissa had suffered. Through the Orb of Empathy, Alissa had caused Rorke to experience all that she had been made to feel. So just as it was impossible for Alissa to free herself of the remembered agony imbedded in her psyche, Rorke also was incapable of expelling those surrogate memories of pain and degradation from his own mind. Still tasting the bitter horror with perfect clarity, Rorke ruminated on the vulgar brutality Tenchi had forced upon Alissa. Rorke bemoaned her fate, one that was now an enduring part of his own.

Rorke could barely tolerate the lingering intensity of his intimate knowledge of Alissa's agony, hidden knowledge that the Orb of Empathy had reveled in full. He now shared that pain as if it were his own, a pain both alleviated and accentuated by their love for one another. Rorke would be forever burdened with the shared sensation of Alissa's unspeakable torment. The images and feelings that Alissa imparted to Rorke through the Orb made him not only a witness to Tenchi's crimes but a twin victim.

From the corner of her eye, Alissa glimpsed Rorke's short, broad form drawing nearer. Concluding her prayers, she straightened to greet him with a warm expression. "Good Morning," she said pleasantly.

"Good Morning." Rorke echoed the salutation but with a troubled frown. "I wish you wouldn't go so far from the protection of the main camp. I worry about you. I worry even when you're standing next to me, much less when you're out of sight. How are you this morning?"

A thin smile pulled at the edge of her lips and Alissa answered, "Better."

Hours before almost anyone else was awake, Alissa had slipped quietly outside the camp's protective perimeter, escaping the potential of its unwanted scrutiny. She informed the sentry of her professed need to defecate and, insisting on her privacy, refused his concerned proposal to accompany the princess and guard her safety while she satisfied the intestinal obligation. Out of sight, Alissa buried the Orb of Empathy and covered the disturbed soil with a random arrangement of leaves and branches. Convinced that it was too great a risk to keep the Orb, she hoped that hiding it would forever prevent its future discovery and abuse. She concealed the magic sphere to keep anyone from ever being able to again possess her mind and body through use of the Orb, and perhaps to keep her from ever doing the same to anyone else, unlikely as that might seem.

"I wish I could do more to help you," Rorke complained, "to restore your well-being entirely and take all your hurts away." The lapidescent features of Rorke's face were carved with the harsh inscription of his deeply mingled love and sorrow.

"You have done all that anyone could," Alissa explained sympathetically. "Your love lifted me out from the bottom of my despair." Her eyes glistened with tenderness as Alissa gently laid her hand over Rorke's cheek. The silken touch of her fingers against his rough skin did much to smooth away the tension engraved upon the surface of Rorke's distressed face. "If there is some means by which my liberation may be fulfilled," she continued, "it will require more than any mortal can supply, even one as committed and generous as you. Jeroboam says that only God can fully resurrect the remains of my soul, and I believe him."

Rorke wondered about the practical truth of God's healing in which Alissa now placed her confidence, but he was moved toward faith by the soft yet compelling intensity of her voice. "And this ritual Jeroboam wants you to complete, it will help?" He asked skeptically.

"The baptism? Yes, I believe it will." Alissa nodded.

"I'm glad." Rorke expressed his support with muted optimism. "And it looks as if it is time, for Jeroboam is coming this way."

A few seconds later, they were joined by the paladin priest.

"Well friends," Jeroboam expressed in greeting, "it is a glorious day, is it not?"

"We shall see," Rorke murmured uncertainly, then continued with greater assertiveness. "Perhaps we can make something good of it if we try. I'll leave you two alone; I know you have important matters to talk about and business to attend to."

"Thank you Rorke," said Alissa. "Please have the camp packed and the men ready to move when I return from the river. We will leave for Braemar immediately after the ritual."

"Yes, my lady." Rorke stood at attention and answered the princess' royal order with the respect and obedience she deserved. Dismissed, Rorke pivoted on the heel of his boot and began to walk away.

But Alissa called Rorke's name, drawing his gaze back to her. Their eyes locked, fixed tightly upon one another, and for a moment all else in the world was excluded from their sight and expelled from their awareness. Each had the other's full attention as Alissa said, "I love you." More than hearing those precious words with his ears, Rorke felt the honesty of them reverberate within the interior of his heart, accepted the weight of their truth, and ascended on the buoyancy of their exquisite joy.

Rorke swallowed the knot in his throat and repeated her simple words of profound affection in a pledge of unmovable commitment. Moisture swelled behind his eyelids but Rorke turned to depart before anyone could witness the first tear fall.

"He is a good man," Jeroboam commented to Alissa, "and a good friend to you."

"The best," she asserted. "Rorke has helped me more than you can ever know. He sacrificed so much of himself just to reach me and to try and rescue me from oblivion. I am extremely grateful to him but I regret that helping me had to hurt him so."

"Yes," Jeroboam agreed. "Rorke gave what was needed no matter what the cost to himself. That is love, the kind of love God can offer you in infinite measure and that we should all imitate in our interaction with one another. Through his example, Rorke has taught you how to truly love. Use what he has taught you. Use it to help your people. And through your acts of love and mercy, bring glory to our Lord."

Alissa failed to respond. Instead she continued to stare ruefully in Rorke's direction and wonder what future their love might enjoy. So much damage had been done and so much remained unresolved that it was difficult to envision what form of expression their feelings would be permitted to experience.

"Are you ready to start your life over again," invited Jeroboam, "by accepting God as your Lord?"

"I guess so," Alissa answered in a quiet murmur.

"No," Jeroboam insisted sternly. "Although I know your life remains in turmoil, you can have no doubt when you make this choice. You must commit to Him without reservation or reluctance. But remember, once you accept Him, you will no longer have to rely upon your own strength to survive life's storms and challenges. The weight of your suffering is too great for you; so lay the burden before God and let him carry it. He is waiting for you to come to Him. Are you prepared to let go of your present woe and embrace God's eternal joy? Are you prepared to acknowledge the sovereignty of God and surrender all to Him?"

Alissa straightened, her shoulders pulling back into a posture of unwavering confidence. "I am ready," she replied, her voice firm and filled with conviction.

Jeroboam led Alissa to the river and performed the ritual by which she became an adopted child of God. In being baptized, Alissa became wholly transformed, a spirit still wounded but no longer dying. She was delivered from a purgatory of hopelessness and set upon a stable path of faith, focused not on the ephemeral condition of her human existence but upon the everlasting joy of experiencing her immortal soul now committed to God. The unalterable truth of God's love reached within the core of her ruined heart and roused from its pain-induced hibernation a compelling sense of hope. Not by magic but by belief, Alissa became a new woman, one forged in righteousness, reshaped by salvation, and cast in the light of God's love. She received this inexpressible gift and, through her trust in the Lord, her spirit was renewed.

Her body glittered with sparkling beads of water as Alissa left the river and stood quietly upon a sloped bank carpeted in a youthful, viridescent growth of grass-like sedges and other plants. There, she closed her eyes and lifted up her serene countenance to sightlessly face a cloudless sky, letting the sun rest warmly on her bare skin. Alissa breathed deeply, filling her lungs with the sweet, wood-scented air. White seed puffs blown from the many cottonwood trees floated all around her like large, fat flakes of bright, winter snow. A soothing breeze played across her cinnamon-colored hair, drying the moisture from the shimmering locks hanging loose about her shoulders. Hearing the rippling of the river as the cool, clear water flowed through its meandering course, Alissa felt it carry away her utter despair.

She felt refreshed, physically and morally cleansed. Although the painful memory of her rape remained, along with the ever-present potential for sin, Alissa was free of its crushing grip around her heart.

"Alissa." Standing at her side, Jeroboam spoke her name. He had dressed, although she still had not. To make certain Alissa was listening, he waited for her to open her eyes and focus on his own before he continued. "Being trained by God's love, your trial can yield the fruit of righteousness. As God has provided you with comfort during your affliction, you can be a comforter to your people during their time of hardship. In you, a flame has gone forth from the house of Braemar to light the way for her people. Believe me when I tell you that a righteous queen shall sit upon the throne, one who will lead her people to God and light their way to salvation. And I have seen that you will also be an instrument of God's will in resisting Gairloch's evil. The Lord has opened his armory and brought you out as a weapon of his wrath. All this has been revealed to me and will surely come to pass."

Jeroboam's premonition foretold a future based on Gnostic insight. Alissa listened but neither responded to nor questioned what he predicted.

Instead, her gaze dropped to the soiled garments worn since her capture by Tenchi then cast off before the baptism and abandoned on the ground. The filthy, tattered shirt and pants lay amid a wild patch of flowers, beneath the burnt-yellow peddles of black-eyed susans and the lavender blooms of spiderwort and chicory. She looked down at her clothes, sullied beyond repair, and decided to leave them there although she had not thought to bring something else to wear. Her heart beating in a tranquil rhythm, the pulse of her life steady and confident, Alissa walked back to the camp robed only in God's grace.

The campsite had been bundled up, the provisions stored and the horses made ready to set forth back to Braemar. In the clearing of the grassy glade, the cavalrymen awaited Alissa, standing rigidly at attention in two parallel rows of ten evenly spaced soldiers that formed a human colonnade bracketing a path that led to Rorke. The cavalry captain held a gift of new clothes for Alissa, although he had not expected her to come back from the river naked. It was an unexpected sight for all but they met the challenge well and received her with dignity. The visual spectacle produced a few audible gasps of surprise but these startled reactions of dismay were quickly suppressed by the marshalling of their honor and military discipline. The poise and bearing of Alissa's person did more to edify the soldiers than the baring of her flesh did to arouse any lustful desire in these worthy men.

A fresh resolve shone brightly in Alissa's emerald eyes and an aura of victory enveloped the physical splendor of her exposed body. Filled with new life, Alissa radiated the brilliant fire of a remarkable new presence, one of power and peace united, of might joined with mercy. She bore the light of a woman possessed of strength without brutality, of passion without capriciousness, of courage without ferocity, of wisdom without arrogance, and compassion without weakness. Alissa no longer appeared battered and stunned by her ordeal but was instead beautiful and inspired. She had been made pristine by her divine renewal. She had prevailed over her earthy pain and become a paragon of indomitable strength and beauty, one as wise as the wicked yet as gentle as a dove.

As Alissa passed through their ranks and down the aisle they created for her, the soldiers dropped to one knee and bowed their heads in reverent respect. Rorke, however, stayed on his feet, his steady gaze fixed on Alissa's face as she fearlessly approached.

"My lady," Rorke greeted her and tipped his head. He was amazed by her, and born of that amazement, an irrepressible smile of amused admiration flickered at his lips. "Per your instruction, we are ready to follow you home to Braemar. But I humbly suggest that it might be prudent, and proper, for you don these clothes before we leave."

Rorke handed Alissa a cavalry uniform taken from one of the dead soldiers who fell when they engaged the goblins and gnomes in battle.

Alissa accepted it, her eyes twinkling with the subdued humor she caught from Rorke. "Am I to be one of your soldiers now, as you once suggested back in Braemar, on the day we said goodbye to each other, when we were alone in the stables."

"No, my lady," Rorke sobered and answered gravely. "You are *my* commander, a warrior princess who I will serve with my life, and with my love. You have my absolute and enduring loyalty in both."

Alissa slipped into the shirt and pants and pulled the sturdy, black leather boots over her feet. Then, like a soldier preparing for battle, she accepted the burden of a chainmail hauberk carried upon her shoulders and worn beneath a green surcoat bearing the heraldic crest of a lion. After fitting a vambrace over each forearm, Alissa buckled a studded leather belt around her waist and felt the comfortable, satisfying weight of a broadsword resting at her hip. She pulled back her long hair and tied it in a ponytail behind her head, then gloved her hands in supple, black leather.

When she finished, the soldiers stood in unison and saluted the princess. With authority, Alissa acknowledged the act of military etiquette, returned the confident gesture, and ordered the men to mount their horses. Seeing her command carried out, Alissa took a seat atop the pitch-black horse that had carried her from the goblin encampment, a strong, spirited steed well trained for war.

From his own saddle, Rorke said goodbye to Keenan, Lukos, and Jeroboam.

"Are you sure you don't want to take two of the horses," Rorke urged the trio. "They're without riders and you're welcome to them. It's a small payment for the help you've given us."

"No," Keenan declined the reward. "I appreciate the offer but to avoid detection and the trouble we'd likely encounter by more openly crossing Gairloch's territories, we will be moving deeper into the forest as we continue on our way to castle Gairloch. The horses would only hamper us in the thick woods. Cutting through Dolmendie Forest will take more time but we'll be safer from the White Elves. So I think it's worth the inconvenience."

"True," said Rorke, "but these woods harbor their own dangers, and they get worse the further in you go. So beware and be careful."

"We will," promised Lukos; she was familiar with many of Dolmendie's perils.

"Then farewell friends," Rorke answered. "I hope we'll meet again, and good luck on your quest, Keenan."

"Thank you," replied Keenan, "and may your journey take you safely home."

Rorke trotted his horse into position beside Alissa. Organized in a tight, defensible formation, Rorke and Alissa led the other soldiers as they began their passage back to Braemar.

Chapter 8

"I can't believe you're alive." For the third time, Donovan repeated this joyous expression of disbelief. During these redundant declarations, the king held his daughter in a prolonged embrace as if to assure himself that Alissa was real and not a figment of his imagination conjured from a strange mental brew of far-fetched hope and dismal heartache.

On the road home, Alissa and her escort encountered the massive army Braemar had mobilized to march against Gairloch. Recognized by the sentries, she and Rorke were quickly brought before the king. Donovan received her in his field quarters, a large tent set within the center of the huge military force. General Morgan and the wizard, Aragon, were with the king and witness to the happy reunion of father and daughter.

Finally, the king released his treasured offspring and stepped back, regaining his composure and a better view of Alissa. Then, much to the cavalry captain's dismay, the king hugged Rorke and slapped the soldier heartily across his broad back.

"Thank you," Donovan told Rorke with great enthusiasm. "Thank you for bringing my daughter back to me. I can't begin to tell you what this means to me, to see her alive and well." His smile wilting with the memory of his grief, Donovan returned his attention to Alissa and explained, "We thought you were dead."

"I'm sorry Father," Alissa expressed with compassion. "The troop escorting me to Parhelion was attacked by a large band of Gairloch's monsters. I alone survived and was taken prisoner by the goblins and their master."

"I feared as much," Donovan groaned. "You poor girl. When I heard you were missing, I dispatched Rorke and his men to find you. But we received reports that they too had been killed. Thank goodness those reports were wrong. Never in my life have I been so happy to have received such bad information. But where is your brother? Nolan also went to search for you."

"Nolan was unhappy with our company. So he chose to leave us." Alissa explained simply.

The news shocked Donovan. "He abandoned you?"

"Yes. And we have not seen him since. I am surprised he did not return home."

"If he has, we have not come upon him." Donovan's voice was heavy with disappointment. "And it would have been hard for him to pass by this crowd without noticing us."

"I would think so," Alissa agreed, as she considered the multitude surrounding her outside the private tent. "What is going on here? It appears as if every citizen of Braemar is camped upon this plain."

"Not all, but nearly so," acknowledged the king.

"Why," Alissa inquired with concern. "Why are you here? Why have you made our people abandon their home?"

"Because I thought it was the only way that remained to defend it," Donovan answered. "Believing that both you and Nolan were dead, we decided to make our last stand against Gairloch. Without a royal heir and seeing little hope for the future, we decided to attack Gairloch rather than wait for death to come to us at Emperor Torrin's pleasure. I must admit I was surprised at how willing our people were to dare challenge the forces of Gairloch upon its own soil, although they must surely understand the slim chances for our success. They all appear eager to fight even though they seem to appreciate the likely prospect of our failure and that the price of failure will be the death of our kingdom. But now that you are alive, maybe there is another hope. Maybe our army should turn back from this undertaking of potential calamity."

"Sire, I do not think that would be wise," General Morgan interjected.

Alissa cut him off before the general could continue his protest. "My life or death alone should not determine if we go to battle. Braemar's best interests should be the motive by which you decide to commit its populace to war and launch an offensive campaign of such unprecedented proportion."

"Of course," conceded Donovan. "But if we go back now, you can still marry Parhelion's Prince Tynan as planned. And with our kingdoms wed, they will finally commit themselves fully to helping defend Braemar."

Alissa shook her head, denying the proposal. "I do not believe that avenue of hope will be open to us any longer. No, you were right to mobilize Braemar for an attack against Gairloch, a final assault that may determine our future once and for all. It is time for us to strike back against evil in the name of justice, and trust that the Lord will be with us, using our efforts to promote His will and advance the good of His children." She spoke with a stoic resolve and an armor of iron conviction around her heart.

"To war," Morgan exclaimed with enthusiasm, giving his support to Alissa's counsel. "And let Gairloch's minions know the thrust of our swords."

Donovan ignored him, his attention remaining focused on Alissa. More than ever before, Donovan saw that there was much more to his daughter's character than the lush beauty of her outward landscape. Beneath that surface lay vast deposits of stoney determination, rich reserves of energy, and an immense aquifer filled with a healing spirit.

"Then war it is," Donovan agreed, choosing to trust his daughter.

"I guess maybe we'll be able to help Keenan in his quest after all," Rorke remarked, more to himself than to anyone else, as he ran his callused hand over the broad rolls of flesh behind his thick, muscular neck.

Aragon was amazed to hear Rorke's masculine voice utter Keenan's name. Fate had taken another unexpected turn. And the wizard now had hope that fate was finally leading them all in the direction he wished to go. Aragon stepped forward and his presence seemed to fill the room as he commanded Rorke's attention. "Who is this Keenan of which you speak and tell me about his quest."

After listening to all that Rorke had to tell, Aragon excused himself and left the tent. He was eager to share this unexpected news with others he knew would be glad to hear it.

Aragon's mother, Marketa, and Quinn, Keenan's father in all but biology, had left the town of Abandon together and gone to Quinn's home in the Tissama Mountains. When they failed to find Keenan there, Quinn explained to his wife, Midori, that he and Keenan had agreed to go to Gairloch with Aragon but they were attacked by goblins. In the attack, Quinn and Aragon had been separated from Keenan and later learned from Marketa that Keenan had continued on to Gairloch without them. After sharing this grim tale with his frightened family, Quinn and Marketa left to continue their search for

Keenan. Reluctantly, Midori stayed behind with the other children. In their pursuit of Keenan, Quinn and Marketa had, like Alissa, run into Braemar's immense army. In talking to the soldiers, they discovered that the wizard Aragon was working with the king to add his magic to Braemar's might. With further inquiries, Quinn and Marketa sought out Aragon. The wizard convinced them that staying with Braemar's army offered the best hope of finding Keenan.

Tonight, Aragon found Quinn and Marketa near one of the many cooking fires, sitting together as they ate their evening meal. Without preamble, he gave them the good news. "Keenan's alive," Aragon announced bluntly.

Startled by the wonderful declaration and its implications of hope, Quinn stood up quickly. The plate of food fell from Quinn's lap to the ground at his feet and was left forgotten in the dirt. "You found him," Quinn exclaimed joyously. "Where is he; take me to him."

"Keenan is not here," Aragon informed them. "But I have received news of him. A troop of Braemar's cavalry returned tonight. They reportedly spent several days with your son."

After having swelled with such great optimism, Quinn seemed to shrink now that he realized Keenan was not as near as he had wished. But Aragon's news was still good. It was the best he had heard in a long time and Quinn clung to it like a lifeline.

"Thank the World Spirit he's all right," Marketa sighed with genuine relief. "Tell us what you've heard. How is the poor boy," asked Marketa.

Aragon laid his long, thin fingers over his mothers shoulder as he answered. "They report that he is well, both healthy and strong." Aragon paused, then looked at Quinn. "In fact, they said that Keenan helped rescue Baermar's Princess Alissa, who had been captured by a band of goblins. The cavalry captain, a man named Rorke, regards Keenan as a hero and a friend."

Quinn ignored the talk of heroism. "Where is Keenan now," Quinn demanded, his voice rough with worry

"When Braemar's soldiers left him," explained Aragon, "Keenan was headed north toward Gairloch. Apparently Keenan still plans to confront Torrin and steal his axe. Although I think such disclosure was unwise, he revealed his intentions to Rorke and asked for help. However, the cavalry captain was not in a position at the time to provide such assistance, having a duty to return the princess to the Braemar's king. But despite Rorke's refusal to accompany him, Keenan is no longer making the journey alone. Rorke told me that a holy man from the north who goes by the name Jeroboam is traveling with Keenan along with Keenan's wife."

"His wife!" Marketa cried out in elation, surprised and delighted by the revelation of Keenan's unexpected marriage. Smiling, she gave Quinn a brief hug.

Disappointment pulled the features of Quinn's warped face into a bitter scowl. "Keenan has no wife. It must be the wrong man. This Rorke must have met some other Keenan."

Aragon's eyebrows lifted in a patronizing expression. "Another Keenan," Aragon scoffed, "also on a mission to Gairloch to acquire the Maul of Murgleys. That would be a rather preposterous coincidence, don't you think? And Rorke was quite accurate in his physical description of your son. Rest assured, it's your Keenan and somehow he's managed to find the time and a reason to take a bride."

"What's she like," asked Marketa, pleased that her grandson had found love in a journey through a land of such grave peril.

"Her name is Lukos. Rorke says she is youthful in her figure and pretty of face but also shrewd with an air of worldly wisdom beyond her age purchased at the price of much personal pain. He described her as a nice girl but also tough and good with a sword."

With an air of mounting frustration, Quinn shook his head. He was concerned about the choice Keenan had made and how this commitment would affect his son's life. He was nervous about the girl's character and how it might influence Keenan's own. Quinn was also disappointed he had not been able to attend the wedding of his eldest son or even meet his daughter-in-law before the couple married. And Quinn was worried that perhaps he had pushed his son into marrying before the boy was truly ready. Keenan couldn't really know this girl. Whatever courtship had taken place, it was too rash and seemed to have come at the worst of times. Still, a merry hope lived inside Quinn's heart born of the wild possibility that Keenan's sudden marriage might offer his son real love and happiness.

"Was she one of Rorke's people," Quinn inquired of Aragon.

"No," answered Aragon. "Along with Jeroboam, she was with Keenan already when Rorke encountered him and Keenan introduced her as his wife."

Astounded, Quinn asked, "And he's taking this girl to Gairloch?"

"So it seems," Aragon replied. "In fact, she claims to have been there before."

In disgust and exasperation, Quinn kicked his discarded plate, sending it rolling on its edge like a wheel across the ground. "Oh this just gets better all the time. Anything that has come out of Gairloch in the past twenty years can't be good."

"Don't judge too quickly," Marketa gently cautioned Quinn. "You haven't even met the girl. Trust Keenan; he's a good boy, a smart boy, and I'm sure he wouldn't befriend, much less marry, someone evil."

Quinn snorted. "I'm not so sure. Look how quickly he got himself mixed up with Aragon."

Aragon ignored the insult. "You may be right Quinn, but at least we know Keenan is alive."

"Yes," Quinn agreed, trying to calm himself. "Where did Rorke last see Keenan and the others? We should waste no time pursuing their trail."

"No," Aragon replied. "Rorke said they planned to arrive at Gairloch by hiking through the heart of Dolmendie Forest. We would have almost no chance of finding them in that thick mass of wood. It is best if we stay with Braemar's army and arrange to intercept Keenan when he leaves the forest to reach Gairloch's castle. Braemar's army will help us find Keenan and it should provide all of us the protection we will need as we draw closer to Gairloch. Our original strategy of quietly slipping into Gairloch and secretly making off with the axe no longer seems possible. But with Braemar's help we can still achieve our goal."

"I don't care about that," grumbled Quinn. "I just want to find my son and take him home."

"Trust me," Aragon assured him, "staying with Braemar's army will give you the best chance of rescuing your son. A search of Dolmendie Forest would be too difficult and would take too much time."

"I suppose you're right," Quinn reluctantly conceded. "But I don't think we'll make it to Gairloch before Keenan does."

"We may," argued Aragon. "The forest has elements that may slow him down and give us a chance to overtake him."

Quinn stared into the flames of the campfire flickering beneath a cooking iron kettle. Brooding upon the dim prospects of his son's survival, Quinn nodded. A grimace clenched his unfortunate face. "Yes, and those 'elements' have just as good a chance of killing Keenan as they do of slowing him down."

With heartfelt compassion and encouragement, Marketa took Quinn's large hand within both her own and squeezed firmly. Surprised by the strength and warmth of the old woman's touch, Quinn listened as she told him, "Don't worry; we'll find Keenan. And take courage in the fact that he is no longer alone."

THE MAUL OF MURGLEYS

Two weeks after having parted company with Rorke and Alissa, Keenan, Lukos, and Jeroboam left the peril of Dolmendie Forest and made their way cautiously toward a far greater danger. They were cut, filthy, and battered from their hazardous trek through the dense woodland, weary from the journey and the challenges they had been forced to battle along the way. Bodies sore and spirits low, their greatest trial was yet to come.

Although more widely spaced now, trees still provided cover for the intrepid trio. But as they inched nearer to castle Gairloch, the land seemed to be giving up its life, as if succumbing to the spread of some invasive disease. The vegetation lost its verdure; the normally green grasses of early summer had here turned brown and brittle. Only a few leaves dotted the twisted branches, clinging stubbornly to an unhealthy source of life, and the scarce fruits and blossoms to be found were colored in unnatural hues.

The sky was broodingly leaden, cold and hard, like the sword hanging sheathed at Keenan's hip. His anxiety growing, Keenan would have felt better with his sword drawn and held in hand in case something hostile should come upon them unexpectedly. But Jeroboam had warned him against it, advising that even with the sun hidden by the clouds, a glint of light reflected off his sword could betray their position and arouse the suspicion of Gairloch's defenders.

Still more than a half mile away, the enormous castle loomed before them, dominating the achromatic vista, shouting with extravagant grandeur and flamboyant color in a land otherwise rendered mute. Here, Gairloch possessed the only voice, while that of the World Spirit, nature, and moral men seemed to have been permanently silenced.

Ahead of them and below the dull, gray weight of the morning sky, dark trees stood naked with skeletal limbs spread open and empty. Their exposed bodies appeared frozen and dead, like inert stands of petrified wood. Around the castle, the trees sometimes moved as they ought not to because there was no wind. Yet the branches swayed and reached out almost as with purpose. Overhead flew a long-necked egret, leaving the lake from which castle Gairloch drew its name and headed toward the purer waters of neighboring Loch Eriboll in search of fish or frogs on which to dine. Even the bird's snow-white feathers appeared drab, its vibrancy veiled by the dawn's heavy ashen drape.

Set against this lackluster landscape whose features had been drained of their natural dye, the castle's immense walls gleamed with smooth stone decorated in bright and boisterous banners sewn to display a blue griffon emblazoned over red background. And atop the castle towers, gilded spires sparkled with golden radiance as if constructed to replace the sun.

Creeping through the tall, discolored grass, Keenan saw the castle and the enormity of his challenge was suddenly made manifest. With new clarity, Keenan finally realized the impossibility of the task he had chosen to undertake. Viewing the apparent impenetrability of Gairloch's walls and imagining the strength of the unholy forces that dwelled within, Keenan was struck by the ridiculousness of his self-appointed mission to steal the Maul of Murgleys and to kill Emperor Torrin with his own axe.

In Gairloch's far-reaching shadow, Keenan felt powerless and insignificant. His confidence wilted and his hope grew cold. Emotionally, Keenan stood at a crossroads of duty and dread, of determination and despair. But with a grim resolve to complete what he had begun, Keenan forced the possibility of failure from his mind and refused to give up, refused to surrender to his fear.

"Stop," whispered Jeroboam, grabbing hold of Keenan's arm and forcing him to crouch closer to the ground. "For now, we should go no further. Today we only came to have a look around and get a sense of what we're up against. Let's try to maintain this distance and circle the perimeter of the castle, looking for possible points of entry or other information we might use to our advantage."

Keenan signaled his agreement then looked at Lukos to be sure that she would follow. Her skin stretched tightly across a face strained by tension, Lukos grimaced with disgust but acknowledged her acceptance of the plan with a brusque nod of her head.

After spying out the castle's formidable exterior and concluding their risky reconnaissance, the three would-be thieves went back to the relative security of the thicker wood to wait out the day's end, discuss their options, and consider strategies for breaking into Gairloch.

Without a word, they sat down amid the strangely gnarled branches and twisted tree trunks, surrounded by a coiled silence in which monsters seemed surely gathered to strike. The gray sky hung over them like a death shroud, covering Keenan in a sense of doom. His spirit lay mired in depression. Nerves strained and bone weary, all three were tense and tired.

Lukos was the first to speak. "Do you see now how hopeless it is? Gairloch is a fortress like no other. No force can break through its defenses and penetrate that cursed stronghold."

"Its strength is nothing compared to God's," answered Jeroboam with quiet assurance. "The castle walls would melt like wax in the presence of the Lord. Take heart and have faith, Lukos, for we will get into the castle not by magic or by might but by the will of the Lord."

"Great," Lukos grumbled, fatigue allowing an opportunity for her old skepticism to reassert itself. "So what has the Lord planned to achieve this miraculous entry?"

"That has yet to be revealed," Jeroboam replied with equanimity. "So let us work together toward its discovery. Keenan, what do you propose we do?"

"Well," he began hesitantly. "Tonight is the new moon; so it will be very dark and Lukos will no longer change into a wolf at nightfall. She'll be free of that transformation now for about another two weeks. We could wait until dark, sneak up to the castle, and climb over the walls."

Lukos growled at the idea but it was Jeroboam who dismissed it. "I don't think that will work. The walls are quite flat and terribly high. Even if we could find a rope, fashion a grappling hook, and locate a spot to serve our purpose along the mighty walls of smooth limestone, the ascent would require a lot of time and the sentries would surely see us. At best, they would arrest us when we reached the top. But they could just as easily use their arrows to shoot us down or simply cut the rope and let us fall to our death."

"I suppose," sighed Keenan. "Then perhaps we can gain access into the castle by the route that Lukos once escaped. We could crawl through the sewers that connect to the Pit, then sneak out of the Pit and into the castle's interior."

"Absolutely not," Lukos almost shouted. "The sewers alone would probably kill us. You don't know what it cost me to escape the Pit. You don't know what it's like. I may have agreed to go with you to Gairloch, which is crazy enough, but I'll never go willingly into the Pit and I'll be damned if I'll let you do it either. Besides, even if you survived the Pit, it would be almost impossible for you to get free and into the castle proper."

"I have to agree with Lukos," Jeroboam remarked calmly. "From what she has told me of the horrors populating that unholy place, we should avoid the Pit as we would death itself."

Lukos was surprised but encouraged by Jeroboam's unusual display of common sense in rejecting Keenan's suicidal schemes. She began to hope they might give up this foolish mission all together and leave this nightmare realm behind so as to begin a new and better life away from Gairloch's evil.

But Keenan persisted. "All right," he conceded irritably then paused in thought before continuing. "Under cover of the night, we could make our way to the gatehouse, quietly kill the guards, and slip inside that way."

Jeroboam pondered the idea and admitted, "That has potential. It is at least the best suggestion yet. But it too is very risky. The plan relies on perfect stealth along with a good working knowledge of the gatehouse's design. We'd also need to know the number and location of the guards we can expect to confront. Sadly, I'm not very confident in this proposal's likelihood of success either."

"All you're doing is shooting down my ideas," Keenan complained. "Instead of criticizing my suggestions, why don't you two help me think of a way to solve the problems and make them work?"

In the face of Keenan's anger, Jeroboam responded with patience. "We're trying Keenan and we do want you to succeed. But we don't want to rush into anything too hastily." Before continuing his dialogue, Jeroboam swatted at an insect that landed on his neck and scratched the bump upon his flesh that the creature's sting had left behind. "The castle's main gate was quite a sight, wasn't it? Did you see that statue they were building about a quarter mile outside the gate? Silly question, how could you not see it? The thing must be over forty feet high. And it is rather ingenious how they have gone about building it. It looks like they piled sand around the statue as it was being constructed to give the massive figure support and allow the artisans to reach the top without cumbersome and dangerous scaffolding. Now that the statue is complete, they are hauling away the sand to unveil their masterpiece. The head and chest have been uncovered and it appears to be a statue of Emperor Torrin. Lukos, I noticed that you seemed to study the imposing sculpture rather intently while we were near it. What did you think about that grand statue of the emperor?"

"I think Torrin is an arrogant ass," she answered.

Lukos' opinion elicited a brief snort of laughter from the paladin priest. "Yes, the statue seems to be a proof of his megalomania," Jeroboam replied. "Emperor Torrin considers himself to be unbound by any law, that he reigns above everyone and everything, that the commandments of God and nature are beneath him. But as I hope you've learned though our studies, pride is a stumbling block, not the cornerstone of strength. Did the statue inspire some idea within you Lukos," Jeroboam asked astutely, as if he knew the answer before uttering the question.

Lukos stared at Jeroboam for a minute, saying nothing. She was reluctant to give him what he wanted. But in the end, she refused to lie, although a month ago such a small sin would have meant nothing to her.

"I counted at least a dozen White Elves," she began. "They bring the slaves out in the morning along with the skilled artisans. The slaves are mostly humans. They are marched up the hill around the sculpture and carry buckets of sand back down to the bottom, dumping the buckets in wagons that carry the sand away."

"So what," asked Keenan. "How does any of this help us?"

"Does it help us Lukos?" Jeroboam inquired intently.

Grudgingly she revealed her solution. "We could go down there tonight, climb the hill, and hide out at the top by the statue. I'm sure they leave the buckets at the work site when the crew quits for the day. They're not worth much and who would steal them? We could each take a bucket with us when we climb the hill. In the morning, when the slaves are brought out to work, we could blend in among them and act as if we are part of the work detail that has been assigned to haul sand. Then, at the end of the day, when the slaves are taken back inside the castle, we simply go with them."

"That's brilliant," Keenan exclaimed quietly, his excitement evident.

"Not really," Lukos protested feebly. "We'll be locked up with the other slaves too. We may be inside but we'll be prisoners. And we'll be unarmed. We can't risk taking our weapons with us because the slaves are probably searched before being taken back into the castle. So we'll have to leave our swords and all our supplies here. Even if we're lucky and we manage to fool the guards, we'll be locked up and powerless to find Torrin and steal the axe."

Keenan crawled over next to his wife, wrapping his arms around her in an affectionate hug and kissing her grime-smeared cheek. "It is brilliant, and so are you," he told her. "I think we can pull it off."

"Yes Lukos, it is a good plan," Jeroboam agreed. "Once we're inside the castle, I'm sure the Lord will provide a means for our escape."

Frustrated by fate as well as by the obstinacy of her companions, Lukos shrugged off Keenan's embrace and stood up, shaking her head with weary disappointment and dull defeat.

"Lukos, did you see any women among the slaves working on the statue," inquired Jeroboam.

"We were too far away to tell."

"But you're worried," Jeroboam asked gravely.

"A little," she said, downplaying the danger. "A few extra workers in the crew at day's end may not seem too strange. The elves will just think they miscounted. But if there are no women among the slaves and I show up, it will raise suspicion. I'll be taken and questioned."

"Then you should stay here," Keenan urged her vehemently.

"Drop it Keenan," she snapped. "I already told you that wherever you go, I go. So don't ask me to stay out of Gairloch unless you're willing to do the same." She spoke in anger but with love.

Keenan stared at Lukos, amazed again by his wife and the devotion she displayed for him despite her fears. She had become his faithful ally in the extremes of good and bad fortune, as well as in all that may lay between fortune's far boundaries.

"I can alter my clothes," she continued, "bind my chest with strips of cloth, and cut my hair. If I'm not inspected too closely, I'll pass for male. Besides, plastered in all this dirt, we probably all look the same anyway." Lukos shrugged, putting on a brave face. But as she walked a few yards away, Keenan could tell that she was frightened as well as angry about the task the three of them were preparing to undertake.

Keenan moved to follow her. But Jeroboam asked permission to speak with her first. Keenan nodded his consent, unsure how else to help his wife.

Lukos met Jeroboam with aggravation and questions. "I don't understand," she moaned in desperation. "I've prayed for God to take this trouble from me, but we are headed straight into Gairloch anyway. Why would God give me the hope of everything I ever wanted only to have me give it up? Why did God bless me with knowing Him and finding Keenan only to return me to Gairloch and have it all taken away again?"

"If you want what is best for your life," Jeroboam asserted with somber compassion, "wait for the Lord to work it out His way. Have courage and wait for the Lord, trusting in His wisdom, secure in His steadfast love. You must completely submit your life to God before seeking His blessing, and before choosing to resist evil, so that you may do so under His authority."

Unflinching, Lukos stared the knight cleric in the eye. "If I do, if I surrender to Him fully and I pray, then will my wishes be fulfilled?"

With gentleness in his own, Jeroboam met her demanding gaze and behind it glimpsed a soul in turmoil. "Prayer may not give you what you want. But it will mean that you are never alone when you face your troubles, and it will give you the strength you need to pass through the storms of life be they inconvenient or calamitous."

Chapter 9

The plan Lukos devised proved successful. She, Keenan, and Jeroboam blended with the other slaves toiling to uncover Torrin's statue. Although utterly fearful of discovery, the imposters' unannounced enlistment in the work party went unnoticed by the White Elves assigned to oversee the laborers. If the slaves took notice of the newcomers, they kept the information to themselves.

Nearly a week had past since the three friends were voluntarily enslaved with the other prisoners and no reliable opportunity for escape had yet presented itself. During the day, they shared in the work of their fellow slaves and at night joined them in their cages. The White Elves thought of these slaves as disposable livestock, unskilled laborers that could be worked until their bodies gave out and then discarded. So the slaves were poorly fed, ill treated, and barely kept alive with any care at all. They housed these second-rate commodities in slave quarters that reflected their inferior worth and throwaway importance.

The six stalls were designed as thick-walled, brick enclosures ten feet wide and thirty feet long with a forward barrier made of iron bars and a metal gate. A three-foot wide metal grille ran the length of each room and a fetid sewer flowed beneath the grating, providing a convenient place to dump the slaves' refuse, which at times might include the very bodies of their deceased companions. Flies buzzed around the room, dancing delightedly in air fragrant with the putrid odor of death and decay. A faint, disquieting melody of flowing water played upon the edges of the sewer's stone conduit, swirling thickly over and around the varied debris within the deep channel. The sewers were filled with a languid stream of rot and ruin that drained the castle and bled into the Pit, making this prison, both figuratively and literally, merely one level removed from the Pit, a place where law and morals have no meaning. Carrying from the Pit an effluent increased in volume and vice, the overloaded sewers open into the river, discharging horrors and waste of every kind, excrement, corpses, garbage, even rejected forms of life. The drain was an unsettling link to the Pit and the doom it represented. And from that sewer beneath the grated floor of the slave quarters, sounds often emanated that invited the mind to entertain thoughts of terror and death.

The cell rooms of the slave quarters were crowded, with fifteen prisoners to a stall. They contained a hodgepodge of people, old and young, men and women, some very sick and others relatively healthy. But all shared a hopeless quality. Lulled by depression into an apathetic stupor, few had the energy to take an interest in anyone else. Theirs was an existence focused almost exclusively on daily survival and even that seemed to receive only lethargic attention or concern. They were a people with no hope or comfort to ease the sorrow of their unfortunate fate, one of unending servitude under the whip of merciless masters. Eaten away by the corrosive poison of life inside Gairloch's immoral den, nearly all the slaves were lean-ribbed with only rags to cover the withered flesh of their tormented bodies. Even those still strong were marked by a forlorn disposition bred of their bleak existence.

To help prevent the slaves from building friendships and through such alliances become a potential threat of riot or rebellion, individuals were picked at random by their jailors to share a selected cell at the end of each workday. Chance seldom brought Keenan, Lukos, and Jeroboam all together in the same room at day's end, thereby complicating any effort of escape.

Last night, Jeroboam and Lukos, along with thirteen others, were selected to be roommates. However, Keenan was forced to accept the company of others. For some reason unknown to them, the slaves were being kept inside today rather than taken out to work at uncovering the sand from around the enormous statue of Gairloch's celebrated emperor.

With brooding apprehension, Lukos considered various possibilities for securing their freedom. But her body and brain were dazed with fatigue produced from lack of food and restful slumber combined with days of backbreaking labor.

Jeroboam spent his time, as he often did, speaking with his fellow sufferers. At the moment, he consoled an old man with one blind eye that was fixed and useless. Puss filled sores dotted the man's arms and legs. And from the elderly gentleman's drooping lips, a stream of saliva drizzled past broken, yellow teeth and down a grimy chin. But he spoke coherently and Jeroboam listened. As with this man, Jeroboam had given his sympathetic ear to several others sharing their confinement, being also willing to talk and pray as needed. Even after only a few days, some found relief in Jeroboam's company and the paladin priest also tried to provide illumination for the dark emptiness of lives lived unlit by faith. At times, Jeroboam was even able to coax his jailors into conversation. From these varied exchanges, Jeroboam learned much about the castle he had infiltrated. For instance, he learned about the great hall, once called the wizard Prelature, where the emperor was said to often spend his time in mysterious entertainment or endeavors, perhaps plotting victories for his people or engineering tools for their success.

Torrin and the White Elves dwelled in sumptuous magnificence, a glaring contrast to the wretched squalor of the slave quarters and the filthy austerity to be found in the military barracks set aside for goblins and gnomes. Gairloch was a divided castle, with one division raised in glittering opulence and the other built of gloomy destitution. Yet both halves were depraved in their fundamental nature and centered around the evil nucleus of Emperor Torrin.

From a position of proud dominion, assured of their inherent supremacy, the elves lived lives of fantastic decadence. Theirs' was a world of constructed splendor devoid of any beauty wholesome and natural in its creation. With unbridled extravagance, its architects and builders transformed Gairloch into a temple of shallow glory and artificial majesty, a place befitting a people of supremely pompous thought and cold, hollow souls. Below splendid tower-chambers of perfected luxury sat red-roofed buildings with marble-walled rooms decorated in gorgeous furnishings and bejeweled with marvelous art expressed in music, sculpture, and paint. Padded in silk draperies and a kaleidoscope of countless colorful pillows, great banquet-halls were equipped with long, low-standing tables arrayed with rich delicacies served on golden platters. Here the White Elves hosted lavish orgies in which they would feast in the abundant pleasures of food, wine, and flesh. In arrogant contempt of any moral restraint based in reason or religion, the White Elves reveled in perversions of every earthly good.

The White Elves amused themselves by playing at recreations peculiar and corrupt but with equal fanaticism applied themselves to an ambitious campaign of conquest. What discipline Gairloch's ruling class exercised in life seemed reserved for military training. Dedicated to the demanding art of war, White Elves called into the army formed an elite fighting force of unequaled skill. With ruthless determination, these erudite soldiers were drilled in military tactics and made to practice their combative talents. This commitment to warfare was further revealed in their development of magical and biological weapons such as goblins, gnomes, and other monsters, fantastic creatures of unholy origin and sinister purpose, abominations conceived in madness and nursed on the milk of hatred.

As in the act of empire building, the White Elves' love of strength and violence also manifested itself in games of gladiatorial competition. The castle housed grand amphitheaters where beasts and men were made to battle in bloody sport for the amusement of the elves. Extravagant theaters were fabricated so that their stages might present outrageous performances of torture and depravity. The White Elves dedicated themselves to pastimes that were predatory or perverse, unwholesome excitements in which they would gorge themselves upon these foul pleasures. Through the sophisticated gratification of these animal sensations, the White Elves perfected the barbaric refinement of their naturalness. All this was a part Gairloch's glory under the rule of Emperor Torrin.

The emperor's overlord, Chang, strode into the large, oval-shaped hall that two decades earlier had ceased to serve as the wizard Prelature following a massacre of heinous intent and ruthless execution. His face grave, Chang came to see the man who had carried out that massacre, made himself a wizard of unequaled power, and crowned himself as emperor.

The domed ceiling of the hall was painted in a complex design and held aloft by magnificently carved pillars. The throne at the far end of the room sat empty with the infamous Maul of Murgleys resting against the arm of the golden chair. The rows of benches had long ago been cleared away and other, less innocent furnishing provided in their place. In the center of the strangely equipped room, Torrin was hard at work, exerting his creative energies, exercising his dark passions, and sweating over a new conception of horror.

In this room, Torrin engaged in the heedless exploration of forbidden realms, realms of magic and applied physiology that no man was meant to penetrate. With knowledge of nature and mastery of magic, he carried out experiments of depraved anatomical manipulation. He created unclean things developed from mortal men but no longer human, things possessing only a tenuous linkage to their lost humanity, the products of a monstrous evolution induced by Torrin's insanity and incantation. But humans were not the only base material used within the unhallowed hall to produce biotic innovations. A proof of that diversity currently lay upon the operating table.

Torrin's servants at Prakrit, the former kingdom of the dwarves, had captured several giant scorpions and brought them to Gairloch. Torrin worked on one now. He was in the process of implanting the torso and head of a goblin onto the decapitated body of a giant scorpion. Keeping both halves of his biological invention partially sedated but alive, the mad surgeon performed the delicate procedure with supernatural precision and unctuous care. Torrin was assisted by two White Elves while three other attendants helped restrain the semi-conscious creature their emperor struggled to create.

Upon reaching Torrin, Chang bowed, then waited patiently for his emperor to acknowledge him.

After several minutes, Torrin picked up a towel and wiped away the black film of ichor and blood covering his hands. Once clean, he turned his dissecting gaze on Chang. The elvin overlord wore heavy battle armor decorated with gold inlays hammered into bold patterned grooves etched upon the steel plates that protected his body. Chang glittered with military strength. But behind his armor, the man of eloquent ferocity also appeared troubled. A sheen of sweat covered Chang's face, a face that always appeared as pale and hard as bleached bone.

"So, what is your report," Torrin demanded irritably. "Whose army is foolish enough to march on Gairloch with the ludicrous hope of challenging me in my own home?"

Chang shifted his weight. His armor clinked softly as pieces of metal plate rubbed against one another and creaked as the leather straps holding the steel suit in place moved with the elf's repositioning body.

"It is Braemar, Sire," Chang delivered the dire announcement, his words flavored with an inconsistent blend of practical apprehension and merciless anticipation, "but only Braemar. They do not appear to be joined by any allies. Our scouts saw no banners belonging to the kingdoms of Parhelion or Garonne. However, they could still pose a threat. Although we don't have an accurate count of their forces, the size of Braemar's army is considerable."

"Nonsense," Torrin dismissed Chang's warning. "The only reason we have not yet annihilated Braemar is because they were able to successfully hide behind their own castle walls. Now that they have wandered far from that relative security we'll be able to put an end to them once and for all. Coming here is a strange move on their part, one that we can take great advantage of, even with our own forces spread somewhat thinly between here and Prakrit. But I wonder what has given them the courage to stir from their hidey-hole and brought them out into the open with the vain hope of challenging me."

The creature on the operating table, newly created by Torrin, began to more fully regain consciousness. It struggled against Torrin's assistants as they fought to restrain the awakening beast. One man held its tail, immobilizing the danger of the large, poison-filled stinger. One man clung to each of its powerful goblin arms and two final attendants grabbled with its insect body and legs.

Distracted by the noisy scuffle, Torrin turned to confront the gruesome product of his unholy handiwork. Unflinchingly, Torrin stared into the creature's face, into eyes agleam with murderous determination. In one quick flash, the emperor's hand shot forward, closed around the monster's throat, and squeezed with unnatural vigor. As he held its thick neck in his suffocating grip, Torrin spoke to the beast, his voice hypnotic in its deep timbre and ruthless insistence. "You are mine. I made you. I own you. You live at my pleasure, you kill at my command, and you die at my whim."

Torrin may have intended to continue his motivational dialogue but his listener lost consciousness. The monster collapsed beneath the intense pressure of Torrin's fingers clenched mercilessly around its windpipe.

With the creature adequately subdued, Torrin released his grip. Speaking to the nervous attendants, Torrin said, "Put him with the other five gorpions." That was the name Torrin had given to this biological amalgamation created by magically fusing two life forms into a new exotic crossbreed. "And feed them well," he continued. "We may soon have work for these pretty pets. I may use them to help welcome our uninvited guests from the south."

As the others struggled to carry the gorbion away, Torrin returned his attention to Chang. But the look on Chang's face told Torrin that his overlord was still concerned about the mysterious source of Braemar's newfound courage. Chang's doubts annoyed Torrin and the emperor silently longed for the company of someone more his equal. Although Torrin enjoyed being the source of his people's confidence, he was sometimes wearied by the task of inspiring them. What a joy it would be to have a peer of equivalent strength, yet one who could be trusted to remain a servant of unquestioning loyalty. Torrin longed for the great pleasure of spending his time with someone more like himself, someone by his kindred nature better equipped to appreciate Torrin's own greatness.

Torrin shrugged, forced for the time being to be content with Chang and to feed the overlord the bravado he required. "It doesn't matter what brought Braemar out of hiding. The fact remains that it will make our work of conquering them that much easier. What is the position of Braemar's doomed army?"

"It is close, Sire, and moving rapidly. They could reach the castle by nightfall."

"What fools they are," Torrin insisted. "Living so long in fear of us must have driven them insane, for they have no idea what they're doing, no concept of the death that awaits them. Let them come like lambs to the slaughter. We will prepare for the gathering of the storm, one that will rain down death upon the kingdom of Braemar. Chang, I want you to bring all our people inside and lock down the castle. Prepare our forces to defend the walls. After Braemar's useless siege has worn down their soldiers and thinned their numbers, our armies will march out and finish them. But let's not kill them all. I want prisoners for slaves and experimentation. I'd particularly enjoy working my creative magic on any members of their royal family that may have been dim-witted enough to lead this army. Once this ridiculous incursion is put down and their army is defeated here, we'll be able to take Braemar's castle with ease. Then we can discuss whether you should remain here with me in Gairloch or if it would be more to our advantage to appoint you as seneschal over Braemar and have you rule that part of my growing empire for me."

Entertained by thoughts of his own ambitions, Chang grinned in reflection of his emperor's confidence.

Braemar's army did arrive that night and quickly set its craftsmen to work assembling a variety of war machines. Huge bonfires were kindled and set ablaze. Trees were chopped down, hewn into massive timbers, and shaped into thick planks of wood. Aragon invoked his magic to lighten the weight of the immense building materials, making the various construction projects easier to complete and allowing them to progress with greater speed. Energized by an edgy yet eager expectation, Braemar's army worked through the night, preparing themselves for battle beneath the luminous, watchful eyes of the distant castle lights.

As morning approached, a swarm of sunlight began to crawl along the exterior walls of the castle, lighting its towers and battlements in a bloody, crimson glow. Glistening in gilded armor as polished as the White Elves' military skill, sentries patrolled the ramparts and looked down contemptuously upon the massing invaders.

Handlers, horses, and men hauled the siege towers and catapults into position, spreading out Braemar's war machines to minimize the risk that the destruction of one might spread to another through fire or the fall of collapsing timbers.

Aragon instructed the soldiers to light additional bonfires and to pile them with as much green, leafy vegetation as could be scavenged from the diseased terrain surrounding the castle. The wizard then used his magic to take control of the gray-black smoke issuing from these smoldering fires, concentrating the thick blanket of fog above Braemar's army to hide the number of its soldiers and conceal their movements from the attentive eyes at watch on Gairloch's walls. The overcast of smoke hung in the stagnant air. Held in place by wizardry, it offered some protection from Gairloch's archers. Unable to sight specific targets, Gairloch's defenders were forced to fire blindly into the protective cloud in hope of hitting the men advancing beneath that thin shield of camouflage.

The earth reverberated with the barrage of catapult fire. The ground echoed the thunderous impact made as each boulder Braemar launched into the air struck its target or buried itself in the dirt short of its mark. In exploding clouds of dust and debris, heavy stone shot slammed into the shuddering walls. The invader's catapults also hurled other projectiles into the castle such as pottery vessels filled with noxious combinations of burning sulfur and quicklime. And Braemar let fly incendiary shells that delivered the weapon of fire to their enemy. The effects of the ammunition Braemar flung at Gairloch were amplified by Aragon's magic. Stone shot hit the defensive barrier of Gairloch's barbican and detonated with wizard fire, a crackling, jade-colored conflagration that blasted fine cracks into the fortified walls.

In other locations, amid a storm of arrows flying in each direction, siege towers were rolled against the lower walls. Framed by the regularly spaced, square merlons of the crenellated walls, the elves released their arrows with deadly accuracy and waited with edged weapons to repel Braemar's attempt to board the parapets and enter the castle.

Beneath sheltering shields, more of Braemar's soldiers pushed forward a battering ram set on wheels and fashioned from a large, tree trunk tipped with an iron point cast in the face of a lion. A lethal cataract of arrows combined with boiling oil poured from immense copper vats descended upon the brave men as they hammered at the castle gates. The cruel waterfall broke over them, drowning many of the soldiers in death while the fearless survivors continued the assault in the absence of their fallen comrades. But even they were forced to abandon their charge when fire fell from above and ignited the battering ram in ravenous flame.

Within the prison of her slave quarters, Lukos listened to the noisy bombardment and the distant clamor of the vociferous battle. They were strange, frightful sounds that made little sense to her for Lukos had never before been witness to a siege.

"What's happening," she asked.

"It would seem that Gairloch is under attack," Jeroboam answered calmly. He continued to prepare for his evening prayers.

"Attack!" Lukos gasped in shock, as if she believed an attack on Gairloch to be impossible. Certainly such a thing had never happened during her sixteen years of residence within the castle. Surprisingly this unexpected turn of events failed to give her hope. Somehow Lukos felt the hour of her death was now near at hand.

Keenan remained locked in another cell, separated from his wife and friend. Keenan thought of his family and let his mind drift back to their lonely mountain homestead, the place of his birth, where Keenan had grown from a boy into a man, one possessed of a restless spirit dissatisfied with the commonplace comforts and routine challenges of home. Now he wanted to go back. He wanted to take Lukos home and build a life of innocent pleasure like the one his parents had enjoyed. Perhaps it was a simple life but one far better than that lived by many others in the world. However, although Keenan had lost his appetite for adventure, he remained determined to fulfill the duty that had brought him to Gairloch.

As the day progressed, Braemar suffered heavy casualties yet seemed to gain little ground. With the night's approach, Braemar's army pulled back from the castle, issuing a temporary ceasefire so that it could make camp, rest, tend its wounded, and get ready for the next round of fighting that would come tomorrow.

To awaken the day, dawn lightly kissed the sleeping sky, and with its warm, gentle touch raised a rosy blush upon the blue skin of the morning air. The tenderness displayed by the heavens was not, however, shared by the landscape of war it illuminated. The ground was scattered with the dead, charred and twisted corpses, the bloody bodies of soldiers who had been stabbed and hacked, and lifeless lumps of flesh bristling with arrows.

Impelled by duty if not by hope, King Donovan and his military leaders marshaled Braemar's forces to repeat their assault upon the formidable castle and arrayed its soldiers in marching formations once again. Amid the booming cannonade made by the continuous fire of Braemar's catapults, once more the intrepid invaders took up the battering ram and manned the siege towers.

As the morning hours and Braemar's troops grew depleted, the siege evidenced little progress in breaching Gairloch's defenses. Then at last the persistence of Braemar's catapults achieved results. In an emerald blaze of wizard fire, another enchanted boulder struck the side of the castle with a deafening impact. In its aftershock and with a loud rumble of cracking stone, the stubborn wall buckled, swaying back and forth before a large section gave way and collapsed. As foot soldiers and cavalry charged forward to fill the gap, boisterous cheers were raised in unison by all of Braemar's men. However their elation, like their offensive momentum, proved to be short lived.

Leaping and clambering over the fallen rubble came a seething mob of bloodthirsty devils. Goblins and gnomes poured through the breach in Gairloch's wall. Ignited by the mad passions of their depraved hearts, the monsters unleashed their weapons in a firestorm of furious rage that threatened to consume Braemar's army in a devastating inferno capable of reducing their ranks to mortal ashes.

With strength of heart and tenacious resolve, Braemar's soldiers resisted the onslaught and began forcibly advancing on the enemy. But soon after they began to push back the mongrel creatures, the castle's main gates opened and released a new outburst of violent chaos.

First through this new opening came a pair of gruesome creatures of unknown origin, their form both somewhat familiar yet also hideously alien. The beasts, although mammals of some sort, had no more fur upon their pink flesh than would a newborn human babe. Each beast wore a harness of heavy chains buckled about its huge, muscular body, bodies vaguely similar to a bull's but four times such an animal's normal size and weight. Furthermore, they ran on legs structured and jointed more in the way of a cat than a bull and behind them dragged a long, rat-like tail. Their heads loosely resembled that of a pig but with horns and an eagle's hooked beak in place of a snout. With grisly claws and snapping beaks, these unearthly horrors did rend and gnaw the bodies of well-armored men. These abominations tore through Braemar's ranks in a pell-mell riot of death, leaving a wake of bloody carnage that littered the ground with mangled bodies and deep pools of precious blood.

Following behind these massive beasts were Torrin's newest hybrid creatures, the six gorbions, each formed from the body of a giant scorpion and the upper half of a goblin. Moving under the swift speed of their six legs, the gorbions lashed out in a deadly frenzy using tails equipped with poison-filled stingers and powerful arms outfitted with swords and hatchets.

Next a barbarous tide of goblins and gnomes surged tempestuously through the gates. With ravenous shrieks of bloodthirsty fury, these long-armed monsters and hellish, scaly-hided fiends clashed with Braemar's stout bodied men. And behind this frenzied throng of detestable creatures, White Elves, mounted on horseback, brought up the rear of the charge leaving Gairloch's gates.

Throughout the escalating battle, the catapults continued to fire. A stray boulder that greatly overshot its target crashed into the roof of the slave quarters. Where Jeroboam knelt in prayer, raising his petition for deliverance to the Lord, the boulder slammed into the overhead beams. Thick shafts of splintered wood joined by jagged shards of fractured brick and mortar fell from above with fatal force. But with light-footed grace, Lukos dove, snatching Jeroboam out from under the falling wreckage and rolling with him to safety.

Beneath a shroud of grit and grime, Jeroboam smiled broadly before hugging Lukos in a hearty embrace of great affection. Holding her by the shoulders, Jeroboam then kissed Lukos enthusiastically on the cheek. "Praise the Lord, for He has granted us our freedom," Jeroboam pronounced breathlessly, his reverent gaze turned up to the blue sky framed by the large, ragged hole in the roof and partially shattered wall.

Lukos scrambled to her feet and pulled Jeroboam up after her. Together, they quickly scaled the rubble slope of the crumbled brick wall and escaped to the roof through the wide, gapping hole. As several other slaves ran off, Lukos pounced from the roof onto an already shaken guard. Swiftly, she disarmed him of his dagger and used it to slit the elf's throat. As another guard ran toward her, Lukos turned and threw the dagger with uncanny precision. It struck the oncoming guard in the neck and dropped him wide-eyed to the pavement.

From the fallen elves, Lukos and Jeroboam each took a sword. The pair claimed their new weapons just in time to content with two more angry guards. These protectors of the prison were brought down in a hasty flurry of death-dealing blows.

Relieving one of the fresh corpses of his weapon, Jeroboam was now armed with two long-bladed scimitars. Lukos took the other sword, intending it for Keenan.

In the remaining intact cells, Keenan and the other slaves pressed against the bars, trying to get a better view of what was happening in the corridor. Lukos heard him shouting and she rushed to find her husband.

"Find the key," Lukos yelled to Jeroboam.

"I already have, my dear," said Jeroboam, holding it up for her to see and moving toward her with a quick, decisive step.

The lock resisted at first but with a little effort the mechanism finally released and allowed the gate to swing free. En mass, the slaves tried to push through the narrow doorway, squeezing through and scattering in every direction.

When Keenan at last made it out, he kissed his wife and took her extra sword. "Come on, let's get out of here."

"Are we leaving," Lukos asked hopefully. It was difficult to hear her over the urgent cries shouted by the prisoners in the other cells, desperate souls pleading for their own emancipation.

Keenan shook his head. "First we get what we came for," he explained. "We need to find Torrin's axe; then we leave. But where should we look?"

Based on what he had learned from his talks with their jailors and the other slaves, Jeroboam answered the question. "I think our best bet would be a place once called the wizard Prelature, a great hall where the emperor is said to spend much of his time."

"Yes," Keenan agreed. "I've heard mention of it too. Lukos, do you know the way?"

"I think so."

"Good," said Keenan, "then let's go; lead on."

"Wait," Jeroboam protested, his objection resolute. "First let's free the other prisoners."

Keenan scowled at the idea. "We don't have time for that. More guards are sure to arrive at any moment."

Jeroboam refused to yield his position. "We must help these people; it's the right thing to do. Don't deny them what the Lord has granted you."

"Arrg," Keenan growled in frustration. "All right; but hurry! Maybe their escape into the castle will help divert attention away from our own exploration."

Once the other slaves were freed, the three loyal companions began their search for Torrin and his cursed axe. On the move with swords in hand, Lukos led them from the wretched squalor of Gairloch's inferior neighborhoods into the regions of constructed luxury reserved for the White Elves. Cautiously but with haste, they ran past the gladiatorial amphitheater where Gairloch's people indulged their affections for barbarous sport and cruel theater.

They hurried through the tangle of passages and cobble lanes, ran past colonnades of marble statues and around elaborate fountains that trickled with water tinted phosphorescent blue. Their swift tour of the castle took them by copper trimmed conservatories and beneath balconies embellished in gold leaf ornaments. Having never before seen anything like it, Keenan marveled at Gairloch's wealth and grandeur. Despite his fear and resentment, Keenan felt himself unwillingly impressed by Gairloch's intimidating charm.

When a group of elves threatened to intercept them, they ducked inside a building through an unlocked door. Luck was with them for the building appeared empty. Alert for danger, they crossed the mosaic floor of intricately detailed, brightly colored tiles. The room was supplied with furnishings of remarkable workmanship and exotic design. Incense burned, emitting hypnotic fumes, seductively fragrant smoke that leisurely coiled and writhed in the tranquil air. Brilliant frescos with strange figures molded in painted plaster watched them from the walls. Exiting out the back of the building, the three friends huddled nervously beneath a steep, tiered roof of red tile before deciding where next to turn. Off to their left, Jeroboam pointed to a flight of stairs that lay beyond an open doorway within a tall, stone tower.

Climbing quickly, Keenan and his friends were halfway up the stairs when their luck ran out. Goblins could be heard pursuing them from below. The creatures jabbered eagerly in their debased dialect, a sound extraordinarily disturbing in its alien tone and feverish tenor. When Keenan and Jeroboam turned to look for the approaching threat, Lukos shouted at them with utmost gravity to follow her and run faster.

The air wafting up the tower was drenched in the foul stench of the nightmarish minions. Impatient for the attack, propelled by large feet and viciousness, the goblins surged up the stairs with wicked weapons clutched in their huge palms. The excited babble of these wild creatures echoed through the close stairwell and mingled with the reverberant sound of their cruel, crazed laughter.

Near the top, an exit revealed a stone walkway suspended high above the ground. The lofty catwalk led to another, larger tower one hundred feet way. With death closing in behind them, Keenan, Lukos, and Jeroboam dashed across the arched bridge connecting the two turreted towers.

As they passed through the doorway on the other side and into a wide room housed within the other tower, Jeroboam stopped. He urged Keenan and Lukos to go on without him. "Keep going! I'll hold them off for as long as

I can and give you a chance to get clear of danger."

"You can't fight them all," Keenan protested emphatically. "They'll cut you to pieces in an instant."

"No weapon forged by man," said Jeroboam, "shall prosper in its work against me while I walk in the will of the Lord. We came here for a purpose, Keenan; now go and fulfill your mission."

"But you'll die if we leave you here," Lukos declared.

"If it's the Lord's will that I die today, you can do nothing to prevent it."

Tensing with trepidation, Keenan tried again. "We need you if we're to defeat Torrin and capture the Maul of Murgleys."

"No," Jeroboam said with uncompromising insistence, "you'll be able to overcome the wicked one because the Word of God now abides in you. Remember well what I have taught you, dwell securely in your instruction and in the hand of God's grace."

"But," Keenan complained.

With a stern look, Jeroboam cut him off. "Keenan, have faith. It's the only magic I've ever needed."

Catching sight of their prey, the goblins yowled with sadistic zeal. Pushing and shoving against one another, the goblins crossed the threshold and poured onto the bridge, moving with a swift, lopping gait. Seeing the grotesque aberrations that pursued them, the young married couple finally heeded their friend's instruction. Keenan and Lukos fled, their grief and fear for Jeroboam subdued by their own need to stay alive.

As Keenan and Lukos took flight, Jeroboam turned to face his attackers. He made his stand just beyond the door, slicing the air with both swords in a daunting display of boldness and skill. He felled his first adversary with a single blow even as he stabbed at the second.

Jeroboam's swords flashed back and forth in a poetic flourish of lethal grace. Moving with adroit swordsmanship, the blades of his long scimitars whirled and cut. He stabbed and slashed as his limber body leapt, turned, ducked, and spun in an amazing dance of expert dexterity and unparallel fighting skill.

Although he parried well the goblins' less competent strikes, their numbers provided compensation for their lack of talent and the monsters succeeded in inflicted painful wounds upon the doughty priest. Before he could hack the creature's arm away, a mace smashed into Jeroboam's side puncturing flesh, cracking ribs, and stealing his breath. But he kept fighting, one sword ripping open a goblin's throat while his other blade stung deeply into the abdomen of a different beast.

A glancing blow carved off Jeroboam's left ear and would have smashed his collarbone had the priest not, at the last second, turned aside from the path of the descending axe. Warm, wet blood ran in a heavy stream down Jeroboam's neck, soaking his shirt in red. Continuing the battle, his courage undiminished, he ignored this wound and his other injuries.

When the combative fury finally ended, Jeroboam remained on his feet with the grisly corpses of fifteen goblins strewn in a circle around him.

Laying down his weapons, Jeroboam dragged two crumpled bodies from the entryway. Then he closed the thick, nail-studded oak door and shot the heavy bolt into place, sealing himself off from the bridge.

Wounded and tired, he climbed the final twenty steps to the top of the tower. Leaning over the crenellated wall, Jeroboam gazed out over the castle grounds, hoping to catch sight of his friends amid the disorder growing inside Gairloch. But in the turmoil below, he saw nothing of Keenan and Lukos.

A tumultuous battle of mammoth proportion raged outside the castle's main gate but Gairloch had yet to fully repulse the invaders. Taking heavy casualties, Braemar's frontline had managed to bring down the pair of giant, unknown beasts released from Torrin's store of evil. Only two of the gorbions survived but there remained a few thousand goblins and gnomes led by an elite corps of hundreds of White Elves.

Over bloody heaps of mangled flesh and bone, King Donovan directed a second wave of foot soldiers and cavalry in a gallant charge against Gairloch's defending army. Rorke and Alissa were with the others who joined their king in his forward press upon the castle.

Cries of horror and pain echoed through the gray, misty vapor of smoke hovering now in less cohesive form above the combatants. When the legs of his horse were cut out from under him, Donovan was pitched to the ground, where he continued to fight on foot. Alissa watched in helpless horror as a sword struck her father in the head and peeled back Donovan's scalp to reveal the chalk-white bone of his skull.

Alissa put her heels to her horse and galloped ahead in a despairing effort to help him. As she drew nearer to her father, a White Elf drove a spear through the king's dying heart. A malicious smile broke upon the elf's face, his skin as cold and pale as a winter moon.

Next to where her father died, a goblin wielding a spiked club struck Braemar's flag-bearer in the head. The blow crushed in the left side of the soldier's face, killing him instantly. As he fell, the flag-bearer tossed the long, wooden staff with its honored cloth displaying Braemar's lion standard into the air.

Alissa dropped her sword and spurred her black horse to greater speed.

The heel of the flagpole hit the earth. But leaning low in her saddle, Alissa plucked the staff from the air before the flag itself could touch the ground.

Having gained the prize, Alissa reined in her horse. Riding in a tight circle, she held the banner high for all to see. The clangor of battle could not drown out her anguished cry of grief nor her more determined shout of defiance, a call of hope that rallied her people to her now that their king had fallen.

As goblins and gnomes closed in on her, Alissa aimed her horse at Gairloch's gates, putting her heels to its flanks and propelling it forward in a reckless stampede. She rode with the banner held aloft. Flapping in the breeze, it trailed behind her in a rousing show patriotic valor.

Storming the gates as a force of one, Alissa shouted in a voice that carried far. "The Lord reigns," she cried out with repeated passion.

The grave faces of Braemar's fighting men looked with reverential awe upon the young woman of heroic courage. Then Braemar's army surged forward behind her, sworn and tested soldiers loyal to their new queen. Rorke and his troop of cavalrymen were the first to follow her.

Flanking Alissa on each side, they cut their way through the goblin horde. Just past the gates of Gairloch, Alissa reined in her mount, holding Braemar's banner high and summoning her people to her in a beckoning gesture of audacious encouragement. Riding in a circle, hacking at the encroaching enemy, Rorke's horsemen surrounded Alissa in a protective ring until more soldiers could arrive.

Mounted, Aragon left the open battlefield and, joining the offensive push, rode his horse toward Gairloch's open gates. Seeing Aragon make his move, Quinn snagged a horse and gave chase. Quinn believed that the wizard intended to search out Torrin and that finding Torrin might lead him to Keenan. Sharing Quinn's deductive reasoning, Marketa also managed to retrieve a riderless horse and took it for her own. Climbing into the saddle with ease despite her age, she raced to catch up with Quinn.

All three made it safely past the gates but by now mayhem engulfed the castle yard. The combatants clashed in a storm of violence, a huge frenzied tempest that ranted and raved with the passionate cries of suffering and slaughter, horrible shouts of butchery and bereavement.

Fighting desperately to survive the riotous bloodbath in which they were now engaged, Quinn and Marketa became separated from Aragon. Now on foot, Quinn led Marketa away from the battle, deciding that they should hunt for Torrin in the place where Quinn had left his former friend over twenty years ago. For some inexplicable reason, Quinn was certain that tracking down Torrin offered the best hope of finding Keenan.

Aragon shared this belief. On the other side of the fierce, interior battle, wielding his sword and black wood staff, Aragon fought his way free. Taking a different route, he too headed for the wizard Prelature.

Drained of blood and energy, Jeroboam slumped to the floor with his back braced against the tower wall, intending to rest a bit before continuing his search for his friends. Grasping his swords, arms folded over his chest, Jeroboam closed his eyes, feeling wearier than he ever had before. His thoughts drifted in a reflective current of memory. He saw the face of his wife, dead and buried now for over seven years, yet in his mind her beauty remained undiminished, as did the love his heart held for her. She had also been a servant of God, but the Lord had called her home. Jeroboam couldn't begrudge Him that, but he longed to be with her once again. That joy to be found in the afterlife was something Jeroboam looked forward to nearly as much as the anticipated rapture of joining the Lord in His heavenly kingdom. Jeroboam wondered how much longer he must labor in the world before his faith would finally be rewarded in eternity. Tears welled in Jeroboam's eyes, the longing for his parted wife weakening him in a way that his physical injuries could not.

The strident sound of fighting grew closer, distracting Jeroboam from his personal heartache. The furious noise rose from the bridge Jeroboam had recently defended. New defenders now held the bridge, a big-bodied man of middle age and a short woman of a more advanced lifespan. Both fought with swords against a hostile mob of goblins and gnomes.

The pair was trapped between the monsters and the door Jeroboam had bolted shut. Perhaps in a cry for help or as a final declaration of love, the big-bodied man began shouting Keenan's name, his voice thick with tender longing and a choking sense of failure.

The man's tormented shout for Keenan surprised Jeroboam but revealed with little doubt that the pair must be the boy's family or friends. Jeroboam stared down at them, unsure how to help but knowing that he must despite his personal fatigue in body and spirit.

"Trust in the Lord," Jeroboam advised himself as he leapt atop the wall. "And praise His righteousness," he cried, jumping bravely from the tower to the bridge below. Spread eagle and brandishing his swords, Jeroboam plummeted toward the deadly skirmish. As the priest fell, he saw a gnome raise the point of a spear aimed to receive him.

But his comrades' pushing to get at the other prey jostled the gnome at the last second, moving the tip of his spear safely aside when it was but mere inches from skewering the descending priest. Miraculously, Jeroboam landed on his feet, his arms bent so that his elbows slammed down on the gnome's shoulders, cushioning Jeroboam's fall.

His strength renewed through faith, Jeroboam wasted no time in using his swords to help the others persevere against the loathsome mutants. Quinn continued to swing his own sword like a man chopping wood, his brawny muscles flexed and released, doling out his powerful energy with devastating impact. In one stroke delivered with the force of a father's love, Quinn cleaved a goblin completely in two. Marketa fought too, exercising her weapon with a vigor and skill that were surprising for a woman of her age.

"You're friends of Keenan," Jeroboam asked while fighting.

"His father," Quinn replied.

"His grandmother," cried Marketa, "is he here?"

"He's on his way to a place once called the Prelature," said Jeroboam, "to confront the emperor."

Looking up from the ground far below, Aragon saw his mother and the two men fighting for their lives. He saw also that they would soon lose that fight.

Aragon raised his staff, pointing to the bridge. The irradiant gem affixed to the staff's apex flared to life and began to glow with a mysterious light. In a voice of power and command issued with enthusiastic vehemence, Aragon shouted an incantation. His hand lifted with a quick gesture and wizard fire flashed from his fingertips. The brilliant bolt of emerald light blasted the center of the arched bridge in a shuddering explosion of intense, magical force. Stones, goblins, and gnomes rained down from the gap in the broken span of rock and mortar. Quinn and Marketa were able to step back from the breach in time but watched in stunned silence as the walkway fell out from under Jeroboam's feet. The priest seemed to hang in the air for a moment, long enough for Quinn to reach forward and grab Jeroboam by his bloody shirt. But the tattered fabric tore apart in Quinn's grasp before he could drag Jeroboam back to the shelter of the fragmented bridge. Quinn and Marketa watched with pity as the priest fell.

Although enervated from the long day's exertion of his magic, Aragon called upon his power once again to help free his mother and Quinn from their precarious perch of lofty elevation. Aragon focused on the door in concentrated thought, using magic to pull back the bolt and thereby enable the door to once again be opened. They waved their thanks to Aragon before passing through the exit he provided them. Marketa and Quinn then continued their search for the Prelature.

Threatened by the shifting shadows, Keenan and Lukos made their way through the portico that would lead them finally to the Prelature. As they approached their ominous destination, the sound of incoherent mumblings and a sinister chuckling brought them to a sudden halt.

Heavy footfalls and labored breathing announced the forbidding figures before the goblins and gnomes came into view. The goblins' bulging, blood red eyes glistened with a burning fire and the gnomes' cruel, reptilian eyes sparkled with exhilaration. Three of each, the freakish creatures attacked in a murderous ecstasy.

Without hesitation, the foremost gnome swung a huge mace at Keenan's head. Having a brawny form and born of barbaric stock, the gnome's strike was conveyed with incredible force. Instinctively, Keenan blocked the attack with his sword but was knocked to the ground by the crushing impact. From that vulnerable position, Keenan rolled to avoid another strike, then stabbed his sword through the gnome's leather jerkin and into the scaly, underlying flesh.

Quickly, Keenan scrambled to his feet, swinging his weapon frantically as other enemies assailed him. With its wicked blade, a goblin opened an ugly gash across Lukos' face. But she kept fighting and her sword tore through the tough meat of the goblin's slick, mottled skin.

Two White Elves walked through the open door of the Prelature, moving confidently and carrying crossbows. The insolent expressions engraved upon the opalescent skin of their faces proclaimed the White Elves' certainty of their superiority. They each took aim and fired.

Both bolts from the crossbows hit Lukos, one in the stomach, the other in the chest.

Her silver eyes went wide and bright with pain as she staggered back in shock. Then a goblin's war hammer punched her in the side, splintering her ribs and collapsing her lung. Hurled backward between two pillars and beyond the sight of the ongoing conflict, Lukos landed with a hard thud upon the cold cobblestones.

Although Keenan cried out to her while continuing to fight, she barely heard him. Dazed and dying, Lukos tried to get up but could not compel her body to answer her heart's desire. Fear crawled though her guts like worms through a corpse. As darkness began closing in around her eyes, Lukos urgently called out to God.

"Please Lord, please help me," she prayed, her silent, pleading words tripping over one another in a rush of desperation. "Let me save Keenan. Save us both. Please don't let me die, not now, not now that I have so much to lose. I love Keenan so much. I've finally found someone to love, someone who loves me. Keenan wants to take me home with him, to meet his parents, brothers, and sisters and become a part of his family. And there's the child. I'm carrying Keenan's baby. I never thought I would, but I want this baby; I want to be the kind of mother I never had and give it from the start the love I found so late. My life is finally worth living; don't take it from me now."

Breathing became more difficult, ragged gasps for air. Frightened, Lukos felt her body growing cold. No answer was given to her prayer. But Lukos began to realize how blessed she had become, how much the Lord had already given her, all those things she was now so afraid to lose. With this thought, she felt herself wrapped in the supreme comfort of God's love even as she shivered with the sensation of her life bleeding out into that unknown realm of death. In these final moments, the Lord was with her now more than ever before; she sensed his close, intimate company and contemplated the hope of eternity in His presence, a gift purchased through faith alone.

"Thank you Lord; thank you," she whispered in reverent awe, her fading energy almost gone. "What can I do for you, Lord? You've done so much for me, but that's not what life is about, not where my focus should have been. I am satisfied in you. You are my all, my everything. My God, before I die, what can I do for you? How can I serve you?"

In her mind's eye Lukos saw a full moon and felt her dying body begin to stir toward the wolf. Then, in the vision, a sun emerged behind the moon, engulfing it in fire, a golden corona of light that overwhelmed the lunar image.

As the sun's revealed glory began to overcome the moon, a voice both strange and recognizable spoke inside her mind. "You're free. The nature of your flesh shall no longer have dominion over you. You are a child of God and the freedom I give you is placed in your hands alone for you to use. You now have power over the animal within you. Through your faith, the chains of the flesh are broken; the shackles of the beast are unbound. Live, and with your life let your faith remain in Me. Use what I give you to serve Me. Help your husband, resist evil, fight for peace, and with love declare your faith to all."

As Lukos listened to the commanding voice inside her head and gazed upon the mental overlay of moon and sun, her strength increased. Her breathing grew stronger and her injuries seemed to heal miraculously. Lukos gritted her teeth and tore the crossbow bolts from her stomach and chest, grimacing with pain and marveling at the supernatural mending of her flesh that followed their removal. Her body continued to change into the semblance of a wolf, but this time Lukos could control the transformation. It was difficult, but Lukos was able to shape and direct the form in which her body expressed the wolf. More significantly, she retained an awareness of her human self. Recognition of her personality, her soul, remained intact.

A strange, intense vitality welled up within her, invigorating Lukos with fierce power as her shape shifted into a new, semi-wolf form. Her face stretched forward into a jutting, canine-like muzzle crowded with long, jagged fangs. Mottled in a patchwork of shaggy, coffee-colored fur, her altered physique increased in size and assumed distorted proportions. Muscle mass and strength became greatly magnified. On elongated arms, her enlarged hands sprouted thick, razor-sharp claws.

After firing on Lukos, the White Elves dropped the crossbows and drew their swords. With one remaining gnome and goblin, the White Elves pushed Keenan's back to the wall. Outside the door of the Prelature, they struck at Keenan with teasing brutality, like a cat playing with a mouse before finishing off its prey.

A terrible howl of primeval fury exploded from behind them, diverting their attention. All turned in the direction of the blood chilling sound. Upright, but running in a crouched gait similar to a goblin's, Lukos rushed to help Keenan. She attacked with a wolfish fury.

The vicious, pointed teeth of her protracted jaw closed around the neck of a White Elf and tore out the milky white meat of his throat in one violent jerk of her head. As Lukos bit the elf, her right claw ripped open the belly of the goblin. The eviscerated goblin dropped to the floor as intestines spilled from its slashed abdominal cavity. The gnome and second elf stabbed at Lukos but with little effect. Howling with inhuman rage, she batted the White Elf and sent him flying through the air. The elf slammed against the stone wall, breaking his spine and caving in the back of his skull. Her rage undiminished, Lukos pounced on the gnome, the last remaining enemy. As it swung an axe at her, Lukos seized the monster by the arm. Holding the arm in her vice like claw, she bit through the limb just below the shoulder, severing the appendage. The gnome's strangled cry of pain was quickly silenced as Lukos released the detached arm and brought both her fists to bear in a pair of bone-crushing punches to the gnome's temples.

Then Lukos turned her attention on Keenan, who had stood in mute horror watching the frenetic craze of the shockingly bizarre wolf creature. After issuing a deep, throaty growl, Lukos snapped at the air in a ferocious display of hungry teeth.

Unable to move, Keenan stood frozen as Lukos approached him. She closed to within inches of her husband, scrutinizing him closely but with a look of uncertainty, as if her memory were weakening.

Lukos sniffed Keenan, filling her nostrils with his sent. He felt the heat of her breath against his face but did not recoil for Keenan recognized the truth of her essence in her clear, gray eyes.

Secure in the constancy of her love, Keenan reached out to his wife. "Lukos, it's me. I don't understand what's happened, why you've changed in this new way and before the full moon. I'm only glad you're alive. Maybe this new transformation happened because you were dying or maybe it was your love and your need to help me that brought on the change. It doesn't matter. The danger's gone now; you can change back. I love you Lukos. Come back to me."

A menacing, low rumble issued from the back of her neck. Drool dripped from her gaping, blood-smeared maw.

"Lukos," Keenan pleaded, focusing on the purity of her crystal eyes. "Don't give into the wolf. Take control of it and be my wife again. I love you."

Tears welled in her eyes as Lukos struggled to regain full possession of her mind. Caught up in the wild enthusiasm of the kill, Lukos had begun to lose her human awareness during the bloody brawl. Having been given a long leash on which to run, her animal nature was now reluctant to yield to Lukos' moral restraint. But Lukos managed to choke it back, reversing the frightening metamorphosis and returning from her lycanthropic state.

As her body melted back into its former human beauty, Lukos embraced Keenan. Clinging to him, she kissed his neck with warm, gentle lips of a natural shape and texture. In a voice distorted with both relief and remorse, she whispered her undying love for her husband. Sobbing with joy at having saved Keenan, she ramblingly confessed regret at allowing herself to be nearly overwhelmed by the wolf.

"It's all right," Keenan assured Lukos, his words trustworthy and true. He disentangled himself from her embrace. "I never doubted you or our love. Now let's find the Maul of Murgleys and get out of this evil place."

From the far side of the spacious room and perched atop a raised dais,

Torrin sat on the golden throne once reserved for the archprelate and watched the small drama playing outside the Prelature's doorway. Although mildly surprised by its outcome, the scene failed to significantly arouse the emperor's interest.

With a casual indifference born of his infinite conceit, Torrin viewed the man and woman's approach without concern despite the unique capacity for violence Lukos had already displayed. Torrin's self-possessed calm was so complete that Keenan and Lukos were a third of the way into the room before they even noticed the emperor's presence.

Once they saw him, Keenan and Lukos froze, their weapons held out in a defiant gesture that lacked conviction.

Without moving from his chair, Torrin looked at Keenan and knew instantly that the boy was his son. The unexpected knowledge crystallized in Torrin's mind as clearly as he saw the youth standing before him. The emperor read Keenan's thoughts, learning who he was and why he had come.

A malicious grin twisted Torrin's lips as he rose slowly to his feet, looking down upon his uninvited guests. The emperor was crowned with a small, silver diadem and dressed in a dark blue robe with bright steel pauldrons protecting his shoulders. Around his neck dangled a silver medallion cast in the image of finely detailed eagle wings that enwrapped an oval shaped, blue-green stone.

Torrin spoke and lifted his hand in a purposeful flicker of sudden movement. Keenan and Lukos ducked instinctively. Behind them, Torrin's magic slammed shut the heavy doors and shot a timber across their interior surface, barring anyone else's admittance to the Prelature.

"You're my son," Torrin announced ceremoniously, his words infused with pompous amusement. "How kind of Quinn to raise you for me. I'd almost forgotten about the old traitor. Is the ugly coward still alive; is he still on the run from me? You're alone, so he obviously didn't share your bravery in coming here. And that may be an encouraging indication of your superior intelligence. For I hope you're not as foolish as the fools who raised you."

Keenan could not speak. Stultified by the impression of power Torrin conveyed and the emperor's supernatural knowledge, Keenan suddenly perceived his own abilities as feeble and his intentions useless.

"I remember your mother," Torrin continued, "an elf named Midori. I enjoyed her for a time. She was a talented lover. But the indulgence of pleasure occasionally brings an unanticipated cost. And here you are."

Torrin reached back and idly fingered the hardwood handle of the axe leaning against the throne behind him. Then he gripped the weapon and dispassionately dragged it out in front of him, as if placing it on exhibit. Keenan saw that the steel axe-head was constructed with a leaf-shaped pike at the top and two curved blades, one half as long as the other. The metal shimmered with a pale, blue light and seemed to hum with the pulse of some strange, latent energy.

Telepathically exploring Keenan's mind, Torrin continued to examine the information at the surface of Keenan's consciousness. Torrin's incisive gaze pierced Keenan's thoughts and laid bare his secrets.

"So you've come to take my axe from me," observed Torrin. "And would you also use it to continue a family tradition of patricide? Am I to die at the hands of my embittered child who I unwittingly abandoned in my ignorance so many years ago? You might find that a difficult plan to execute. So let's finish the introductions and maybe chat awhile before you make your vain attempt upon my life. I am rather busy at the moment. As you may have noticed, we're entertaining friends from the kingdom of Braemar, and they'll expect me to make an appearance soon. But it's important that parents make time for their children. And I wouldn't want you to feel any more neglected than you already do."

Quinn and Marketa found the bodies outside the Prelature and considered it as proof that Keenan had made it this far. But the doors to the dreaded chamber were locked and would not open. Together, Quinn and Marketa picked up a marble statue and employed it as a battering ram against the stubborn doors. With frantic resolve and unbridled desperation, they pounded on it repeatedly, producing a loud, rhythmic cannonade but no entry. The timber barring the door creaked and cracked but would not give way.

Torrin, confident that his life was eternal, his power unequaled, and his greatness indisputable, expected all who encountered even the mere mention of his name to swoon with wonder and tremble with fear. Although his name alone may not evoke such a response, Torrin's presence did profoundly affect those in his company. Keenan regarded the emperor wizard with fear and fascination. He remained appalled by the atrocities committed under Torrin's rule but discovered now that there was also a curiously appealing quality about the man as well. Enthralled by the emperor, both he and Lukos ignored the incessant knocking that came from the doors behind them.

"I see you've brought your wife along to meet me," Torrin remarked. "She is a most unusual girl, remarkable even. And I am curious as to how this changeling would account for her existence. However, I must admit some initial disappointment that my progeny had chosen to marry a dog. I never liked dogs very much. But I have learned that you can train a dog and even the most insipid of canines can be made useful. Have you trained your bitch well Keenan? Does she perform to your satisfaction?"

"Leave her alone you sick bastard," Keenan yelled back, finally finding his voice.

Torrin responded to Keenan's fearful protest with mild mockery and a disingenuous attempt to pacify his aggrieved son. "No, unlike you, my parents were married at the time of my conception, although that fact hardly improved their parental worthiness. But I meant no disrespect. As I said, with her special abilities, Lukos is a very remarkable girl. In fact, she seems like someone who might feel quite at home here in Gairloch. Perhaps you could too. Gairloch has a great deal to offer and you would be a prince, heir to my illustrious throne."

"Never," Keenan shouted with indignation, his nerves raw.

"Don't be so quick to renounce the name Murgleys and relinquish your birthright," admonished Torrin. "I can give you a world to rule and a paradise in which to play." Torrin spoke with boundless arrogance, as if his invitation were irresistible.

Using magic, Torrin projected his thoughts into Keenan's mind, manifesting them visibly inside his brain. He forced Keenan to contemplate unplumbed possibilities for his life. Projected with tangible substance, the mental pictures seemed to become reality, taking on a vibrancy of color, texture, and smell. In a virtual existence, Keenan experienced enticements of compelling potency. In scenes placed before him by Torrin, Keenan saw himself as prince of Gairloch, living a life of sumptuous luxury and sexual excess. In orgies, he gorged himself on a banquet of female flesh. Keenan saw himself living out all the other pleasures that could be purchased with wealth and power. Kingdoms bowed to him and any property or thrill he might desire could be his.

Then from somewhere within himself, something else called out to Keenan. The scriptures he had heard read by Jeroboam raised themselves in Keenan's mind and he gave them voice. "Better is one day in God's house, in His love, than thousands spent in the poverty of riches offered by you or by this world."

"Don't feed me that religious claptrap," Torrin snarled, "you self-righteous whelp. I'm the only god you need concern yourself with. You're not holy, neither of you. The threads of evil are woven through your souls. Don't deny it. I can smell it as a bee senses nectar. And oh the odor is so sweet. It's there in that cruel corner of your heart that you keep locked, except when no one is looking. Open the gates; let loose the Beast. Let it show you the way. Evil is only a word that the weak use to condemn what they themselves are too fearful to exercise. Power. Join me, and you'll gain power beyond your wildest dreams, power that will let you freely indulge the very impulses that in your cowardice you now deny, power to satisfy your every desire."

A cloud lifted from Keenan's mind and he saw Torrin's true nature more clearly now, saw him as a man of dark ambition and cruel amusements. In his defense, Keenan lifted the shield of faith and armed himself with the sword of the spirit. "God's grace is sufficient for me," Keenan said stoutly, remembering more of Jeroboam's teachings. "And I shall have no king or father before my Father in Heaven."

With boredom Torrin waved Keenan's moral declaration aside. "Then you'll have to die," he promised, bringing up the axe and taking a step forward.

To protect her husband, Lukos sprinted forward in a feral effort to sink her sword in Torrin's flesh, screaming wildly for his blood. But a bolt of blue lightening flashed from Torrin's hand, catching Lukos in the chest. Blasted off her feet by the magic burst of light, she was pitched backward and thrown to the floor. There, unconscious and enveloped in an eerie luminosity, her body convulsed with spasmodic twitching. Keenan ran to her, keeling at her side in the hope that Lukos could be saved.

Exhausted, Marketa dropped the statue she and Quinn had been using as a battering ram, forcing him to do the same. Now Quinn charged the door alone, hammering at it with his shoulder. Again and again he tried, endeavoring with all his might. The doors shook from the impact, as if taunting him, making Quinn believe in the hope of admittance but yet unwilling to deliver on that promise. Quinn screamed with pain and despair as he collided with the door once again. The bones in his shoulder splintered, but so finally did the barrier. The timber snapped and the doors were flung wide. Carried by his own momentum, Quinn stumbled through the door and fell to the floor. Marketa rushed in after him.

Keenan turned and shouted. "Dad!"

At the sight of Quinn and Marketa, Torrin paused in his advance, dismayed most especially by the presence of his mother. But the emperor quickly masked his astonishment with an antagonistic air of nonchalance.

"Well how nice," Torrin remarked with cruel sarcasm, "this is becoming quite the little reunion." He studied Marketa with narrowed eyes filled with disdain.

Slipping something from her pocket, Marketa walked toward Torrin despite his cold reception. Tired and wounded, she moved with an awkward gait. Her heart knocked wildly against her chest, like the beating of an angry fist against an unyielding door. But disregarding her fear, the aged and weary woman persisted.

"Torrin," she called to him with gentleness. "Please don't hurt the boy; let Keenan be. Let him live and be happy. There has been too much killing already. Let it end Torrin. I know there is more to you than what you've become. Perhaps it's not too late to save yourself from ruin. Lament, repent, and amend your ways. Please Torrin. You're my son and I still love you."

"And I curse you," Torrin growled with immeasurable malice. "And I will delight in all your deaths." Hat saturated Torrin's heart and his voice dripped the blistering venom of that dark emotion.

"I'm so sorry." With tears in her eyes, Marketa sighed woefully but she stood firm. "Repent and be at peace in the mercy of the World Spirit." Then Marketa revealed the object removed from her pocket, a sling fitted with a rough stone. It whirled around her head in one quick revolution before she discharged the small projectile. With remarkable accuracy the stone struck Torrin in the forehead, catching him completely off guard. Staggered by the blow, Torrin dropped his axe and swayed uncertainly on his feet. But he was fast to recover and lashed out with magic at Marketa.

She dodged left and managed to avoid Torrin's first bolt of magic. But propelled by his volcanic temper, Torrin lobbed several more. Detonating in a shower of light and stony debris, the hail of magic exploded against the room's pillars and walls. However, the fit of anger robbed Torrin of his aim and caused him to miss his target again and again.

Into that maelstrom of magic, Aragon entered the Prelature. Silver runes shimmered like flowing mercury along the wizard's black wood staff. Aragon shot back with wizard fire, a dynamic outburst of power that severely challenged Torrin. In a barrage of magic energy, the brothers battled one another. Making an effort to escape the crossfire, Marketa pulled on Quinn's uninjured arm, urging him back toward the door.

When the stone slung by Marketa struck Torrin, Lukos regained consciousness and the mysterious luminosity faded from around her body.

Exploiting the distracting furor of the brother's dual, Keenan managed to snatch Torrin's axe without his notice. Touching the axe made Keenan's skin tingle and caused his stomach to clench with revulsion. Furthermore, he heard a strange sound coming from inside his ears, a faint, lyric buzzing, a song sung too softly for Keenan to comprehend. It was the axe that sang to him, and knowing it was evil, Keenan did not want to understand the verses of its whispered corruption. So he resisted the urge to concentrate upon the compelling voice. He wanted to throw down the blade, but held firm to the vile weapon, believing that he must remain true to the terrible business he had taken it upon himself to complete.

Keenan meant to use the axe against Torrin but it proved impossible for Keenan to approach him through the chaos of ricocheting magic. So Keenan moved back beside Lukos. Then like Quinn and Marketa, they too struggled to get clear of the destructive volley cast by the contending wizards.

Caught between the two brothers, the room's pillars were bombarded by magic. Weakened by the collapse of several central supports, the ceiling caved in. And the wreckage momentarily separated Torrin from his enemies.

In the distance, a horn sounded. Repeated several times, the echoing trumpet call delivered a lamenting announcement of failure, a forlorn declaration of defeat.

"Braemar is retreating, and so must we," Aragon advised the others. "Let us flee from Gairloch while we still have a chance. All of you, quickly, follow me."

Chapter 10

When the horn signaled Braemar's retreat, war withdrew from the horror-haunted castle. The bold invaders abandoned any hope of victory and now fought only to escape the nightmare of combat and failure surrounding Gairloch, that devastating zone of fighting and fatality that Braemar had been forced to acknowledge it could not endure. Even Braemar's most courageous began to turn and run in fear of total defeat. Alissa did her best to rally the troops into an organized retreat that might at least forestall their utter annihilation. Working in concert, she and Rorke gathered the scattered remnants of Braemar's depleted army into a more concentrated force so as to enhance the dismal likelihood of their survival.

Bodies blanketed the ground like fall leaves in the forest. In a seething mass of greasy plumage, thick flocks of crows descended on the battlefield, eager to dine upon the banquet of carrion. Washing over the heaps of ruined flesh in great, rolling black waves, the pitiless birds used their beaks to strip meat from fresh corpses. The harsh call of these repellent birds pierced the ear like cackling laughter that mocked the fallen soldiers and their wasted lives.

In his own flight out of castle Gairloch, Keenan became separated from Lukos and the others. However, Keenan had no time to seek out his friends or to entertain concern about their safety for he was being chased by a horde of monsters numbering nearly a hundred strong. These goblins harried him with singular intent, with a dedicated ruthlessness that could not be distracted by the initial availability of other prey. Most certainly it was because Keenan still carried the Maul of Murgleys that these unnatural beings pursued him with such relentless purpose.

Keenan avoided capture thus far only by his luck in getting hold of a horse's reins and taking swift possession of the forsaken steed. Spurred by Keenan's demand and its own terror, the exhausted horse was barely able to stay in front of the pursuing goblins. He galloped blindly, hurrying without any deliberate destination, seeking only to outdistance those that hunted him.

Propelled by the awful might of their savage muscles and iron sinew, the goblins strained to catch Keenan; plunging recklessly through trees and underbrush, they bounded over the land. The powerful legs and huge arms of the goblins' horrid bodies flexed with ferocious vitality, showing no hint of fatigue. With a gnashing of cruel, slavering fangs, the goblins fixed their baleful, red eyes on Keenan. Roaring and snarling feverishly, the wild cries of the demented creatures advised Keenan with dreadful certainty that the goblins were rapidly closing in on him.

Kicking mercilessly at his horse's belly, Keenan screamed at the beast to go faster. The poor animal struggled to comply and gained some success in pulling ahead of the murderous mob. But Keenan knew this burst of energy could not be sustained very long. He sensed the horse was nearing the limit of its strength.

Terrified, Keenan considered dropping the axe, letting the goblins have it back if relinquishing it might save his life. But Keenan hesitated, remembering why he had come to Gairloch and the people whose future might depend upon his actions. He had not stolen the axe to prolong or enhance his own life. He had done it to help reduce the threat of evil in the world, evil he felt in part responsible for because of his heritage. Keenan had vowed to take the axe, sworn to strip his father of that hateful tool so that the emperor's power to do evil might be thwarted. So many had sacrificed so much to help Keenan fulfill that pledge that he could not now abandon his promise.

In its agitated, overextended stride, Keenan's horse planted its hoof poorly causing its ankle to twist. Stumbling from the excruciating pain, its forelegs buckled, bone snapped, and the lame horse crashed to the ground under its own momentum. The uncontrollable fall pitched Keenan forward. In a rough landing, his face scrapped the forest floor, filling his mouth with dirt and blood. The axe flew from his hand and bounced a few feet outside his reach.

Dazed, his head spinning, his body aching, Keenan scrambled to get up. He quickly plucked the axe from a tangle of green shrub and took off on foot, running in rebellious desperation yet knowing he could never outdistance the goblins.

As he ran, the axe seemed to whisper to Keenan from inside his head, its beckoning voice growing more familiar and insistent. It was Torrin's voice, tempting Keenan once again. The whispered entreaties now urged Keenan to use the axe, to wield it in defense of his life, to fight back against the horrific creatures closing in on him. *You must use the axe*, the voice warned. *It is your only hope of survival; only the Maul of Murgleys can save you from your enemies. The axe will make you invincible if only you would use the power you hold gripped in your hands. Using the axe will grant you authority over not only the goblins but others too, and the acceptance of that authority will set your soul free.*

Clenching the axe tightly in his sweaty palms, Keenan could feel its malignant evil, a tingling sensation that sought to penetrate deep below the surface of his skin. Past nerves and muscle, the corrupting influence of the axe tried to worm its way to the very core of Keenan's heart. But even knowing it was wrong, he wanted to use it anyway. Scared beyond the strength of his forbearance, Keenan realized with inescapable clarity that he must use the axe or die. No other hope remained.

Keenan reached the water's edge of Loch Eriboll and was left with nowhere else to run. Perhaps sensing the danger of the axe, the goblin aggressors reduced the pace of their sadistic advance. Showing uncharacteristic caution, the monsters amassed in a semicircle around Keenan. Their prey trapped, the goblins moved in slowly for the kill.

Keenan reared back, hoisting the Maul of Murgleys over his right shoulder. The axe blade glimmered with an intimidating blue pulse. Bunching up with physical energy, Keenan's arm muscles compressed. Straining against the accumulated tension of his body, Keenan gritted his teeth. The veins stood out in his stiffened neck. The heat of Keenan's blistering stare was further inflamed so that it now blazed with the white-hot intensity of his emotion. Then, with a defiant roar, Keenan swung the axe with all his might.

The blade cut through the air with a loud whoosh and a reverberant hum of unknown power stored within its polished metal. The goblins pulled back even though none were near enough to feel the lethal cut of that magical blade.

As the axe completed its arc, Keenan turned his body away from the goblins and let go, throwing the axe farther than human strength could carry it. It flew spinning through the air, traveling an unnatural distance beyond the lakeshore and out over the waves.

A mermaid, a noble creature born of the natural world, broke from the lake in a terrific spray of water and leapt into the air. In an exquisite flash of beauty and with a dexterity of astounding grace, the mermaid took hold of the axe before plunging back into the great depths of Loch Eriboll. It happened so quickly, Keenan might have believed it merely a delusion of his fevered mind if not for the spreading ring of rippling water that marked the spot of the mermaid's passage.

Having done all that he could do, Keenan dropped to his knees in the water. For him, the war against evil was over. He had stood firm unto the last and could only pray that some good would come from what he had done with his life. Burying his face into his hands, Keenan waited for the goblins to hack him apart and bring his story to an end.

Leering and slavering, the goblins lumbered forward brandishing weapons of percussion and incision. They growled and gibbered with excited fury, a loud and terrifying sound that blocked out the noise of a swiftly approaching horse. With great alacrity, the rider dismounted. Dropping from the saddle before fully reining in his horse, he hit the ground running. Before the goblins could react, the lone defender charged into their midst.

It was Aragon. Speaking words of potent magic, the wizard circled his staff in the air around his head and then struck the base of his charmed, silver-tipped rod against the earth with tremendous force.

The staff detonated in a flesh-searing shockwave of destructive energy. Forming a wide circle two hundred feet in diameter around Aragon's staff, an outpouring of emerald light flared in all directions. Aragon incinerated the goblins with magic. The monsters' tough, slick skin began to melt off the bone, their bodies dripping like tallow candles before erupting in flame.

At the sound of the explosion, Keenan instinctively fell forward into the protection of the lake. He felt the heat of the blast wash over him but he kept his head down, holding his breath and unwilling to witness whatever new calamity was taking place behind him.

Silence followed the shrieking horror of the goblins. Reduced to ashes, the goblins were gone and the fire also died. In the peace that came after the fearsome roar of magic and death, all that could be heard was the rhythmic lapping of waves breaking against the lakeshore.

Exhausted, his energies spent, Aragon leaned heavily upon his blackwood, rune encrusted staff. A light breeze ruffled the ragged edges of his dirty blue robe and Aragon swayed uncertainly on his feet for several minutes before he felt confident enough in his strength to raise his head and open his eyes. It was several minutes more before Aragon could hazard his first step. Gradually, Aragon's vitality renewed itself but it would be days before his strength would be fully replenished.

Keenan sat in the water, his expression dazed. His hair was singed and he had minor burns across most of his back but otherwise Keenan was unharmed.

Aragon made his way across the charred ground and headed carefully toward the lake. Once there, Aragon waded out to Keenan, then shakily offered his hand to help him up.

As the youth stood, Aragon greeted Keenan with goodwill and avuncular affection. "That was a close call if ever there was one, young Keenan," Aragon remarked, patting his nephew tenderly on the shoulder. "Those goblins were all over you like stink on a skunk, weren't they boy? But you did well. Yes, you did quiet well indeed. Your father, Quinn I mean, would be very proud."

Keenan shook his head, his eyes downcast. "But the axe," said Keenan, "it's lost. I failed to destroy it," he complained, his voice infused with somber disappointment.

Aragon favored the boy with an encouraging smile before answering. "It doesn't matter. You accomplished the next best thing and proved your worth in the process. It was a remarkable feat considering the circumstances you were under. The axe has been successfully removed from Torrin's custody; that is the important thing. I am confident that the maids of Loch Eriboll will keep it safely sealed away. The mermaids have no love for Gairloch and would have no interest in using the axe themselves. They can be trusted to secure the axe from any hands that may want to exploit its power. It's over Keenan; you have finished your quest."

"Good," he sighed. "I want no more adventures."

Aragon laughed. The gentleman enchanter gave Keenan a wink and a nod as if acknowledging some unspoken wisdom that had passed between the two men. "I understand your attitude, and it's a sign of maturity. I hope the future will be kind enough to accommodate your wishes."

"What happened to the others," Keenan inquired uneasily.

"I had to leave Quinn and the others so I could follow you. But I believe they made it out of danger. They were headed for cover in Dolmendie Forest when I last saw them.

"I know where they might have gone," suggested Keenan, "to the place where Lukos and I last made camp before entering the castle."

"Then my honorable friend and nephew," said Aragon, "let us go back and see if we can find them. You may lead the way. But I'm afraid we'll have to walk, as my horse seems to have disappeared."

When Braemar's army began its retreat, Gairloch's forces refrained from immediately giving chase. Selfish of glory, the White Elves coveted the individual credit for this triumph and desired the unshared pleasure to be had in the final slaughter of Braemar's army. So the goblins and gnomes were pulled back within the castle and a sizable corps of White Elves assembled to pursue their enemy. These preparations afforded Braemar a modest head start, although they formed no illusions of hope from this brief reprieve.

Skirting the edge of Dolmendie Forest, Alissa led her beleaguered people in a hurried pace but with a discipline that controlled their panic. The new queen succeeded in putting several miles between Braemar's army and Gairloch's castle before the White Elves could be seen gaining on them in the distance.

However, as the White Elves approached and prepared to engage the enemy in what would be Braemar's final battle, another army joined them from the south. The cautious kingdom of Parhelion had come at last to Braemar's rescue. No longer liking their odds for victory, the White Elves abandoned the fight and returned to Gairloch.

As their armies intermingled, Braemar's people greeted Parhelion's soldiers with shouts of joy and hearty handshakes. Filled with gratitude and respect, Alissa stared with astonishment as the commander of Parhelion's army rode toward her on a tall, well-dressed horse. The commander was Prince Tynan, the man to whom she had been promised not so very long ago. Although to Alissa, it seemed like years rather than months since the interruption of her journey into marriage. So much had changed since then that Alissa looked on her betrothal as the memory of a different person.

Tynan surveyed the threadbare remnant of Braemar's collective might, a tattered scrap of what had once been a large cloth of sturdy fabric. "Where is Donovan," Tynan asked Alissa. "Where is your father?"

Alissa's gaze was sharp and her words steady as she answered. "The king is dead. He gave his life in battle."

His mood sorrowful and reflective, Tynan paused before responding to this unhappy news. "I am very sorry," he said finally. "And I understand your grief, for my father too has died. King Cameron became sick, an illness that consumed his body rapidly. Despite all our efforts to save him, my father died.

After burying my father and hearing that Braemar was marching on Gairloch, I marshaled our army to aid your cause. Alas we came too late to help you in your assault on Gairloch, but at least we came in time to offer you safe passage home."

"And we thank you for it," Alissa replied honestly. "Although I fear there will be little safety now for us at home. There is almost no one left, no hope that we can defend our home against the invasion that will surely come in retaliation for our assault upon the emperor's castle."

"Then let us marry now," Tynan proposed, "so that your people can be assured of their security."

"No," Alissa refused, "you don't know all that has happened. Much has changed. You are released from your promise to marry me. I am damaged and as matters stand you have little to gain through an allegiance of marriage with Braemar."

"It doesn't matter what has happened," Tynan countered. "The past can be buried with the dead. What matters now is the future of those that yet live. We can rebuild together, grow stronger together. Marry me today and give our people hope for their tomorrow."

Torn by her conflicting loyalties, Alissa turned her gaze in search of Rorke. Nearby, he sat astride his horse. Like all those around them, he listened to her conversation with Tynan. The features of Rorke's face sagged under the weight of renewed misery.

With love evident in his eyes, Rorke met Alissa's probing gaze. Then in somber silence, the cavalry captain nodded his consent, demonstrating that Rorke understood Braemar's need to be greater than his own. For the good of others, Rorke and Alissa sacrificed their own love for one another.

Facing Tynan once again, Alissa straightened her posture in a regal manner of gentle grace. "I accept your offer of marriage," she announced confidently, "and would gladly have you as my husband and my king."

Smiling, Tynan gestured for his second in command to come forward and officiate the rite of marriage. King Tynan and Queen Alissa dismounted to stand before him during the ceremony while all watched the union of their kingdoms.

During the impromptu nuptials, Nolan arrived on the scene just in time to see his sister wed. Lost in Dolmendie Forest, Braemar's angry, young prince had wandered without direction, blindly following deer trails that led him nowhere. The haunted forest had stretched the limits of Nolan's sanity. Taught and frayed, that delicate cord ultimately snapped beneath the strain applied by Dolmendie Forest. Having weeks to chew on his own bitterness and shame, Nolan went mad, blaming Alissa for all his troubles, certain that she had been the one to cause his downfall. In his rambling solitude, Nolan spent his time muttering imagined conversations with himself, building fanaticized alliances against his sister. Or perhaps the voices with whom Nolan spoke were real and it was the whisperings of the sinister forest that had somehow led him to be here at this particular moment in time. Regardless, Nolan was convinced that Alissa had ruined him, that she had seduced his heart with a hope of love that she then betrayed by allowing her body to be defiled by another. Alissa stole the one thing he wanted most and now could never have. For that, Nolan swore he would punish Alissa with extreme severity.

Lifting a spear, Nolan charged his sister, crying out with indistinguishable words of furious revenge. Although lunacy now distorted his suave features, Alissa recognized her brother but was unable to make sense of his obvious intention. Immobilized by her confusion, Alissa hesitated and would have been killed had her newly wedded husband not intervened.

Tynan leapt in front of his bride, unselfishly shielding her from danger. Impaled by Nolan's spear, Tynan's chest erupted in blood. His heart pierced, Tynan died quickly. Lifeless, the king's body slumped to the ground dragging the spear with him.

Howling with frustrated fury, Nolan leapt at his sister, his hooked fingers reaching for her throat. Recovering her senses, Alissa raised a sword against her brother and brought an end to his troubled life, wiping out Nolan's rage and injured pride in a single blow of her double-edged blade.

Keenan led Aragon back to his abandoned campsite, where true to his prediction, they found the rest of their family waiting. Upon seeing him, Lukos rushed to hug Keenan, covering his face in kisses of elated affection before yielding her place to Quinn. The bones of his left shoulder being badly broken, Quinn pulled his son close to his barrel-chest in a firm one-armed embrace. Marketa wrapped her small arms around both father and son before going to welcome her own son, Aragon.

"I was so scared," Quinn croaked with emotion. "I thought I might lose you forever."

"I'm fine Dad," said Keenan. "I'm sorry you were worried. I'm sorry for all the pain that came from my decision to take the axe from Torrin. I know you're angry with me, but I still believe it was the right thing to do."

"I won't be angry," promised Quinn, "if you tell me that it's over."

"Yes, it's over," Keenan assured him. He explained how Aragon had saved him and that the Maul of Murgleys was now hidden away in a safe place where Torrin would never find it.

His opinion of the wizard modestly improved, Quinn directed his attention at Aragon. "I still resent you for dragging us into this mess. But I thank you for being there when my son needed help."

"You're welcome," acknowledged Aragon. "After all, you, Keenan, and I are family, the people who we should be able to count on in our time of need."

Quinn grumbled but said nothing further as he reached out to tentatively shake the wizard's hand.

Turning back to his son, Quinn asked, "Are you ready to go home now Keenan, both you and your wife I mean." Quinn smiled amiably at Lukos. "I'd like to get to know my daughter-in-law. And we should start building you two a house of your own as soon as possible. I imagine you newlyweds will want more privacy than you'll get living in a house with your mom and me along with all your brothers and sisters."

"I'm not going back to live with you Dad," Keenan announced unexpectedly.

"Why not," Quinn inquired, the features his unfortunate face lined with increased parental concern. "I thought you said this business with Gairloch was over."

"It is," Keenan told him. "Don't get me wrong; I'm done with adventures. I'm not interested in trying to be a hero anymore. But this experience has taught me that I also don't want to hide from the world either. And for now, going home would seem like that. It would seem like I was hiding. Maybe in a year or two I'll come back home to live with you, but not now. I need to be a part of the world first, if that makes any sense. For example, in a small way, I felt like my work at Marketa's orphanage did some good, that I made a difference in people's lives."

"You make a difference in our lives," argued Quinn.

"I know," replied Keenan, "and I love you Dad; you know I do. But I shouldn't only want to help the people I love. That seems somehow selfish. Don't you think? So if Marketa will let me and if Lukos is willing, I'd like to go back to Abandon and continue working at the orphanage."

"You're always welcome," Marketa stated fondly, pleased by her grandson's decision and the kindness of his motives.

"All right," Quinn agreed. "But on your way to Abandon, you'll have to stop at home and see your mother. She'll want proof that you're alive and well. And she'll want to meet Lukos; the whole family will. Marketa, you and Aragon should come too. That way you can go back to Abandon together and keep each other safe during your journey."

"Lukos, what do you say," asked Keenan.

"That sounds fine," she answered. "I trust your judgment."

"What's wrong then, you look sad."

"I'm not," Lukos told Keenan. "In fact, I'm very happy to hear that you like helping children. I'm sure I will too. It's just that I was wondering about Jeroboam. Do you think there is any chance he might have made it out of Gairloch alive?"

"I wish I knew," Keenan replied with regret.

"I believe we met your friend," Marketa suggested. "In truth, he helped save our lives. Inside the castle, we fought together against some of those dreadful creatures on a bridge that collapsed. I'm sorry, but your friend fell and I don't see how he could have survived." Marketa laid a warm, commiserating hand on Lukos' shoulder. "Who was he dear? Tell me about Jeroboam; tell me about your friend."

Picking up his pack, Lukos removed Jeroboam's Holy Book and caressed its worn leather-bound cover. Responding to Marketa's sympathetic prompting, Lukos explained their friendship with the paladin priest. Lukos recounted the story of her baptism and of how Jeroboam had opened her eyes to God.

"He did so much for us," Lukos murmured sadly. "I can't believe he's gone."

"It sounds as if you learned much from him," observed Marketa, "that he touched both your lives in a profound and meaningful way. It would appear that Jeroboam was an even better teacher than he was a skilled warrior. Take comfort in the fact that you can keep his memory alive by remembering what he taught you and sharing that wisdom with others."

"But there is so much I don't know," said Lukos, "so much I don't yet understand about the God he introduced me to, about the God I've accepted as Lord over my life. How will I learn?"

"You have his book to guide you," Marketa remarked gently.

Dejected and a bit ashamed, Lukos shook her head. "I don't know how to read. Keenan, will you read the book to me, will you teach me to read it for myself?"

With a nervous urgency, Lukos pressed the book into Keenan's hands.

After flipping through its many pages, Keenan shook his head and frowned. "I can't," he admitted dismally, as if he had greatly failed her. "It's not written in the language of the elves my mother taught me nor is it written in the common tongue. So I don't know what it says any more than you do."

"May I see it," asked Marketa and Keenan gave it to her. "I have never seen this particular book before. But long ago when I lived at Gairloch, before the castle became what it is today, I spent some time studying ancient and obscure texts. I've seen this language in some of the old documents I studied then. It will be difficult, but I think with time and effort I can decipher at least some of this book for you. If you'll allow me Lukos, I would like to help translate your book and teach you to read it for yourself."

"Thank you," Lukos accepted. "I'd like that very much."

"Good," said Quinn. Nervous that they were still in danger, he sought to end the conversation and put their party in motion. "Let's go home."

Within the towering stone-block walls of castle Gairloch, Chang lined up the prisoners of war. For inspection by the emperor, the elvin overlord assembled the unlucky soldiers captured during Braemar's failed invasion. Torrin would take what he wanted for his own exploitation and leave the rest for Chang to determine their appropriate use.

The examination of the prisoners took place outside the gateway to the Pit, that labyrinth of terrifying tunnels and chilling catacombs. Through a series of iron gates, the prisoners overheard whispering echoes of the unwholesome things that made their life within the bowels of the castle, those subterranean chambers forsaken by Gairloch's rulers and transformed into a prison of darkest terror.

Frightening sounds escaped the underground world of horror and death, the sounds of weaker beasts being preyed upon, torn apart, ripped open, and crying out in anguish. Torrin found this soft melody of pain oddly attractive for it stirred his own predatory hunger, his cruel primitive desires. The prisoners, however, experienced an altogether different reaction, just as intended. They had been assembled in such close proximity to the Pit so as to instill within the prisoners a fear of hidden dangers, of horrors yet unknown, and to hint at fates worse than slavery.

In his evaluation, Torrin observed that all the prisoners were openly terrified or attempted to disguise their fear behind masks of poorly manufactured bravery. There was only one exception, one man who did not tremble nor pretend with false courage. A small man with a scraggly beard, he appeared to be about forty years of age. A large clot of dried blood covered the spot where his left ear had recently been shaved off.

"I don't like the looks of this one Chang," Torrin asserted his displeasure, "and he doesn't appear to be worth very much. I suggest you cull him from the herd."

Still the man did not flinch, despite the menace of Torrin's close scrutiny and the death threat he implied. The man's placid response further nettled Torrin's animosity.

"Why are you so calm," demanded Torrin, "your freedom is gone, your life nearly over."

"Your walls do not confine me," answered Jeroboam, "just as the flesh does not imprison the soul. For a soul controlled by the Spirit of God lives in peace and freedom no matter the circumstances of the flesh. I am always free for the Spirit of the Lord is in me. It is you, Torrin, who are a prisoner, a slave to sin. Sin shall continue to be your master unless you repent and offer your life to God."

Torrin stared at him, astounded by the man's idiocy and the strange similarity his word bore to those voiced by his mother in the Prelature. "You are insane. You have nothing but your delusions, whereas the world is mine to rule."

His manner so serene and satisfied even in his defeat, Jeroboam seemed to regard Torrin with a kind of pity, which the emperor found curiously unsettling. "All that you revere," said Jeroboam, "earthy power, pleasure, and wealth are counted as loss in comparison to knowing the Lord God. Do not place your love in the things of this world, because the world will one day pass away for both the weak and the strong. But he who is filled with God's Spirit, seeking to do His will, shall live forever."

Torrin was struck by the air of formidable authority and steadfast character that sat so easily yet so unexpectedly on the small, soft spoken man. Torrin could perceive nothing terrible in particular about the man that should at all seem threatening, but a nervous doubt twisted inside the emperor's dark heart the longer he faced Jeroboam.

"You are a fool," Torrin scoffed, unsure why he bothered to waste his time in debate with this worthless peasant. Perhaps it was only to prove something to himself. "You set your hope on some make-believe god because you're too weak to take power into your own hands and exercise that power for individual gain."

Jeroboam spoke with perfect confidence, his body battered but his spirit unbruised. "If I am weak, then I will rejoice in my weakness for it has brought me closer to God and demonstrated His strength. I boast not in my own strength but in God's. Through my weakness, His power can be revealed. I can attain perfection not through my own works but through His saving grace. In my weakness I have always been either helped or comforted by God. Through His holy example I am able to assist others in dealing with their problems and share His truth with them as I endeavor to give aid or consolation."

Torrin considered devouring Jeroboam in the fire of his magic, but something stayed his hand and the emperor pursued an alternate path of punishment. "Well we will put your bold assertion to the test," Torrin smirked, "because you're going to the Pit. See what good you and your god are able to achieve there."

"I go by His will, not yours," Jeroboam remarked. "My hope is in Him, a hope that is accessible even to you. God can change what would otherwise seem unchangeable. It may be too late for anyone else to help you but it is never too late for God to help, if you would only yield to Him in faith. The fruit of the Spirit is still available to you if you would choose to reconcile yourself to God, denounce your own authority and accept God's sovereignty over your life, and seek to do His will instead of your own."

Torrin's pride fortified the wall around his heart keeping out the truth of Jeroboam's counsel. "Chang, take this useless thing to the Pit," Torrin commanded. "He won't last the day. But maybe he'll learn a lesson in the nature of power before he dies."

Alissa led her people home. King Tynan's body was wrapped in cloth soaked with preservatives and returned to Parhelion for a proper burial. With Tynan's death, Alissa became queen of Parhelion. Some questioned her authority to rule over her husband's kingdom but in time all accepted Alissa. Most opposition evaporated when Tynan's mother publicly gave her support to Alissa's assumption of the throne and acknowledged Alissa as Parhelion's rightful monarch. Tynan's mother knew that she herself could not rule with effectiveness during these troubled times, at least not with the effectiveness that she saw her daughter-in-law possessed with great abundance.

Fearing that two kingdoms could not be adequately defended, Alissa chose to abandon castle Braemar entirely and transplant all her people to Parhelion. When Emperor Torrin launched his retaliatory attack on Braemar, he found the castle empty and took possession of it without a fight.

It would be over a year before Rorke and Alissa would marry. To do so any sooner would have appeared disrespectful of Tynan's memory. Alissa ruled her new kingdom well. Her unfailing courage, positive attitude, and moral guidance had the power to embolden the hearts of all her citizens and to refresh their collective spirit. Without doubt, they would need her strength for the future challenges promised by the threat of Torrin's expanding realm.

THE END

Learn how the saga began…

Read the exciting Prequel to **The Maul of Murgleys**

Death Brand
By Scott C. Ristau

On sale at:

PublishAmerica.com, Amazon.com, Borders.com, BN.com, Target.com, Buy.com, and elsewhere